My Blue Coiling Snake
My Empty Room

My Blue Coiling Snake
My Empty Room

LYNN CRAWFORD

CLOVER
HEIGHTS

My Blue Coiling Snake, My Empty Room

For information contact:
Clover Heights Publishing
www.cloverheightspublishing.com

Publisher's Cataloging-In-Publication Data
(Prepared by The Donohue Group, Inc.)

Library of Congress Control Number: 2021910269

Crawford, Lynn, 1954-2017, author.
My blue coiling snake, my empty room / Lynn Crawford.

ISBN 9781736054505 (hardcover)
ISBN 9781736054529 (paperback)
ISBN 9781736054512 (ebook)

Gay couples--California--San Francisco--Fiction.
Spouses--Death--Psychological aspects--Fiction.
AIDS (Disease)--California--San Francisco--Fiction.
Grief--Fiction.
FICTION/Literary.

Book design by 1106 Design
Cover art by Susan Synarski

Printed in the United States of America

9 8 7 6 5 4 3 2 1

For Ellen

PART ONE

1

My plans for a dignified death, I must admit, were copycat. The particulars of it were my own, but the lightheartedness, the lift that came to me when I thought about it and planned for it, came from a story I heard on public radio. An older woman was determined to take matters into her own hands. Why let a stupid terminal illness run the show? Every sentence was recorded in my mind, and would replay. I called her Alma.

Her grown son was the one to tell the story. "She had style," he said. "She had love." She would call him when the time felt right to her, and invite him over for his favorite meal. He knew what this meant. They had agreed upon the cue. Pot roast. But each time, it shocked him that she actually did cook a roast, complete with carrots, potatoes, and onions pan-roasted in the juice. She would urge him to the turquoise formica kitchen table and seat him where his father used to sit. Then, she would fuss. She would get out an everyday plate but wipe it first with a fresh towel to make it shine. She would place the roast and the vegetables in serving dishes, and present them at the table instead of preparing the plate at the stove, which was how she served the family, years ago. The family being the two parents and him. And now just him.

She would never accept his urgings to sit down and have a little with him. "No, you go on," she would say. "Sons should outlive their mothers." She would set the lemon-meringue pie on the opposite end of the table, squeeze her son's shoulder, and go out.

At this point in the story the son pauses. There is a breath that catches in his throat. Just one. And then he goes on. And I go along with him. Once this broadcast got inside my head, it never quit. Some stories just go right in. Later, they pop back into our lives. We find the parts that are right for us, and then we go on. The story seems to go by fast, but like a song, it can keep replaying. It can become your song. You can become a mockingbird, singing parts of the story. Territories become yours, and then you live them. Or not.

Unlike the mockingbird, I don't sing for everyone. Only for involved parties. If Jay were alive, he would have known when I was getting obsessed. He would have sensed a restlessness in me as I lay beside him in the morning, and he would have asked what was on my mind. I would have said, the Pink Lady from the Radio. And he would have ruffled my hair, and I would have settled myself in the crook of his shoulder, and I wouldn't have had to say anything more, because he would have been there when the radio was playing, he would have heard the story too, and he would not have been shocked. We would have listened to it together, then I would have refused to talk more about it. Yes, I hate to admit it, but that's the truth. He would have wanted to come to some sort of understanding about these things; in fact he did want that, but I wouldn't talk. I was too afraid. And now, I'll do what I didn't allow him to complete.

But that's another story.

She would go into her bedroom and change out of the blue knit outfit she wore to what she called "her old ladies move their bums" class. She

4

would put on an elegant pink silk nighty, knee-length, purchased especially for the occasion. She would crawl into bed, fold her hands across
her chest. Her son could see from the kitchen that the light was still on.
There would be a gleaming glass of water next to her, a bottle of pills.
The base of the glass was thick, and made the light falling from the lamp
into the water glow like fire at the base.

Then he waited. He sat in the kitchen, tense, pretending to read the
paper. After an hour he would hear her moving around in the bedroom.
Soon she would appear in the kitchen doorway, wrapped in a pink
chenille robe he swore was the same one she'd had when he was a kid,
though he hoped not.

She cleared her throat. "Another dress rehearsal, I guess. If it keeps
going like this, I'm going to need a new dress."

No pink nighties or chenille robes for Jay and me, two men, four
sideburns, one deadly illness, shared. But that lady was with me, I was
sure, as I left the cottage where Jay and I had lived for years, and went
down the steps early, to meet the taxi, so the driver wouldn't have to wait
for me. I'm so slow. And waiting is so difficult. Waiting can take forever.
I was sick of waiting. A year after Jay had gone on, I was still waiting. I
wanted to go. I was sick, and I was tired of it.

When the driver popped out of his car to take my bag, I was smiling,
broadly. My cheeks were flushed. A crow was cawing from the neighbor's
roof, and there was something easy about that. I didn't know him, he
didn't know me, it was an easy love. Hello, goodbye, my darling.

2

I HAD SETTLED ON THE FAIRVIEW. I never had occasion or opportunity to go inside, which was good. It meant nothing to me. Just an old, if fancy, hunk of a hotel on Nob Hill. When I called for a reservation, I did have a moment of sheepish regret for the trouble my plans might cause them, but in fact, I had already thought carefully about how to minimize all that. Especially for the staff. When the clerk took my credit card number and other information, I stopped worrying, and even started to feel like someone who was just making plans to get out of town, change the frame, get a new perspective. Strange, but true. I felt like a man on the go, a guy set free. And Alma, my inner Alma—ever consistent, rarely complacent—was all for it. All for going actively, and by choice. Just feeling her there with me, I relaxed, and as I relaxed, the clerk's voice grew less formal, more friendly, more truly welcoming.

A week later, when I headed toward the hotel, I didn't look behind. That was that! I told myself. I really believed it. I got in the cab and left.

The driver was playing the radio quietly. A ballgame. Something I didn't care about. So far so good. All systems go.

By the time we got down Market past Church, I noticed that the announcer's voice sounded like Alma's son. For a moment I considered asking the driver to change stations or turn down the volume, but it wasn't that loud, and soon I was drifting off, closing my eyes against the mid-afternoon glare. Whatever happened to him, I wondered. It had been years since his story had aired. Did he have any idea that it still might be a real hit with some people? That some people, like me, might even take it as an actual jumping-off point for themselves?

Better that he not know, I decided. Better that he not trouble himself about other people's choices. I wouldn't want him to take that on. After all, my choices are my own. And his mother's were his mother's.

What I did feel bad about, what I do feel inclined to apologize for, is for taking a story that was once his, and adding to it and subtracting from it according to my own needs. And now Alma, my Alma, my muse, the one who I have named, is clearly not one and the same as his mother. His mother has not only morphed but been replaced. I took liberties because the original story is, after all, theirs. It's not Alma's account. We can't really speak for her. We will never know what she was actually thinking when she went into her bedroom alone and lay down in bed with the sheet pulled up to her chin. We can only imagine.

I forced myself to sit up straight and look out the window. Enough with Alma, I decided. Who knows why she changed her mind so many times. What mattered was like the son said: she was always in earnest. Ultimately, her time did come. Now, it was time to claim my own journey. Get myself where I was going.

I watched the traffic and the street and let myself go a bit blank. Me, William Lifton, age forty-five, on my way to a decisive solution, was letting myself be driven. I was not driving myself. There was no force of will on anyone's part. My mood, my decision, my executive actions, everything was lined up as naturally as waves in the ocean.

I actually fell asleep several times, lulled by the braking and surging of the cab. And that was fine. It showed me how ready I was to go. Street signs and centerlines dissolved into an ad on the radio for tires, a distant siren, forsythia at the edge of a yard when I was five. Who knows why? Why any of it? And Alma again, popping back in at an intersection. Franklin and Bush, body and soul, waking and dreaming. The traffic halted.

Thank you, I told her. But I don't need you now. You can go. You have given voice to so many things for me, but it's time now for me to go my own way.

She didn't. She didn't do much of anything, except bother my heart. She had gotten into me, under my skin, into my imagination. She might as well have been sitting beside me in the flesh, stroking the hair on my arm in the wrong direction.

"Go!" I hear myself say. Emphatically. "Get up and go!"
The driver eyes me in the mirror. He thinks I am talking to him.
"We are jammed," he says, patiently.
"Sorry," I mutter. "I'm too hot."

He turns on the air conditioning. I stare down into my water bottle. My afternoon fever is beginning to take hold, I realize. Of course, Alma isn't in the cab. She's in my head, in her own apartment there. She's my friend. Imaginary, perhaps, but with me nonetheless. And maybe this time, she needs me. She needs me to imagine her. To see her laying in her bed, staring at her pill bottle, her water glass. After a while Alma's eyes close. I see her eyeballs rolling back and forth under her lids. Is she looking for her husband, Herbert? I've searched my own darkness for Jay, many times, in just that way. So lonely. She rolls over onto her back, hands crossed just below her breasts, or where her breasts once were.

Enough! I open my eyes a slit, check out the people crossing at the intersection. Wind in their hair, stray papers blowing in the street. No one talking to each other. Sometimes that's such a relief.

But not right now, for Alma. She's got my ear, even if I can't see her. She wants to tell me things in her own way, she is saying. That's what she wanted from her doctor. Just to hear her out. Two or three sentences! Is that really so hard to take?

It's the fever talking, I remind myself. It makes me hear things.

She pushes on. "All I wanted to say is that when I went to the doctor, I knew something was wrong. Ever since Herbert had died, I'd been shrinking. When I walked down the street in a breeze, my clothes flapped. But when I told him exactly that, the doctor laughed. Maybe he thought I meant to be funny. Everyone loses weight when a spouse dies, he said. The ninny. Well-intentioned maybe, but a ninny."

A week later he showed her the results of the scan, and there it was, plain as day. Cancer, twinkling in her bones like green stars. "Of course, I'd suspected," she said. "That's why I had the appointment! But still, I was shocked. I'd always had such a good attitude. Courage and Forbearance." But there were things in this world that were a lot bigger than her, she realized. Tiny stars, twinkling.

I reach out to take her hand, startling myself awake; but, it's my own hand I am holding. I'm alone in the backseat of the cab. A crowd roars softly on the radio. Hands folded in each other, I drift in its whirlpool of sound. The cab continues on its way.

So does Alma. "There is more," she says. "So much more." She is coming at me every which way now, talking, sitting beside me, lying in her bed, audible, invisible, living in her own dream, which of course is really my dream, as I float further and further away from any sort of location, any sort of resistance or questioning or reason or sense. She is just there, accompanying me, telling me a story from inside my own head. Radio broadcast from a non-linear location, I think. Crazy, yes. But at this point, who cares? We are drifting together now, all mixed up, time and space and fever and calm.

Peacefully, I ride the silence the rest of the way to the hotel. I forget all about Alma. She just disappears. Peacefully. Forgetting about her, and forgetting about me too, my own story, my own plans, I am just bumping down the road. Turning corners. No red lights now. Going.

3

THE CAB TURNS INTO THE CIRCULAR DRIVEWAY. The hotel is huge. Columns, orderly rows of windows, limestone, flags. It looks like a national monument. As the driver angles the cab between vehicles, I gather myself up. Briefcase (a distraction, a disguise, a fake). Raincoat (second hand, purchased at Buffalo Exchange. More downtown professional than I would ever have worn). A shopping bag with a few cold drinks. Ginger ale, apple juice. The sickroom stand-bys.

Just as the cab rolls to a stop, I pop out of the back door. And my foot goes right into the flower bed. Fancy enriched soil, recently watered. I laugh. A little touch of the earth before my ascent!

A doorman rushes up, offering a towel or handkerchief. I wave him off. I'll keep it, I say. A souvenir of my visit. I have to keep waving him off.

For a second I just stare up at the face of the hotel. Windows sparkle; a long white ribbon of vapor trails across the blue October sky. Behind me, out on the street, the traffic surges through the intersection. From the sound, I know the light has changed. I'm shivering a bit now. But everywhere is inspiration, the energy of people on the move. The cab driver has popped open the trunk, the bellhop is already swinging my bags onto his gleaming brass cart. A half-dozen women in business suits pour out of an airport van, their laughter ringing against the stones of the drive.

"Keep the change," I tell the driver, paying the fare, then handing him some Franklins rolled up in a few tens to throw him off. He offers to take the artist's portfolio from under my arm, but I decline. It's unlikely that he'll ever figure anything out, but I wouldn't want him to think he'd assisted me with my plan. Besides, I want to carry the portfolio myself, so the desk clerk can see me with it. I want him to believe the story I have told, if only so that he too will feel no responsibility for what happens later. The portfolio is heavy, though. Each time the breeze smacks into it, I am twisted nearly off my feet. I concentrate on walking as normally as I can into the hotel. An open door to a place of coming and going. The doorman stands with a wide smile for whomever passes.

The clerk stares at the computer screen, waiting for my reservation to pop up.

"I wrote ahead, weeks ago," I say, pushing the confirmation number and my credit card across the mahogany counter.

Without looking up, he answers that he is sure everything is fine, the system is just a little slow today.

From his tone, I can tell I must sound in need of reassurance.

"Cool it," I say to myself, but I'm still on edge waiting to hear I've got the exact room and view. And a key to the roof.

I pat the chest pocket of my overcoat, making sure the copy of my letter to the manager is still there. I knew my request for a key might seem odd, so I wrote ahead. I paint cityscapes, I had said, and need a hotel in San Francisco with a balcony room facing northwest. If possible, I would also like access to the roof. I mostly plan to work in my room, as it would probably be windy up top, but it would be helpful now and then to have recourse to the bigger perspective.

I enclosed several color copies of my alleged work. I thought that was a convincing touch, even though the only effort I made was to rip a few pictures out of an art magazine and take them to the copy center.

The ruse, to my surprise, went without a hitch.

Still, when the manager called to say the hotel would be happy to accommodate me, I felt guilty. Lying has not been my specialty before now.

The printer starts up, zipping on the counter.

"Here it is," says the desk man. "Top floor room. And a key to the roof for you."

But just as I turn toward the elevator, he asks me, "You're an artist?"

I shrug, pulling deeper inside my coat. Now he'll make a little eye contact with me and see what I don't want him to see: fish cheeks, dull hair, burning eyes. Meanwhile, he's got the body of a circuit party boy.

"I want to doublecheck something for you," he adds, punching at his keyboard, screwing up his face as he reads.

I force myself to approach the counter again, hoping I don't break into a sweat. Everything has gone so well.

"Do you really want the top floor room?" he asks. "We've given it to you as an upgrade, but I see here you originally requested a balcony room in the old section. In the new section you'd be higher up, but there's a tint to the plate glass that would change the color and light of the view. I bet you wanted the balcony for the natural light, plus the bridge and ocean scenery."

He raises his eyebrows expectantly, proud of his attention to detail. I mumble my thanks. I'm grateful, but it's hard to have him look at me. I'm happy when he gets back to his paperwork.

It's then I notice the wall clock behind him. Big crisp numerals on a white face. I wait for the big hand to pull back, as if gathering strength, then leap.

It's the bellman who opens the curtains. Seeing the balcony stops me for a second, tip in my hand. Then we resume our patter.

Once I'm alone, I find I'm still pretending. I fiddle with my bags, unfold then refold a few things, just to soothe myself.

I set my toilet kit on the bathroom counter. Beautiful veins in the marble. I run my hand over them. Jay had gorgeous veins.

The marble is cold to my touch.

I lay my face against it anyway.

Grief, and clinging, one more time.

And then the shits hit again.

I make it onto the toilet.

Head touching my knees.

The usual shakes.

I pull myself up, refasten the diaper, which is still clean. Ridiculous little moment of pride.

I fill a glass with water, sit back down on the toilet lid. Sconces, like upturned seashells, sweeping coral-colored light up the walls.

I need a little time, to rehydrate and renew.

I open my kit, lay a few things out. Comb. Toothpaste. Floss. Lotion. Razor. And not one fucking bottle of pills.

No more.

"Let there be a feast," I say.

More and more viruses, drinking my bloody fucking wine.

When I go, they'll go too. So, let them have a last supper.

I set my toothbrush upright in the glass.

Time to approach the view.

The balcony doors are mullioned. I rub my thumb along the smooth surface of the wood. I can almost hear Jay comment, "Great paint job. Good restoration."

I stand with my chin against the muntin, staring out at the divided view. To the left, an office building. To the right, blue, rising up at the end of a street which drops off and then suddenly there it all is—the Headlands, floating above the bay, skirt of fog upturned in the afternoon breeze. The bridge is there too, but my eyes are on the hills, already beginning to green after one October rain. I can almost smell the wet shoots poking up between the bent dry stalks.

Spring in a dying season.

Mount Tam.

Jay is there now.

He was always drawn to big bright overlooks.

Each Easter, we would go, hiking up to a grassy bald spot where we'd spread an old wool blanket and lay side by side on our bellies, reading the paper, dipping into our bag of scones, cheese, fresh-squeezed juice. Lupine everywhere.

I close my eyes, reaching in my mind for a stem, wishing I could drag that cobalt-blue flame across his bare back one more time, making him jump up and grab the blanket, like he did that once, tumbling me off, laughing as I rolled over and over down the hill.

"Ready for me?" he'd said, straddling my waist when I'd come to a stop, nipping me on each ear.

As I stand here now, warming the brass of a door knob in my hand, I pretend it is him, his hand, reaching for me.

"Open your eyes," I tell myself. "He is not here."

"Only thin glass between you," argues another voice.

I rest my forehead against the pane, watching the glass mist up from my breath. It almost startles me. How can there be so much life still left in me?

But there is.

I press down on the knob, which is really a lever like a long narrow wing. I hear the lock disengage, but when I pull, nothing happens.

Safety latches, plus a bolt near the floor.

I pause. Is this a prohibitory sign?

They come free, but not before a little doubt creeps in. I picture the sudden speed, everything streaking by. Adrenaline, sharp as ammonia or crushed juniper berries, up the nose. My fingers, clawing the air, trying to cling.

But I've come to see our lives pass through our hands like water anyway. Choosing to live at least one second facing forward would be extraordinary. At least for a man like me.

Wrapping my coat around me, I step out into the wind. I am testing myself, in the full light.

As I stare at the ground, I feel the chill ocean air rushing at me.

I am simply a man taking in the air, I try to say with my posture, aware of people moving around their offices in the opposing building.

Tonight they will be gone, asleep, oblivious.

I check the street, up and down.

Nothing very familiar. I drove by this place a handful of times in fifteen years, talking with friends, not noticing much. No memories to snag me.

Drawing a deep breath, I look again toward the Headlands, which are different now, fainter. The fog, thinner and higher, more dispersed. Behind it, the mountain seems to fizz, atomized, broken into particles. But not the despair.

My sturdy weapon.

I approach the balustrade.

The portico is directly below, jutting out over the front drive, exactly as anticipated.

A limousine, long and sleek, pulling out from under.

Swing low, I whistle through my teeth, a sort of giddiness coming over me.

Laying a hand on the rail, I close my eyes, steady myself against a sudden wave of fatigue.

And relief. I've done it. This day's tasks.

4

I WAKE, MY HAIR WET, A TERRIBLE CRICK IN MY NECK. For a few seconds I think maybe I am at Sidney's, getting a haircut, leaning back over the sink while she washes my scalp with her strong hands.

A painting of Fisherman's Wharf is opposite me.

Definitely not Sidney's.

It seems to be the middle of the night.

I prop myself up, remembering now.

I am still wrapped in my coat, the balcony doors are open.

Fucking cold.

I swing my legs off the bed, shoes still on. I sit for a few seconds, brushing off the coverlet as I let an intention form.

Shut the door.

All the lights surprise me. Bright offices. Pedestrians bunched at the crosswalk. Streams of traffic.

Only 8 o'clock.

I turn my back on it for now, go into the bathroom to rinse off my face, towel my hair.

Fucking sweats.

But that's why I dragged a whole suitcase. Dry T-shirts, fleece pull-over, flannel bottoms.

Then I crawl in under the covers. Turn on the TV. I read somewhere that listening to the sound of a human voice can calm the heart rate.

I listen with my eyes closed, the flash of changing scenes registering not unpleasantly through the skin of my eyelids. Soon I am drifting, picturing Sidney's little haircutting stall again. One of my regularly scheduled pleasures—a trim in a chair at the back of an art gallery! What a great mix Sid and her lover hit on when they opened that place.

No wonder it's on my mind. This night began there, two months ago, when I saw that painting. A man sitting in a chair, ghostly pale, surrounded by fruits and butterflies. A gray towel or shroud was piled on his head, half-folded, half-tumbling down his cheeks.

It could have been a mirror.

"We're selling this for Alejandro Mazon, a young Cuban artist from New York," Sidney said. "What do you think?"

I nodded. Sentences the color of moon or bone unraveled in a rambling hand across the night of the painting:

> *Suicides have already betrayed the body . . . Like carpenters*
> *they want to know which tools.*

At home that afternoon, I collapsed on the couch, peeled off my socks. Already I was paying for my excursion. Spikes up the calves, plus that all-too-familiar sensation in the feet, as if I'd walked home over hot coals. No way to get away from it.

I slouched for a long time, eyes wandering the room, touching the spines of my books, skins of fruit on the table, drooping limbs of the cypress framed in the window. Not consciously casting about for a tool, I riffled my junk mail. *From heaven there fell three apples,* said an ad from a healing center. *One for the person who told the tale, another for the person who listened, and the most beautiful of all fell into the abyss.*

Fell, and has not stopped.
That passage, still whistling, deep in my ears.
Unobstructed, in a time of many obstacles.

That was what the pale man was thinking when I woke later that afternoon and caught him sitting on the edge of my dream. Unobstructed. Like a carpenter, he wanted to know which tools. The shroud piled on his head was more precarious now, threatening to drop its grayness entirely over him. Meanwhile, the fruits and butterflies carried on, annoyingly colorful, out of reach.

I sat up, trying to wipe him from my eyes. Drastic tools, I thought. Drastic, if I am going to cut through my various fogs. Double infections, I think of them, the one viral, the other habitual, life-long. My tendency to cling to the past, making museums of my passions, my epiphanies. Suddenly, I knew I needed means that would give me no choice, once I had chosen. Something that will yield at least one sensation of hurtling forward, air bursting in the sinuses like after a dive, nothing else possible, just one vividly present second before blackout, and then nothing. No going back. On yourself, to yourself.

The plan came to me in a moment of waking and stillness.
I am, after all, my father's son.
Taking my time.
But unlike him, choosing my time.

5

My father was a grocer in a corner market. My mother was too, but most things seemed to revolve around his timetable, as if he were the only one.

My mother and I would be peacefully absorbed in our individual tasks when suddenly my father would come hustling in red-faced from the back room with some request or other. It was rarely a matter of real urgency—mostly we'd just drifted too far from him into our own thoughts and daydreams as we swept aisles or trimmed lettuce. Later, I would understand the need for connection that drove him in these moments, but when I was a kid my thoughts would scatter like small birds when I heard that tone in his voice. "*William, it's time to stack apples*" (never mind that I had already sorted out the bad ones). "*Joan, are those checks ready?*" We'd have to hop to it, not because he was a violent man, but simply because he expected it and would wait next to you tumbling the change in his pockets until you complied.

Even so, there was something unyielding in my mother, an unruffled line to her shoulders as she dropped her own chore and took up his as if none of it were worth getting upset about. Outwardly accommodating, she inwardly resisted his pressure. Sometimes this had the effect of calming him, but there were times, especially when I was a teenager, when it only made him more demanding and her more closed, stubborn, bitten-down. I knew it could go on for hours, him pushing, her preserving her composure, until finally she would throw down her rag or whatever she was doing and stand with her hands on her hips, eyes flashing. *"Now what is it that can't wait?"*

At which point he would become magnanimous and happy in direct ratio to how upset she was. He would reach for her, gently pulling her to his chest, her fists wedged up between them as he petted her hair, speaking in soothing tones, suggesting she take a break. She would stand there with her cheek against him. Balance would seem to be restored, but I could see her face, the reddened cheeks, the pressed-together lips.

Turning my back on them both, I would head for the back room.

The full force of my resentment wouldn't catch up to me until he finally did relax. When he wanted to rest, he damned well would, propping his feet on the desk in the back room. "Slowness is divinity," he would say, drifting off. I hated that phrase then, even as I squirreled it away deep beneath the surface of my anger, to be retrieved later. At the time, the sight of his chin dropping onto his chest repulsed me.

Nothing like those young delivery guys, lean and hard in jeans. I'd wait for them on hot summer afternoons, confused by my eagerness to help them unload their crates, our shoulders brushing, the smell of their sweat making me restless for hours afterwards. I'd be up and down the block, launching my skateboard off sharper and higher corners. Or I'd throw myself into the hardest physical labors in the store, building muscle, muscle that I'd hide behind at school.

Once I had loved my father's arms, their solidity. But now I felt so far from him, his baggy pants and hair oil and the lopsided grin he had for certain women customers. His whole body would enliven as he bantered with them, counting out their change with an extra flourish. My mother would be right there—it didn't seemed to stir animosity between

21

them—but a sort of hopelessness would come over me, a secretive lostness from which I knew he could never rescue me, for the lives of our bodies would be different. I didn't know yet, clearly, how, or why.

I felt it acutely, though, every time I had to lead one of those tattooed delivery guys in from the backroom, packing list in hand, to ask my father for his signature. I can still see him, elbows on his newspaper, glasses sliding down his nose as he leaned on the counter, reading. There would always be a lag before he would acknowledge us, for even though he often gave the impression of being driven, when he was slow, he was uncompromisingly slow. As we waited for him to finish a paragraph or two then stretch, yawn, and rummage around for a pen, I would stand, arms crossed, tensely aware of the guy next to me, his tobacco smell and T-shirt. Trying to ignore what might be rearing its head, literally and figuratively, I'd stare out the window, fighting the color in my face, cussing my father under my breath for the way he was taking his time.

Now it's my inheritance, and it makes me want to laugh. Here I am in a ritzy hotel, taking my own good time, and if it weren't for him, and for my mother too—their slowed-down life, or at least, the small square footage in which they passed their days—I would not have the sense of entitlement I have. Entitlement to my own time, to bide my time, choose my time, mark my time. It's mine.

The day after tomorrow. No more waiting for Nature to take its course.

I straighten the edges of the pretzel bags, my gleaming pop-up altar to my ancestors.

And I see my father again, right before he lifts his eyes and looks straight into the face of who or what has come for him.

6

A KNOCK.

Before I can collect myself the light snaps on and I am blinking at a woman in a powder blue dress. A uniform. She has a small tray in her hand.

"I'm not taking any meds," I mumble, pulling the covers up to my chin.

"Sorry, sir!" she says, backing away.

Realizing where I am, I grin at her, amused that I would actually think a nurse would wear a dress and apron these days. I'm half in childhood.

But she shakes her finger at me playfully, as if I am naughty.

"Don't do anything I wouldn't do," she calls out with a polished pleasant briskness as she closes the door.

I laugh, suddenly aware that she has chosen to take my grin as flirtatious.

I do have my moments of doubt. I don't need one right now. Yet, I have learned to let them roll through, in waves, if need be. Sometimes the waves lap at my edges, quietly.

"Don't push," says a soft voice inside of me. "You don't need to strain. The issue will take care of itself." As my mother used to say, "Bide your time."

"Yes," says a more pragmatic voice, "but while I wait for the Big Celestial Bus, who will take care of me? Friends? Volunteers? Community Services? Everyone is so busy. I don't want busy."

But they will come.

And so will the fevers—the deliriums, phantasms, memories, and confusions. Here and there, now and then, up and down. No wave without a crest and a trough, said Alan Watts. And waves of grief and memory and sickness and oblivion, of coming and going and everything else in between. I have slid down every slope. Well, maybe not every slope, but I don't want to check that out. I will take care of myself, so to speak.

There is a hush in the room. Heat, a cart in the hall, traffic below. For a second it feels like a hospital at night.

But the bed is covered with the clothes I had unpacked earlier. Neat squares of sweatpants, sweatshirts, flannel shirts, robe, socks, pants. Extras of everything. Entirely unnecessary. Except that when I packed, I couldn't stand the caved-in look of the bag with just a few things in it. It was depressing. I was afraid it would put me off my plan.

Now I just want it out of the way so I can have more room on the bed. I throw the bag in the corner and crawl back under the covers. My plan says to rest. I will rest.

I turn on the TV, fiddle with the remote.

Strong throat of a young man. He empties a bottle of spring water onto his upturned face, sun behind, the sparkling fluid spilling over his chin onto his chest as he drinks.

I'm sold. I turn off the sound so I can watch without the noise. Hold onto his hips. It's over in a few seconds. Then a cop show, with flashing lights, two men smoking in a car.

I shut it off, roll onto my side, look out the double doors. Stars barely visible, given the city lights. But there are a few. How many light-years away? I could be looking at the time of Columbus up there. And down here, the breaths of Jesus and Hitler and everyone else in between are blowing across the headlands. Particles of DaVinci, Einstein, the hated great aunt, the one well-loved . . . and so why not Jay?

I've asked myself that for months. I wanted Jay, my Jay, the flesh and blood Jay who was so beautifully formed, with well-defined muscles and a tongue articulate in all ways. The scent of his hair, his way of groaning that was a sexy growl, and the skillful hands of a tradesman. And I can only find him in the fantasy of mixed up memories, dreams, tumults, griefs, scents. The yawning black hole of loneliness.

One night after he was gone I lay on my back on Kite Hill, wishing I could find the light of a year in which we were both still alive, had just met.

Emptiness came over me as I lay there, cradling the back of my head in my hand. With more strain than pleasure, I began to pull at my dick.

No Milky Way that night either.

For a while, I fell asleep, and then for a longer while, I lingered in half-sleep, neither waking nor dreaming. A sheet of light was falling through the double doors. Faintly antiseptic, fluorescent, sometimes luminous too. The TV was still on. I lay very still, watching the dark, as if the missing or the missed could appear.

"I will come to you," Jay said once, while I was sitting on the edge of his hospital bed. Even though the room was warm, I had the arms of his burgundy sweater draped over my shoulders. I leaned in closer so I could hear him.

25

"I will be waiting for you," he added, gazing at my lips.

I dabbed at the sweat in his hair with a washcloth. The beads kept coming.

"Do you hear me?" he asked, squeezing my arm with surprising strength.

"I'd like that," I heard myself say, but I couldn't hold back my despair. I didn't believe he would be waiting for me, any more than I believed he was waiting for me before we met.

"We met anyway," he said, eyes crinkling.

PART TWO

Make me to hear joy and gladness;
that the bones which Thou hast broken may rejoice.
Psalm 51:8

7

We met at a dinner party. I almost didn't go. I'd been heaving boxes all day in the office supply store where I worked, and I stank. Not only of sweat, but also dust. Dullness.

So, I tried to back out. I called Clive, one of the hosts, and told him I was filthy from work, with no time to run home to West Detroit for a shower.

"Filthy is good!" he'd teased. "Just come!"

He gave me a rundown on who was coming. A classical music dj, who I knew only by name, from the radio. Some academics, who along with Clive and Thom, his partner of twenty-five years, had just returned from a conference in New York, at which the recently deceased Christopher Isherwood had been honored. (Clive was one of Isherwood's biographers.) Also coming was a school teacher, a painter, and, he joked, a few representatives of rough trade.

And where in that line-up did I fit?

I was a part-time stock clerk, a part-time student. Clive and Thom were both English professors at my commuter campus, big-wheels in their fields. As much as I was flattered to be invited, I was intimidated. Yet when I opened my mouth to decline, the words didn't arrive. Underneath, there was such hunger in me, a hunger for examples, for inspiration, for something other than a coming out story. How did two men love each other, live together, make a home together, for over twenty years? That was longer than my parents had been together, before their lives were cut short by a drunk driver.

In the end, my curiosity was truer than my fear.

Or I wanted it to be.

I drove to the party in a wet snow, telling myself that if I wanted to worry, I should give up the focus on my sweaty shirt and pick a real danger, like the slush that was right under my nose on the Southfield freeway.

Clive opened the door and in swirled a bright cloud of flurries ahead of me. "Those aren't mine," I said jokingly. Ignoring my awkwardness, he touched a finger to the brim of my cap.

"But they are sparkling!" he said, staring wondrously. Then meeting my eyes, he smiled. Nothing like the smile I had seen on campus, where the discreet academic half-smile ruled. I grinned back, bashful and aglow, as though he had said I was sparkling. It was the snow that was beautiful, of course, yet I wasn't going to turn my back on the luck of being mixed up in it, decked out. A young man. I stomped my feet on the porch, knocking the snow off my boots.

Thom popped out from behind Clive, and giving my scarf a tug, he pulled me into the vestibule. "Get going," he said, pointing me toward the hubbub in the living room as he took my coat.

For a few moments, I just stood at the perimeter of the gathering in my stocking feet, letting my eyes adjust to the soft light. Candles flickered; real paintings gleamed. Until that moment I'd never been in a home with real art. I hadn't even thought about it. In fact, as a kid, I'd thought my mother was a real doyenne for making a special trip into downtown Detroit every year to check out J. L. Hudson's selection of old masters. Of course, they were reproductions stamped with fake brush marks. But because of her, we had Rembrandt's *The Man with a Golden Helmet*, a Renoir mother and child, a Brueghel, and several DaVinci sketches. Definitely a cut above the neighbors, whose tastes tended toward bug-eyed poodles and toreadors on black velvet. She was a wonder, my mother, and I'd been proud of her.

Clive swept me up by the arm and led me around, a dozen names and faces swimming past in a blur. A real estate agent, an engineering professor, the classical music dj, a therapist, an artist, an attorney. Then he went off to mingle and I ducked into a side room, lured by the sight of an antique reading lamp bending lily-like over an easy chair. Bookshelves ran the entire length of the house; opposite them, a long row of mullioned windows reflected the light. There was even a rolling library ladder, the kind that fastens to a track up near the ceiling.

The transformation of a suburban sunroom into a library was such an oddity to me, such an insistence on being one's own eccentric self, that to me it seemed almost as queer as being queer. I stood in the middle of the room, my eyes skipping from shelf to shelf. Snowflakes bumped against the windows behind me, and for a minute, without thinking, I registered the sound as that of moths, beating against the glass in their rush toward light.

Glancing around the room to make sure I was alone, I started up the ladder, scanning the shelves. There seemed to be a general order to things . . . the psalmic era, the Renaissance, the Restoration, then Early America, and Stonewall . . . Hardbound, paperback, leather-bound. But unconventional things were mixed in too, hinting at personal associations. Old debates, odd attractions, complex affiliations—one author leaning up against another—randomly, or deliberately—who knew? I imagined there were clues everywhere to the inner workings of Clive and Thom's bodies and souls, and to their relationship. I could only guess—but guess at them, I did! What a joyful little snoop I was, climbing around in my tight dirty jeans, accused by a title right under my nose. *A Spy in the House of Love!* Yes!

Clive walked into the room just then.

"Busted!" he said. "Caught totally red-handed."

I froze. Cheeks flushed, I gave him an inane grin. I can still feel it. And my heart pounding. "Guilty as charged," I said, as lightly as I could.

"And glad of it, I hope. How's the view from up there? As you look out over the crowd you could probably take an inventory of who is getting bald under the thatch." He ran his hand through his own still-dark hair. "Hosts, too," he added.

From what I could see, he still had a full head of hair. It took me a second to realize he was simply trying to distract me from my own insecurities.

"What's in your hand?" he asked.

"Oh, just something it landed on when you came in," I confessed. "That's about the extent of it. But I do like how it looks. Worn leather, gilt letters."

"In other words, you like the clothes. Who's wearing them?"

"Herbert Spencer?" I said, reading the cover. "That was my grandmother's maiden name!"

"Herbert, or Spencer, or both?" he teased.

Awkwardly, I started down the ladder, book in hand. He continued to stand in the doorway, resting against the frame, contented, it seemed, just to watch me and enjoy a quiet moment. Such a simple thing, really, yet it met a longing in me I didn't know I had, or even what it was. All I knew is that I was ablaze, not just my cheeks now, but all of me. I had been caught in a moment of quiet derring-do, and Clive had seen it, my earnestness, and liked it. And his eyes were still on me, my worn work-shirt and jeans, my muscles, and banged-up hands. He cocked his eyebrow, playfully, appreciatively. There was nothing complicated or intrusive. And even though I am almost certain Clive forgot about that moment within a few minutes, it lights me up yet again, all these years later. I was no longer waiting for some delivery guy to show up in the back room of my father's store. Except for the book in my hand, I had become one of them. And that was good.

Just as I reached the bottom rung, Thom stepped in, dish towel slung over his shoulder.

"Did you chase Bill up that ladder?" he said to Clive, cheerfully feigning a rebuke.

"If I were twenty-five years younger, I might have," said Clive. "What of it?"

"Well, if I were thirty years younger, I would have, too."

Then he planted a big smooch on Clive's cheek. "But I guess we're stuck with each other now. At least in the kitchen. I need your help with the escargot. We're about to eat. And as for you," he said, wiggling his finger at me, "I suspect you might have trouble finishing up with whomever you have in your hand, before dinner. If so, you will have to come back."

"Definitely," concurred Clive. "It's Herbert Spencer, and he always takes time."

"Oh, good old Herbert. Big-side whiskers, I believe. But if I remember correctly, a nice frontispiece," he said, winking at me.

"Just take Herb home with you," said Clive. "He hasn't had much action for a while. He's an old guy. When you get tired of him, bring him back to us."

"Where he belongs," added Thom, pulling Clive out of the room.

Herbert accompanied me to the dining room, where Thom seated me by a drama professor and the classical radio show host. Already they were trying to top each other, arguing about the exact year in which Louis XIV had warned that because dinner conversations could become volatile, blunted knives were more appropriate for table settings.

"I'm sure it was 1669," said the professor.

Oh my, I thought. Eyes down, I took as long as I could to unfold my napkin and spread it across my lap. They gassed on and on. What blowhards, I thought, with youthful superiority. No way was I going to play student, I thought, even if they were brilliant. Sourly, my mind latched onto that stupid date, 1669. As I repeated it snidely to myself, my brain obviously recorded it, and here it is now: 1669! Hah!

I had left work in good spirits, but now that mood had all but vanished.

A woman seated across from me picked up a butter dish and offered it to me. There was nothing yet to butter, so I gave her a quizzical look. She subtly glanced toward the professor, then touched the butter knife, which was resting on the edge of the dish. I realized it was pointed right at him.

"You feel safe tonight?" she asked playfully, in a low voice.

"I do now!" I said, taking the dish and setting it down between me and the professor. "I feel very protected, thank you!"

Clive had briefly introduced me to Miko in the living room, saying she was the guest of honor. After three years of work, she had just completed a still life of three pears, which was now resting on the arms of an Italian provincial chair at the end of the table. I had already more than noticed the painting—it was stunning—but now, with Miko watching me, I made a point of reveling in it.

"I want one of those pears! They look ready to eat!" I exclaimed.

"Help yourself," said Miko. "There are three on the plate."

"It feels like I can see every cell in each fruit, yet they all blend into one variegated glow. How did you do that?"

"Very slowly, with a brush of three hairs. Cat hairs," she added, modestly looping a long strand of shiny blue-black hair behind her ear.

"But she persevered," said Mitch, her husband, a microbiology professor from campus. "For three years. Dot by dot."

"Sometimes it felt like a very long game of connect-the-dots," she said.

Resting back in his chair, Mitch gazed at her admiringly.

"And who was the cat who helped?" I asked.

Her eyes lit up. "Murphy. He was Mitch's cat, before we met in Tokyo."

"Now he's all hers," Mitch said, stroking her arm. "The real marriage was between the two of them."

She placed her hand on Mitch's. They looked so peaceful together as they resumed listening to what was going on around them. Finally, I calmed down a bit too and began to take a more open-hearted interest in the other guests.

The dj was now addressing himself mostly to his plate. He seemed to be assuming that someone was listening to him—he cut his eyes my way once or twice—but he didn't seem to want or expect a response. And I wasn't actually taking in much about what he was saying. Mostly I was picturing him in the confines of a radio studio and imagining how well his job suited him. No interruptions, not much dialogue. Yet I did hear enough to gather that he was brilliant, and that this gift must have set him apart from others for much of his life. It was setting him apart now, making him seem aloof and unlikeable. Even so, he was trying to work against all that. Earnestly, if awkwardly. Abruptly he broke off and zeroed in on me.

"What do you do for a living?" he asked, staring at me through dirty glasses.

"I work in a stockroom to put myself through school," I told him. Fully expecting that that was going to be the end of his interest in me, I was ready to turn away.

But he was surprisingly persistent.

"Good enough," he said. "A good reason to work in a stockroom, if you have to have a reason." He took off his glasses and began to polish them with a handkerchief. "I grew up in Pontiac," he added, as if that explained something. We both fell silent.

"Have you seen any good movies lately?" he suddenly asked. "What gym do you go to in your end of town?"

"Usually I'm too tired after work to do either," I said. I barely remembered the last movie I had seen. My comments about it were at best, vague. Yet he nodded and seemed to listen intently, even ponderously. Embarrassed for us both, I looked around for a convenient distraction. When the men who had been to the conference together burst out laughing, I angled my body their way, glancing briefly at the dj. "The City!" I said, as if that explained everything. And he nodded, as though it did. We turned our chairs for better listening and I imagined we both felt alleviated of a conversation that had reached a natural limit.

This is what I gleaned. There were five-star reviews all around for the phenomenal nudes at the Metropolitan. There was some debate as to whether the marble member on Hercules wrestling Antaeus was as fascinating as the literal member of a drunk guy in the bushes of Central Park. Despite his remarkable style of whacking off by pulling on a strategically attached red ribbon, with a cluster of jingle bells on the other end, which rang quicker and quicker, his performance was, according to one authority, "Operational, not operatic." Everyone seemed happy to move on to the topic of the Continental baths. That report was delivered mostly through sly glances, raised eyebrows, and alluring refusals to tell more.

"I saw Bette Midler perform there ten years ago," the dj said.

"That's oral history!" someone teased.

"Yes," answered the dj, in a serious tone.

"Where's Joe?" piped up another man, diverting the group.

Thom answered. "He called and said he couldn't come because he is still recovering from a flu he caught at the baths."

"He must have got his head wet," somebody joked. We all groaned.

Thom stepped into the gap that followed, throwing his arm around Clive's neck.

"After all these years together, we're still into simultaneous orgasms," he announced.

With perfect timing, Clive looked at him and added, "Yes, but in different cities."

Everyone laughed, and even though it seemed like everybody had heard this joke before, either from these men, or elsewhere, they seemed happy to hear it again. I thought it was funny too, yet I also felt a little uncomfortable. I was hardly prim or naive, but I was still in search of models for a gay life, and this joke or confession by my admired professors confused me. Was this the secret of their long-lived love? Partly I hoped that their joke was just a joke. Yet as they turned to go into the kitchen, they gave each other affectionate looks that seemed tinged with a quality of reassurance. And that made me think, their affection must be hard-earned.

"I was thinking about what you said earlier," the dj abruptly announced. He was fiddling with his napkin, eventually folding it into a little crown.

"What did I say earlier?"

"About that movie."

"I'm all ears," I said, trying not to look surprised. I had already forgotten what movie I had talked about.

"Did you notice," he said, "how the narrative structure of that film is comparable to Beethoven's 'Emperor' concerto?"

"No, that one went right by me."

"Well, you see, the concerto begins with a cadenza, and of course everybody, at least in Beethoven's time, knows that you don't start with a cadenza! TAKE NOTE! the music is saying, right from the get-go. But then there's that problem," he said, pausing, looking me intensely in the eye now.

"What problem?" I felt forced to ask.

"How do you sustain that kind of energy for forty minutes?" he asked, arching his eyebrows.

"Aha . . . ," I said. "I have a feeling you might know something about that!" He didn't laugh.

"Contrast!" he exclaimed. "Big contrasts of mood, passion, tentativeness! Remember the first movement? So deliberately pompous, public, open? 'This is not to relax!' the composer is telling us. I am not here to comfort you! Then, suddenly, that unearthly magic of the second movement—choral, muted, private—like a protected space! So marvelously intimate!" He dropped his voice almost to a whisper. I had to lean in.

"'Where can we possibly go from here?' The composer himself seems to be wondering that very thing as he then begins to stutter through the notes, searching for what he needs for that tremendous forté. Make no mistake—this is intentional! By allowing us to hear him stutter, he deepens the intimacy. He opens the curtains, letting us see him in the very act of creation!"

Triumphantly, he gazed at me. And I was impressed. He had spoken so plainly about what must be a complex thing. Of course, I had no idea what he was talking about, no idea of what I could possibly say in response. Yet, he seemed to know that, and my lack of deeper knowledge seemed fine with him. Perhaps because of this acceptance, and because of the joy of self-expression that had welled up in him, exuberant, but not begging for admiration, something in me shifted, too. It was fine that I was just sitting there, attending. I was just me. That may sound like an overstatement now, and it was certainly something I had no words for then, but it restored and built upon the feeling that had come to me in the library. I felt grateful, even blessed. And at that age, that was a very good place to be.

"Listening to someone talk about music is not the same as listening to the music itself," the dj suddenly added, almost apologetically. "You don't need a single word for that."

"I know nothing about classical music," I said. "As if you can't tell. I don't know much about any kind of music, actually. I listen to my radio in the car."

Picking up the crown by the flap, he let the napkin unfold over his lap. "I will play the concerto on my show at five on Wednesday. You can hear it then," he offered. "On your car radio."

A year or so later, I would hear him on the radio, explicating the Emperor once again, and that time, I took notes, keeping them as a sort of souvenir of that evening. But that actual evening a handsome man seated a few places down at the table suddenly piped up.

"I'm a high school teacher, and I'm always telling my kids to read the book I'm talking about. Reading it will be better than listening to me talk about it." He had dark gleaming eyes. Wavy hair, deep chestnut luster. Tousled. Loose. Everything said loose. Easy. His curiosity seemed easy. Whatever came across his path would delight him. Was it randomness, was it spontaneity, or sheer randiness? And which did I want? Maybe all of it, my body answered, as he flashed me a roguish grin!

"Want some?" he asked, picking up the bread basket. The end of the baguette was stiffly pointing right at me. Mika suppressed a giggle. In that split second of a pause, he picked up the baguette himself, ripped off a hunk, then held out the basket to me again. But I was staring at his jaws and lips, enamored of how he worked them, powerfully. I forgot all about the bread, even though he kept holding the basket out to me.

A man with an appetite, I thought. He seemed to want everything! I followed the muscles of his neck down into the V of his shirt. He was watching me, too. Merrily. He ran his tongue over his lips, just for the fun of it, it seemed, then took a big sip of wine and swished it around before flashing me another grin.

I picked up my own glass and ran my finger around the rim before I took a sip. And returned his grin.

I thought he looked like a coyote, which was rather absurd given that I had never seen one. And I would never see him that way again. At any rate, though he was muscular and lean, he was not lithe like a coyote. He did not dance in and out of place. He did not have pointy ears, but his interest in what was going on around him gave him a pricked up quality, an agility and alertness.

"I hope you don't mind if I listened to all of that. I like how he put things," he said.

I rubbed the back of my head and looked away. He started to laugh at my unfeigned ponderousness, and I was still thinking of coyotes. The nipping affection of a brother in the pack. There was nothing to do but shrug my shoulders, show my own teeth, and join in the laughter of being caught out. Suddenly, I felt lighter, looser.

***

Throughout the evening that roguish grin became something the entire party worked for. While Clive poured the rare and expensive wines, Thom presented the corks to Jay for his approval. Others vied with their best witticisms and deliberate crudities. The attribution of so much subliminal power to one man annoyed my egalitarian spirit, and, more honestly, intimidated me. I refused to give him much face. In other words, I was enchanted.

It was he who again insisted upon me with his smile, and even a wink, when the appetizer was brought out to great exclamation. Looking down into his plate, Jay patted his belly.

"Mmmm," he said. Escargot.

Grabbing a baguette, he ripped messily.

I stared at the arsenal of miniature silverware next to my plate, then glanced around the table to see how others were going to deal with it. Even the plate itself was odd—a pansied porcelain affair with a dozen potholes brimming with melted butter and shells. Looking at my face, Jay cracked up.

40

"Dig in," he whispered, shoving the baguette at me. "It's just a poor excuse to eat lots of butter and garlic."

Nothing had ever seemed quite so endearing as the way he then proceeded to sop his bread as the rest of the company delicately poked with tiny silver tongs and forks. Fishing out a shell with his fingers, he sucked vigorously, a little dribble on his chin. Sensing my eyes on him, he waved his pinky, capped by the empty shell, then irreverently dunked it up and down in the melted butter.

We sat watching the butter sluice onto the dish, bound silently in our mischief like two voyeurs.

Happy and relieved to find a co-conspirator, I was sluicing over, too.

Catching wind of Jay's snagged attention, the drama professor piped up.

"Who was that I saw in the car with you last Monday, Jaybird? Didn't think you were such a chickenhawk."

"Huh?"

"Southfield Freeway, about 4:30 pm. Young dude. And he was in the driver's seat. Can you believe that? Our Jay?"

Jay screwed up his face. "Sounds great, but I can't remember."

"Ah, the luxury of plenitude. 'I can't remember,' the good man says."

"Oh, now I do," said Jay, ignoring the professor's tone. "I made a deal with a student in my remedial reading class who runs around smoking dope and gutting tires. Promised I'd teach him to drive a stick if he read six books and didn't skip class. I didn't think he'd do it, but I had to keep my word."

At the time I didn't think too much about Jay's story. I was too busy watching his lips, the way they rounded over each word. He was good with his mouth, just the right tension in all the right places. Maybe he'd like a little appreciation in kind, I fantasized. I'd always been good with my mouth, too.

Given proper inspiration, I had my arenas of confidence.

8

JAY LEFT BEFORE ME. I was standing in the vestibule pulling on my boots when the door opened and he stood under the halo of the porch light, shoulders dusted with snow.

"Could you take me home?" he asked, stomping his boots, breath roiling in the cold air.

"Sure," I said. "Battery dead?"

"Not exactly."

We headed out the door. A whole new world was underway. Mountains of snow drifted across the long narrow drive. Tall pines with heavy white epaulets stood quiet sentinel.

I was just about to point out which sleeping mound was my rusted-out Ford when I slipped. Reflexively, I grabbed for Jay, trying to keep from going down.

"Excuse me," I said, hanging onto his coat as I scrambled for footing.

"You don't need an excuse," he said, keeping his arm around me until I was steady.

Then maybe a few seconds longer.

Or was I making that up? Had he really said what I thought he said?

I pried open the car door and the competitions began almost immediately: who was butch, who was faux butch? I gunned the engine; he shoved snow off the back window with a sleeve. I got out and chipped ice from the windshield; he kicked beards of frozen slush from the wheel wells. I pulled chunks of ice from under tires; he helped me with his bare hands.

By the time we got around to negotiating the long driveway, I sat behind the driver's wheel—and he sat out on the hood, legs crossed, swinging a foot, pointing the way through trees and swirling snow.

Captain, my captain. It was a brave new world.

Once out of the subdivision, I asked him which way.

"I don't know," he said, suddenly sounding silly.

I glanced at him. He hadn't seemed drunk.

"You did say you'd take me home?" he asked.

"Yeah?"

"To your house?" he said, rubbing his hands together.

Could I be a little denser? I turned on my blinker and made a fast left. The hind end of the car slid out, fishtailing. He put his hand on my thigh. The car righted itself.

So did I.

"My, my," he said, checking out the bulge. "Any girl with an imagination would run."

By 4 am we were standing by the stove as I stirred hot chocolate, leaning into him. Things had gone even better than anticipated.

"I give stars to my best pupils," he said, wetting his finger and touching my forehead.

"What makes you so sure you're the teacher?"

"I'm eight years older."

"True," I said. "But I have my ways," I added, slipping a hand under the robe I had loaned him. "I enjoy administering examinations as well as taking them."

He leaned against the edge of the table, arms crossed as he stared at my lips. Then raising an eyebrow, he met my eyes.

"So, what's the first question?" he asked.

When I woke at 11 am I was surprised to find him still there, reading in bed. It seemed like amazing good luck. I lay there a few moments, pretending to be asleep, afraid that when we finally took note of each other the joy of the night would vanish as we each felt compelled to arrange a face. I watched him from beneath my lashes, enjoying the sight of him as long as I could—fresh, relaxed, in repose. I fully expected that as soon as I spoke or made a move, I would see his jaw and neck muscles tighten even as he smiled or bantered. If he stayed for breakfast, the border guards would most certainly arrive, each of us conducting a suppressed but implicit scrutiny of the other's purpose, permits, intended length of stay.

Despite my best intentions, it seemed the process was already happening. When he realized I was watching him, he put his finger to his lips.

"Shhhh," he said. "Don't tell. And no expectations, okay?"

I flipped over on my belly and raised up on my arms to look at him.

"That's an expectation," I said, mustering a grin.

He palmed my forehead and gave me a gentle shove.

"My truck is still over at Thom and Clive's."

I fell back on my pillow. "Oh," I mumbled under my breath. "Now I see."

"But I do want to finish this chapter," he added, burrowing under the covers.

My spirits leapt, but so did my anxiety. I wasn't used to bringing guys home so soon, never mind having them linger on in the light of day. Night was better. I could use candles. The heavily upholstered furniture I had inherited from my parents would recede into dark corners. But come morning, there it would all be, slumping around the living room like a family of possums, too bald and patchy for even the earthy genre (ferns, antiques, avocado-tint refrigerators). I used to fool myself into thinking the fringed lampshades, antimacassars, and dilapidated (but still enthusiastically floral) couch made a sort of delayed Janis Joplin statement—but that delusion quickly evaporated in the neon glare of the disco age. The effect was clearly Early Grandmother.

The couch in particular dismayed me. First, because it had outlasted my parents. Second, I consequently couldn't seem to get rid of it. I couldn't stand the thought of my parents being dead for almost ten years while that damn couch continued to carry on, too cheap to last well, too rude to expire gracefully.

Which, of course, in circumstances like these, was a major, if understandable, embarrassment.

While Jay read, I hopped in the shower and made my plan. I would lure him to the kitchen for eggs and toast, then scuttle him out the side door to the car before he had a chance to check out the front room.

As soon as I stepped out of the tub, I could hear Handel's "Water Music" on low in the living room. I ran out, toweling my hair. There he was, sprawled nude on the couch.

"I like it," he said, gesturing around the room. "Where'd you get all this stuff? I expected brick-and-board bookshelves, maybe, but lace-edged pillowcases?"

He flung his arms comfortably over the backs of the cushions and kept looking. I knotted the towel around my waist.

"My great aunt did the lace," I said sheepishly. "I was named after her father."

"It's refreshing," he said.

I blushed.

He caught my vulnerable look.

"Let's go eat," I said. "The coffee is on."

While I was flipping my eggs, Jay took his plate back to the living room and curled up in a stripe of sun on the couch.

"I like it in here," he called.

Awkwardly, I sat in the easy chair opposite him.

"Makes me want to be a cat," he said. "There's so much to look at. I'd like to leap up on your bookshelves and rub up against the spines and paw open your cupboards. Snoop around."

He cocked his head as he read the titles, a hank of black hair falling over his forehead.

"Such variety," he said. "*Richard's Bike Repair* . . . *Anna Karenina* . . . Ram Dass, Chekov, *Jane Eyre*. And what's this?"

He walked over to a shelf, plate in hand; pulled out a yellowed magazine.

"*Practical Beekeeping*? Now there's a concept. I wonder who's writing for the impractical beekeepers? . . . And here's a whole row of *Reader's Digest Condensed Books of the Year* . . . 1954 . . . '55 . . . '58 . . . I used to read those when I stayed with my grandparents!"

Great! I thought. Welcome to the mausoleum.

But I leaned back in my chair, watching him, a slow smile spreading across my face. He was enjoying himself, floating the titles out into the air like toy boats on a pond, playing more and more expansively as he became aware of my intentness, my pleasure in his play. Suddenly I had a glimmer of how hungry he was to display this buoyancy, to have it seen. Unlike me, whose sense of being known has so often relied upon sharing my history, he seemed eager to convey sheer energy, to have it delighted in, unsquelched; to see himself ripple the field of another's vision. I was happy to lay back and oblige.

"Thomas Hardy . . . the Hardy Boys . . . Gide," he continued. "And here's Stephen Crane, sidled up to our old friend Walt, the Good Gray Bard. Now that could be racy! Did you know Whitman was a nurse in the Civil War? I always did love a nurse with good hands," he said, winking at me.

"And what's this, next to Kafka? *Psychic Discoveries Behind the Iron Curtain*? Such filing! And *Man and His Symbols*, by Carl Jung . . . Maybe that's why I slept so well. Lots of dream fragments floating around. I don't usually sleep so well the first time."

"Usually . . . and how often is that?" I teased, arching an eyebrow. "You do seem to know how to fascinate the men."

One side of his mouth pulled up in a half-grin. "Yeah. My problem is finding men who fascinate me."

"I see. And I have the honor of putting you to sleep best of all . . ."

"No, no, no, that was a compliment, really. It was hot, messing around with you . . . but more than that. I must have felt at ease . . ."

He paused, raking his fingers through his hair. He seemed to be hunting for words, the right footing.

"It's true, I've done my share of club-hopping," he said. "But that gets old . . . guys shouting coming-out stories over a loud bass, followed by some acrobatics to see who's gonna be on top. Then what? Maybe you have something in common, maybe not. What I was trying to say is that this place is my idea of a funhouse, really. Some people fall in love simply because they love the same books, you know . . . I always liked that idea . . ."

I blushed. He hunkered down over his plate, bit into his toast. We sat for a few minutes listening to the music, letting his comment hang in the air, mingle with the melody. Looking back, it seems we both needed to veer off for a few seconds. The relationship was new, after all. Neither of us knew what to do with the latent intensity of that moment, if and how to hold it. I wanted very much to ask him the simple and logical and important next thing—what books did he love—but I felt shy, afraid it would put him on the spot, seem too fetching after what he'd just said.

He, meanwhile, was heaping more jam on his toast. I could hear his knife sliding around, scraping bottom, tinkling the glass as he dug around for the last glop. Lifting a loaded-up square to his mouth, he crunched down, vigorously working his strong jaws, the sound audible above the music.

47

I shifted in my seat, distracted, watching myself grow uncomfortable. The loudness of his munching took me aback, threw me off, made me feel involuntarily annoyed. At the time I couldn't stand my own pettiness, but I see now how the presence of so much appetite in that room must have been overwhelming, unfamiliar, almost sacrilegious amidst the revered but dusty artifacts.

A vague inarticulate sadness began to well up in me, against my will. I forced myself to listen, trying to understand, pushing against my closedness. The crunching bounced off the walls, stirring up hollows and empty places. It was making me feel twitchy, crazy, almost violent, in a silly sort of way, like when someone on the bus is munching through a bag of chips, blatantly having, taking, and you're forced to sit, waiting for your stop, realizing you're suddenly outrageously hungry—you had no idea you were that hungry—and you think any minute you might just stand up and rip it out of their hands and scream, "Gimme that!"

I could feel the blood flushing my neck and face; my palms were starting to sweat.

The stereo clicked off. Crossing his knife and fork, Jay set down his empty plate with a clatter.

"That was yummy," he said, almost inanely. Then he stretched out his legs, as if for something to do. For the first time he appeared a little restless. The quietness seemed a bit awkward for him, tense.

My mouth opened, words flew out, in a hearty unfamiliar voice.

"I like a man with appetite."

Well, at least I'd like to be able to, I thought to myself.

Jay clasped his hands behind his head and gazed at his toes, grinning sheepishly as he wiggled them. With his arms up like that he looked so exposed, his belly little and soft and white beneath the solid ribs. My eyes wandered, traveling the line of hair to his dick, which was dozing, sleepy head lolling on a thigh. A wave of protective tenderness ran

48

through me. Years later, when I read the Tibetan saying, "We each have been each other's mother in another life," it was this moment that came back to me. My eyes dropping to Jay's dick, pillowed on his thigh, and the protectiveness I felt.

Jay capped off his stretch with the semblance of a long yowly yawn. He tilted his head, loosening his neck, as if he was trying to get (or appear) more comfortable.

It hit me what a self-absorbed jerk I was being, not only that morning, but for a long time. It hadn't occurred to me that Jay might need help opening up too. Here was this beautiful man, pouring over the open book of my life, brightening each moment with his easy curiosity, and when my time came to ask what was on the shelf inside his heart, I'd sat there, obsessing about shyness and chewy noises.

I took a gulp of juice, trying to clear my throat. I didn't usually like orange juice, but had pulled it out of the freezer for Jay. The harshness, the acidity, felt good.

I looked over at him, so nakedly enthroned on my couch. He appeared suave, self-assured. But he'd actually said very little about himself, even though he seemed comfortable. And I noted it was my house he'd invited us to, not his. I wasn't sure what to make of this—an embarrassingly messy bed, a roommate, a tendency toward secrecy, privacy, control—but I did note the lack of transparency, and attribute it at least in part to my perverse inwardness, my lack of probing and inquiry.

Meanwhile, my moment was sliding by.

I struggled, suddenly desperate to get over myself.

"So tell me," I said, kick-starting myself. "What's your space like?"

He shrugged his shoulders, gazed out the window.

"No big deal," he said, twiddling his thumbs. He'd bought an old house in Rosedale Park five years before; devoted many hours to stripping the woodwork down to the natural oak, exposing the mantel, restoring the original French doors between the dining and living rooms. He claimed enthusiasm for these tasks, but his voice sounded peculiarly flat.

"That's a labor of love," I said, watching his face closely.

"I guess so," he said.

"What's to guess?"

"Oh, I don't know," he said, sounding pained, not with me, but the whole subject, or maybe the struggle to get it into words. He picked up the empty jam jar, turning it over in his hands.

"I guess it's kind of an arranged marriage," he finally said, fixing on the label. "More of a labored love, rather than a labor of love. With time I've come to really like it, but it wasn't my idea. My father had decided it was stupid for me to throw money down the drain on rent, so he pestered me into going around with a realtor and fronted the money for a down payment.

"I know I sound like an ingrate," he added morosely, "but it wasn't my timing. My parents were getting ready to move to Arizona. One of those condos where it's against the rules to hang a towel from your balcony. They wanted to see me settled before they left. At least in a house, if not a marriage. The whole thing brings up a lot of guilt."

He sat twisting the lid of the jar on and off.

"Let's talk about something else," he said.

He set the jar down on the table with a wham.

"Sorry! Bottom came up fast," he said.

I raised my eyebrows.

Crossing his legs, he started biting at the web of his thumb. "Sticky," he said, cleaning with his tongue.

As kids, my friends and I would put our hands in our mouths like that, fingers and thumb splayed out around our cheeks, when we played horses. We called it "putting in the bit." We'd buck and frolic around the yard, elbows up, bits in place.

I waited.

He dropped his arms to his lap, holding his elbows.

"It's just that I wasn't out when my father decided to fork over the bucks," he finally said, wrinkling his nose. "He would never have done it if he knew I was a faggot. He's an asshole, but I feel like a cheat."

He absorbed himself with his paper napkin, trying to unwad and flatten it over his bare lap.

"A wrinkled mess," I said quietly. "Sounds like you both feel pretty bad."

"Well, it's over and done with now," he said, giving up on the napkin. Scrunching it into a ball, he suddenly whirled it at me. I tried to catch it, but it bounced from my chest to the rug. Still thinking about his parents, I let it lie as I tried to sink into what he'd been saying, go deeper.

He leaned forward and with a long arm grabbed it back.

"What about you?" he asked abruptly, wedging in a lighter tone. "I've heard all about how out you are on campus."

Unable to keep up, I stared at him blankly.

He wagged his finger teasingly and pushed on, taking advantage of the pause.

"Your advance man was bragging," he said, dangling bait.

"Oh?"

His eyes pinned me, determinedly bright. Pressing him to talk more about his father at this point seemed cruel. I didn't want to be responsible for pulling the switch, making his face go dim.

"Must have been Clive," I said.

"Yep. Before you got to the party. Brave and hunky were his exact words, I believe. He went on and on about how you got the first openly gay poem published on campus. He said it was such a hit, somebody slashed your tires twice in the school lot afterwards, in appreciation."

"Three times," I said, correcting him.

"Jesus! But rumor has it you went right on to hound the librarians into starting a gay lit section. Is that true?"

I rubbed my cheeks, feeling a bit overpraised.

"Am I making you blush? I'm hungry for that kind of courage. The daily stuff."

"Maybe it's not that big a deal for me," I started to say.

"How can that not be a big deal?" demanded Jay, his black eyebrows shooting up. Again, that enthusiasm.

"Maybe I have less to lose," I insisted. *"Freedom's just another word, for nothing left to lose,"* I said, starting to hum the tune to "Me and Bobby McGee."

He cut me off.

"Don't be so modest. Take a compliment!"

A silly grin spread across my face. My cryptic little freedom song had soared right over his head, no questions asked. He thought I was being humble.

He continued on, bent on sharing his first impressions of me.

"I was watching you at the party. You didn't know hardly anybody. People were busy putting on the dog, shining each other on, but you didn't resort to all that posturing. You just sat there listening, a little uptight but very real. I liked that. Meeting people actually seemed to mean something to you, was worth registering with a little anxiety. And you weren't afraid to show it. I'm sick of jadedness, the latest fashion accessory. A lot of guys can't leave home without it."

He paused, looking at me. "You're incredulous, aren't you? Don't you recognize yourself?"

"No. I felt like a self-absorbed neurotic mess at that party."

"Well, to me you were the most confident man there," he said, polishing off his coffee with an emphatic slurp.

I watched his Adam's apple bob alluringly. Suddenly I heard the words like I never had before. Adam's apple. Tight skin, hungry lips, taut unbroken surface.

"Down the hatch," he said, standing up, interrupting my entrancement. He looked down at me, smiling, shaking his head.

"You just sit there a minute and learn to bask," he said, picking up my cup, heading into the kitchen for seconds.

I took off my watch and put it on the opposite wrist. I wanted that awkwardness there, as a prompt, reminding me to bring the conversation back to him. He was incredibly adept at keeping the focus on me.

I decided to take a gamble, go with my hunch that maybe he'd open up more if I went first with the self-disclosures. I'll show you mine, you show me yours: that sort of thing. But talking so much about myself felt seductive, dangerous. Important observations could be missed. I was afraid of getting lost in the headiness of it. I hoped the clunkiness of my watch on the wrong wrist would keep me both sensible and considerate.

"Are you basking?" he called from the kitchen. I could hear coffee dripping into the pot.

"Doing my best!" I replied, pulling the collar of my robe up around my neck.

I thought back over the party. I certainly couldn't dispute the overtness of my anxiety, but didn't feel there was much bravery or choice involved. I would have covered my ass if I could. I was afraid Jay was seeing what he wanted to see.

Out in the kitchen, cupboard doors were banging open and shut. "What do you need?" I hollered.

"Sugar. I see zillions of things but no sugar."

"In the bowl," by the sink.

"I used it all."

"Look on the top shelf, left of the sink."

Things were quiet. Then he started up again.

"I take back what I said last night about you being the youngster. Look at this pantry! Macaroni-and-cheese, soup, canned tomatoes, flour, Crisco, baking powder, and what's this? A jar of barley? Rice, white and brown. Olives, dills, hot mustard, a zillion bottles of spices . . . You've really got this down! I'm a lot older, and I'm still trying to learn food

53

doesn't magically appear in cupboards like fruit on the vine. Except maybe mold. I grow that really well."

I laughed.

"My parents ran a market," I shouted. "It's in the genes."

"I don't know, my mother always had a full fridge. So, what's my excuse?"

You have a mother, a voice silently lashed out in me, shocking in its vehemence.

He came back into the room, sugar box under his arm, full cups balanced in each hand.

I jumped up, relieved for the chance to help. We set the cups on the table, then each took a corner of the couch.

He pried open the metal chute on the box, trying to pour. Nothing. Opening the top, he dug at the impacted mass with the handle of his spoon.

"Don't use this much? Like it black?"

He dumped two huge spoonsful of clumps and granules into his brew.

He couldn't help himself. It was his temperament.

"So?" he demanded. "Did you bask?"

I cradled my foot, picking at a callous. Would it be lying to let him continue to think of me in those ways?

Oh, lighten up, I told myself. It's the morning after. He's entitled to his opinion. Flattery. Roses. Whatever.

Still, I felt like I was inventing, or allowing myself to be invented.

I decided the only way out was to try and live up to it.

Jay's eyes zoomed around the room, out the window, through the trees, back to my face. Loose cannon, I thought.

"What do you picture yourself doing in the future?" he suddenly popped off, Mr. No Expectations.

The future? What a novel idea. It had rarely occurred to me, except in the form of short-term goals, like college graduation.

"Not exactly an eggs-over-easy question?" he asked.

"My experience hasn't exactly led me to believe in it," I muttered.

Jay scooted around in his corner to face me.

Wondering how much to say, I picked up my coffee. It was too hot, but I held onto it anyway, running my finger around the rim.

"What do you mean?" he asked, with that confused half-grin.

I didn't want to look at him. I was wondering if he was going to turn out to be one of those big dumb Golden Retriever types, all honey-eyed and friendly and pawing at the knee, without the least idea of what he was getting himself into. I was used to that. Before the plague, my peers had relatively little experience with death. It seemed that no matter how and when I told the story of my parents, it always caused a major downshift in conversation. Young people, having no idea what to do, would lapse into extreme inarticulate caution, scared to death of saying the wrong thing. Old people would pity me, straining to fix me with unbearably kind eyes and offering cookies and tea, as if I were a child. The middle-aged offered stories with themselves as models of survival, making sure to end on a hearty self-assured note. In any event, I'd always feel horribly humiliated and ashamed, as if I'd contrived the whole sad Dickensian tale to manipulate sympathy. No matter how briefly and flatly I'd put it, my words would stick there in the air between us, my little tin begging cup. I hated it.

Eventually I learned to evade or deflect the topic altogether, tossing off dead mother jokes or flippantly claiming my family was so small it could hold a reunion in a phone booth. Ha, ha, ha. At the time, I tried not to notice people looking away strangely, but later, my cheeks would sting with shame. I thought it was my status they were reacting to, not my way of handling it. Orphanhood seemed the province of children, not people in man-sized bodies.

Jay touched his finger lightly to the rim of my cup, waiting for my finger to come full circle next to his.

"Where are you?" he asked softly.

I glanced at him, then into the dark well of my coffee. It was almost the color of his nipples. I felt like I should say something, but couldn't quite muster it, didn't want to, not yet. I felt hot, almost shaky, beneath the surface. I knew if I stood I'd be rubbery as a colt. It wasn't exactly the question itself, but something in the timbre of his voice, the softness and curiosity combined. It was inciting my courage, in a way I could never have done alone. I could tell the floodgates were opening, whether he, or I, wanted them to.

Suddenly I was up pacing around the room, wanting a life, making one up on the spot, surprising myself with clarity and fervor. Clearly an understory had been growing in me, that layer which persists close to the decaying forest floor, moldy and damp, while the big trees shout and wave their giant green umbrellas so publicly in the daylight above.

I told him everything.

I told about the drunk driver at 2 pm on an April afternoon and how I stood at the kitchen phone, one bite out of a sandwich. I told about the trooper's voice quavering as he asked if I knew Dan or Maureen Lifton. I told about standing there a long time afterward, sandwich in hand, desperately focusing on the green of the lettuce against the cracked wheat, wanting nothing more than to be able to go back to eating my lunch normally.

I told about wondering who to call, who were my father's friends, if his customers knew they were his friends. For him there was no line between the two. I told about my mother's nightgown, still lying in folds on the bedroom floor, and how I was afraid to pick it up, to feel the heat gone out.

And I told about the executor, my uncle, who'd come pushing through the front door, yellow legal pad in hand, surveying the room, consulting his clipboard, clearing his throat two or three times before announcing he'd have to sell the market to pay off their debts. He'd arrange it, he said. Not to worry. He was an accountant. This was the first time he'd deigned to set foot in our house in a decade. We saw him maybe once a year, when we were invited up for cocktails at his white-brick colonial in Bloomfield Hills. Suddenly, there he was, occupying the living room. "Where's the TV?" he'd asked.

"The TV?"

Turns out he'd given it to them, a hand-me-down. Huge old Admiral in a hutch, in their bedroom.

He headed down the hall.

I called after him.

"My mother's nightgown is in there too. Might have some resale value."

He came barging back.

I was sitting on this couch.

He stood over me, head shaking. I could see his fist working around inside his pocket. Hit me, I thought. But he pulled out a little tin, shook two aspirins into my hand. "Firm up," he told me. "You're a man now." Then left.

"No TV?"

Nope. Early that evening some guy had arrived in a van, saying he'd been sent to pick up a TV and could I help him carry it out. I lied. Told him I couldn't find the TV, then went inside and smashed the screen with a hammer.

Recalling the intensity of my impulse, I paused, looking out the window at the huge icicles hanging from the eaves. I could feel Jay's eyes on my back. I remembered how as kids the other boys loved cracking those icy swords over each other's heads. I always hated it. I thought they were beautiful.

"I've never done anything like that since," I said, facing Jay.

"I wasn't worried," he said quietly.

I straightened the drape, pushing it further back. The noon sun was melting the top layer of snow, making it shiny and slick. By night it would probably freeze, form a hard crust.

I glanced at Jay, wondering how all this was going over.

He was sitting cross-legged, gazing down into his lap. Aside from rubbing his palm, he was still.

I asked what he was thinking.

For a while he didn't say anything, just kept rubbing his hand. Finally, he said he couldn't imagine handling all that at thirty, never mind nineteen. He confessed he was in awe of my survival abilities.

"More like liabilities," I muttered.

Ignoring my self-deprecation, he foraged for words.

"I'm not sure if you want to talk about this," he said carefully. "But, well, I've never even thought about having to bury anybody. Is it tacky to ask what you went through?"

He screwed up his face. "I'm sorry, tacky is a crummy word . . . I don't mean to sound so trivializing. It's just that I've never had to go through anything like that. My grandparents were gone by the time I was four. What I meant was, would it be rude or insensitive to ask?"

I fingered the drape.

"Not if you really want the answer," I said.

"I wish you didn't have the answer," he said. "But yes. I'd really like you to tell me, if you feel like talking."

I took a deep breath, spacing out a little as I watched some kids playing Chickens and Fox in the snow on an elderly neighbor's lawn. They were lifting their legs high, crashing through the sunny surface, making a joyful mess of the soft hills. Soon they would run off to their home around the corner, forget about it.

What was all this going to mean after Jay went home? Was it too much, too heavy, too soon?

He was still looking at me, eyes shiny and questioning.

I started pacing around the room again.

"No," I said. "It's okay to ask. I had gone to the funeral home down the street a few hours before my uncle came over."

"By yourself?"

For some reason this fact always embarrassed me, as if it were my fault. "Yes," I confessed.

"What happened when you went inside?"

The first thing that popped into my mind was how some little maple buds stuck to my soles and came off on the lobby carpet. I told Jay how I was bent over trying to pick them up when the mortician appeared. I apologized to the guy but he said it was okay and asked if he could help. I said I thought I got them all. But, of course, that's not what he meant to help me with.

"You must have felt pretty out of it," said Jay.

Laughing nervously, I shoved my hands up inside the sleeves of my robe, rubbing my arms.

"Totally. We sat at his desk and signed papers and made up obituaries, but I couldn't tell you a thing about what was in any of those papers. I could have signed away a million dollars for all I knew."

"Did you even have any idea how much money you had to work with?"

"No. I kept trying to find a way to bring that up but these fluorescent lights kept buzzing. I just wanted to get away from them. Then we went down some stairs that had indoor-outdoor carpeting on them. That's what sticks with me. Indoor-outdoor carpeting. Weird, huh?"

"I don't know," said Jay.

"Well, neither did I. I certainly had no idea I was about to go coffin-shopping."

"Jesus," he said, hugging a pillow to his chest.

"Maybe we should talk about something else," I said. "It's not very romantic."

He winced.

"What's the matter?" I said. "I'm sorry . . ."

"Am I only good for that?"

I was startled by his remark.

"No," I said, embarrassed. "Not at all. But you seemed uncomfortable."

"I am. Why shouldn't I be? We're talking about your parent's getting killed, for God's sake."

I hugged my side and turned red. Suddenly I felt like I was going to cry.

"Come here," said Jay, patting the cushion next to him.

I walked over in a daze and sat down, putting my face in my hands. He placed a hand on my back.

"Try and finish," he said. "I don't want you stuck down there in that basement anymore."

That did it. Leaning into him, I started to cry for the first time in five years.

It was a good half-hour before I sat up and took my face out of my hands. I felt as if the old one had peeled off neat as a nutshell, leaving a new one, rumpled but fresh.

Jay smiled as I plucked the wadded up napkin off his thigh, blew my nose playfully. Stammering around, I tried to find some words to thank him. He told me to just quit it, and with his big hand on the back of my head, hauled me toward him. Mock-dead, I clunked over sideways, head in his lap.

We stayed that way a long time, each of us absorbed in our private thoughts, self-consciousness gone. I felt almost drugged from crying, smoothed out. Specks of dust drifted in and out of a shaft of sun. After a while, the shaft looked like a slanted door. I lingered there, enjoying the sense of threshold. Suddenly I felt his thigh under my cheek getting hot and tight.

I flooded with prickly attention, hairs standing on end. Neither of us moved. Was I imagining?

I drew up my knee, trying to cover my hasty response. Would he think me totally deranged, given all the talk of death?

He took in a breath, shifted his hips.

I wrapped my fingers around his ankle. A turgid vein leapt under my thumb.

His fist, twisting in my hair.

Wild root, pushing up against the back of my head.

Rolling over in my grave, I went right to work.

Afterward, I reached up and grabbed the afghan off the top cushions, settling it over us.

He lay with his head on my chest a long time, letting me stroke his hair. The contrast of its blackness against the sun-washed ceiling, the snow-brightened atmosphere of the room, felt astringent, healthy, like the sting of fresh air on the cheeks after being stuck inside too long.

He mumbled in a dreamy voice.

"What?" I said, curling a strand of hair from behind his ear around my finger. Slowly I pulled it, making his face come up out of my chest.

"Did you know the Victorians made lockets and frames out of their dead relative's hair?" he said. "They'd make tiny braids and weave the braids together into something quite solid. Then they'd put their photos in them. Mourning pictures."

"Did your ancestors do that?"

"I saw it in a book."

We both drifted off again. I let my eyes wander over the spines of my books, not reading any titles, just taking in colors as I felt his ribs moving in and out with his breath.

"So, I want to know your story," I finally said, rousing myself, giving him a gentle squeeze.

He groaned. "I'm sleepy."

"Oh come on," I said, tickling his ribs.

"Not fair!" he said, rearing up, then collapsing on me, making a show of being splayed out and lethargic. "Do we really have to do that?"

"I thought you wanted to go all the way."

"But it's so white bread. Compared to your story, it's all so predictable and boring."

I kept running my fingers through his hair, giving little tugs each time I reached the end of a lanky handful.

"That sounds like the best thing in the world to me," I said dreamily. "Did you go home for Christmas?"

Jay sat up clumsily, his hair every which way.

"No," he said. "They sent a check for the cost of a flight, but told me not to come, since my brother's kids would be there. As if that explained everything. Since I came out to them last year all they can talk to me about is the weather."

I looked into his eyes. Deep brown, with a warm gold ring around the irises.

"There's more than one way to be dead," I said, cupping his cheek with my hand.

Later he would say this was the exact moment he fell in love with me.

PART THREE

9

As it turned out, I never did switch my watch to the other hand. The fact of Jay's strong feet crossed over mine, the heat of his breath against my neck, was better and more true than any story.

That night after taking him back to his Jeep I lay alone on the couch, watching the twilight fill the room.

I remembered a dream I'd had several times, a sky full of quiet stars, then suddenly, as I watched, one would slip. In the dream no sense of wonder came over me, and I knew something was missing, in a way I'd rarely acknowledged by day.

But that night, with the edges of my parents' furniture softened by the dark, I suddenly felt surrounded by a kneeling herd of oxen, cattle, lambs—some sleeping, some attending, like in the nativity scenes I had loved as a child. I remembered the warmth of my mother's hand over mine as we would stand in front of a local church's manger, and she would point out the wise men.

10

I WAKE CLUTCHING THE SHEETS, calling Jay's name.

But no answer.

No sun.

The hotel.

I slip into a half-dream. Nearby is a shoreline, drifted over with snow.
It flows and heaps between big rocks with smooth curves, blue shadows.
I want to lie down there, cool my neck, the fever, against the snow. But
I seem to be standing out on the water, which is frozen, looking back at
Jay, who is on the beach. The background is birchy, like upper Michigan,
but the rocks are Northern California. Time and place are mingled.

I walk out a little further, sensing the current under the ice as it
surges into shore. I am unafraid. Snow covers my ankles, dulling the
neuropathy. Everything is so crisp and clear. I wave to Jay.

Suddenly the drifts close to shore turn into swirling surf. It is beautiful, roiling between the rocks. I am enamored. I don't realize the danger
until I am drenched up to my knees, ice and snow dissolving beneath
me. Nothing holds. A wave, then a larger one, smash onto shore, then
wash back, sweeping me up, swelling higher and higher, engulfing me to
the chest. My coat, trousers, scarf are plastered to me, a heavy dragging

skin I fight against. I call and call to Jay, not knowing if he can hear me, or if he answers.

All the beauty in the world cannot save me.

∿∿∿

After that first night at my house, I waited two days, then three, for him to call.

My body hungered. This was a new thing, my body propelling me to hope. He had said he would call, and I trusted. At work I'd stand at the register mechanically punching in numbers but inside, my cells were swarming in a subatomic daze. His hand around my cock, his breath on my neck, the leap of his pulse under my thumb.

Suddenly the voice of a customer would cut in, asking for change. Startled, I would dole it out, the pressure of Jay's grip unrelenting.

Four days, then five. I almost called, but didn't want to seem too pushy. Then another Friday rolled around.

No answer.

I'd really thought he'd be the first to call.

No answer.

I tried and tried for three more nights, and once, after 2 am.

No answer.

Would you please fucking answer?

Put me out of my misery?

Take me in your hands your arms your mouth your ass, take me anyway you can?

Out of this hotel?

This fucking doubtful place of not-quite-yet?

I started to get pissed. He'd seemed so interested and had more than implied he would call. I thought he owed me at least that. A frank refusal. *It seemed hot but I had second thoughts . . .*

I wondered if he was one of those people who was more interested in witnessing the effects of their charm than really seeing somebody.

By the tenth day I stopped calling. Each time I rang up a charge on the register all I heard was ringing and ringing.

"Yeah?" I said, picking up the phone and shoving it under my chin. I wanted both hands free to continue poking bits of oatmeal out of the sink strainer.

"Well hello," he said suddenly, sounding very hoarse. "Howdy stranger."

I set the strainer down quietly and shifted the phone to my other ear. My heart thudded.

"Well, hi," I said, struggling to keep my voice from going too sour or hopeful.

"So when do I get to see you? I got in late last night and have been tossing and turning since 3 am, wondering how early I could call."

Such urgency, I thought. I'm overwhelmed. Why now, and not the ten nights before?

"Are you still there?" he asked, erupting into a wet cough.

"You could have definitely called earlier," I said. "Like ten days ago. I called you, but you were never home."

"I was in Key West," he said, sounding astonished. "Don't you remember? We talked about my parents? How they sent me money for Christmas, to go anywhere but Arizona?"

"I thought that was for Christmas."

"The gift was for Christmas, the ticket was for semester break. My friend Burt and I went down."

I picked up the strainer and a fork and started poking a tine in and out of the holes.

"Didn't you get my card?"

"No."

"I'm really sorry," he said, putting extra effort into making his scratchy voice sincere.

I flashed on the dinner party, the other men, that smile.

"And was it hot?" I said. "The weather?"

"It is now," he said. "Fever and a bad-ass sore throat. After it all burns off I can't wait to see you."

See you again.

After it all burns off.

11

THE CARD DID COME, two days after the call. I was so relieved. It wasn't a lie.

The water warm but too much traffic.
I can't stop flashing on how you looked when I came in from the snow
  and asked for a ride.
I want to be back in the snow.
The sun is all wrong.
I didn't really want to go.

Simply just to stand again, pulling off a boot with ease, on the threshold of meeting him again.

"But you must have had a little fun," I'd said into the phone.

"Well, yeah, a little. The last night in the motel room, while Burt was out prowling the bars."

I cut in. "Maybe I don't need to know."

"But I was missing you . . ."

"Stop."

"It's not what you think. I'd left my trashy novel at the beach. I found a Gideon's in the nightstand. *The eye is not satisfied with seeing, nor the ear filled with hearing.*"

"You said you were tired of all the traffic."

"Can I be more definitive? All I am doing is lying here thinking about you."

⌇⌇⌇

I want some time with you.
I want some time.
I never did like all the traffic.
I will go in my own good time.
This isn't my time.
My time has gone by.
Carpe diem.

12

W INTER MELTED QUICKLY INTO SPRING. By April we were
seeing each other almost every weekend, showing each other our favorite Detroit area haunts. He took me out for grape leaves, moussaka,
and homemade yogurt with lemon and honey in Greektown, where
afterward we watched a glassblower make a bell with his breath. I took
him tromping through the muddy floodplain woods at Fairlane, Henry
Ford's mansion tucked away on a corner of the University of Michigan-
Dearborn campus. Up against an oak on the banks of the Rouge he did
things to me I'd been too scared to even wish for as a teenager stomping
those grounds. I insisted on reciprocating in kind.

Take me where you always wanted to take somebody but never did, I
whispered into his neck late one afternoon while dancing hot and crazy
in a sea of shirtless men.

A local disco was hosting its first Sunday afternoon tea dance, and
the boys had come out in droves to cruise and chat and jostle and drink
and check out this phenomenon sweeping inland from the coasts. The
scent of clean sweat and randiness hung intoxicatingly in the air, blown
about by a cool spring breeze wafting in through an open door. As Jay
caught my wrist and led me bopping and bumping through the joyful

crowd, it seemed as if nothing could ever stop this wild infectious freedom, this celebration of release breaking out across the land after millennia of oppression and hiding. We were drunk on it, drunk as innocents with the first heady taste of wine on our lips.

As we reached the door, I turned back for one last look. A moon-blue spot hit the spinning crystal ball above the floor. Suddenly the music stopped. A zillion darts of light flew out into the pause, making the room tilt and swirl. Dancers turned up their cheeks, shoving their faces into the smear of tiny fleeing stars, letting themselves be plastered, slithered over, altered and entranced as they undulated to the beat of a song already gone. Slower and slower they moved shoulders, hips, and feet in the enchanted silence. A cluster of men had stopped entirely, wrapping arms around each other, sliding hands down the backs of each other's pants, swaying and throwing off heat as they became their own expanding nebula. Jay slid his arms around me and we swayed too, watching until the next tune came blasting out and the crowd went wild, wagging sassy fingers at each other and the sky, lip-synching in unison, *I will survive.*

Jay and I mouthed the words too as we boogied out the door, me behind him, hands on his hips.

~~~

Exiting. And the ache of so much unexpected sun pouring in.
Don't think, I tell myself.
Just go.

~~~

Out in the parking lot, my eyes almost bursting in the bright sun. Screening with my hand, I let Jay swing an arm around my waist and propel me across the crowded lot. For the first time in my life, I totally

73

forgot the stream of traffic buzzing by, the possibility of being seen in the arms of another man in a public place. It wasn't until I heard Jay's keys against the car door that I came to, a flush of retrospective anxiety sweeping through me as I glanced over my shoulder. I said nothing, though, as I slid into the Jeep.

Out we sped along Hines Drive, that green park beltway through the burbs where bikers, ball teams, and families all mingle at the edge of the road, drinking beer and soda, playing radios loudly, polishing motorcycles and cars in the late afternoon sun. Jay scanned the ballfields as he drove, riding the brake.

I scanned too, nervously glancing at the tangled shrubby fringes of the outfields, wondering where we might be headed. After a few miles I decided I'd better speak up.

"I know I've been throwing around bold invitations, but I was imagining something more private."

"Oh?" teased Jay. "So what was it you had in mind just a minute ago, before you said that?"

"Shut up!" I said, shoving my hand under his arm, tickling him vigorously.

"You just wait," he said, fending me off with an elbow. "I wouldn't even think of taking you here. I've been here lots of times. You said to take you where I'd never been with anybody. Obviously, that's not here."

"Great. And on the way we get to visit sights of coitus past," I said.

Grinning, he pulled over onto the gravel shoulder, pointing to a covered pavilion sheltering a dozen picnic tables.

"Yep. And here's one of the real hot spots," he said. "Lots of action. Especially each June, when I bring my seniors here for their graduation picnic, along with any parents who want to go. We play volleyball, and they put on plays that make fun of me. Very illicit."

I laughed. He pulled back into the traffic and headed west, talking animatedly about his efforts to arrange special field trips, something resented by teachers who were more worn down. The students loved it, though.

"You are really jazzed about your job," I said.

He smiled, kept driving, grew quiet.

Suddenly I became aware of how I always seemed to need to spell things out, either in my head or out loud, rather than just letting them be. Jay, on the other hand, communicated his feelings less by labeling them and more through his voice and face and gestures as he told a story. I liked that about him then. He could just have his enthusiasm, without analyzing or explaining everything to death. At the time, it pulled me out of myself in a helpful way. His quietness following my remark made me uncomfortable, but in a good way. I could feel my urge to fill up the space, chatter, make a verbal bridge between us. Instead, I laid my hand on the back of his neck, rubbing it as we rode, eyes ahead.

Oncoming traffic was thinning out. The lawns and slopes of the park grew deeper and more empty. After a while we turned off Hines Drive entirely, taking a narrow two-lane road I didn't know. Out we flew past half-built western townships and water-filled cornfields, driving until the road turned to gravel and the day to dusk. I sank back in my seat, happy to let myself be taken further than I'd imagined. Head lolling against the window, I let my eyes wander along the long skinny ditch at the side of the road, full of a black and twisting rope of water. Unexpectedly, just as the sun emptied itself from the sky, the surrounding fields of standing water turned liquid gold for a few shiny moments. I rolled my window down, wanting the sweet night air against my skin, the music of tiny frogs. Jay took my hand.

Eventually we came to Ann Arbor, the outskirts. I didn't immediately recognize where we were. I'd visited a dozen times in the past few years, but always took the freeway, never this back route. I'd grown almost dozy, listening to clods of spring mud thud against the floor boards. Then suddenly, the hush of pavement underneath.

I sat up. Jay finally spoke, pointing to a little white house as we passed beneath a cozy corridor of wide-branching trees, lit from beneath by streetlamps.

"Robert Frost lived there for a while," he said. "Two roads diverged in a yellow wood, all that."

Then over a stone bridge, railroad tracks, Huron River.

"Lots of cars at the Gandy Dancer, maybe a wedding," said Jay. "Used to be a waiter there, my junior year. Good sand-dabs. Worked the same shift with my girlfriend, the last one I made a pretense of having. We were a good match. She was perky and smart, anorexic, didn't want sex. Somebody had hurt her, maybe the stepfather. So, it wasn't an unkind arrangement for either of us. I don't know if she ever got what the deal was with me, though."

He turned off Division, cutting through a student neighborhood of old Victorians. I pictured him there, after work, escorting his girl-friend up to a door, making quiet excuses as to why he couldn't go in. I imagined him walking away, feeling slightly guilty but relieved, his friskiness swelling with each step he took under the trees. I put myself in the picture, walking toward him, our eyes not directly meeting, but definitely taking each other in. I'd notice his boots, his long gait, thick belt. I'd be drawn to the way he moved, the jut of his hipbones, slight roll of his shoulders. I'd think about luring him up onto one of the big wrap-around porches cluttered with bikes and recycling and broken wooden chairs. There, in a pocket of darkness.

He would probably find me incredibly juvenile. I would have no hip collective household or artsy studio in which to seduce him. I was just a commuter student from the lowly satellite campus, in for the day, a tem-porary frolic. He probably wouldn't even take a second look. We would pass, and I would walk on alone, enviously staring up at the houses, just as I always did here, jealous of all the terribly interesting and important and diverse conversations being bantered about inside.

"Come here much?" Jay asked, startling me.

I shrugged my shoulders.

"Each school break. I call in sick at work, make a daylong pilgrimage."

I cringed, hearing myself use the word pilgrimage. It made me sound like such a novice when I wanted to feel sexy and assured.

Jay pulled up to a stop, stared straight ahead, both hands on the wheel.

I turned my head, gazed out the side window. Try not to obsess, I told myself. He's quiet at times. So look around. Enjoy.

A large gabled house on the corner was ablaze with light. As we idled, I leaned forward, snooping. It was all so different from my neighborhood, where the small brick houses closed up tight after dark, curtains and blinds drawn in double layers. Here, everything was open wide, illuminated for all to see. In the dining room, I glimpsed a lively chaotic group huddled around a table. Allen Ginsberg grinned amiably down from one of many posters on the wall. The light was rosy and warm, diffused by a batik bedspread slung beneath the ceiling lamp. Upstairs, a lone reader sat in a chair, mantle of light falling over his shoulders.

I craned my neck, trying to get a better look. The muted, envying side of me was creeping in. I wanted to be that man, free to set aside my books at any moment and go wandering these streets for hours, peeping in yellow-lit windows. They were eyelets, inlets, invitations to a hundred possible worlds.

Jay stepped on the gas, moving into the intersection.

"Know where you are?" he asked, pinching my jeans above the knee.

I nodded, inarticulate. We were crossing State Street, the main artery into central campus. A few students hurried along, toting backpacks, laundry bags, food. No big deal, I thought, to somebody like Jay who'd lived here for years. He'd outgrown it, moved on. Unlike me, who always spent my first hour or two here feeling both invigorated and uptight, awkward, out of my league.

Just glancing down State Street brought up so many personal firsts. Until I'd come to Ann Arbor, I'd never listened to live blues, wandered through a street fair, watched a silent movie, bought a gay paper, eaten an avocado. I'd never been in a used bookstore, food co-op, or café. In retrospect, these seem like such little things, typical of many college towns in the late seventies, but to me, Ann Arbor might as well have been Paris. It all seemed so glamorous and sophisticated compared to my neighborhood of barbers, auto workers, postal carriers, veterans, retirees.

Jay hung a left, then another, backtracking through the neighborhood. Stopping in front of a house with a heavy overhanging roof, he peered up at the porch, then let out a guffaw.

"See that dark blob left of the door?" he asked. "That's my old chair. Must be nothing but rusty old springs by now. My former housemate Al got involved with a woman who lived here. After a while, he moved in with her and took that chair with him, without asking me or my seven other housemates. Of course, there was a big hoo-haw, with demands that he come back and confess his sins at a collective dinner. I can't believe that old thing is still there."

I laughed along with him, in a false knowing tone. Of course, I had no idea what it was like to live in a student co-op. Unless you counted my present co-habitant, an eighty-one year old Croatian widow, my landlady, who lived in the downstairs flat. In exchange for outrageously cheap rent, I mowed the lawn, shoveled snow, put up screens, signed a probably illegal contract to never have a woman stay overnight. She had no idea why it was especially easy for me to satisfy the last requirement. Occasionally, I would glance out my window and find her going through my trash, hunting for beer bottles. After being cursed at in English and prayed for in Croatian, I learned to take the bottles to the campus recycling center.

Jay pulled away from the curb, a nostalgic look on his face. I averted my eyes, staring off into the darkness beneath the dash. The last thing I needed was the specter of my landlady butting into my mood, making me feel embarrassed about my circumstances. When Jay turned on the blinker, I tried to shake myself, make myself look at him, hopeful that at least one or the other of us could find something to say that would distract me out of my funk.

His eyes were on the road ahead, unwavering. He seemed elsewhere now, too, gone away into himself. I felt a little stab under my heart. I couldn't blame him. I wasn't contributing much. Why wouldn't he be bored with me? My sudden moods and self-preoccupations.

We drove silently into the campus core, skirting Hill Auditorium. I stared out at its long wide steps and Grecian columns, then ahead at its more modern counterpart, the Power Center, an out-of-place cubist wonder of ugly mirrored glass walls. I didn't know who dreamed up their companionship, but the Power Center was definitely trying too hard. Like somebody else I knew.

Relax, I told myself. At least I knew what it was like to live and work in the real world.

That was the line I'd fed myself the first few times I came to Ann Arbor, and it had worked then, allowing me to stick around long enough for my defensive superiority to subside. When I realized most campus shops were well-stocked with students who had to work, just like me, I'd calmed down a bit. With time, I'd even developed a new way about me, a greater casualness, an improved sense of entitlement, as I browsed in bookstores, lingered in a café, learning the pleasures of spreading a New York Times on a little glass table before me as I sipped jasmine tea.

Even so, this passage was not without cost. One night I dreamed I was sitting in the Central Café, one of my favorite spots on Main Street. I was with my friend Sarah, who lived on campus. As I savored some huevos rancheros, I glanced out the window and saw my father, lugging a crate of oranges. Excited, I pounded on the glass, waving. He peered at me for a second, then kept walking with his load, apparently not recognizing me.

The mood of this dream had definitely seeped into me as Jay and I drove through the heart of campus. By the time we were rounding the curve by University Hospital and starting down North Observatory, it had become an encroaching gloominess. I could feel my vitality, the playful raunchiness that had helped me begin this whole escapade, slipping away. I wanted to be back inside that frisky self with the bold sexy propositions, but I'd been taken over again by my monsters. I thought with intimidation about Jay leaving Ann Arbor after five years, moving back to the city, taking trips to the coasts. I envied how he was such a smooth ambassador, negotiating with equal ease the streets of the inner city, burbs, country, college town. I felt a gulf opening between us at that moment, a gulf of my own making. I grew more and more subdued, pulled in, angry at myself. Why did doubt always have to betray me?

Meanwhile he was silent, absorbed with his driving. On our left was a wrought-iron fence, holding back more darkness. As traffic picked up, I stared into the onrushing lights. My skin felt cold. I pulled on my jacket. Feeling a tension in my thighs, I tightened and released them. Wanting to harden up, I started to blot out Jay, making him into a pair of hands on a wheel.

Spying a parking space, Jay ducked into it, turned off the engine. He leaned across me, hand on my thigh, staring out the window on my side of the car. He talked haltingly, stuff about why he'd picked this dorm. I barely registered it. I stared down at his hand, the hairs on the backs of his fingers.

He went on. "Most freshman wanted to live here because it was co-ed," he said, but he'd chosen it for its original leaded glass, the wood moulding. His voice trailed off, sounding oddly husky, hoarse.

I grunted a few uh-huh's, trying to cover my glum raw melancholy with a muscular reticence. Later he would tell me he thought I'd lost interest, that he was dragging the whole thing out too long.

He kissed me on the lips quickly, sat back in his seat, put on a grin.

"Ready?"

Giving my thigh a hard squeeze, he opened the door, jumped out.

A wave of anxiety surged through me. I sat anchored in my seat. A dorm? I couldn't imagine. No way. Where would we go? A janitor's closet? The shower-room?

I rolled up my window.

He locked his door, came around to my side.

"Come on," he said, drawing a lightning jag in the dust on my window.

Then he ran across the street, away from the dorm, into the fenced-in dark.

I ran after him.

It turned out to be a cemetery, an old one. Big oaks, cedars, a few clumps of hard old snow making vague swatches of light in the dark. He took me by the hand. Our shoes made little sucky noises in the squishy spring grass. A cold wind was picking up, high in the branches. I tried to let it fill my chest, relax. This was infinitely better.

It was even darker away from the street. Jay picked his way between headstones, stopping now and then next to a tree, looking, considering. Finally he started to talk, his voice still hoarse.

"My roommate kicked me out of the room a lot," he said. "He'd take it over every weekend afternoon so he could screw his girlfriend. When I'd complain, he'd say I could have someone over too, if I wanted. Of course, he didn't really mean someone with a dick. In the fall and spring I took refuge over here a lot, with my books. There was a big sugar maple I'd lean up against. I felt like such a weirdo. I thought there was probably nobody else like me, except maybe some old faggy alcoholics in a smoky bar far away in Greenwich Village, so I'd better work it out with Jane. But then I'd just end up over here, by myself."

He trailed off, stood rubbing his palm, looking down at it, a hank of hair hiding his face. For a long minute I watched him, my belly tightening,

81

remembering his hand, its thickness and callouses and long wide bones. Behind all his smoothness and grace I could see the lonely young man he had been, could see the limits of my imagination, thinking I was the only one who had felt that different.

Suddenly I grabbed his wrist, pulling it behind him as I leaned against him, tree at his back. I shoved my tongue in his mouth, lips hard against his. I slipped my hand inside his jeans, over his ass. He grabbed my other wrist, pulling it behind him too, our thighs pressing against each other. I tried to wriggle my second hand down his crack but he fought me, forcing my palm to twist outward, away from him, still inside his jeans. My knuckles ribbed clumsily against his tailbone as he kept me there, kissing him fiercely, our cocks pushing hard against our zippers until we couldn't stand it anymore and he pushed me down, thumbs digging on my clavicle.

Undo me, he said.
You undo me.

I came bursting out of my prison.
I followed the direction of my hands.

You have big hands, he said.

I had to grow into the bigness of my hands.

Sometimes the hands give first
before the rest of us gives too.

I stood tucking in my shirt-tail. Low humid clouds scudded across the crescent moon, cutting off the horn. It surprised me when he took out a little black comb, dragged it through his hair. Gently, tentatively, I took his hand. We stood side by side, kicking at little tufts of grass, both of us being awkward together.

〜〜〜

So when did the body become the prison?
The body the house the prison?
Stinking drop of spittle, bile and froth, drying in a fever's heat.
I got laid (out to dry), people say.

I would not be too ashamed to plead for it now.
Undo me.

But no.
Long and slow.

By my own hand.
Can't you see?

I am trying to take things back into my own hands.
Where are you now?

I came bursting out of my prison.
He undid me.
He undid me.
He undid me.
The body the house the prison.

〜〜〜

Looking through the eyes half-closed, the fringe of lashes. Dark bars, keeping me in. No. Keeping him in. Memory of him, over and over, parting his hair with a little black comb in a cemetery where it was spring and the sap was running up from the dead. All that gristle and lace, femur and pearl, transmuting up through the soil, the solid veins of trees, the soles of our feet. We didn't think of them then, they who were underfoot, or of ourselves, how we were them and they in us. For me, a minor miracle, that forgetting. My bones, finally urgent and young.

<center>~~~~~</center>

I began to ask more of him. At least three nights a week, then five.

"Take me for granted," I urged one morning as we slow-danced to a tune on the radio in my kitchen. "I want to be yours, all yours."

He put his hand on my chest, splaying his fingers, keeping me at a slight steady distance as we swayed.

"Whoa, Nelly," he said softly. "How can you be so sure? After only a couple of months."

"I just know," I said, stretching my chin across the gap, straining to rest it on his shoulder, the cloth of his shirt.

"You haven't even seen the worst of me yet," he said, slowing us to a gentle rock, one foot to the other.

"So, what's the worst?" I asked, gazing abstractedly over his shoulder at the buds on the elm outside my window. Pricked up ears of tiny green dogs, I was thinking.

He lowered his arm, unclasping our hands, leaned against the counter. Forced to attend, I stood back, surveying the full length of him.

"Okay," I said. "How bad can you be? Do you hit people?"

"No!"

"Steal money for drugs?"

84

"No."

"Fuck little boys?"

He shot me a dirty look.

"So, what's the big deal?" I asked, tugging on his big finger.

He shrugged, suddenly sheepish, eyes roving the ceiling in wide silly arcs.

"For all you know, maybe I turn into a maniac sometimes and throw things."

My eyebrows shot up.

"At people?"

"No."

"Walls?"

"Maybe . . ."

"Well," I said, glancing around at my dishes. "We just won't buy expensive things, will we?"

He couldn't suppress a smile. A new tune came on, a livelier one, at a galloping Romper Room pace. Grabbing his hand, I pulled him toward me, commandeering us around the room, me stepping in, him stepping back, a faint look of alarm and perplexion on his face.

"Don't forget," he said, stumbling along, trying to find his balance between my crazy dips and swirls. "I have my job. Friends. Other things. I need some time. We need some time."

I nodded, and smiled, refusing to stop.

~~~~~

I could give him my time but not some time.
Gleam of sweat on a feverish cheek.

The structure of the bones the beams the house the living room.
The plaster cracking in the heat and falling.

How different I am, he was, stripped to the bone.
Whoever thought to love the flesh.

It's not about thinking, he said.

Or was that me.
My part.

Forgetting the lines and roles in the heat.
I need some water.

They poured water through the windows the doors of his house when he
was gone and there was nothing but the bones, a smoking pile of rubble.

It is not a myth that in some cemeteries at night it is possible to see a
blue light flickering above the graves. Gas releasing.

You drive everything into the ground, he would say. Always explaining.

And you, I'd answer. Content with bare bones.

Or was that me?

13

By May, we were spending at least half our nights at Jay's house. At first, he'd seemed edgy and subdued, self-conscious about the circumstances of his ownership, but I didn't care. I was happy to get out from under the eye of my landlady. Granted my own set of keys, I came to view his early reluctance to take me home as an endearing idiosyncrasy, his way of trying to control the pace of things. Mostly he was so regular; it was reassuring to know he had a few quirks.

Both of us favored his place on work nights. There was a big oak table in the dining room, with plenty of room for projects and books. As the end of our semesters approached, we often worked late, with a few quick distractions thrown in during breaks to "settle the body," as Jay described it.

Usually it was me who knocked off first. While he graded papers, I'd soak in the claw-foot tub, relaxing with his copy of *Leaves of Grass* or *Tales of the City*. Wrapped in a towel, I would kiss him only lightly on the hair before I went off to doze, his tabby cat Emily curled up next to me in the bed. I wanted to prove that I could leave him alone when we were together in the same space.

The lightness of my kiss, however, was not without effort. Sometimes, when I was almost asleep, I would find myself jerked awake by an energetic little man in me, barely containable, who would leap up out of my dream-body, threatening to call out to Jay: "See! I was almost asleep, without you!"

Not wanting my enthusiasm to betray me, I would roll over with the sheet wrapped tightly around me. Sometimes I actually was asleep by the time Jay came padding down the hall.

The house itself was a mission brick bungalow in a once-optimistic neighborhood of wide streets, big maples, and modest houses built in the thirties for mid-level auto company managers. A mix of black and white professionals had been slowly moving in, renovating, bringing new life to an area others had fled due to fears of rising crime and plummeting property values. Jay had had to fight his father over location. His father finally acquiesced, deciding to be glad there was at last some interest in his offer of a down payment.

Jay continued to anguish, however, about having taken his father's money before coming out to him. This anguish seemed at play in the fervor with which he'd stripped every surface in the place. The mantle, sills, moldings, and floor were a beautiful glowing oak. The wood was so much the centerpiece, furniture seemed almost incidental. An uncomfortable Danish modern couch, a friend's storage problem, was pulled out from the wall at a haphazard angle. A half-dozen Windsor chairs, waiting to be refinished, were scattered about, with a few lovely but unmatching antique tables and chests. All of this seemed arranged not for any particular comfort or design, but for ease of access to the baseboards and sills, the never-ending pleasures of sanding, buffing, oiling the wood. Projects. It was the home of a man who liked projects more than laying about, a man who liked to do.

I often felt a little restless there, unable to sink in, settle down, which is why I both liked it and gravitated to the tub. Conversely, at my place, Jay would head straight for the couch. Often, on Sundays, while I cooked dinner, he would stretch out, shoes on, swearing he'd be in to help me soon. I knew it would only be a matter of minutes before the funny sweet sounds of his snoring would come floating into the kitchen. When, finally, I called him to dinner, he'd sit up in a disheveled heap, rubbing the back of his neck, looking surprised. He never took naps, he'd say bewilderingly. Was I mad that he hadn't helped?

No. Not then. I loved giving him those moments of drift. My puttering alone in the kitchen seemed part of making that slippage possible. It seems so strange now to think that those times really only lasted a month or two. I was so happy. I wanted it to go on and on. I added extra garlic to everything, joyfully crushing the cloves, peeling away the delicate papery skins, slicing the heavier translucence of the pulps. As tomato sauce bubbled and pasta water boiled, I imagined a tangled arbor of grapes tumbling over my head, the low hum of bees lazing between the vines.

One evening, when dinner was ready, I turned off the stove. Grinning, I went in to him as he snoozed with his big sneakered feet considerately jutted away from the cushions. Catching a shoe between my knees, I started ripping at the laces.

His eyelids fluttered.

"Stay a while," I said, tugging on the heel.

He stared at me blankly, letting his eyes clear.

"Just make a commitment."

"To what?" he asked, belly-up, scratching his navel.

"To what's already happening," I said, struggling with the sneaker, trying to pull back the tongue. I got it off, but he twisted free, rolling off the couch and racing down the hall to my bed, me behind him. With a thud he hurtled himself onto it, the mattress still bouncing as I pounced on him, only to be flipped on my back, arms pinned above my head, shoe in hand.

He straddled me. "Always stirring up trouble, aren't you?" he said, giving my wrists a few shoves into the mattress.

I squirmed, play-snorting.

"Can't just let things be, can you?" he asked, bearing down harder.

"Yep," I said, thrusting with my hips. "Always poking and prodding."

He let go with one hand and grabbed back the sneaker, diving onto his belly next to me, clutching the shoe under his chest. I flung myself over him, chin shoved in next to his ear.

"Gimme," I said.

"No."

"Now," I said, jamming my hands under his belly.

"No," he said. "I'm sleepy."

"Sleepy?" I said, mock-incredulous. "You admit it! But of course. The C-word is in the air."

"C-word?"

"Commitment."

"I thought this was just about a nap."

"It is."

"Uh-uh," he said. "You're stirring up a stink again."

"Take that back!" I said, squeezing him around the waist, renewing my attempts on the shoe.

He bucked and heaved, trying to throw me off. Both of us were huffing and laughing but growing more heated.

Finally, I hooked a finger in the shoe.

He yanked violently, jerking it out from under him. I lunged, shooting out full length on top of him as he flung it in the corner, out of reach.

We both lay collapsed, panting.

"I can't believe you did that," I finally said, surprised by a note of real hurt in my voice.

"Look who's talking! People who don't want trouble shouldn't dig in the rubble," he said, voice muffled in the sheets.

"Or maybe," he said, starting to wriggle his ass slowly under me, "you just like trash."

14

WE TOOK OUR BOWLS OF PASTA out onto the front porch. I had a sated blurry feeling, a sense of resolution in my body, familiar and gratifying. We sat side by side, not talking, slurping with bowls up close to our chins.

It was twilight. A neither here nor there time, I told myself. But necessary, part of a natural progression. I smelled the night air on the grass, listened to water from a sprinkler splat on hard cement, watched lights blinking on a plane. Everything seemed to hang motionless, suspended between a blue and dark heaven.

I set my bowl down, half-empty.

Jay kept shoveling, seemingly oblivious. Suddenly he paused, fork in the air, and looked directly at me. I raised my eyebrows.

He glanced away, placed his bowl quietly on the step between his feet. He stared off into the street, absently snapping a twig from the shrub next to him. I glanced in the opposite direction, feigning interest in a car flashing its brights at a kid on a ten-speed. Out of the corner of my eye, I could see him plucking leaves from the stem. They fluttered down into his bowl one by one, sticking like dark stars.

"He loves me, he loves me not," I said, venturing a cheek against his shoulder.

He didn't lean into me, or answer. We both stared at the bare stick twirling between his fingers. I reached over. He half-handed it to me. I played with it, shoving my thumbnail into the fleshy bark, feeling it crinkle under my push. It was too dark to see the raw greenness of the skin beneath, but I wanted it, was picturing it anyway.

He cleared his throat, looked into the sky, rubbed his cheeks with both hands.

"It's not that I want to see anybody else," he announced. "This week. This month."

Stopping abruptly, he reached over, took back the twig.

"It's just that I don't want to have to know what that means yet, I don't want to be pushed," he said.

"I understand," I said, not really sure if I did, but willing to be happy. My heart went leaping and crashing ahead anyway, plunging into hope.

And next? It was singing. Next?

~~~~~~

A leap of faith.
A walk on air.

I wanted to be in love.
I wanted to stay in love.

Put your right foot in,
take your right foot out

put your right foot in
shake it all about.

I am shaking
I am shaking

Up here on the edge
shaking

who or what to hold me

breath of roses
plume of yellow exhaust hovering above the city
exhalations of dogs, lilies, murderers

my lover's white shirt
a fog hanging over the bay

shroud

I would rend
with my feet

Leap of faith
walk on air.

~~~~~

I was sleeping. No running sores or weeping lungs or fungus-laden toes.

Just falling off that ledge, swiftly and smoothly, from waking into sleep. Traffic ebbing and surging out on the freeway, an ocean of coming and going, dimly heard, gathered into some half-perceiving place. Dreams of going, and not alone.

15

I WOKE ONE MORNING AT JAY'S to the sound of sawing and the splatter of rain against the window. His side of the bed was empty. From the top of the dresser Emily coolly assessed my reaction. Ten o'clock, late for me. I had never slept with a man so skilled at rising and slipping away without alerting me to his absence. But then again, more often than not, other men—or myself—had meant to communicate departure, whereas with Jay, I knew he wanted me to stay, even as he went on with his day, at his own pace.

Pulling up the shade, I sat on the edge of the bed, looking out through the streaks. It was the sort of spring rain that pulls green up and out of everywhere, fuzzing once-stark branches with a leafy softness. I loved the way the leaden clouds darkened and deepened the green, but also made it surge with a barely contained light, the yellow becoming more yellow, too. The shrubs flaming at the edge of Jay's yard must have been forsythia, not witch's broom, but the two mingle in my mind, the broom flaring wildly on the coastal hills of California in late winter, which I always loved, for the way it brought me back to that morning at Jay's. To wake in a house already alive, the smell of coffee drifting in from the kitchen, the sound of a beloved happily absorbed elsewhere, puttering with the knowledge of you there, under the covers, the eaves pattered over by rain!

I drew on my drawstring bottoms and padded through the house to the basement stairs, following the shoosh-shoosh-shooshing of a handsaw. Halfway down the steps, I stopped. Jay's back was to me. It was bare, the muscles moving neatly under the smooth skin as he ripped the saw in and out, in and out of the timber. I sat down on the cool linoleum step. The scent of Douglas fir was intoxicating. He still had on his striped pajama bottoms, work boots, thick safety glasses. I had never seen him working in his shop. There was serious machinery—planer, table saw, biscuit joiner, sanders—plus a whole wall of neatly hung hand tools. Of course, my eyes were on the best hung. It was such an easy turn-on—I couldn't help but smile. He was so agile, the saw sliding back and forth, never pinching to a stop in the tight wood.

When the end of the board flopped off he stood, chest heaving, catching sight of me. I grinned. Sawdust flecked the hair on his arms, the little ridge of fur disappearing under his waistband. I probably still have a few shreds of that flannel in my ragbag at home. White, shot through with fine blue stripes. Ridiculous to some, I suppose. Why save what only seems to throw into high relief what can't be saved? But I can't help myself.

I couldn't, I can't, take my eyes off him as I came down the stairs. He stood with his pajama bottoms hanging low over one hip as he wiped the sweat off his forehead with the back of one arm. In the other hand was the saber of his saw, dangling down. Like a horny ruthless swashbuckler, even with the goofy safety glasses, fogged-over. I almost remember it that way. But when he stepped forward with one eyebrow cocked and eyes not breaking my gaze he didn't need any special effects. He was more than enough for this boy to handle. I could see his erection tenting up the front of his pants as I picked my way around the lumber and tools on the floor to slip my hand inside his waistband.

"Got some hardwood for me?" I said, backing him up against his workbench. Tasting the sawdust on his lips, I slowly worked my way down. I was in the mood to worship.

He was just knocking together a table, he told me afterwards. No big deal. A political theater company he had been involved with for three or four years in Ann Arbor was having its usual May Day reunion. On Saturday, he was going to help do lights and sound for a performance at a UAW hall in Detroit. They would have an after party at his place on Sunday. Felice, one of the powerhouses of the former company, had gone on to develop a show written and performed by union members about their lives. It was a big hit at union conferences and meetings all across the state. Felice occasionally pulled in various members of the old company to help, including Jay and his former roommate Steph, a pianist. He knew I had to work, but if I wanted to drop by the UAW, or spend the night on Saturday and then be there on Sunday for the reunion . . .

He tossed off the invitation casually, as he jostled around behind me, drying himself off from the shower. I was eyeing myself in the mirror, trying to finish my shave. I wasn't paying much attention, truth be told. It wasn't that I didn't want to meet his friends, of whom he had spoken many times as his first chosen family, the kindred spirits he'd found after leaving home, coming out. It was just that I'd been happily absorbed in something he had said a few moments before about how he'd been using the hand saw instead of the power saw in hopes that he wouldn't wake me. I didn't want to yield my little reverie to even the thought of anyone else. "Dream any trees?" he asked, bright eyes on me in the mirror as he'd rested his chin on my shoulder, squeezing me around the waist with one arm.

I'd tipped my head back. He'd caught it in the basket of his big hand, drawing my hair up through his fingers. A thousand winking stars tugged open under my scalp. I didn't want to be anywhere but there, that day, with just him, and the stars.

In the vigor of health.

16

"DREAM ANY TREES?" he had asked.

Not then.

But now, I do. I see them, rising at the edge of an open field. Gray at first, barely distinguishable from the low-lying fog filling the field.

Then a clearing. Some sun.

The day I am remembering is brilliant.

Fall.

The air is crisp. I hang my head out the car window, drink it in like a dog. I am maybe ten. My father and mother are in the front seat, talking. It is Sunday, we are out for a drive. Nothing much is happening, except happiness. We are happy. The sun falls into me, slanted.

We stop by a woods. A sprig of trees, really, left standing at the edge of acres leveled for a subdivision. Soon, quick cheap rows of blonde and red brick houses will march in uniform over fields once cleared for beans or corn or cows. Detroit and suburbs are sprawling outward, more and more each week.

My father steers the car down a bumpy track into the woods, eyes on a heap of upturned trees and shrubs. A bulldozer is parked half-pushed into the pile. I turn around, look back at the land behind us. It is orange and scraped, like a desiccating hide.

An unlikely paradise, really.

But my father's love for such places fills me. The broken beauty there, so like his own. I watch as he jumps out of the car, slams the door, stands for a minute scratching his belly, taking the air.

It smells of torn-up roots and dirt and wood.

He lets out a happy sigh.

My mother comes around the car, takes his hand. She winks at me, in playful conspiracy. I know she is trying to stop him from scratching a hole in his T-shirt. We both know this is impossible. He is always scratching his scar from the war, where the shrapnel entered.

Gripping the back of my neck, he gives me an affectionate shake, steering me down the muddy tracks of the bulldozer toward the pile of tree limbs.

I am his, his gesture says.

I like it. More than he knows. The solidity of his hands, his compact strength, the uneven lope, a lope that is due to his wound, yet somehow makes him seem a bigger man to me.

I walk beside him, feeling his contentment in my own body. I am just ten, but I sense, intuitively, in that way that children can, his mood has something to do with the war, some correlation between the dug-out pits of houses, the trench in which he had been shot, the land which would soon be healed over with turf and cheap homes, this time for vets from Viet Nam. I can feel the ache and solace in him, coming together.

He picks up a walnut, tosses it at me.

It falls open in my hand, along a puckered seam.

My mother plucks some Queen Ann's lace, sets it in her hair.

My father adds dried thistle.

I trail behind, flinging milkweed in the air.

Together, we fill our trunk with the hacked-off limbs of young, uprooted trees.

At home, we unload the firewood, each of us taking a turn to saw, carry and stack it; then, to tend a stew in the kitchen. I flit happily from house to yard, chopping wood, chopping carrots. As a family we are used to working together, each contributing what we can. When my father tires, he plunks down in a chair, shells a few nuts; I take up the saw. My mother pauses too, has a smoke. Standing with one hand on her hip, gazing up past the garage at some jay in the Colorado spruce, her eyes narrow as she exhales. The blue-green tinge of the needles seems to fill up something behind her eyes.

Thinking of my mother's mood now, I know it belonged to all of us. I recall my father looking up from his shelling, sensing it, wiping the sweat from his forehead on his sleeve, and she turned and looked at him, and then both of them turned and looked at me as I worked. And between us passed a vigor and a pleasure that would underlie that spring morning in the basement with Jay. Just the bare scent of it, in the sawdust, without any actual memory of the parents, or child. It was as if they had been absorbed into the air itself, the light slanting in through the streaky windows of the basement and shining down from the florescent tubes of the shop onto the shoulders of the two men receiving from each other what had been made possible, what had been prepared, by some day out of mind.

But still there.

Hard not to cling to.

Worship.

The simple pleasures of a healthy man.

17

WHO WANTS TO SHARE? I didn't. Not one inch of my private time with Jay. When he first told me his friends were coming the next weekend, I was less than enthused. What can I say? I was in that possessive period of early love. Besides, the tone of his invitation had seemed tentative, more like an afterthought. I didn't want to intrude. It was a reunion, after all.

Of course, curiosity soon got the best of me. By that afternoon, I was helping him varnish the table. By mid-week, we carried it out to the yard, settling it in the grass between the apple tree and cherry. The moon shone down through the branches, nearly full.

Back in the house, we stood at his bedroom window, looking out at the table. A satiny cloth of light ran its length. It floats up now, as in a dream, luminous, waiting for plates of food, hands in the bread, gossip and songs.

I put my hand on his back.

He is quiet.

We look at his table.

18

ALL WEEK THE TABLE FLOATS UNDER BLOSSOMS, beckoning. I get it in mind to make a fish stew. My mother's recipe, in her big cast iron pot. On Saturday I'm up and out before Jay. As I sneak back into his room to get my keys, he props up in bed, sheet around his waist.

"Where are you going?"

"My secret," I say, grinning from the door.

He runs his hands over his face. He has to get going too, pick up equipment, take it to the hall.

"Come here," he says.

"No," I say. But I let my eyes drift down his belly, once, slowly.

"Later," I say, lifting an eyebrow as I turn to go.

"Not fair!" he calls after me.

"Make due!" I shout from the front door. "Just save some for me," I add, poking my head back in.

I drive away, picturing the cool blue sheet, him slipping beneath.

It's the warmest day yet. Already people are out in their yards, jackets off, doors flung open behind them, flats of seedlings set out in the sun. I am eager to make a gift of it to Jay, who will spend it inside, in a windowless hall, doing a good deed. As I drive I am planning my surprise, a feast for him and his friends. When I'd asked what he'd intended to do about food, he'd said they usually threw together a tuna salad, some rice and beans, whatever was around. No big deal.

At the market I decide to show him what can really be done with whatever's around. I fill my basket with the freshest of foods, those I can offer simply, just as they are. Asparagus—fresh, no sauce, with wedges of lemon to pique that turgid sense of spring. New potatoes, sandy and small, good for roasting in their skins. Strawberries, uncut, with caps of green. Parsley. Bread, crusty, unsliced, to be pulled apart in great wads, a light dust of flour coming off on the hands. Unsalted sweet butter. Thick heavy parcels of fish, another of bones, hefty under my arm.

I walk to my car, everything fizzing with light—the black shimmering road, skins of fruit in my bag, striped awning. I am humming as I slip the key into the lock. Humming with new life, finally waking from a long subterranean grief as a new energy comes bursting through.

It's then it comes to me. Though this market is like the one I grew up in, I've lost the ache. I am no longer mourning those who have gone, my parents, the life I knew with them. There is only a good ache, for things to come.

"Make like a bird," my father would say, on a good day, throwing his arms out wide, no pain of adhesions pulling.

Out of the lot, breeze in my hair, I drive with the windows down. Stop by my flat, gather some clothes, the recipe, the pot. The air in the closed-up rooms is tight. I can't wait to get back to Jay's, fling open the doors, put on some music, start the stock.

Emily darts from the shrubs as I stride up Jay's walk. Catching whiff of my new potential, she sniffs at my calves as I open the door, eyeing my bags. For the first time, she deigns to mark me with her cheeks, claim me. She troops in behind, my pal from counter to fridge as I wash the leeks and berries and fish, her green eyes wide as I pick up a skeleton by the tail, lower it into the pot. I buzz around the house with her all day, cleaning and cooking and changing the sheets as the bones simmer, dissolving into a rich broth.

When Jay comes home, I want the curtains lifting in the moonlight and breeze, I want the house adrift in scent like a boat in full sail.

So much seems possible.

~~~~~

On my desk at home is propped a postcard I picked up at the art museum last year, a still life with skull, leeks, and pitcher. An underlying rosiness like apple blossoms shines through the bone yellow skull, infusing the table of white.

If only I could sing the happiness of that May into both of us now.
Me and the virus.
Companions to the end.

Too late to bargain, too soon to give up.
High noon, strong wind.

Are you cold too?

Small dumb beast.
Your planet, dying.

Maybe I should have sung to you more.
Maybe I could have found the one song that would have lulled you,
made you quiet and calm as sheep in the hills.

Would you have stopped wanting more?
Struck a peace, called off the troops?

If only you could have been happy with fewer of you,
small things, less busyness.

Your world would have lasted.
Our world.

But look at us.

I wanted it all too.

～～～～～

By the time I got to the hall that evening I was aching to see him. As
I crossed the big crowded room looking for him, people swirled by in
their Saturday night best, steelworkers and their wives, black and white,
young and old. The convivial spirit of the place flooded into me. I had
resolved to keep my activities of the day a surprise, play it cool, but by the
time I located Jay amidst the tinkle of glasses, clatter of plates, laughter
and talk, the odors of fried chicken and fish, perfume, whiskey and beer,
I was fairly bursting with the combined exuberance of my day and the
energy in the hall. All I could do was beam at him as he finished talking
with an old guy who was leaning over his lightboard.

Jay hadn't seen me yet. As he listened to the old guy his eyes were
shining and serene, his body relaxed into sympathy with the old man's
story of recently losing his wife. Jay wasn't saying much, but it was all
there, in his body, the genuineness of his concern.

It was the old man who nodded to me first.

"Think you've got a buddy here," he said to Jay.

Seeing me, Jay lit up, put his hand on my shoulder.

"My partner," he said, the overtness of his introduction taking me
by surprise.

The old guy shook my hand, then ambled off, probably thinking I was Jay's assistant. To me it didn't matter. Jay's intention, the openness he seemed able to feel here, pleased me. Given how careful he had to be around school—I was proud of him.

"Lonely old guy," said Jay, oblivious to my amazement. Tilting back in his chair, he folded his hands behind his head, eyeing me up and down.

"So, where's my surprise?" he asked, long legs draped over each corner of his chair.

"Have to wait," I said, pulling up a chair, brushing my arm against his calf as I bent to retie my shoe. He leaned over the light board, torso pressing against me as he pretended to fiddle with some cords. I raised back up, my face passing close to his and he inhaled.

"You smell like sun," he said, looking at my hair, smiling.

"And what's all this you're in the middle of?" I asked, my eyes sweeping the hall. Behind him, around us, the crowd swirled, people passing platters, guffawing, clinking glasses. The faces of union leaders, Walter Reuther and others I didn't know, watched from their portraits lining the cinderblock walls. I was a bit in awe—there was a kind of festiveness and camaraderie I had never seen elsewhere—or rarely—since: a crowd of a thousand black and white people, sitting at tables, in groups of eight or ten, mostly of one race or another, but hopping across aisles to lean over a shoulder, tell a joke, forge an alliance, join in the wave of laughter pattering over the heads of all. And here was Jay in the middle of it.

"How many of these events have you done?" I asked.

"A half-dozen," he said, pushing a paper plate of cherry strudel toward me.

"I saved you some," he said, swiping up some red goo on his finger, sucking it off with exaggerated flair.

"I hope it's a big piece ...," I said, staring at his lips, remembering that morning.

"Very," he said.

Just then the lights flipped off and on.

"Showtime!" he said, pulling his cue sheets toward him.

I leaned back, arms crossed, stretching out my legs, letting the moment open and spread through my body.

~~~

I had gone to the hall that evening without much thought of anything beyond the lovely but small drama that was unfolding between Jay and me. To me the show was simply a diversion, entertainment. At first—as performers had risen up from the audience and come singing and dancing down the aisles to take their places center stage, to stand or sit on boxes Jay had made—I had been more focused on Jay, the expertise with which he slid the levers up and down the board. As the performer's faces shifted from blues to greens to gold, to me it was as if Jay were personally bringing a whole world to life.

Absurd, of course. I was all wrapped up in him. But later, after I had gone back to Jay's house alone, leaving him and his friends to strike the set, the worker's faces and stories and songs kept swirling up in me, playing to some deep music in my body as I tossed and turned in his bed. I felt as though I were still awake, still beside him, watching the show, hearing the stories of people much like those who had shopped in my parent's store, until I rolled over, draping my arm over where Jay should have been, and woke, realizing I had come home, to his house, alone.

I turned over onto my back. The shadows of leaves were tossing and shifting in the moonlight on the walls. The room felt crowded and busy, as if with layers of spirits. Closing my eyes, I kept seeing one woman performer in particular, talking of how she longed to hear the human voice after a day operating a drill punch. The noise had not only made her half-deaf, she'd said, but lonely.

Suddenly I found myself falling more deeply in love with Jay. Caring about this woman's story, he made an effort to bring it to light—with minimal attention for himself—bridging a gulf I had felt, or rather feared, between us.

In half-sleep I remembered that Jay's grandfather had briefly worked as a security guard at the Ford plant where my grandfather had been a welder for twenty years.

Had they been lonely, too?

I rolled over, pulling Jay's pillow over my eyes as I watched the grandfathers recede into a dream, walking together across a gray parking lot, lunch pails in hand.

They re-emerged, this time on stage, wearing the faces of a black man and a white man, arguing about union dues. Jay shifted beside me, focusing a spotlight.

I pushed the pillow aside.

I am certain our grandfathers would never have spoken to each other, Jay had said, earlier in our relationship.

Why not? I'd protested.

My grandfather liked his uniform. The stripes. Silver buttons.

I lay on my back, picturing Jay's grandfather, his heavy coat. The moonlight in the bedroom turned to snow, piling on his shoulders. He was peering through the tangled ivy on a chain-link fence. Just beyond, strikers walked, frost on their breaths, each wearing a hat identical to my grandfather's fedora.

As a boy I had loved to touch the brim of that hat. The dull gray softness of it.

I opened my eyes, searched for the clock. Jay had been right, I thought. Our grandfathers would never have spoken. I liked him all the more for having the guts to say it, for not smoothing it over.

We were two halves of a single complicated history, I told myself.

The walnut my father threw me, falling open in my hand.

〰〜〜

Lunch time, San Francisco.

The traffic below picking up, workers pouring out of buildings. Everyone reaching for a door. Fresh air, hot pretzels, apples shiny with wax. Women's heels quick on cement. Men brushing elbows as they wait at the curb.

All that, long ago and far away now.

No, here. Sixteen floors below.

Get a grip.

Hungry. I am still hungry.

Surprise of an appetite.

Thin shit for months, but suddenly even garlic smells good. Room service, making a delivery across the hall.

I didn't even think to bring something. Heft of a brown paper sack. Peanut butter and jelly in the old school cafeteria. My nose in the bag, inhaling. Crinkle of wax paper—a hundred sandwiches opening as kids' voices hike and ring and make a din. Later, years of city lunch breaks with coworkers and friends—mu shu, dim sum, sushi, quesadillas, menudo—everyone reaching.

Happy birthday! Platters of garlic noodles and salt-roasted crab steaming in a crab-orange room off 46th on Judah. Turning pink in a long row of faces wishing you well.

It is not so easy to die.

∼∽∿∼∼

Falling open again.

That clear bright night at the hall.

People pouring out to their cars.

Jay and I leaned against my Ford, hands in our pockets.

I didn't want to leave. Not just Jay, but everyone, and the feeling we had made together by watching in the dark hall, what is difficult, hopeful, what might be changed. There was a yearning in the air, a yearning of terrible beauty.

Jay reached up, gave my shoulder a little shake.

"See you at home," he said.

Home.

A deep hush filled the inside of the car as I drove away.

19

THE PARTY ON SUNDAY MADE PEOPLE want to stay and stay. I wanted it that way, the day opening out into more and more hours, the light going out of the sky gently and being taken up by the candles and dim lamps in the house as the people moved inside laughing and carrying conversations—along with empty pie pans and gallons of wine—from Jay's table on the clover-sprinkled lawn to the kitchen.

The house had a hum to it now, water rushing through pipes, singing from another room, the sound of someone scooping coffee, a door opening, another closing, wood floors warmed by bare feet dancing, and an hour or two of singing along to Motown, swaying.

Everybody loved the food. We talked a lot, too. I found myself drawn out to tell story after story. Mothers or fathers who had died, work, injustices, love affairs; Jay's friends made me feel like it was something, really something—not in a standout sort of way—but tribally.

As the evening drew to a close, Jay's old housemate, Stephanie, sidled up to me in the archway to the living room.

"What a surprise!" she said, admiring the wedge of strawberry pie on her plate. "None of us could have pulled this off," she added, beaming. "Our art is in other arenas. Jay lucked out."

"So how many years have you had these May Day reunions?" I asked.
She raised her eyebrow.

"I didn't know we did," she said, a funny mystified smile coming over her face. "Is that what Jay called this?"

I nodded.

She laughed.

"He told us it was his housewarming. We've been waiting ever since he moved in—how many years ago? Three?"

"A housewarming?"

"He said he wanted us to meet you."

It was my turn to be surprised. She stood smiling up into my face, a small woman with long black hair and hazel eyes. I still remember her eyes; there were dark flecks and green fibers that seemed to make up a view of a sunny lawn with people cavorting. Something very Sunday in them.

We looked across the room at Jay. He was sprawled on the couch, shirt unbuttoned, face relaxed as he listened to the cluster of friends around him talking. I realized again how much of himself he had to keep inside each day when he went to work.

When he saw us looking he tilted his head back into the cushions, giving us—me—warm eyes and a lazy grin that made me swallow.

"He's showing you off with this party," said Stephanie.

I grinned back at her, color rising.

"I feel like I've just been confirmed," I said.

~~~~~

He closed the door.

I went up behind and slid my hands into his front pockets.

"I'm in love," I said.

We stood swaying a little. The music was on low. He was humming quietly off-key. We both stared out the porthole of the thick wood door into the street. The day had been warm but the night dew on the asphalt sparkled as if it still could frost.

He reached his arms behind him, clasping his hands in the small of my back, hugging me.

"I want this forever," I said.

"You're infatuated," he said. "You're much too young and attractive to get married. Besides, who wants some replica of a fifties marriage?"

But then he began a kiss which lasted down the hall into the bedroom and on into the next morning.

20

THE SEASON CHANGED ABRUPTLY. It was still May—the burst cases of buds filled the cracks of sidewalks and spilled from under the fringe of crabgrass when I tried to sweep Jay's drive, the shriveled rusty bits sticking to my broom—but an early heat wave was on. Cherry blossoms drooped with extravagant weariness, littering the lawn as the wild chaos of spring came undone.

We weren't quite ready for it.

Each day at school my shirt was damp against my chair; Jay's kids were stir-crazy. I was lucky—the end of my term had come early, but Jay still had a few weeks to go. In the evenings we sat at his big oak table, windows wide open as he graded papers and I read. On the night I am remembering, I drank a little wine, then went to bed before him, falling asleep to the sound of crickets.

I was startled awake by the doorbell. As my eyes searched the room for the clock—2 am—Jay was already climbing out of bed, cramming himself into his jeans, padding off down the hall. Groping for my shorts in the dark, I went stumbling after him, reaching for the bat I kept by my bedroom door until I realized I wasn't at home.

As I came down the hall, he backed away from the little window in the front door.

"It's okay," he whispered. "One of my crazy kids. Just stay out of sight."

I ducked onto the living room couch. Humid night air rushed in as he cracked the door.

"Hey Eddy. It's 2 am. What's the deal?"

Some mumbling, out of earshot. For a while I couldn't hear anything, just secret night noises, some scuffling, maybe a squirrel or cat, rummaging under a bush.

"No," I finally heard Jay say.

"Please," said the young man, voice hiking. "You gotta let me stay."

He went on, something about everything being all fucked up at home.

"No," said Jay. "But I can take you to a shelter. In the morning, I'll come. Help you figure something out."

I watched Jay standing patiently, one hand on the door, the other rubbing the back of his neck. As his posture relaxed, the door swung open a couple more inches. A wedge of light from the porch fanned out across the floor, onto the corner of the couch, my foot.

Maybe I jerked, I don't know, didn't know, even then, right after, when I froze, trying not to call attention to myself.

There was a pause, suffused with the scent of lilac.

Crickets in the night air.

I held my breath, staring at the tiny checkerboard grid of the window screen, its pattern burning itself into my eyes.

Your move, I thought.

Then footsteps, pounding down the stairs, a fuck you hurled behind.

"Shit," said Jay. The screen door banged as he took off down the steps.

I crept to the front window on my knees. The kid was racing full tilt down the street, strong arms and legs pumping. He was sleek, with a well-muscled chest under his sleeveless T-shirt. The sight of him running with Jay in pursuit stirred me, I must admit.

Jay was behind, hindered by bare feet. As the kid cut into an alley, Jay gave up, stood catching his breath under a streetlight before hobbling back.

"That's Eddy," he said, throwing himself onto the couch. "The one I taught to drive a stick."

We sat in the dark with the door open, listening for footsteps. Jay picked flecks of tar from the balls of his feet.

"Enough excitement for the night?" he asked apologetically.

"So, what do you do now?"

"Try to calm down, figure it out in the morning."

I went to him, stood behind the couch, kneading the tight cords of his neck. I thought about saying something about how the light caught my foot. As he relaxed under my hands, I listened to the trees tousling in the breeze, let my mind drift and go drowsy. Sensing a flagging in my fingers, Jay grabbed my wrists and pulled my arms across his chest.

"Thanks," he said, catching a few hairs from my arm between his teeth. He grazed a little, ponderous or calm, I wasn't sure.

Finally, we shut the front door, trundled off to bed. I fell asleep quickly, waking once just before dawn as Emily thudded onto the mattress from her perch on the window sill. In the gray light I could make out Jay, lowering the sash. The last thing I heard was the brass lock sliding into place.

When I woke again, it was after nine. The room was sunny and warm, almost stuffy. There was an apple in Jay's place on the pillow, a little note. I flung open the window and lay back, letting the fresh air bathe my skin. The prior evening came back to me, the boy, the sight of his arms and legs pumping. I let myself linger and dwell. At his age, I would have loved to have been Jay's student, bring him gifts, only half-knowing why.

Later, I would try to hang onto that feeling, to buffer my rage.

<center>~~~~</center>

Did it happen three nights later, or maybe a week? I don't recall, but Jay still had two more weeks of school to go. I'm sure of that. And that it happened on one of our nights apart. We were in the habit then of taking a few nights off each week to see other friends, or spend time alone. I'd spent the evening happily puttering around my flat. Jay had had plans for dinner and a movie with Thom.

At 1 am, the phone rang.

"I'm sorry," he said.

"For what?" I said, propping myself up, instantly awake.

"I need to come over," he said, keeping his voice steady. "Something's happened."

Knocking the lampshade askew, I turned on the light. "What?" I asked.

"Don't make me tell you on the phone," he said, voice quavering.

My gut still twists, thinking about it.

"It's 1 am. Why now?"

"Everything will be all right," he said.

"Sounds like it," I said, already angry and scared.

We hung up. I bumbled around my room, bumping into open drawers, putting on my pajama bottoms, flinging them in the corner in favor of a stiff pair of jeans. I brushed my teeth, almost shaved but decided to keep my prickly edges. My face looked flushed in the mirror.

I went out to the kitchen. Turning on the old-fashioned stove light, I sat in the dark at the table, looking over at it, wanting its candle-like comfort. My mind raced, turning over each moment of the past few weeks like rocks. What had I been missing? What were the signs? Could he really just end it in the middle of the night? My secret heart didn't believe that, but my body did. My body was preparing for an end. My hands flitted through the previous day's paper, trying to fold it, clear the table. They seemed to have a life and mind of their own, nervous and unfocussed.

When I heard his keys in the door downstairs, a shock of alertness ran up my spine. Reopening the paper, I stayed glued to my seat as he came up the stairs, not calling out to him. I felt a little cruel as I let him walk through the dark flat toward the light in the bedroom, calling hello.

He came treading back into the hall, toward the kitchen. Seeing me sitting there, he hesitated in the doorway, then flicked on the overhead light.

"Jeez, I said," screening my eyes. "It's the middle of the night!"

"Sorry," he mumbled, hitting the switch. He looked big and tousled, a bit deranged as he strode into the kitchen, eyes darting around at me, the cupboard, the stove—an animal vigor rolling off him as well as a stench, smoky, undefinable, bizarre.

"Where's my mug?" he blurted.

"Your mug?"

"I want it," he said, going over to the sink, making a din as he rattled through the pots and pans on top of the dish-rack. "Where is it?" he asked, an odd panic rising in his voice.

"Oh here," he said, retrieving it, holding it in his hand carefully, the handle hooked through his finger. He stood staring at it with a strange fixity. It was just a cheap blue ceramic mug, but he set it on the counter as if it were an heirloom.

"Do I still have clothes here, in my drawer?" he asked, heading toward the hall.

"Excuse me?" I said. "I can see you're hot to trot but I didn't know I was supposed to have them all ready in a brown paper bag by the door for the Big Drop. The Big Dump."

He spun around, stunned and confused, looking at me as if I had just materialized in the room. His eyes seemed glassy, bloodshot.

"What the hell's the matter with you!" he blared.

"Me?" I said. "You're the one who comes stomping in here at 1:30 in the morning stinking like God knows what."

"I stink!" he said. "You just wait. You think I stink!"

"If you're going to do this in the middle of the night, could you at least give me the courtesy of sitting the fuck down?"

I shoved a chair out from under the table toward him with my foot, the legs screeching on the linoleum.

"You sit the fuck down," he erupted, grabbing the chair, slamming it back under the table.

Before I could shoot up out of my seat he was already bent over the stove, head on his arms, shoulders up around his ears. His ribs were starting to quake.

"I'm sorry," he was saying. "It's just—"

The catch in his voice at that moment made the bottom of my stomach drop. Suddenly I understood that something was horribly wrong, something different than I'd thought. Quickly I went to him, laying a hand on his back.

"Don't," he said, lifting his elbow, fending me off.

He straightened up, covering his nose and mouth with his hands, eyes shut, apparently reeling, dazed, gathering himself in. Backing up, I pulled out the chair, sank down, eyes riveted on him.

After a few minutes his breathing seemed to even out. I leaned forward, slid my hand into the crook of his elbow, tried to pull his hands away from his face, draw him down.

He took a deep breath, opened his eyes, searched my face.

"Sit down," I said softly.

He shook his head. "I have to go," he said, blinking. "I'm sorry . . . there was a fire."

"What do you mean, a fire?"

"I came home—there were fire trucks everywhere—cops, fire marshals—it was already out. Hoses all over the street. Mud. The lawn's a mess. They didn't even let me cross it. It's all roped off, until they investigate. Heavy smoke and water damage. They asked me to come down to the police station—they have a drunk kid in custody who won't identify himself. They think he broke in the back, set the fire, then freaked out, called the fire department. They picked him up on his bike a few blocks away. I called you from next door. I came here, right away. I have to go . . ."

As his face started to crumple I stood up, slid my chair over to him. He sank, cradling his head on the table, a sob hiking up in his body like a wave, building and building without cresting. He was fighting hard, trying to stay on the surface, refusing to be dragged under. Saying his name as tenderly as I could, I hugged his head to my belly, leaning over him, trying to make shelter with my body.

He held his breath, stopped shaking. His muscles seemed petrified.

"Just breathe," I whispered, rubbing his back.

"Tell me everything is fine," he said, words muffled.

"Everything is not fine," I said. "Your house just burned down. It's not supposed to be fine. But we'll deal with it. You'll be okay. We'll do it one step at a time."

Everything was going to be all right, I thought, at least for a moment. My hands held his head firmly to me. It was throwing off an enormous heat. Beneath the ashy stench of his hair I caught a whiff of him, pure him, the oils and sweat intensified by fear. I wanted to bury my nose in his hair, squeeze him tight as a horrible joyful relief swept through me. This sort of disaster, I could do. I could be of use. I had skill.

"You're still here," I said. "Still here. That's what counts."

But he wasn't there, not all the way. He tolerated me a few seconds more, then leaned away, stood up.

"I have to go," he announced shakily, wiping his cheeks with the back of his hand.

Suddenly I remembered Emily, in her window seat, preening with the back of her paw. He had said nothing of Emily. Almost blurting her name, I stopped, turned away, looked at the clock, trying not to tear up. I heard him fumble in his pocket for his keys.

"You're not going alone," I said, spinning around.

We descended the stairs, me leading.

It was a warm night. I insisted we take my car. He said he had to get something from the truck. I got in my car, started the engine. I watched him in the rearview mirror, coming up from behind, jacket wadded in his arms. I leaned over, pushed open the door. He slid in. A loud yowl erupted from his jacket—Emily's head popped out. She glared up at me, wild-eyed and indignant, ears flattened to both sides.

"We should probably just go," said Jay, clamping his hands around her.

I could barely keep my eyes on the road, I wanted to keep looking at the two of them. Jay stared straight ahead, a glazed look on his face as Emily kicked and bashed about between his hands. I didn't think about it at the time, but the way he was holding her was making me a little uneasy. But, of course, he was in shock. I tried to make him talk, be himself.

"Where was she?" I asked.

"Out."

"How'd you find her?"

"The neighbors."

"Where'd they get her?"

"Under a bush."

"The little marauder."

I slipped my hand under his collar. His skin felt cold, despite the warm night.

"Want my jacket?"

He shook his head.

I rolled up my window.

The ashy smell intensified. After a few blocks, I turned on the fan. Inside the dull roar I could hear something ticking in the vent, maybe a dry leaf. For a half-second the sound was almost comforting, as if we were sitting by a campfire, twigs crackling. Then the present came leaping up, the reality of flames racing over Jay's beautiful wooden floors and antiques, the spindles and boards stripped and smoothed by his hands; devouring photos, letters, his childhood collection of seashells, rocks, a robin's nest, egg intact for twenty years . . .

Trying to break my chain of thought, I shut off the fan. Jay's head was turned toward the side window. Emily had hunkered down under the cage of his hands, a dark lump.

"What are you thinking?" I asked, hooking a finger gently under his collar.

He lifted a shoulder, not quite a flinch, but still perceptible. His neck had gone totally rigid, didn't loosen under my hand. Suddenly I wanted to haul him over next to me, gather him into my arms. I knew it would be the wrong thing, but I couldn't stand to see him feeling so violated, in need of a shell. Afraid of what I might do, I took my hand away, put it back on the wheel.

"Could you answer?" I finally said, unable to keep a note of fear from creeping into my voice.

Out of the corner of my eye I saw him sit up straighter, glance at me.

Okay, I told myself. Just calm down. Most people in his shoes would be in a daze.

He cleared his throat, answered almost matter-of-factly.

"I was thinking maybe we should drop by the school first."

"The school?" I said, surprised.

"My list of parent phone numbers is there."

"Why would you need those now?"

"In case it's one of my kids at the station."

"Even if it is," I said slowly, "the cops aren't going to expect you to arrive with the right phone number. Your house just burned down. You're doing a lot, just to show up."

He looked at his hands.

"But you don't really think it's one of your kids, do you? They just voted you favorite teacher of the year. They love you."

"Maybe that's the problem," he said, in a strangled voice.

I shot him a swift look.

"What do you mean?"

"Eddy," he said.

"Eddy?"

"It has to be him, down at the station."

I pulled the car over, under a broad maple, out of the streetlight. It all came rushing back, the pounding in my ears merging with the memory of the kid's feet pounding down the stairs. Strong arms, slender hips . . . My face, incredibly hot in the dark. I sat with my hands on the wheel, unable to breathe, all of me contracting around a single point: had the kid seen my foot as the door swung open? I broke into a sweat, wanted to retch. For what seemed like the first time that night, I could feel Jay's eyes on me.

"I know what you're thinking," he said. "Don't go there. I would never do that."

Briefly our eyes met. I hadn't been thinking that, not until he'd mentioned it . . . The men at the dinner party, teasing. My own lingering in the bed, the morning after the kid had come by. If I could think of the boy that way, what about Jay? I swallowed several times, about to say what, I wasn't sure.

"I wouldn't do that," he repeated, catching me by the chin, making me look at him. Suddenly he was there, behind the eyes.

"I know," I said shakily.

But I didn't know, I didn't know what to think at all. He let go of my chin. Both of us stared down at Emily. It seemed I should say more, but I was falling into a hole, tumbling with no clear perspective. He didn't seem to notice. He started to pet Emily, scratch her between the ears.

With uncanny timing she pushed up to meet his hand, then twisting around, bit him.

⁓⁓⁓⁓

Cursing, he jerked back his hand. She slithered down under the seat. He let her go. I restarted the engine.

We crept along beneath the trees, houses and parked cars passing in a blur as I drove like an automaton, debating if I should tell him about my foot, warn him before we got to the station, or if that would only be selfish, a way to insert myself into the center of his troubles. It seemed the most I could do was steer, brake, use the blinker. The undersides of the leaves were a hallucinogenic green in the street light. Everything seemed a little unreal.

We pulled up to a stop.

No words came.

"Go," I heard him saying. "The light has changed."

I wanted him to keep talking to me. I want him now, in this hotel. Telling me I can go, the light has changed.

He began to direct me to the station, and soon, I pulled into a space right next to the door. He got out quickly. We looked at each other through the glass. I curled my hand, half-waving, half-beckoning. I have to tell you something, I mouthed through the glass, leaning across the seat. He waved too, thinking I was saying goodbye. I watched him disappear into the station.

A few cars came and went. Emily stayed under the seat. I stared at the wall in front of me. The sickening image of my foot kept flooding in, the way I had just sat there, a deer in the headlights. Why hadn't I moved? Or maybe I had, a little reflexive jerk at the touch of cold light. Enough to bring the whole damn house down, though. One way or another. And Jay had been so clear, don't let him see you. He had asked only one damned thing of me.

As the minutes ticked by, the guilt became unbearable. It wasn't me who lit the fucking fire, I told myself. It wasn't me who answered the door at 2 am. Most people wouldn't have dared, or bothered, at 2 am. Not in Detroit. Unless you knew someone was coming. Unless it was a regular thing . . .

I shifted in my seat, ashamed to be doubting him, betraying my own sense of him. Of course, he was capable of admiring some student's ass, but mess with it . . . ?

Suddenly I imagined starting the engine, ramming the car through the wall. I belonged inside. If I were a wife or a girlfriend or even just a friend, I would be inside. I stared at the fluorescent light falling in hard squares through the station house door. Angry tears blurred the edges. It started to rain. I unrolled the window, watching it pour in sheets through the light. My sleeve was getting soaked, but I didn't care. I was doing the most that I could, which was nothing.

The shower stopped. A few minutes later Jay emerged, flung himself into the car. "Get me out of here," he said, sinking into his jacket.

I sped down Seven Mile, turned onto Telegraph. The early morning commute had just begun, headlights and brake lights bobbing about in spray from the tires. One fast food joint after another loomed up, bright ugly islands in the wet and dark. Nothing seemed inviting, a place where one man might comfort another openly.

Jay tugged at my sleeve, pointing to the lot of a pancake house on the other side of the road. At least it was mostly empty, dimly lit. I parked at the far edge, backing into the space, facing the few cars parked next to the door. Jay was starting to shiver. I ran in, got him hot chocolate. He sat holding it without drinking while he talked.

It had indeed been Eddy at the station. When they'd taken Jay into the room where they'd been questioning him, the kid had been slumped in a chair, arms crossed, looking very frightened. "Why?" Jay had asked him. The kid had stared at the floor, tears in his eyes.

A couple of cops had then led Jay to a different room, offered him coffee. An older cop in street clothes followed them in. He said it looked like Eddy had broken in through the side door, set the fire with some papers. He must have panicked, called the fire department. Some cops had picked him up several blocks away on his bike, his jacket smelling of smoke. At first, he'd tried to run, had denied everything, then said he had to do it, to keep those faggots off. All three cops watched Jay's face carefully.

"Are you a homosexual?" one of them had asked.

Jay looked at me, face turning red as he tried to keep speaking.

"I lied," he said, voice cracking. "I told them that had nothing to do with it. But, of course, it did. I knew the kid had energy for me. I wasn't sure what to do. I didn't want him to feel ashamed of who he might be, think he was bad, the only one. I wanted to give him a chance to talk, let him know he was going to be all right. But he never dared, and neither did I, not one damned word. Even with the driving lessons, the talks after school. But I was worried about him. The way he kept escalating, coming over. I was trying to back off, cool things down, think of what else I could do. I shouldn't have been so fucking nice. Now see how it looks."

He paused, the skin at his temples flickering as he clenched his jaw.

"I told them I'd refused to let him in that night, had offered to take him to a shelter. They kept pushing. Why hadn't I let him in? Had he ever been in my house? Could anyone corroborate my story? I told them you were waiting in the car, had been there that night, would be willing to talk. The two in uniform really got off on that. Had a sleepover on a school night with your boyfriends, huh? Guys night out? How nice. Stuff like that. The older guy stopped scribbling notes, told them to knock it off. But one of the assholes just couldn't reel it in. You brought him here with you? he asked, incredulous. "Your boyfriend? Are you homosexuals?"

"I'm not lying," Jay had told him.

"But are you?"

"What?"

"A homosexual. Queer."

"What's that got to do with it? I'm the one who's out of a home now. I didn't do anything."

"We could examine the kid, you know. Full body."

"Wouldn't find any. Not mine, at any rate."

"You expect us to take your word for that?"

"Jesus, he's a kid."

"Should have thought of that earlier, buddy. Or maybe we should check you too. Would you like that?"

"Fuck off. I can't believe this."

"By the way, want to tell your principal first, or would you like us to? We'll call and warn him about you at 9 am, regardless."

"What?"

"We'd be going you a favor, buddy. You admit you have a guy in your bed while a kid's there in the middle of the night, and now you have the nerve to bring your fuck buddy here in the car with you as if we want something with him too? Are you nuts?"

"I'll call a lawyer," said Jay.

"Go ahead," said one of them. "Like publicity? Want parents, kids, all the principals in the area to know? Even if you'd win, who'd hire you? The nail salon?"

I took the cup out of Jay's hand and set it on the dash. Curling his fingers into a fist, he sat with his other hand clamped over it. I reached over, cradling his hands in mine, unfolding the fingers.

We sat that way for a long time, neither of us able to speak or move. Dawn filled the sky, humid and gray. The windshield steamed over. I cracked a window. The glass began to clear. A few cars came into the lot. I changed my mind, rolled up the window. I didn't want to see what was out there, didn't want it looking in at us.

Turning to face him, I asked what he wanted to do. Tucking his hands under his arms, he said he really had no choice. He would just go to school. Tell the truth. He had nothing to hide.

His matter-of-factness stunned me. I wasn't sure if he was being brave or naive. From things he'd said before, I'd had the impression his principal was the type of nice guy who disliked controversy.

"Maybe you shouldn't go yet," I said, thinking out loud. "They could hardly expect it. You don't even have clean clothes. You could just call, tell them you need a couple of days. It would give us some time to think. We could call Thom and Clive. They'll probably know a lawyer. Not that you've done anything wrong. But if they're going to act like assholes, we should be prepared."

Jay blanched. I stopped talking.

"I don't want to fight," he said stiffly. "I haven't done anything wrong. I shouldn't need a lawyer. The kid is a mess, everyone knows. The truth should speak for itself. If they don't believe me after seven years of working together, then fuck them."

He paused, shifted. The thought of him losing his career as a teacher left me speechless.

"But I can probably nip this thing in the bud," he said, "if I just show up, talk to them."

"I don't know . . . ," I said, trailing off. I didn't share his faith that things would be put right. I told myself it was his call, that he was the one who knew his workplace, but I couldn't shake my fear that he believed things would come out okay simply because they should, or because he needed them to.

"Before we do anything," I said, "I need to eat. So do you."

He shook his head.

I insisted: "At least rinse your face, comb your hair."

He twisted the rearview mirror, looked at himself.

I opened my door.

He followed suit, moving slowly.

I handed him my comb as we walked across the lot. Inside, he headed for the john, I chose a booth. The place was nearly empty. A bored young waitress arrived with sticky laminated menus. My eyes went straight for the pictures, unable to take in words.

Jay slid into the booth, hair wet and shiny under the lights. He looked a little brighter, if stubbly. He started riffling through his wallet, piling up credit cards, paper scraps, old stamps on the fake woodgrain table.

"What's up?" I asked.

He said he needed to call his insurance company. His voice was a little tremulous. I pushed the menu toward him. He glanced at it distractedly, went back to the wallet. The waitress came. I ordered pancakes. She turned to Jay. "Same as him," he said, not looking up. She held out her hand for his menu. He glanced at her blankly. "The menu," she prompted. Flushed, he handed it back, asked for directions to the phone. She tilted her head toward the lobby. I watched him turn the corner, fighting an urge to go after him, hand him a coin to call Thom and Clive. I made myself look away, at the window, trying to think about what to do next.

The window was dirty and huge, with streaks of gray. Beyond I could see the lot, some cars, the whiz of traffic beyond, but nothing my heart wanted. No ruff of trees, forsythia, anything green, the soft lift of a breeze.

I covered my face in my hands, sank back in the booth.

"I have to leave," he was saying.

I opened my eyes, blinking. I must have nodded off. He was standing by the side of the booth. A plate of pancakes was steaming up into my face, smelling of oil.

"What?" I asked, rubbing my cheeks.

He wedged into the booth. "We have to go," he said. "I have to get to school and get that over with so I can get to the house. The insurance people will be there by eleven."

I looked at my watch, ran my fingers through my hair. "Can't we at least take five minutes?" I said. "We need the fuel."

He sank back in the booth. I dug in. He sliced a few rough squares off his stack, pushed them around with his fork, trying out various configurations. His mind seemed suddenly busy.

He glanced over his shoulder, then leaning across the table, whispered that the insurance company would be sending out an arson investigator.

I put down my fork. "Why are you whispering?" I asked, an angry tone leaping into my voice. "You have nothing to be ashamed of. You didn't set the fucking fire."

He reddened, but after a few seconds his shoulders dropped, as if he had heard the protectiveness in my anger.

Pressing my luck, I pushed my plate aside, suggesting again that we call Thom and Clive.

He waved me off, saying he was more worried about getting over to his house and boarding it up before things got stolen or wrecked even more. He started to rattle on, picking up speed, thinking out loud about what he would need for the job: plywood, locks, nails, door hinges. On and on he went, obsessing about idiot practical details—how he needed to get done with the school so he could get to my house, get his truck, go the bank, get cash for the hardware. He kept saying "I, I, I," as if he had to do it all alone.

I cut in.

"Can't you just hire someone?" I said. "Get some help? You look like a wreck. We should go home, get some rest."

He shot me a look, flagged the waitress.

"What?" I said.

"Home?" he said.

"I'm sorry," I mumbled, turning red. "I meant my place. It's yours, as long as you want."

"I think the insurance gives money for a motel," he said, looking at the bill, counting out some change.

"Don't be silly," I told him. "And what about Emily?"

"We'll both be fine," he said, struggling to pull on his jacket. "I can't deal with this now."

Heaving himself up out of the booth, he headed off for the register. Clumsy with fatigue, I scrambled after him.

At the school he hesitated with the door swung open, one foot in the street. We'd parked right in front, instead of in the faculty lot. A few early-bird students were crossing the dew-slick lawn, heading for choir or clubs or simply the front steps. I watched his eyes follow them, thought I saw a tear beading up on his lower lid. I almost put my hand on his arm.

But then he got out, closed the door, gave me a nervous grin. I found myself smiling back, fighting off a look of worry and approbation. I even flashed him a thumbs up. What else could I do? I will always remember that moment, for as helpless as I felt, what came to me then was a simple love, a letting go, a willingness to wait in the moments when he could not.

"I'll be here," I called after him, through the open window.

~~~

I had no idea how long it would take for him to return to me. In the end, it would be years, really, though in fact he would return to the car in a matter of minutes, thirty or so.

The nine o'clock bell rang. The rowdy, heated din of teenaged voices drifted out over the grass. The day was already muggy and hot. I stared up at the school, its tall stately windows and sand-colored brick. In earlier days it had probably been elegant, but now its face was sooty and stained. I ducked my head down, looking up at the third-floor classroom Jay had pointed out as his. From that angle I could see only ceiling, banks of florescent lights, but could picture its cozy clutter, its half-dozen barrels spilling over with a tangle of purple-tongued plants, maybe coleus, inside the circle of desks—Jay's effort to make something lively at the center of things. It hit me once again what an extraordinary teacher he was, what a vital world he created for his students, even if for just a few hours a day.

I looked away, up into the trees, trying not to let the thought of him losing all this overwhelm me. After a while there was only the heavy dull hum of cicadas in the air, a hot day beginning. I lapsed into silence, waiting.

～ぃ～～

He came loping back across the lawn, mug in his hand, gym bag slung over his shoulder. Something about him looked different. After a few seconds I realized he was wearing a fresh white T- shirt, still creased from where it had been folded.

Heaving the bag into the back, he climbed in.

"Had a chance to duck into my room, grab a few things," he said, letting out a pressured sigh, raking his fingers through his hair.

"Hot," he added sympathetically, looking over at me, the startling blue alertness of his eyes surprising me once again. I felt myself stir. He looked wonderfully roguish, his blue-black hair falling to one side, his jaw rough with stubble. I wanted to grab his chin in my hand, hear it bristle between my fingers, forget the day that was ahead.

"Got my mug," he said, grinning sheepishly as he held it up in a toast. A little ripple of relief ran through me: he seemed like himself again. Making a pretend cup of my hand, I toasted him back, knucklebones to porcelain.

"Look," he said, digging around in his front pocket.

Out came a keychain with no keys, a shiny Petoskey stone dangling from it. He draped it over my palm. It was the usual sandy-gray, cool as ash, a piece of old reef worn down by the waters of a million years. I turned the fossil over gently with my finger.

One of the senior girls had given it to him, he said quietly. Kids had kept coming up in the hall, saying they were sorry. The news had obviously spread. The girl had pressed the keychain into his hand, saying it was hers, slightly used, but she wanted Jay to have it, to remind him there would be new doors.

He broke off, swallowing several times.

Over his shoulder I could see some kids lining up along a classroom window, staring out at us. Instinctively, I lowered my hand before I placed the stone back in his.

"Those kids really love you," I said.

"Yeah," he said, drifting off a minute, then shaking his head as if to clear it.

"So, onward," he said, shoving the keychain back in his pocket.

I started the engine.

We headed for his neighborhood. Jay opened the glove compartment, started rummaging.

I asked what he was looking for.

"Paper and pen," he said, "to make a list for the hardware."

I suddenly realized he hadn't said a thing about what had happened with the principal.

"Everything's under control," he said, for probably the tenth time that day.

"Just as expected," he said, the principal had given him the week off. They'd talk in a few days, after the police had had a chance to clear things up.

We went another block, but still he didn't elaborate. To him the matter seemed over and done with, his mind already on to the next thing. Finding an old pen, he sat scribbling on a piece of tattered bag, trying to make the pen work. I drove along, biting the inside of my lip. Did he really believe that the principal was only being responsive to his needs, rather than covering his own ass, biding his time until the investigation was over?

"What about the police?" I finally asked, trying to keep a neutral tone in my voice.

He stopped messing with the pen, looked over at me.

"Jesus," he said. "I'm sorry. There's so much on my mind, I forgot to tell you the good news. The cops told the school that Eddy had retracted his accusation before I'd even gotten to the station. He'd seemed pretty drunk. Of course, that's all in my favor."

We raised our eyebrows at each other.

"Thank God," I said, letting out a breath, trying to share his sense of relief. Even so, I could feel the heat rising in my face. It made me sick to think of him sitting in that room alone with the cops, them knowing about the retraction, but toying with him anyway, piquing his anxiety.

"So, the cops had called the school, before you arrived?"

"Yes."

"What did they say?"

"They'll go out to the school today and tomorrow, to interview some teachers, check my reputation. Purely routine, the principal said."

He unscrewed the top of the pen, blew into the stem, trying to force down some ink.

"Doesn't that make you nervous?" I asked.

"My colleagues respect me. They'll back me up."

He sounded reasonable, but his voice was tight, his body agitated. A few seconds later he shut the glove compartment with a bang, startling us both. I couldn't help but feel it was me he wanted to shut up.

"Sorry," he mumbled.

"No, I'm sorry," I said, unsure of what either of us was really apologizing for, but the tension between us subsided anyway.

We drove silently under the tunnels of maples and oaks, each in our separate worlds, coping in our own ways, me worrying about the security of his job, him making his list. He looked so brave and vulnerable, smoothing a scrap of bag over his knee, trying to flatten the wrinkles. I focused on the battered dusty pen between his fingers. Don Quixote's lance, I thought. David's sling.

He jotted a few words, nothing dreamy. Hammer. Nails.

As always, he was pointing himself forward.

21

Usually, when I turned onto Jay's street I would feel my body downshift and relax, happily anticipating our visit. The houses in his neighborhood looked so solid and square, with their light-dappled lawns and broad-leafed trees soughing in the breeze.

That day everything was terribly still, the short-cropped grass burning in the heat, the houses drifting away somewhere inside themselves, blinds drawn, no old people out pulling weeds, children wheeling bikes, parents carting groceries into the house. For a few seconds my body was a dumb beast, a fledgling habit of hope surging into me like a strange cool breeze. As I leaned forward in my seat—my back was soaked—Jay reached across, plucking my shirt up off the skin. How good it felt, the touch of his hand, just at the place I couldn't reach myself. Both me and the house had changed under those hands, the knots worked over, the surfaces stripped then flooded with the vitality that could make dull stressed wood leap to life again, strong warm oak.

Without realizing, I began to drive more and more slowly, pulling back from what was up ahead.

"You don't have to go slow," said Jay. "Not on my account."

We were only a couple blocks from his house. I picked up the speed, instantly agitated. I reached for his hand, but he was biting his thumbnail, leaning a bit forward.

I tried to reassure myself. Just because the house had burned didn't mean our love would burn out. It wasn't a sign, I told myself. Yet of course, I knew our relationship was young for such tests. For both of our sakes, I tried not to dwell on it, kept my eyes straight ahead.

From the corner, all that was visible were two white trucks and a van parked out front. Yellow police tape fluttered between stakes at the edge of the ripped-up lawn.

Then Jay's house came into view.

Roof, ivy, mission brick, barberry shrubs, juniper, yew—it was all there, plus more. Workers in blue caps were scaling ladders, boarding up windows. In the open door a man was on his knees, repairing the lock and frame.

Jay was out of the car in a flash. I rolled up the windows partway to keep Emily in, then went after him. In the street the smell hit, something like formaldehyde, mixed with smoke and the fresh odor of wet upturned dirt, an exposed inside-out smell.

Jay paused halfway, screening his eyes as he squinted up at the raw yellow plywood nailed over the windows. A couple of workers at the foot of a ladder gave him a nod.

"What's all this?" Jay asked, his voice flat and dry.

"Fire clean-up," one of the crew answered, flinging his cigarette butt in the grass.

Jay flushed.

"What I mean is, who the hell ordered this work? I'm the owner."

The workers exchanged a quick glance.

"Hey Henry," one of them piped.

Both of us looked toward the door as a man in a suit popped out, briefcase and flashlight in hand, leather soles gritty on the steps.

"Are you Jay?" he asked, extending his hand.

Reluctantly Jay shook his hand, shoving a fist in his pocket.

"I'm sorry," said the agent, nodding toward the house. "Things aren't great, but better than they probably seemed last night. Major smoke and water damage, but nothing structural. A few months' work with a good contractor. I can supply names."

"I have my own contractor," said Jay stiffly.

I shot him a surprised look.

The agent paused, rubbing the back of his neck. Changing tack, he gestured toward the foot of the porch.

"Some students came by. They brought flowers. They seem to think the world of you."

Jay looked away, rubbing his chin. The steam seemed to go out of him for a second.

The agent dug around in his briefcase, pulled out a clipboard.

"I need your signature to authorize the work," he said, uncapping his pen, holding out the contract.

"What work?" said Jay, suddenly turning back to the agent, narrowing his eyes.

"The work these guys are doing to secure the premises, mop up, take out the debris."

I winced inside at the word "debris." Jay scowled down at the contract.

"What if I had wanted to do the work myself?" he said. "Isn't this a bit after the fact?"

"You gave me the go-ahead this morning. You probably forgot. You've got a lot on your mind."

The agent began reeling off what would be needed: water vacs, special dehumidifiers, fans . . .

"Can the equipment be rented?" said Jay.

It was my turn to look away. Why couldn't he just accept the help?

A glimmer of frustration flickered through me, a feeling that would become all too familiar—but then, it was just a flicker, tempered by the patience of new love.

Jay caught the look on my face.

"I don't care how good their guys are," he muttered to me. "They're not going to be as careful as someone working on their own property."

I kept my mouth shut as he glared up at the house, jingling the change in his pants.

"I want to go in now," he said abruptly, starting for the door.

"I should go with you," said the agent, following. "You'll need a flashlight."

"I want to go alone," said Jay, holding out his hand for the agent's flashlight.

I didn't know what to do. Did he mean to exclude me?

I took off after him up the stairs anyway, half expecting to be ordered away; but, we entered the dark living room together.

Three workers came heaving toward the door gripping a tarp loaded with chunks of plaster, cinders, melted red plastic. Both of us stepped aside, making room, our arms one careful inch apart. For a quick second Jay glanced at me, our eyes meeting—just barely—but enough, as he lowered his shoulders, leaned a little into my heat.

Following the beam of his light, we could see the air swirling in tall drifty pillars of ash and dust. Eyes streaming, we pulled off our shirts, wadding them up over noses and mouths as we hacked and blinked.

He skimmed the walls with the light. They were streaky with smoke and water but unburned. Suddenly the couch loomed up, drenched to a sodden lurid maroon.

Jay gave a startled little laugh.

"Well, Hello Dolly!" he said. "You're still here!"

He grinned at me over his bare shoulder. Just moments ago he'd been all tight with rage and rigidity; his ability to toss it off in a second stunned me. I melted once again.

"This can all be fixed," he muttered, moving on into the dining room, ignoring the crunch of plaster and cinders under his feet.

I lagged behind in the dark living room, needing to look more. Waiting for my sight to adjust, I took in the couch from the corner of my eye, a sickening dread spreading out from the center of my chest. That night, my foot, the light pouring in. It was all so obvious from that angle. Suddenly I felt swallowed up, engulfed by my guilty fear. If he knew, would he leave me?

I could hear him elsewhere in the house now, rummaging.

〰〰

"Tell the truth," I hear him teasing me now, from the other side. "Isn't there something you're not recalling? Something you always forget.

"Are you coming?" he'd called from the other room.

And came back, shining the light in my face.

〰〰

The dining room had clearly been ground-zero. The table where Jay had sat night after night correcting papers was now a heap of char. The walls were scorched, plywood covered the window. I realized the completed stacks of finals with Jay's careful comments, jokes, grades were smoke now, too. But as we moved through to the hall, we found a scattered sheaf, and then some individual sheets, wadded up, and finally, in the kitchen, a can of lighter fluid from the garage.

This was the only point at which Jay's propulsion seemed to flag. Picking up one of the sheets, he uncrumpled it. I couldn't see his face in the darkened hall, but I imagined what it must have felt like to know his students' work had served as tinder. A chill ran down my spine as I pictured Eddy standing with the can, surveying the dining room, the papers, perhaps leafing through them, selecting a few.

"Oh Eddy," Jay said, crunching the paper back up in a wad. "Eddy, Eddy. We should have talked . . ."

The words caught in his throat as he coughed in the ashy air. We both stood there thinking of the boy, just hours before, perhaps hesitating in the same spot, scanning a page, a sneer on his face. By the time he'd reached the dining room, he'd broken into the garage, smashed the glass of the side door. What had he wanted?

Probably even he didn't understand. Obviously, he had sensed something in Jay, something about the kind of man he was. Did he want him—or to be him? Maybe both. In any event, it was Jay who had ignited this confusion in his heart and dick. And it was making him crazy, one minute lusting for it to happen—the unnamed thing that could change him, suck his breath away, make him more of who he was—the next minute, he was terrified, wanting to throttle it, douse it, destroy.

I imagined he'd stood for a second, gazing at the table, into the living room at the couch, down the hall to the unmade bed. I saw him vividly as he began to rip and tear the papers, fling the fuel around, lighting the match, watching it all go up, his classmates' words, years of harshness, cootie boy, sissy, cocksucker, flamer—he let it all go until he couldn't take it back. He wanted to take it back, the flame into the match, but all he could do was call the police, and flee.

I didn't want to understand, but I could. I thought of some guys from my own middle school, three bellicose jocks, and an obvious sissy, Eric, who it had been rumored they cornered each afternoon on their way home from school in a little patch of neglected woods beneath an underpass. They called him Knees. "Knees, Knees, Knees," they would bellow when he walked into homeroom. Eric would be brave and grin, trying to be a good sport, but his grin seemed false, garnering the ridicule of the whole class. I had lived in terror that I would be next. I was constantly adjusting my walk, or praying I wouldn't pop a boner in the gym shower. One day Eric just didn't show up at school anymore. A few years later I heard that he had overdosed on heroin in his new high school.

Eddy had been different, though. His rage, going outward. I looked over at Jay. He was bending over, picking up something. His back, long and bare.

"The phone," he said, holding it out to me, a chunk of melted plastic. Eddy must have flung it down the hall, after calling.

Mutely, we both looked at it.

The rest of our time in the house that day was spent in the basement. Hanging the flashlight from the clothesline, Jay set me to work drying hand tools while he went more carefully over the machines with rags. Eventually, I went upstairs to his closet and dragged out a suitcase, filling it with photo books, documents, a few clothes that would prove to be permanently stench-filled. I had his permission, of course. But he stayed with his tools, with his sense of what would help him move ahead.

It was me who carried the flowers from his students to the car. He sat in the front seat, eyes averted as I laid them in the back, as if even a look would broach too much tenderness.

With no mention of motels, we drove to my house.

~~~~~~~

When Jay woke from that first troubled sleep after the fire, he would find me moving quietly about my room, emptying half the drawers in my bureau, making room in the closet. I was humming. I'd like to think it was a solemn comforting song, but truth is, it was probably "Oh What a Beautiful Morning."

I had slept, but not enough to restore a clear-edged sensitivity. I was just relieved he was with me. To Jay, watching me through one eye, face half-flattened on the pillow, I must have seemed like a happy but perilous spider, testing my web.

I sat on the far edge of the bed.

"I'm glad you slept," I said, wrapping my hand around his ankle.

He drew up his leg.

"What about you?" he said.

"Okay."

In fact, I had been half-awake all night, alert for any sign of anguish in him, ready to curl my body around his. But he had stayed submerged, remote.

I gave his ankle a little squeeze.

"I hate to bring this up," I said, "but I have to leave for work. Should we try to get you some numbers—a lawyer, your union rep—in case you need them today?"

He groaned, pressing his fingers against his temples.

"*We* are not going to do anything," he said, swinging his legs out of bed, drawing on his shorts. "*I* am going to go back to the house. And you are going to go to work."

"But what if Eddy's parents make a stink? The kid's in hot water. He lied once—he might do it again. The police are going to keep digging."

"There's nothing for them to find out," said Jay. "And they're definitely not going to find what really should be found out, which is how I really did fail."

I started to shake my head.

"I did fail—failed Eddy, my job, myself. My whole fucking masquerade of a life."

He grabbed the edge of my comforter and pulled it up over the rumpled covers with a surprising violence. Something in me unclenched, relieved. This felt real.

"Fucking house," he said, plunking down with his back to me on the bed as he yanked on his shoes.

"It was never my idea in the first place," he said, anguish in his voice. "What am I going to tell my father?"

He sat for a second staring down at his feet.

I came around the side of the bed and sat down next to him, refraining from putting my arm around him.

"Nothing, if you don't want to," I said. "At least not for now."

"Saying nothing is what got me into this whole damned mess in the first place. Saying nothing to my family for years about who I really am. Saying nothing to the kid. Fucking driving lessons. I had my chance and blew it."

He stood up, examining his face in the mirror over my dresser.

"But maybe it's not too late," he said, jamming a comb through his hair.

"What do you mean?"

"I want to talk to Eddy," he said. "That's the only thing that could put this right."

"Oh no you're not," I said. "At least, not without a lawyer, some witnesses. Jay, there's more here at stake than this kid's coming to terms with who he is."

"Yes, there is," he said, turning to face me. "I have to be able to live with myself."

"But can't you see? If you try to make contact with Eddy right now it could be taken the wrong way. It's not right, but that's real. You have to go slow."

"I don't know how to go slow," he said, closing one of the bureau drawers I had left open. There was a tone of real torment in his voice.

"Why don't we go back to your original plan?" I suggested. "I'll meet you at your house after work."

Reluctantly he agreed.

But later that afternoon, when I arrived at his house, he was nowhere in sight. In his room I was surprised to find two tired-looking women sitting on his bed with clipboards, going through his clothes, making an accounting of his possessions for the insurance company. My "friend" had left hours ago, they said. He'd meet me at my house. As I went down the hall I could hear them go on with their inventory: "blue shirt, Oxford cloth, yellowed armpits. Four T-shirts, one with holes. Six jockey shorts."

What about piss stains? I thought to myself. No wonder Jay had left. So much, being dragged out into the open.

It was me, as it turned out, who made most of the trips back to his house. Jay showed up to deal with tradespeople when required but shifted into a surprising antipathy toward the place. His old feelings resurfaced, his sense of it having never really been his idea, his project, in the first place. Whatever interest and investment he had, had been tainted, interfered with, first by his father, now by the fire.

"Everything I touch turns to shit," he would say, dragging my brokendown chaise lounge into my yard. He barely moved that first week after the fire, rising only to make the most necessary calls, to eat and to piss.

Having expected him to be up and at it, I was secretly pleased when he was not. I had patience with this sort of contraction. I thought I understood its familiar rhythms from the loss in my own past. But now, I was to be the caretaker, or at least that's what I was trying to be.

Remembering a wide blue bowl that had been my mother's, I retrieved it from a cupboard, set it on the kitchen table. I filled it daily with fresh offerings—strawberries, bananas, oranges—and was pleased each night when I returned home from work to find it gleaming, emptied, clean. To me it was the blue open heart of our home, the refuge and domicile I was extending to Jay.

Since Jay couldn't bring himself to go on any of my search parties of his house, I went by myself, several times, filling boxes and dishpans with unbroken bowls, unburned books, fragments of pottery he'd loved. I tried to wash what I could, then aired things in the yard, taking in the books each night before the dew began to settle. Since they smelled too foul to store in the flat, I kept them in the trunk of my car. Jay thanked me, but could barely bring himself to investigate my progress. And given the results, I didn't encourage it.

"I don't know why you bother," he said one night after we'd come inside. "Stuff is just stuff."

I looked around my living room, eyes resting on my great-grandmother's Wedgewood vase, the slate blacks and blues, the tiny cut figures of gods and fawns and Dianas dancing below the rim. To me such objects were all that was left of my family. Spinning down my path of assumptions, I disbelieved his detachment. So, besotted with my own presumably deeper knowledge of loss, I missed this important way that we were different.

22

"TAKE YOUR TIME," I told him often that first week, wishing I could comfort him more.

But he was too ferocious for that. One flash now of his face as he lay on his back trying to come. Straining, flushed, determined. *I will not be damaged.*

I looked away, hand working. His fist suddenly over mine—tighter, faster. Was it the specter of the schoolyard bullies, making it difficult for him to come? Why did they always have to appear when two men love?

Afterward, we lay spooned in the late-fading light of mid-June, him adamantly around me. There was an ache in me to talk, to draw him out. But it was clear he wanted to quiet me, and so I gave him what calm I could, pretending to fall asleep.

"I'm not going back," he said quietly to me one night over dinner.

I stopped with the serving spoon in mid-air.

"I don't want to work anymore where I can't be myself," he said, pulling apart some bread.

I had struggled to refrain from asking him about school all week. Clearly, he had not wanted me to probe. But the tension of not knowing had been mounting.

"The principal helped me work out a confidential settlement with the district," he continued. "If I resign, they won't pursue any action against me. If I don't work in the field, they won't have to give any compromising job recommendations."

He started to eat. I stared at him, trying to take hold of what he was saying.

"This is a real turnaround," I stammered. "You were so sure they would back you up."

"I don't really care what they think anymore. I'm not comfortable with what I did—or rather, didn't do."

"But that doesn't make you a bad teacher. This isn't fair," I pushed.

"No, it's not," he said, persisting. "And that's why I don't want to be part of it anymore. I can't live that way one more day—shutdown and afraid."

"There was good reason to be afraid," I said.

"Sure," he said. "But did I bother myself about that? No! I couldn't figure out what to do, so I just burrowed into my snug little life. And then, I failed Eddy."

He paused.

"I don't know how to answer for that," he added, meeting my eyes in such a straightforward way I could feel my stomach drop. At a loss for words, I studied his face in the early evening light, seeing angles I hadn't seen before.

I reached across the table, took his hand.

"Brave pal," I said.

"I know you probably think I should stay and fight," he said.

"It did occur to me," I said.

He let go of my hand, sank back in his chair.

"I don't know," he said. "I had my chance with Eddy and I blew it. What good would it do to drag him or me through even more of a mess? This way, we can both just go on. He has no prior record. They'll probably let him off with some counseling through a diversion program."

He looked down at his plate.

"There's really no good choice," he said, voice tense and dry.

"No," I said.

"Except to live differently," he added. "No more hiding. God—I've shut up about so many things, my whole life, without even knowing it. In high school, I never even told my parents I might want to be a woodworker."

Pushing away from the table, he stood up and took our water glasses to the kitchen. I listened to him refill them, stared out at the toss and dazzle of the trees.

"I've been thinking," he said, walking in slowly, balancing the brimming glasses. "Maybe I should sell the house, after the repairs," he said, setting down the glasses. "Jim just told me about this guy we used to know who moved to San Francisco. He buys houses on the cheap, often from probate, then makes his money by fixing them up and selling them. I would love that."

"You would do a good job," I said, the haste of my response giving me away. Everything in me was on alert.

Jay caught my tone.

"But that's a dream for a different day," he said, his turn now to reach across the table, take my hand.

"Can you stand for me to be lost a while?" he asked, raising his eyebrows.

The appeal in his voice for my understanding, even approval, would always have the power to instantly disarm me.

"Take your time," I heard myself say, once again.

Later that night, he let me ease into him, long and slow.

There was something different in the way he wanted me.

In the morning, when I woke, I was surprised to find him spooned close to me, still asleep, this time me around him. It had been a while since he had been relaxed enough to allow this.

I lay without moving, savoring the moment. The sun was filtering in through my curtains. I drifted, remembering every precious day we had spent in Jay's room over the past months. Often, I would wake before him, immersing myself in the quaver of light passing though the uneven glass of the old window by his bed. In the weeks just before the fire, that window had seemed to transform, age and change into something beautiful and gentle and slow, faintly green, liquid, flowing. With him in my arms then, all my past trouble and grief had seemed like a silly dream from long ago, far away, in a time when I had been deeply mistaken, or very young.

When he woke, I squeezed him tightly.

"I want to grow old with you," I whispered in his ear, stroking the flat of his belly.

He didn't answer.

My heart started to sink, but just then, he grabbed my hand, pinning it to his chest, keeping it from straying lower.

"What about now?" he said, that deep lascivious undertone in his voice. "Right now?"

Right then, I got stiff against his ass.

But I wasn't going to let that distract me.

"I want more," I said. "A future."

Suddenly he was up on all fours, straddling me. Looking at me with mock severity, thumbs pressing into my shoulders, he flipped me over, ass up, knees between mine.

"Let's not get there too soon," he said, sliding his hands under my hips, grabbing my cock as his tongue rimmed my ear. "Didn't you ever want to do something dangerous?"

My answer, already in his hands.

23

BUT IT WAS A VOLATILE TIME.

After the first few weeks, he began staying with his friends Rick and Mike at least three nights a week. He said he didn't want to overwhelm our young relationship.

I was on his nerves, I could tell. One night as I was reading in the living room at twilight, he came in and snapped on the overhead, voice full of anger as he groused about how I always had to have it so dark.

Another night, as I set his place at the table, he told me to stop fussing like a nervous hostess.

"Okay pardner," I said, tucking in a napkin under the knife.

He stopped in his tracks, chair half-pulled out from under the table.

"Stop it," he said quietly. "I can't think of my being here right now in those terms."

I sealed my lips. He was right, of course.

But not entirely, I thought to myself. I bought new sheets and a pillow for him, anyway.

Within the week, he announced his arrangement with Rick and Mike. By the end of June, he told me they had invited him along to San Francisco for a few weeks, while they checked it out as a place to live.

It was a great opportunity; Rick had a friend who needed house sitters. There was room for me in the van, but both of us knew I couldn't get free of my job, and while he was solicitous, and disappointed, there was no disguising the vitality that was sweeping back into him.

How could I oppose it?

He called often. First from campgrounds and truck stops along the way, then from their rambling house overlooking the bay. As he laid out on the deck under pines, he described to me what he could see—Bay Bridge, barges, tangles of freeways, tall buildings, block after block of pastel-colored houses winking in the sun.

"A vista!" he exclaimed, looking down Liberty Street toward the green slopes of Dolores Park, lined then with dozens of tanning men stretched out on their bellies. "They call it Dolores Beach," he said, laughing.

One night he even phoned me from a club, holding the receiver out to the room so I could hear the pulsing music, the laughter of the men (as if I could miss it). The excitement in his voice was both contagious and disturbing.

I tried to echo his thrill in those calls, telling him how much I wished I were there with him, packed up against the other boys at the bar, the nude beach at Land's End, the gay pride march. But more than anything, I just wanted him to come home.

"Maybe you want to stay," I said to him one night as I lay on my bed, listening to him enthuse.

"I do," he admitted. "But not without you. We're going to stay an extra week, but that's it. It's all going by so fast."

There was an awkward pause. An extra week felt like forever to me. Sensing something, he quieted down, asked about my day.

As I listened to myself tell him my own good news (I had been selected for a paid internship in the fall at an educational book publisher in Ann Arbor), I could hear my voice go flat. Suddenly I was back to feeling like

I did when we first met—hardly glamorous. And though he was happy for me, it was easy for me to discount the appreciation in his voice as simply run off from the joy he was feeling in San Francisco.

Two days before he was supposed to arrive, I let myself into my flat and was surprised to find the table set with two places and warm pots on the stove, but no Jay.

My heart leapt. By the time I had changed my clothes he was bounding up the stairs, a garlic braid in hand.

"Left this in the car," he said breathlessly, presenting it to me. "Remember me?" he added, a sheepish grin on his face.

He looked fantastic. The Castro had clearly been an inspiration. His hair was trimmed shorter, making it look blacker, much thicker than I had remembered. And he was sporting a mustache, almost grown in. His color was bright and he was beaming, practically turning himself inside out as he struggled with dinner, never his forté. He kept darting back and forth to the living room, pulling from his bags various ingredients and gifts—jars of sun-dried tomatoes, salsa, olives, gourmet mustards; a strand of puka beads; gay papers and porn; some poppers; a tape of Sylvester.

Dinner was as bright as he, with everything orange and red—placemats, napkins, flowers, pasta sauce, tomato fusilli. And a very stale loaf of sourdough. "Just because," he said, "it's the thought that counts."

I was touched. No, floored. Not only was he full of his adventure— he seemed happy to share, eager to bring it all home to me! He was so exuberant, laughing at himself as he noticed for the first time the very red meal he had cooked.

After dinner, he plopped a package in my lap, watching my face avidly as I opened it.

A black leather vest, with a Harley-Davidson T-shirt. Just the sort of thing that I loved but would never have bought for myself.

He pulled me over to the mirror, tugging off my shirt, holding open the vest for me. As I slid into it, he stood behind me, eyes all over me.

"Have you been a bad boy?" I said, unable to stop myself, avoiding looking at him in the mirror.

"You're my bad boy," he said. "And I'm going to help you break some of your rules."

"How?" I asked.

Taking my hand, he pulled me back toward the table.

"By getting you out of here," he said, beginning to clear the dishes with a clatter and gusto. "By starting over in a new place where I can kiss you anywhere I want."

"What's wrong with right here?" I said, standing beside him at the sink, offering my cheek.

"That's my line," he said, giving me a gentle elbow to the ribs as he continued scraping garbage off the plates.

When I didn't stop hovering, he knocked me with his hip, then grabbing at the belly of my T-shirt, began drying his hands, pulling me closer each time his fists gave a little twist inside the shirt.

"Right here is just swell, too," he said then, kissing my neck, the wetness of his hands in my shirt brushing my belly.

"For now," he added.

He knew I was scared. He knew me better than I'd thought.

We didn't talk about it anymore that night.

Within the week he pitched his proposal.

Unless I wanted to go with him in September, I could follow him to San Francisco in a year, after I had finished my internship and school. He would put his house on the market, then go on ahead, looking for a property to buy, renovate, resell.

"Of course," he said, "I would make no claims on you. I couldn't expect you to wait, to curb your needs in the months between."

Both of us crossed our arms, stared at our shoes. The evening sun filtered in around us. I let it fool me a little, pretending we could stay within its peacefulness forever, my eyes playing connect-the-dots with the paint spots on his sneakers.

"Something is telling me to go now," he said. "You could come for visits. At Christmas. My treat."

I sat plucking at a rip in my jeans.

"So?" he demanded, poking me in the ribs.

"So what?"

"So, what do you think?"

"I think that boy Eddy really did succeed."

"What do you mean"?

"In taking you away from me," I said, hating myself for that voice, the smallness of it, even as I said it.

Jay shoved my foot.

"Listen, you snot. Come here," he said, pulling me by the arm.

I hunkered down, Emily's technique when about to be prodded out of bed.

"I don't want us to be like that," Jay pleaded gently. "I want you to come."

I tipped over with my head on his lap. He ran his fingers through my hair. I took the comfort, but for the first time in our relationship, I felt myself holding back from him in a big way.

A month later, we stood by his truck saying goodbye.

It is early morning.

He is ready to leave. His house is on the market. He has bought a cap for the back of his truck, which is jammed with camping gear, clothes, what is most essential for his first few months. At a rest stop out on the freeway he will meet up with Rick and Mike, who have rented a U-Haul truck. They will go in caravan.

I have just given him a present. I had wanted to give him something old—something to salve the loss of his own things. Maybe a fossil, or a rummage-sale butter dish webbed with fine cracks like whorls on a finger. At a resale shop in Ann Arbor I had found what seemed to be a hunk of old ivory carved into a Tibetan version of a recorder. The shop-owner had said it had been traded in by a trekker. I had no idea it was a thigh-bone trumpet, carved from human bone. I was simply drawn to the deep umber oldness of it, the sense of it being handmade. I had envisioned Jay fingering it whenever he felt lonely. I had planned to say that breathing into it would help him conjure up all that endured from the past, including us, as he tried to go forward.

Now that moment is here, and all I can do is hand it to him with a lump in my throat.

I don't know what to make of the funny soft smile on his face. He holds the bone in his hand, shaking his head a little.

"What?" I finally say.

"I saw one like this at the Asian Art Museum in San Francisco," he says, rubbing his thumb down the shank.

"You are so fucking amazing," he adds. "All this change is not exactly making you happy, but you go out and find me something that trumpets it anyway."

I cross my arms, speechless. That was not the meaning I had intended, not at all.

Sensing my inner shift, he looks up at me. The maples bow over us, last night's rain still slipping from the leaves. Trees, grass, sky—everything is heavy and green, or leaden. My legs are thick trunks. Things seem to be moving without me.

He reaches for my arm.

"If you need me to stay, I will," he says, almost with a sob.

The word "need" runs me through, in the same jolt as his touch.

Suddenly I can move. I lay two fingers across his lips, shooshing him, then take him into my arms. I don't care who sees us—my landlady, the neighbors.

I stand there a long time after he is gone, looking at the cracks in the bark.

How beautiful it is, the dark against the green.

PART FOUR

24

Waking up, the sun flooding over me. A few hours past noon.

Where am I?

For a few minutes, I forget he is gone.

The silver of rain sliding off leaves is in me.

It is still September in my head, with leaves poised to turn, but not yet turned.

Then all fall down.

Something like chips of bone clinging to my cheek.

Smell of tar and ash.

No, gravel.

Asphalt.

Roof.

Oh yes.

Jay is gone. A long time now.

And I am still trying to follow.

Again and again, I watch him go, a private ghost world spinning in my head.

But out there, down there, on the street below the hotel, it is just after lunch, the sun is shining, it is still spring. People are hurrying back to offices and stores. I watch, head propped on the edge of the roof, fish-cheeked, wizened gargoyle. Below, a revolving door goes round and round, taking in the workers. I can almost hear the shoosh of air rushing in. A woman in a red scarf biting an apple. Can almost taste the sharp snap of the Jonathan, the bright skin breaking, the tang and then the dull-gray corridors.

I should get right down to it, I imagine her thinking, as she hesitates in the lobby.

Just do it.

The next thing. What I have been putting off.

But it is not so easy, I could tell her.

More than once now, I have been all set, ready to go.

And then.

My doctor's voice, intruding again.

Was that just a month ago, my doctor saying, dare to hope?

He was starting a new campaign for another drug.

I rolled my eyes.

I felt a little bit cruel. I should have cut him some slack. He's seen the miracle for so many. The virus held at bay, lives regained. Patients getting jobs, taking on dogs, paying off credit card debts.

Then, I come in, skinny-assed, hobbling with my cane, dry tufts of hair. Looking as patchy as that tattooed archaic man they found in ice in the Alps a few years back.

No more experiments, I answered, feeling he should have known better. My system is too sensitive—he'd seen how brutal each round had been—and still, my viral load keeps climbing.

But he kept making his case, offering to hospitalize me while he started me again on the protease inhibitors.

"Maybe it'd go easier this time," he said. "With food and assistance, someone always there to monitor."

A generous offer. He'd have to doctor his records to justify the expense. I was touched.

I looked down at the drug company brochure he had placed in my hand, the pretty air-brushed pictures of fit happy men. For a moment I was overcome by loneliness and shame. Was I a failure for not having the will to go through it one more time—my hopes rising, only to be cut down by the terrible nausea, eye-piercing headaches, wasting from the medicine itself? And all the while, my T-cell count in free fall?

The doctor was looking at me expectantly.

No. In my deepest heart, I knew I was ready to go. Maybe not that day, or the next, but sometime soon, while I still had the presence of mind and coherence of body to do it.

Squaring up in the chair as best I could, I stuck my hand in my pocket, fishing around for the bottle of expired Seconal.

"Is this too old to get the job done, when the time comes?" I asked.

I don't know why, but I guess I expected he would offer to renew the lethal dose as trustingly as Dr. Jeremy had first prescribed it for me, years ago. I suddenly missed Dr. Jeremy. He would have understood. He knew what I had gone through with Jay at the end. And he knew from his own struggle with this fucking disease. There comes a time. How long had it been since Dr. Jeremy had died—two years?

"These would be dangerous," he said, handing the pills back to me. "You should throw them out. They might not work."

His hands returned to his lap and stayed there.

I looked over at his prescription pad. Things were not going as planned. I was becoming a bit shaken. I cleared my throat several times.

"If you renewed," I said, "I would take every precaution—fill the scripts slowly, save up over time, tell no one."

"No," he said.

"Why not?"

"I'm just not comfortable. It's too soon."

"But I'm not talking about today, or tomorrow. I just want some on hand. As you can see, I had the old ones for years."

"I just don't trust your judgment," he said. "You're teary and depressed."

I looked away, shaking my head.

"It's hardly the first time," I said.

His chair squeaked as he rolled it forward a little, compelling me to look at him, his pink gleaming cheeks.

"I'm not giving up on you," he said. "I haven't given up hope."

I have never wanted to kick a puppy before, but for a split second I thought of putting the heel of my boot on the edge of his chair and sending him flying. He had such a shiny face, energy pouring out of it, pink that had spread now, beneath his hair. I loathed him for it, his abundant good health, and then I noticed something.

He was sweating.

I knew then exactly what was going on. It was him who needed the hope. He was on the front lines, and would be, long after I had gone.

"Times keep changing," he said, raising his eyebrows.

"Not that much," I said, but under my breath. Something in me had shifted.

I pulled myself up out of the chair as he wrote a prescription, the one I didn't want.

"Sleep on it," he said, handing it to me.

"Don't I wish," I said, giving him the best mischievous grin I could muster.

We shook hands, and I thanked him for all his efforts, knowing I would never ask him again for what I really wanted.

~~~~

Across the way, a woman in a suit at the window, talking on the phone. She is looking down at the street as if she were watching for someone.

Maybe her lover is coming.

If only I could fling out my arms and join them, the people who are arriving. What an angel!

But no.

It would change everything—a man falling into their day.

How thoughtless could I be?

The best-laid plans (or so I'd thought, arranging for the roof key—a whole story to the manager about being a painter and wanting to do the skyline at different times of day).

Now I have to wait for dark. Again.

Like the woman, back at her desk. She looks restless. Her fingers pecking through papers. I imagine she too can't wait for this day to be over. Her eyes are on her work, but like me, her mind is probably on her lover. How he looked just now, down at the street corner, as they parted. But also when they first met. She wants the feeling of that first meeting to come back. Did he fall in step with her, side by side—or had he cut across her path and faced her for a few seconds? She would like to remember every detail, but she doesn't. Had he looked at her directly, straight into her eyes, or had there been something a little sideways that day, too?

Does it disturb her, not to remember precisely? I imagine her trying, squinting inside, but the more she tries the more the memories seem to fade, like the corners and shadows in her office evaporating from sight as the sun pours in.

I want her to get up and pull the curtain. Who could live in a room like that?

Just call him, I want to tell her. While you still can.

25

STOP THINKING ABOUT IT SO MUCH, I would tell myself, that fall after Jay had left. Just call and tell him. Whatever has been done is all within the agreements of your parting. But instead of picking up the phone, I would lay on my bed, lights out, waiting for him to call, even though I knew it was a night on which we had not planned to talk. I would put on Beethoven's "Emperor Concerto" because it reminded me of the dinner at which we had met. I would play it over and over, trying to evoke the feeling of that night, the way my insecurities had melted. A whole new world had seemed to unfold as we stepped out into the snow together.

He had made me so hopeful.

And then the music would shift. The faces of the other men around the table would come back to me, their eyes shining as they smiled, delighting in Jay's story. I would remember the classical dj, how intimidated I'd felt as he'd described the music, its big contrasts, the shifts in mood from public to intimate, and back again. I could still see him arching his eyebrows as he'd asked, "How do you sustain that kind of energy for forty minutes?"

And how do you sustain that kind of energy over a lifetime? Now, I wanted to know.

Three months away was a long time for a handsome man.

Besides, we had agreed we could sample some candy.

"Just a few bar snacks," I had teased before he'd left, waving my finger at him, affecting a lightness I didn't really feel.

"No main courses," he'd agreed, putting on a comforting sternness.

Later, on the phone, I couldn't keep from probing him.

"Nothing but empty calories," he'd claim. "What we have is very filling."

We would leave it at that, go on with our talk about my internship, his real estate affairs.

But after we'd hung up, I would secretly follow him around in my mind, in and out of bars that I had never seen but imagined anyway, along with men to walk him to his door, a different guy each night. I'd watch as Jay would slide his key into the lock, the other man's hand in his back pocket, until I couldn't take the self-inflicted torture anymore. I'd switch on the light, make myself walk around the flat, trying to shake it off.

I began to hate my room. Everything the way it had been for years. This shelf and that stack, this set of drawers. Everything a bit faded.

For the first time in memory, I was in the mood to rip up my life, turn it over.

But the thought of moving all the way across the country to be with a man who seemed so changeable, so careful not to overpromise—seemed daunting.

~~~~~

Martin was a solid quiet man with wide Slavic cheekbones, not unlike Jay. He was good-natured, easy-going, and when we made love it went so smoothly I felt as though nothing had been broken, or even broken into. We were in parallel situations. His partner was away too, in medical school in Boston. Nothing further needed to be said.

On my internship days in Ann Arbor, we would meet up for coffee or a quick dinner. Sometimes, after just a few minutes of halting conversation, we would fall into simply reading our papers or books, then go back to his apartment. It was as though both of us were re-instituting the rhythms of a longer-term relationship, the moments of easy silence and repose, without earning it from any intimacy we had developed with each other. On a few Sundays I drove out and picked him up and went tooling out Huron River Drive to the cider mill at Dexter, where we stuffed ourselves with powdered doughnuts, then stopped back at his place. Sated with sugar, we messed around, then got down to what we both seemed to long for most—a comforting nap. When I woke and was eager to leave, that was easy too. He didn't protest at all. It was as if I had managed to find someone who was most like what I had feared Jay would turn out to be—chronically cheerful and uncomplicated.

~~~~~

The woman at her desk is rising.

She is leaning on her hands, staring off into some far corner of the room.

Maybe she is looking at a clock.

Counting the minutes?

Yes, I could tell her—time is dragging.

The hands sweep slowly down, then up. A slow angel.

Deliver me, damn you.

Her blond hair swings down in a sheet as she bends over, reaching beneath her desk. I can't see her face now.

I pull my arms up on the edge, rest my head, watching her.

So strange—how I can see her in more detail than I can remember Jay. At least, his face.

When did his features begin to fade?

She has her briefcase up on her desk now.

In her trim suit, the picture of someone who is going places.

Maybe she's decided to leave right this minute.

Fuck work, she might be saying.

Maybe she's going to march right over to her lover's office and catch him by surprise. See the look on his face in that split second before it dawns on him who she is.

She pops open a compact, studies her face.

Would he give her a second look now, just as she is, gray suit slightly wrinkled and all business?

And once the recognition comes into his face—what then?

She wants to know. Is he really there for her?

Or has she made him up entirely out of her own desires?

She hesitates, flecking at something on her lip.

Thinking of his wonderful mouth, again.

In the last days I would swab Jay's once-gorgeous mouth with little pink sponges on a stick. Bony ridged cavern of stench.

She shuts the compact, zips up her briefcase.

To be one of the people who can just pick up and go! Trusted. The secretary never questioning why, or where, or if it's the right time.

But wait—she's coming back. There she is, at her desk again.

She's coming over to the window!

Is looking straight at the hotel!

If she glanced a little higher, could she see me? Her face right up to the glass.

I hold my breath. Maybe her face is the last I will ever see. How strange—a stranger! To see her in such detail.

I pull myself forward on the ledge, the pebbled tar sharp under my knees.

You are beautiful, I whisper.

I wish she could know. The scent of apples is in her hair.

She is turning to go.

I imagine her fear, a little upsurge as the elevator door opens.

But even so, it is all so dazzling!

26

Jay COULDN'T BELIEVE I had never seen the ocean. He drove
me there right off the bat, straight from the airport, even though it was
after midnight. We sat in the parking lot at Ocean Beach, laughing in the
fog. I could hear the surf, can still feel the roar of it pounding through
my blood the way it did that night, raising a little chill. We were really
at the edge, the whole country behind us and then a dropping off into
rolling churning blackness with a few lips of white caps peaking up, folding over, and smashing down out of sight behind the sloping humps of
dark sand. The whole truck seemed to shudder with the force of it, and
the wind, and later, our play.

But first it was good, it was more than good, to sit turned toward
him on the bench-seat of the truck, to smell him and hear the timbre of
his voice as he told me about his day. I reached up and held his face in
my hands. Even in the dark, his eyes gave off light.

Then we flung open the doors and ran through the rough salt air
with cheeks stinging so I could plunge my hand up to the wrist in the
sea. Jay caught me around the waist, and we raced to the truck, shouting and freezing, the wind tearing away our words until all that was left
was a joyous noise.

We made out right there in the truck, enveloped in fog. His mouth, his gorgeous mouth, firm and dry and then slick as we went at it hard, the thunder of waves in my ears as I pinned him against the door, my hand scrunching a handful of shirt and hair as I found the tight bud of his nipple and he cupped the back of my head, pushing me down, the metal of his buckle cold against my forehead. Nipping at his prick through his jeans, I yanked at his hips, trying to pull him away from the steering wheel. Just then a car turned in off the highway, beams swept the lot.

We paused, my face in Jay's crotch, his fingers clutching my ears. I could hear the crunch of gravel under tires, then somebody cut the engine.

I sat up.

No car in sight.

Fog brushed the windows.

"Don't worry," said Jay, smoothing my temple with his thumb. "It's San Francisco. I can take you anywhere I want—or *you* want," he added, grinning.

We were all over each other again in a flash. It was dizzying, my skin, its hunger. I pulled at him, wanting him out of his clothes, out of his mind, out of the cramped fucking truck so I could get at every inch of him, his balls and the bare bubble of his ass and the low-end rasp of his breath as he bore down, letting me in. I flailed for the handle of the door, picturing the dunes, a cove in the sand.

But he was unrelenting, the pressure of his mouth, his hands, around me. We were in a different time zone now—someplace faster, more urgent, a little rough. He was using me hard, almost with a stranger's touch.

I served him with matching fervor, willing to be a stranger, too. Something new was beginning, and for once, I barely questioned it.

During those next two weeks he took me around the city and in almost every place we could, we took each other. Outdoors, at twilight, in Buena Vista Park; and one morning, in the scrub above the beach at

Land's End, our breath steaming like horses; and one night, atop some rocks at Corona Heights, the voices of two men floating up from a hill below, until at one point, we all laughed, acknowledging each other's presence. And somewhere against a tree, eucalyptus scent erupting from the hard-helmeted seeds crunching under our boots.

Afterward, at Café Flore, we sat outside at tables still wet with dew, eating frittata with roast potatoes and fresh wedges of fruit—amazing, such fruit, in mid-winter! And the men in tight T-shirts and jeans, some even in shorts! Jay seemed to enjoy me gaping, to egg me on, pointing out biceps and asses, both of us reveling in a greater density of queers passing through one intersection on Market than in any bar in Detroit.

I went to the john, and was startled by a persistent tapping on the door.

I hurried to finish, jamming my shirt into my jeans.

"Hey, I saw you out there . . . Can I come in?" rasped a hoarse voice.

Belt firmly cinched, I opened the door—and a hand reached in, grabbing the front of my shirt, pushing me back inside.

"No way out but in!" said Jay, letting the door slam behind him as he playfully shoved his tongue into my mouth, hand down the crack of my ass.

A wild adolescent silliness seemed to have overtaken us both, spurring us on in this intentionally sloppy charade of anonymous sex. Soon it would take a confusing turn, but in the first week of my visit, we also romped about town to the wharf, the cable cars, Union Square, North Beach, the usual tourist things, concluding each day at the place where Jay had stayed in the summer, and where he was housesitting again while the lesbian owners were off to Portugal. We'd sleep in a heap, surrounded by dogs and cats while the boughs of tall cypress scraped the eaves.

I loved that house—it would give shelter to some of my deeper hopes, with its walls and mantels and bookshelves happily cluttered with photos of the women's two daughters and nieces and nephews—in skin tones from cream to dark tea. Not so much that I wanted children—but I wanted to know that family would be possible again.

I was especially fond of a photo in the entryway: two handsome silver-haired women linking arms with two men in tuxes and one bare-chested guy in a leather harness—all receiving awards from a nun with a beard. Anyone who came to the door could see that photo. I was impressed—it was hung on a nail, suggesting that there was no occasion on which it would be chucked in the closet. It sounds so tame now, but at the time, after what had happened at Jay's job, it was just the change of world we were longing for.

That Christmas Eve, we joined hundreds of queers and their friends at the Castro Theatre to hear the Gay Men's Chorus perform their campy and serious renditions of holiday music. Crammed shoulder to shoulder, mixing catcalls with old carols, we made a holiday for ourselves and each other under the coppery glowing ceiling of the grand old theater. At one point I looked over at Jay, and both he and the man next to him and the man past him looked back at me, and we laughed at ourselves—big guys in leather jackets, all with tears on our faces from a totally sappy rendition of "Home for the Holidays."

"An Army of Lovers Cannot Fail!" shouted a dyke who leapt up at the end of the encore, and we all hooted and cheered and poured out into the street.

A crowd for the second show was lined up all the way down the block and around the corner. I see them still, the men with cheeks full-fleshed, their backs strong and square, or elegantly lean, as yet unclaimed by the disease that was soon to render many of us gaunt, blind, dead within a few years. We strolled by like generals, inspecting the troops.

"I have a present for you," said Jay, "back at the house."

He had just brought in a tray of sandwiches and beer.

Setting it on the coffee table, he began to organize, mating spoons and knives, aligning them more properly to the plates. It made me smile. It was out of character for him, plus we didn't even need spoons. Seeing me smile, he righted himself, grinning sheepishly.

"Caught!" he said, with an excited shrug of his shoulders. He nodded toward the food.

"Eat up!"

"What's this?" I asked, peeking under a triangle of crustless bread.

"Not the present," he said. "Just a treat. Ploughman's lunch. No big deal. Real cheddar from England, some Branston pickle. I got the idea from a guy in the cheese shop on Castro."

He uncapped the thick bottles of imported brew, handed me one.

"From one ploughman to another!" I said, clinking my beer to his.

Two Cockapoos were already begging at my side. I laughed. Lapdogs! Not quite what I'd pictured for Jay's big city life when I'd been torturing myself back in Detroit. Happily, I broke off a bit of sandwich for them each. Jay was still standing, rocking on his heels as he watched me.

"Have a seat," I said.

He took a swig of beer, then crossed the room to the picture window, drew open the curtain.

Lights on the bridge, skyline, distant hills across the bay quavered in fog.

We both stared out.

"If that's my present, that's pretty damn good," I said.

"Only the best," he said, turning toward me. "I spread a cloth of dark and gold before my lover's feet . . . Or something like that," he said, giving me a silly grin as he scratched the back of his head.

He cleared his throat, shoved his hands in his pockets.

"I do want you to have it all," he said, looking at me.

I stopped munching.

"What I mean is, there's a lot out there. I want you to have what you want of it, without restraint."

I raised my eyebrows, set my sandwich down.

"Well, maybe a little restraint," he said, picking up his silk scarf from the table.

I twisted to look up at him as he came behind me, around the back of the couch. He draped the scarf around my neck, then stood with his hands on my shoulders, looking down at me.

I stared at his lips upside-down, starting to feel a little kink in my belly.

"What's that mean?" I asked.

"It's up to you," he said, pulling the scarf across my throat, then wrapping it round till he held the ends like reins. "I'm going to take you somewhere tonight," he said. "Have an open mind. You don't have to do anything—but you can, if you want. Think of it as my treat. The only catch is, you have to go blindfolded," he added.

He laid the silk over my eyes. I reached up, circling his wrist, feeling the tendons work as he tied the knot. Half expecting his hands to travel, I stretched out my legs.

"Do with me what you will," I said, my prick already at an uncomfortable angle in my jeans.

But he stepped back, breaking off from me.

"First, you're going to relax here with me and have another drink," he announced.

With that, he left the room, Cockapoos trotting behind.

I tilted my head back, peeking under the scarf. Same carpet, of course. A giddy little shiver ran through me. I felt like such a novice. And what about him? He seemed nervous too.

"Drink up," he said, placing a big sweaty quart in my hands.

"So much?" I asked.

"So many questions!"

"You drink some," I said.

"Just do as I say, not as I do," he said. "Besides, I have to drive."

"Where are we going?"

"That's for me to know, and you to find out."

"Whoa!" I said. He was really getting into the swing of things, now that I couldn't see him.

I heard him walk across the room, then back again.

"Here," he said, pushing something into my arms. "Your coat."

"We're really going out?"

He took me by the hand, pulling me up.

I struggled to find arm holes.

He took my hand, leading me out the door to the wooden stairs. I stumbled along, laughing and gripping his arm.

"What is this, a trust walk?" I said, recalling his stories of having his students play a similar game.

He led without answering. I could hear the wind high in the cypress, feel their sway in my own legs as the scent came in through my mouth.

He really was taking me somewhere.

"Is there anyone out here to see us?" I whispered.

"No," he said. "But if there were, it's clear we're playing."

We got to the truck, and he let me in. I slunk down.

"Hey, it's Christmas," he said, knocking his elbow against mine. "You can be as decorated as you want in this town. Sit up and be proud!"

"I don't know," I said, continuing to slump as he drove and talked.

"I'm not sure if you're going to like this," he said. "But that's all right. It just seems like something you should have done, if you've been to San Francisco."

He paused.

"And before you move here for good," he added. "With me."

I was a bit buzzed by now, infected by his light-hearted overtone. Playfully I groped for him, insisting that with him around, I didn't need any extra convincing.

He pinned my hand to the seat. I kept up a mock-struggle, pointing out he was going to have to let go of my wrist sometime to shift gears.

"I think you're trustworthy," he replied.

The truck lurched through a few more intersections, then swerved and came to a halt, engine idling.

Jay pulled off my blindfold.

Warehouses, blank-faced and dirty, lined a wide street.

"You have two hours," he said. "Then, I'm coming for you."

"Where are we?"

"Go figure," he said, nodding toward a building on the corner as he stuffed some cash in my pocket and handed me another quart of beer.

"How will we meet up?"

"Inside," he said. "I'll hunt you down. Just don't lock yourself in any rooms where I can't find you."

"Where will you be?"

"Looking for parking or something."

"For two hours?"

"Slowness is divinity," he teased, quoting my father's phrase, which I had shared with him months before.

He reached over, grabbing the top of my head and giving it a shake.

"Get out of here. Go have a blast. I'll be there at the end," he said.

I stared at the big metal door.

Army gray, with a beady little peephole, un-telling as a pigeon's eye. No signs or names in sight.

Merrily forward, I urged myself, pressing the bell, then standing back a step. The lock-release began to buzz. After a few seconds, the door popped open.

"You need to pull," said a trim guy with blue-black hair. He was holding the door for me, his arm on the panic bar. Attractive veins.

"Hi," I said, smiling inanely, unsure what face I should have for the occasion, whatever the hell it was.

He ignored my smile as he ushered me in.

"Do you understand what this is?" he asked, not unpleasantly.

"Kind of."

"It's a private men's club," he said, looking me over now. "For gay men," he added.

"Okay," I said.

"Are you a member?"

"I'm gay," I said, feeling foolish.

"That helps," he said, friendlier now. "But you have to buy a membership and pass," he added, motioning me on to a cashier's window.

It was bullet-proof glass. A sign above said Eighth and Howard Baths.

Holy shit, I thought, clutching my bag of brew. Of course, I had heard stories, fantasized, read stuff in gay papers, but now here I was, about to enter the famous baths. My mind was racing. Had Jay been here before? What did he mean by this, dropping me here alone? No Firearms, warned the sign below.

Three guys breezed in behind me with gym bags. "You in line?" asked one.

"Go ahead," I said, voice sounding loud and strange.

They pushed by, radiating the slight but tolerant impatience of those who know the ropes. I kept my eyes on a flyer, something about hepatitis studies.

Guys flashing cards at the window were buzzed through an inner door. One man cut me a glance over his shoulder, waiting until I met his eyes before he went through.

I flushed. The tough-looking cashier stood up, passing a tattooed hand over his nubby shaved head.

"Ready?" he asked me, raising a dark eyebrow.

I nodded, fishing around in my pocket for the cash Jay had stuffed there.

"I should walk you through some procedures," he said.

"Sure," I said, grateful for his friendly eyes. A book was open on the counter, so I read the title, upside down. Dante's *Inferno*. Yellow highlighting.

This was getting good.

He pushed a bunch of forms at me, then helped me with what seemed like an endless regimen of membership applications, ID checks, rule sheets, release of responsibility statements. No, I wasn't an undercover cop. No, I hadn't been coerced. Yes, I understood what this place was.

"All the rooms are reserved tonight," the guy said apologetically. But I can get you a locker."

He ducked out of sight.

I had to wait for him to let me in. There was no handle on the outside of the door. You couldn't just go in or out, at will. Something about that really hit me, contributing to my growing sense of entering a place beyond my usual volition.

Going through the door, I could already hear the music, its driving sexual beat, pulsing through the walls.

I entered a cove-like room with slot-boxes like in a bank vault, only warmer. He already had a box open for me on the table.

"Put your valuables in here," he said.

Then handing me a thread-bare towel, he pointed down the dark hall to the locker room.

"Go enjoy," he said.

I was losing track of time already.

I had no idea how long it was taking me just to navigate my way to my locker in the dim yellow light.

Or was it red? Maybe both. Bare bulbs, and row after row of gray lockers with men here and there between, the flesh tones leaping out in the rare light. Some guys simply dressing or undressing, others up against the cold metal with each other, fondling, kissing, towels tied at the waist.

Wandering up and down, I tried to keep my eyes on the locker numbers, relieved to find mine at the end of an empty aisle. I sat down, cracked open my beer.

Obviously, time to strip and stroll.

With shaky fingers I dropped my jeans, wrapped the towel around my waist. For a flash I was a teenager all over again, worrying that my dick would be too small, or worse, a huge giveaway in the shower. But here, I was safe. Ostensibly.

And already hard. Just the smell was turning me on. Musky and male, mixed with the odors of bleach, sweat, urine, deodorant, hot towels. A heady, not dirty smell. And the music was pounding. I could feel a blasting draft of it every time someone went in or out of a nearby door. It pulled at me, bass thudding, jamming in over my fears, my questions about Jay, pulverizing my thoughts, which were already reeling, but it wasn't hard to let them go. Other instincts were welling up. The whole village was dancing.

I threw my clothes in a ball in the locker, hitched the towel around my waist, left the beer.

The showers were behind a bright wall of glass. Well-lit, with everything out in the open, no curtains, or stalls. I could see a half-dozen guys under pole-showers, water streaming down their torsos, a few just soaping up, others keeping themselves hard while they watched one guy doing himself as he got fucked from behind, standing up. Three guys were kissing and rubbing up against each other, massaging each other's balls. Chin on a shoulder, one of them slid a half-glazed look my way, licking skin when he saw me staring.

I pressed on, sucked down a dark passageway by the music, which was throbbing now, coming up through the floor, meeting my feet. Men loomed up, passed by. I couldn't see faces, just a white stripe of towel around a body, or a glint of eye or teeth. That was me too, I realized. A flash in the dark. A shiver ran through my flesh.

The passage dumped me out in what seemed to be a main area. I could see alcoves with porn flickering, other doors and stairs, but what caught me was the surprise of a waterfall raining into a giant whirlpool. Pretty, with rocks and ferns. Guys were cruising the humid perimeter, so I joined them, looking in on the dozen or so men in or around the pool, some submerged, arms slung over the edge, while others were up on the rim, getting sucked or jacked off. No out and out fucking.

I backed up to a wall, loitering as I watched a handsome man slip off the pool's edge, stroke toward the center. The men around the ring were riveted too, some aggressively trying to compel his gaze with their own, others dropping their eyes seductively, or sullenly, or both. The question floated there between us: whom would he choose? One guy let his long legs drift up, break surface, playfully wriggling his toes. My prick butted against my towel, rooting for this one. I was happy when he won, though all I could see from that point on was two wet bobbing heads as the handsome guy came to port between those sinewy thighs. (That image would stay with me for years, resurfacing each June when those huge, beautiful mosquito-like insects with long floaty legs bump along the ceilings. My prick would swell improbably at the sight of them, and I would laugh, suddenly remembering those men.)

But that night I moved on, restless to survey the whole scene, and more than a little afraid, I suppose, of becoming a sitting duck. Saving the steam room for later, I opted instead for the stairs.

The second floor was a maze of narrow halls with long rows of doors, open and closed. I walked fast, acting unstoppable, but my eyes were darting back and forth, scoping out the little rooms. In those with open doors, guys lounged ass up or belly down on platform beds, eyes toward the hall, skin drenched in the crimson light of a bulb over each mirror. I took them in as pieces rather than whole—the tight muscles of an ass, a wet prick lolling, an indentation in a wide chest, a clenched hand. I saw a sheet drop to the floor, and for a second my body recalled Jay sweeping back the curtain just hours before, telling me he wanted me to have it all, to the fullest. Suddenly my eyes welled up. As I passed the doors that were closed, I tried not to think of what he might have been doing behind one of them this last fall. He wanted me, no matter what else he had done—that seemed clear.

I headed for the stairwell.

On the landing was a saguaro cactus skeleton. I had never seen the real thing, only pictures. It had Christmas lights twined in the hollows, shining out through the holes. I paused, looking at it, my whirling senses steadied for a moment as I listened to some guys on the steps gossiping. A thick furry man was enthusing about the concert at the Castro, and a tenor he hoped to lure to his home for a meal. The glow was still in him, a big, blustery, infectious, *joie de vivre,* and as I went on up the stairs, I found myself thinking, I would like to have friends like him when I moved here.

On the third floor, I entered a cavernous black room and was immediately assailed by what seemed to be a huge roiling animal of many heads, limbs, pricks, and assholes writhing under tiny red lights. I was overcome by the sheer quantity of thrusting, sucking, and fucking as the beast thrashed and splayed itself from a central mass into a maze of nooks and crannies, oozing the smell of alcohol, poppers, sperm, lube, sweat. Goosebumps all over, I stood fascinated as a daisy-chain of guys at the heart of it all fucked doggy-style on a platform bed, maybe six in a row, while men wedged in underneath, sucking and licking their balls. They, in turn, were jerked off by hangers-on at the edge. I waded into the room a few steps, packed in on all sides by gyrating flesh, not realizing I was trembling until I was touched lightly on the arm.

I looked to the side to see who it might be, but before I knew it a head shoved in up under my towel and my dick was stuffing a mouth. There was barely time for my towel to fall. I came in a pop, like a teenager.

Hot hands gripping my hips, I was angled into an alcove as others reached in but were checked by an elbow. Fingers were all over my chest as a voice yelled into my ear, "I love all this hair." I couldn't see his face, only a dark halo of curls, one of which stuck to my lip as he went down on my nipple then came up again, panting in my ear that he couldn't believe I was still hard. Guiding my hand to a long lean prick, he began thrusting up against me, then broke off abruptly, taking my hand.

"Come back to my room," he shouted over the music.

"My towel," I said. Cutting into the crowd, I lost him.

I was in a rush now, having no idea how quickly time was passing. Extracting a towel from between two feet, hoping it was mine, I made a swipe at my sticky cock, then got out of there.

The stairs were temporarily blocked. A brawny guy in a leather harness was standing over four supplicants on their knees on a lower step. Hands folded in worship, each was bound to the master by a silver chain that ran from their matching dog-collars to a silver ring in the center of his harness. When the master ordered that they could now proceed, they rose en masse, hands still in prayer, as the master backed up the stairs. (Necessary, I suppose, to avoid a silly unskillful tangle of lines. But I didn't think of that then.)

I squeezed by, feeling embarrassingly tame in my little towel, but eyeing a supplicant's watch as I passed.

"Tell him the time," the master suddenly barked from above. I halted, and the man demurred.

Forty-five more minutes.

I ran red-faced down the stairs past the cactus. I just wanted to get to the whirlpool now and submerge. I imagined waiting there for Jay, arms up over the rim, eyes on the door. What would he want to know? Nothing, I imagined, but I would know, and it would make my face go stupid. But why? He had given me permission, I reminded myself. It was just sex, if that's what you could call it. My cock was still tingling, but I somehow couldn't feel the rest of my body.

At the bottom of the stairs I saw a door open and steam billow out. What a good idea. I hurried over. I could let the past few minutes sweat themselves out of me, collect myself, be invisible for a while. I wanted things to slow down.

The hot heat rushed me, and for a second I thought I might drown from the moisture in the air. A patch in the foggy yellow light opened on a bench right near the door. I sat my ass down between two guys who were resting against the tiles. But soon they disappeared in a fresh burst of steam.

I closed my eyes, feeling the sweat trickle down my chest. The music was Latin now, a love ballad. When I opened my eyes, the mist had thinned. Now, I could see a man stroking his own belly, heavy dick hanging, face in repose. Beautiful strong collar bone. The action was slower here, more sensual. A gray head in a crotch, rhythmically lifting. Hard tile, with toes curled under. A ruddy big-chested man reaching toward a pink palm, tracing the lifeline. Lean black thighs and a low throaty laugh. Thick hands kneading a sinewy wrinkled shoulder. There were guys everywhere, thirty or so, on benches, in alcoves, up against the tiles. Steam burst from the pipes again, erasing it all, then a new scene emerged, revealing two men in a corner, long bodies twisting together like the thick turgid stems of lilies.

A wild Brazilian samba started up, and in the center of the room, a man with an inward-turned gaze had begun to dance. He was doughy, and big, with pale skin and hair that seemed the same color. Outside, on the street, few men would probably have looked at him, writing him off as potato-ish and bland, but here, he was moving his hips with an amazing smoothness, and twirling his hand sensually above, in the heat, with his lips half-parted, his belly undulating and open. It was entrancing and beautiful, and for the first time that night I felt joined in some sort of unity with the men around me. Shoulder to shoulder, we were unified by a single vision of this lovely man weaving between us. Numinous, skillful, shining, he was not supremely beautiful in the world's surface sense, nor in our own most brutal preferences for the young, gorgeous, and strong. But there was something in his undulations that could not be overlooked.

When the man next to me put his arm around my shoulders in a brotherly way, I leaned my head back, companionably draping my hand over his knee. I had no idea what he even looked like. My towel was tenting up, but that wasn't news, and really had nothing to do with him. A guy across from me came into view, and I realized he was staring at me, stroking his balls and dick with a meaty hand. He was a hunk, and I was terribly flattered. Squeezing my thumb inside my fist, I played to his gaze for a few seconds, letting my legs fall open. The man beside me leaned over, kissed my shoulder, then ran his tongue up to my ear, asking if we might mess around. Before I had a chance to answer, he took my chin, turned my face to him and began a passionate and almost searching kiss. The roughness of his mustache felt good, but after a few seconds I put my hand on his chest, backing him off a bit, wanting to get a look at him.

It was at this moment that I saw Jay. He was staring right at me. The man next to me, sensing my intake of breath, raised his eyebrows.

"My boyfriend is over there," I whispered.

"What's his name?" the guy asked, pulling a corner of his mustache.

I didn't answer.

He turned, scanning the room. "Hey buddy," he said. "C'mon over. We weren't gonna leave you out."

The samba man came wriggling by, blocking the view.

When Jay reappeared, his arms were crossed.

I beckoned.

He refused, then made a chins-up motion with his head, as if to say get on with it.

I froze.

He continued to stare at me with half-hooded eyes, a determined self-abandon in his face. But, I could see, it cost him. His temple flickered and I knew he was clenching his jaw. Even so, he dipped his head again, more impatiently this time, as if there was something for him in this too.

I put my palm over the heart of the man waiting patiently next to me. As my hand went out, Jay was still looking directly into me, not breaking away, not hiding the glimmer of fear that clearly leapt into his eyes. It was such a naked moment. His willingness to go forward seemed unstinting.

A supreme feeling of immense devotion swept through me.

I whispered to the man next to me that I had to go. We exchanged an affectionate look, then he shrugged good naturedly.

"No problem, buddy," he said, getting up, tightening the towel around his waist.

"All yours," he said to Jay, as he passed by, knocking him lightly on the shoulder. "You've got a good boy there."

I went to Jay immediately. I don't know what I thought I was going to do—maybe straddle him on the bench—but when I got to him he lowered his head, sandwiching his hands between his thighs. I ran my fingers through his hair, then pulled his head against my belly. He didn't reach up to hug me, or push me away. I just stood there, his head in my hands, oblivious now to the other men in the steam.

Suddenly he grabbed my hips, and pulled himself up.

"Let's go," he said roughly, readjusting his towel. "I have a room."

I trotted at his heels into the main area.

"I'm sorry," I yelled at the back of his head, over the music.

He spun around—I almost ran into him. His hands flew up to my chest, and for a second I thought he was going to give me a shove. But he grabbed my nipples instead, holding me in place with a pinch.

"Just drop it," he said, enunciating fiercely as he increased the pressure until my eyes teared, my shoulders curved, my breathing changed. But the pain was good, a cleansing fire.

"Now, where are the rooms?" he demanded, softer now, that familiar tone of bravado returning to him. He let go, giving me a little push.

I led the way up the stairs. It was such an obvious clue, him making me go first, but at the time I didn't catch it.

As we passed the saguaro cactus, I pointed toward the Christmas lights. I knew Jay loved the trappings of the season. He nodded, but still seemed locked away behind his face. The stairs were crowded now, with lots of traffic up and down.

We entered the dark corridor of private rooms and began to search the aisles for the number on Jay's key, glad to pour ourselves into this simple task.

As I entered the room, the sight of my scarlet skin under the red bulb above the mirror startled me. Jay stood against the closed door, arms crossed, looking me up and down before he spoke.

"The gentleman said you've been a good boy. That would be quite unfortunate," he said, looking down his nose in an attitude of mock-inspection.

Trying to play along, I suggested that he examine me, my voice suddenly drying up as I fought an untimely shyness.

"Get up on the table," he said.

I lay down.

"Over," he ordered. "And up. On your knees. And with your head down. I don't want to see your face."

I did as I was told, suddenly *flooded* with a desire for punishment.

I wanted some pain, to match any I may have caused. Ever.

185

"I beg you," I whispered.

He came around the side of the table, pulling my head up with a handful of hair.

"What did you say?"

I didn't answer, just turned my face away.

Still holding my head down with his hand in my hair, he started to play with my ass, every now and then pushing his knuckles up against my crack, harder each time, but then receding, as if he were deliberating. I began to push back against his hand, desperate to make a rhythm of it, but then he stopped for a moment.

Nothing was happening.

Somehow, I knew what to do.

Twisting around, I grabbed him in a headlock and pulled him down onto the table, on his side. Immediately he curled into a ball, me around him. I thought he would cry, but he just lay there, hands between his thighs again. Finally, he said something, but I couldn't hear. The music was still blasting.

"I don't know what my problem is," he shouted this time, to the wall.

I hugged him tighter.

"I'm the one who started this," he said. "I wanted to give you the whole San Francisco experience."

I raised up on my elbow, peering over his shoulder at the side of his face.

"But maybe you didn't want me to take it," I said into his ear.

He winced.

"Or be taken by it," he blurted.

"I'm not taken by it," I started to say, but he cut me off.

"How do you even know?" he asked, swinging his legs over the edge of the bed now, sitting up with his back to me. "You haven't had time to know."

"I just know," I insisted.

"That's what I'm saying," he fired back, giving me an almost disgusted look over his shoulder. "You always think you know who you are—I'm this, I'm that. Doesn't it occur to you that *you* could change? You could get out here and change?"

"And what if I were changing? You didn't seem to like it."

He faltered, staring at the wall, arms crossed now.

"It's my own fucking fault," he finally said. "I had no idea you would leap at it like this."

"That's not exactly how it was," I said, getting a little huffy. "Besides, you egged me on. And what about the other times, when I wasn't here? Were you such an angel?"

It was his turn to look startled, as well as hurt.

"I've never been here until tonight," he said.

"You never messed around these past three months?"

"I didn't say that."

"So, what are you saying?"

"Nothing, unless I have to."

"You have to. You started this."

"I met a few guys in bars."

"And?"

"Usually we went for a walk, talked, sometimes messed around."

Now I was red and burning hot under my skin. It was my turn to sit up, face the door.

"So, you wanted more than sex. You walked, you talked," I said, pulling the towel over my lap, tightening it around my waist as I stood.

He grabbed my wrist.

"Don't go," he said, the words catching in his throat. I glared at him.

"I missed you. I missed you terribly. I missed talking to you."

Suddenly he pile-jammed his head into my belly, and burst into tears.

We lay curled on the bed together for a long time, comforting each other. I stroked his hair, wondering, how many other men had done this with him.

Those last few days before I returned to Detroit, Jay submitted himself to me with an unprecedented intensity—with a sense of wanting to feel the hurt—those are the words that come to me now. Before, his pain had seemed locked away, inaccessible in its full force. But here, at last, was the suffering for all that had been taken from him by the fire, channeled now through the upsetting image of me with another man. I relaxed, and gave myself more completely to our heated grappling, his desire for me to pound into him as if I could tear him open.

I returned to Detroit feeling more powerful and determined to forge ahead. Throughout the winter and spring, as I prepared to move, all I had to do was recall the intensity of those last nights with Jay—the smell of his sweat, the sight of his skin flushed with release—and any molecule of hesitancy in me would dissolve in a gasp.

27

LAYING HERE IN THE HOTEL, even with my eyes closed, I can feel the hour. Five o'clock. That extra hum in the air as everyone in the city packs up, ready to head out. I would like to do that, one more time. Oh God, that surge of vigor at the end of the day.

I pull myself out of bed, go to the French doors. The night is still blue-tinged, young. Across the street, the office building is lit up like a showroom panel of TVs.

Where's the channel starring my new friend? Still at her desk. Seeing her, something in me eases. Though she's not actually a friend, she is familiar now. I force myself to look away, check out the empty offices. I don't need any attachments. She's just a stranger, not a friend.

Wrapping the blanket around my legs, I realize I've heard that line before. Both Jay and I used it, on each other, and to ourselves, about the other men. We were in the thick of it then, in our prime. Those urges seemed only natural, something to be embraced, but also to be kept in place.

Of course, that took a little work, but things were good in those years, really good. We'd paid our dues. It was our turn to breathe easy. Sure, we did hear about an ominous disease, as news leaked out from LA and New York. We were in the crowd outside the Castro's Star Pharmacy, craning our necks, shoulder to shoulder, when the CDC report was taped to the window. But from what we could tell then, the illness seemed to hit guys who'd done lots of drugs and sex.

That wasn't either of us.

Soon after I arrived, I found work more quickly than we'd expected. While Jay spent his days ripping apart the probate property he'd talked about at Christmas, preparing it for renovation, I went off to Macy's, where officially I was a temporary file clerk in the transportation department. Mostly, though, my job was to save the manager's ass. He was a nice guy, not very bright, but with a great all-American smile and plenty of fleshed-out stories about his tricks on Polk Street. He came in one morning waving a document he'd been struggling to write for weeks. It was a mess, so I cleaned it up, and when he turned it in, his bosses loved it—a first. He admitted a summer extra had done it; my job was extended. I was glad to have the cash, plus it was a bonus to be able to use a few editing skills. The hours ticked by pleasantly enough, but for most people on staff, real life began after five.

I'd step off the elevator and into the street, invigorated by the sting of fog as I hurried to the subway, eager to see Jay. I can still hear the patter of dozens of footsteps on the stairs to the tunnel, feel the cool air as I descended, the shadow of the stairwell walls falling over me. Pushing through the turnstile, I'd be pulling off my tie, wondering where we'd eat that night. Years later, when the novelty of waiting by the tracks in an international crush of races, creeds, outfits, and ages had worn off, I still retained a Midwesterner's sense of wonder, along with a pride that Jay and I had become part of this place.

On the train, I especially liked the sideways-facing seats, where I could command a view of the whole car, entertained by glances between strangers, a brushed arm, an offered paper, an inward gaze so fierce it was obviously meant to compel. Back then, you could find a sexual buzz everywhere. If someone caught my fancy, I preferred watching his reflection in the window, where I might see his face, unguarded. Big surprise—I had a thing then for workmen, guys in banged-up heavy boots or overalls, painter's pants, mechanic's uniforms. I especially liked it when one of them was caught without a seat and had to stand swaying in the aisle, hands gripping the rail above, maybe a little skin exposed as his shirt came loose from his trousers and his hips shifted and rolled with the ride. I tried to keep his reflection in view as the window flashed and shimmered with the movement of the train and as the contours of his body began to morph into images of Jay. Odd, I now think. The way the mind is. As if I'd already known that soon he would be a fleeting image, a ghost I would try to capture.

But at that time he was very much alive. I anticipated arriving home, finding him at work, maybe with his arms up in just that way, belly showing below his T-shirt as he loosened a ceiling lamp. I'd imagine him on the top of a stepladder, feet precariously side by side. "I can't let go, but hello," I'd hear him say, grinning down as he struggled with the wires. "I can help you let go," I'd answer, reaching up, shoving my fingers under his belt, playfully threatening his balance as I dragged over a milk crate with my foot. Climbing onto it, I'd begin licking the skin below his navel. I wanted, among other things, to make him laugh. He'd attempt to quell it, so as not to lose his footing, but I'd keep pushing, ridiculously trying to work my tongue under the loop of leather in his buckle, gnawing it, goofing around until he was able to screw in more than the lamp.

The daily miracle did wear off once in a while, of course. Especially after living together for a few months at Jay's house, or should I say, his construction zone. Confined to a back bedroom, we set up a hotplate, microwave, and small fridge, but I was not as adept as Jay at living out of boxes or shuffling through plaster dust on my way to the john. One morning he rounded the corner just in time to see me kick a silty box out of the way as I searched madly for clean clothes.

"Not so fond of cardboard armoires? Maybe the paint fumes are getting to you," he noted, not unkindly.

He came up behind me, wrapping his arms around me, pinning my elbows to my sides in reassuring restraint. "I'm okay," I said.

"You're being a good sport, but I know you'd like a settled home. I knew that about you from the get-go."

It was his idea that we should look for a one-bedroom apartment, cheap enough for me to cover on my own, but big enough for us both to use as home base. He'd stay at his place when he was in a work frenzy, or if either of us needed space. The apartment would be more mine, to nest in and arrange.

Answering an ad in the newspaper for a cottage in the Castro, we walked through a passageway beneath a two-flat building, and I had my first glimpse of a San Francisco invisible from the streets of cheek-by-jowl houses. Suddenly there was the umbrella of green I had been craving—tree ferns, pittosporum, plum trees, heirloom fuchsias, tall Leland cypress. I would learn the names later, but at the time, they were all the more enchanting because they had no names, no categories. A new beginning.

The landlord, an older gay man, sat us down at a little café table under the black bamboo and grilled us in his own polished and paced way. Donald had lived in the cottage for fifteen years, but was taking a break from the city, moving up to the Russian River for a while. He wanted someone capable of maintaining things. Could either of us change a washer? Keep the ferns watered? His love for the little courtyard between the cottage and front flats was palpable; his longing to see it nurtured and sustained in his absence struck a chord in us. He sensed that. On the day he turned over the key, he told us he knew we were right for the place when he saw us look up into the rustling bamboo, then catch each other's eye, faces relaxing simultaneously. Both of us blushed to think we had been observed so closely, but coming from him, an older gay man, it felt like a blessing on our path.

We moved in, or should I say, *I* unloaded a U-Haul full of belongings I'd had in storage, and Jay carried over a few gym bags full of clothes. Within the month, Emily came too, dropped off by a friend who'd brought her along on his flight from Detroit. That night, we stretched out side by side on the bed, talking softly as we listened to her prowl in and out of cupboards, ignoring us both. In the morning, though, we woke to find her staring regally down on us from the crown molding. Somehow having her eyes on us made it feel more like family, though from then on, she tended to act more like *my* cat, marking my legs, fussing at me to be fed. Jay made a few affectionate squawks of protest, but was appeased when she restored his permission to wear her like a stole on special occasions—namely, if he brought her home a doggy bag.

But often she'd have to wait until midnight for that since, after dinner, we'd roam the neighborhoods—Cole Valley, Inner Sunset, the Haight, Castro, Noe Valley, the Mission—checking out exterior paint schemes before it got dark, ogling inner decor when the lights came on. Jay was eager to fill me in on his projects and recruit my opinions. His confidence and enthusiasm reassured me. He didn't seem to miss teaching, and rarely spoke of what had happened.

We stopped off regularly at the Midnight Sun, where we'd stand around drinking, yakking, watching music videos or trash TV with a group of guys we were getting to know. It was such a thrill to just walk down the hill and have that opportunity rather than having to drive halfway across the Detroit metropolitan region in a sleet storm. Later, snug in the cottage's claw-foot tub, we'd share our impressions of the other guys as we'd soak, wetting towels and draping them over our heads to keep ourselves warm as the water cooled.

One night, Jay hung the towel over his entire face, sucking the cloth in and out and making a silly noise as he breathed.

"I have a confession to make," he said, in a goony voice.

"I will hear it," I said, matching his tone.

"I have done something few men in this town have done."

"Mmm, could be delicious," I said, in an aside.

"I have a boyfriend."

"But there are many here like that, young man."

"Yes, but most are not in a couple. If I were to simply observe, I would say that it seems to be regarded as a major sin, a sign of terrible stagnation, a refusal to liberate one's innate potential. One man in the bar even had the audacity to quote some mystic to me. '*Stop boring God*,' he said, when I refused his offers."

I grew still in the water.

"And are you bored, young man? Do you wish for a Boys' Night Out, as some of the couples allow?"

There was a long pause, a pause that he allowed to thicken with tension as I stared at the blanks of his eyes, hidden by cloth.

"In my time I have watched the lazy Susan spin," he said, putting on the tremulous voice of a sage. "I have tasted many dishes, enough to know that one can sample endlessly, without being deeply satisfied."

Towel still over his face, he grappled for the handle of the faucet, turning it on for another blast of hot.

"Wanting leads to wanting," he said, extending his arms now like a man feeling around in the dark, running his fingers lightly down my chest, across my nipples, then under the water.

I leaned forward, kissing him through the wet terrycloth.

"It's a small life, but it's ours, and we like it," I overheard him telling one of the guys at the bar a few weeks later.

28

AFTER THE FIRST YEAR AND NO TREMORS, I set my great-grandmother's Wedgwood vase on the mantle. I had accepted the fact that fate might shake the creamy arms of Diana, the Muses, and me into a pile of spindly bone.

A few months later, with Jay's help, I went one step further, carting my parent's overstuffed furniture out to the curb. Emily was sad to see her favorite shredding posts gone, but I was finally ready to clear the decks, start anew.

For once I was ahead of the fashion curve, having developed a passion for Arts and Crafts furniture. I liked its solid, simple lines. On weekend mornings, Jay and I wandered on foot to rummage sales and antique shops, stopping at cafés along the way to bicker affectionately about whether or not I really needed one more basket. Jay was good at helping me think through what sorts of things would work well, but it was clear that he regarded the cottage as my project. Was he curbing his domestic enthusiasms after losing everything in the fire? He denied this, saying he was happy to reap the benefits of my efforts, since his energy was taken up with renovations on the property he was getting ready to sell.

One fall Saturday, though, something did catch his eye. We were at an elderly neighbor's garage sale. Mabel had lured us in, beckoning to us from her lawn chair just inside the door. Her voice was feeble, but her eyes were alert.

"Just two weeks to Halloween," she teased. "Could I interest you two men in some heels or earrings?"

Tables were scattered with fifties-style costume jewelry, scarves, handbags, housewares. A guy with a shaved head glanced up from a bin, winking at us as he held a chunky necklace of blue cut-glass across his hairy chest.

As I poked through a stack of Fiesta ware, I noted Jay leaning over something in the back of the garage with great absorption.

I went over. He was pushing and prodding now, testing the joints of an oak reading chair. There were no cushions, just a frame, and it was covered with a greasy layer of dust, but it was Mission-style, only twenty-five dollars, and the first thing I had seen grab his personal interest.

"Want me to get that for you?" I whispered, linking my arm through his.

He stared for a minute, then shook his head, moving on with his hands in his pockets. As he stood in front of an old mirror, I watched his eyes slide back to the chair.

"Twenty-five?" I quietly asked Mabel.

"Oh, I guess, if that's not too much for that dirty old thing."

I started to pull out my wallet, but Jay shook his head vehemently at me and motioned me outside.

"I may be back," I told Mabel, winking.

I fell into step beside Jay on the sidewalk.

"I could clean that up for you, I told him. Get some cushions. I'd like to. Plus, its cheap."

"That's just it, he said. It's a real steal. Maybe even a Stickley. It could be worth hundreds. She obviously has no idea."

We raised our eyebrows at each other.

"Should we offer her a little more?" I suggested.

"Whatever we could offer her wouldn't be fair," he said. "Let's just do the old lady a favor and tell her what she has."

She listened to us with a cocked head.

"That old thing?" she said again. "No. That's just cottage furniture. It was everywhere when I was young. I'll give it to you for ten!"

"Absolutely not," said Jay. He insisted he could get her much, much more around the corner at a shop on 19ᵗʰ.

She waved him off. "Phooey," she said, staring at him in disbelief when he told her what prices he'd seen there. "It's not right for them to charge that much."

"But it's the way of the world," said Jay.

"Well, it's not my way. I just want it out of my garage, now! I don't need all that money."

"Your slipper's got a hole in it," Jay pointed out. "Don't you need a new pair of slippers?"

She glanced down at her toe, which was sticking out of a hole. She waved hello to it coquettishly, then turned back to us.

"Keep your eyes off my ankles, young man. How dare you!" she said. "I want you to pay me thirty dollars and take that piece of junk out of here."

Smitten, I paid her while Jay maneuvered the chair out of the garage. Resting it upside-down on his head like a bulky crown, he carried it home with a spring in his step despite the weight. Every Halloween after that, he would leave a cheap but outrageous pair of fluffy slippers from Walgreen's at Mabel's door. To continue this tradition was one of the few promises he extracted from me before he died.

As it turned out, the chair was low for Jay, and made his long legs look even longer, and his knees solid and prominent as they poked up, his large hands hanging over the ends of the arm-rests. It brought out the sprawl in him, something big and relaxed, which made me want to go down on my knees before him. The feeling of his hands cupped around the back of my head, pulling me in, seemed more than enough for one lifetime.

Were we oblivious to the epidemic around us?

Of course not. Every sniffle had us both quietly frightened. And it wasn't long before we began to hear about friends of friends: a night in the emergency room, a dangerously high fever, the appearance of a lesion. An acquaintance from Midnight Sun who was dancing one Friday was on oxygen the next.

That was only the first swell of the wave.

But it left me open and greedy for the most mundane pleasures: squatting together around a pizza steaming in its box on the floor as we took a break from painting a ceiling; newspapers littered across the bed as we sprawled together watching a video, unloading flats of primroses in January, both of us amazed to have flowers, in winter!

Jay had a wonderful capacity to amplify joy.

I remember distinctly one day when we went to our HMO to get flu shots. Not exactly a promising scenario. The line went all the way around the outside of the building. Jay dropped me off to hold a place for us as he parked. A silly little delight went through both of us when we found each other in the long line.

At some point, an elderly Latin lady with dark prescription glasses and a cane appeared quietly at our side and was obviously sticking close. Jay asked her if it was hard to stand. She nodded and rolled her eyes. I volunteered to hold her place, encouraging her to sit on a bench. "I'm afraid I won't be able to find you when it's my turn," she said.

"We'll find *you*," Jay said, offering his arm.

Just then a nurse came along, rounding up the disabled and old.

We waited an hour in the crisp November air, chilly in the shade, hot in the sun. In front of us a thin-lipped man in a crisp golf jacket lectured an almost glamorous Russian woman in a dramatic fake fur hat about the history of the Alamo. Jay and I glanced at each other, entertained at first, but after a while it was painful to hear him droning on and on without once looking at the woman.

"We are very lucky," I whispered to Jay.

He nodded, pressing his shoulder against mine.

We resumed talking happily together until we were well around the building and almost through the doors. On Geary, a fresh breeze was blowing in off the ocean. I remember him licking his fingertip, sticking it in the air as if to test the direction of the wind. We both raised our eyebrows expectantly, having the same thought at the same time: after our shots, we'd pick up lunch, head for the beach.

We waited some more inside the building. Elevator doors slid open, people poured out. It was then a woman ahead of us snagged the arm of a guy rushing past.

"Want in line?" she asked.

He looked confused, running a shaky hand through his spikey hair.

"I was just going home," he said, glancing perplexedly at the crowd. "What's going on?"

"Flu shots," she said. "You look like you could use a shave. What are you doing here?"

He flushed. "Gerald. He's on oxygen. We just got him into a room. We've been in the ER all night . . ."

The woman held onto his sleeve while they murmured together. He was looking off to the side, eyes moving absently along the line until he came to Jay. I noted what seemed to be a flicker of recognition, and then he nodded, maybe in faint greeting, maybe goodbye to his friend. I felt Jay shift from one foot to the other.

"All I can say is people better start getting tested," the guy said more loudly as he started down the hall.

"I'll call you," the woman said, hugging herself as she watched him go.

I looked at Jay, who was now studying a flyer on the wall.

"Did you know that guy?"

He shook his head, shrugged.

"I think he's the roommate of someone I met when I first got to town."

The line surged forward. Jay was ahead of me now. We entered a large chaotic hall where people were fed into a dozen or so nurse's stations. I lost track of Jay. I was rolling up my sleeve, getting ready for my shot, when I spotted him outside, on the other side of the plate glass window. We caught each other's eye just as the needle slid in. He winced in playful sympathy, but when I joined him outside, he seemed agitated, quickly heading for the parking structure.

"What's up?" I asked. All morning he'd been so pleasant, even joyful, unlike others around us.

"I'm ready for this to be over," he said. "It's been more than two hours."

"You sure that's all it is?"

"Two *hours*? That's *all*?" he said, misunderstanding me, sounding irritated.

"I didn't mean that. But never mind," I said, deciding to keep it simple. "You must be hungry. Let's get out of here. I'll find us some lunch, take you to the beach."

"My savior," he said, brightening.

We drove to the ocean with the windows down, blowing off the last-minute stress by singing along to the radio at the top of our lungs.

We walked along the shore, skipping stones in the unusually smooth valleys between waves. The Farallon Islands seemed to be floating on top of the water, just out of reach.

We would keep each other safe, we vowed. We would have to adapt our intimacies, but we felt we were up to the creative challenge. As for testing, we decided to wait. Confidentiality was in question, plus there were no significant treatments yet.

Mostly, though, we wanted more days like this one, as unclouded as possible, for as long as possible.

29

WHILE SOME MEN POURED THEMSELVES into bodybuilding, diet changes, pyramid money schemes, or trips to parties in a well-worn circuit of cities around the world to assure themselves that they were, for the moment, virile, Jay and I immersed ourselves in work.

It took him a few years to complete the house. As hoped, it sold with enough profit for him to take on a new building with even greater promise but needing more repair. This time he hired some part-time help, mostly younger guys who were also refugees from the Midwest. He had an affinity for starving-artist types, which meant they needed some training. As always, he was a good teacher, patient and clear. Soon they were seeking his advice on everything from used cars to used boyfriends. Though I felt a bit threatened at first, mostly I was happy to see him have a new arena for his skills.

It took me longer to find my way. As eager as I was to know the future and have control over it in my romantic life, by contrast, I was fine with the unknown in my work life—perhaps too much so. I told myself that as long I was happy with Jay, I'd be able to cope when my temporary job at Macy's ended. In the meantime, I was free to explore the city with my boyfriend, unburdened by the sorts of after-hours obligations that fall on many professionals.

The question of my work life did concern Jay, however. When was I going to get bored and perhaps blame him for interrupting my fledgling career in publishing?

I tried to assure him that there was nothing I missed about being a low-paid copyreader in a room full of cigarette smoke. Meeting him, and moving to the city, had been an unexpected blessing. I was enjoying a newfound trust in simply seeing what unfolded.

He warmed to that idea—but didn't totally buy it. Why had I worked so hard to get through school, then? What had been in my mind?

The truth was, I hadn't thought very far ahead. Before my parents died, when I first started college, I just wanted out of the store. I was sick of the practical concerns that dominated our family life. When I decided to study literature, I argued to my parents, who had grown up in the Depression, that it was a good pre-law course, but I didn't really think I'd ever become a lawyer. Let them worry about tomorrow, I told myself. I'd take up that concern when I got there.

When it turned out that for them there would be no tomorrow, my vague fantasies of becoming a poet or having something to do with books were submerged as I struggled to untangle my parent's estate. There was no life insurance. When the store was sold, it just barely paid off the debts. I was left scrambling for a way to support myself. Numbly, I packed up their possessions, found work at the office supply store, moved into my flat. Just to graduate would be a big achievement.

But I did, and here I was with Jay, in a gorgeous city. I was making my way just fine, I told him. If I had learned anything during those college years, it was how to roll with the punches, take what comes.

He laid off me, for the most part. I don't know if he detected my underlying vulnerability, but in retrospect, what is important is that he acted as though he did, acted with an almost animal intelligence, moving sleekly to give way, give room.

What arose in that space was my own nettling awareness that while I liked to think I was so at ease with change in my work life, I had in truth become complacent, afraid to risk failure. Without even knowing it, I had been guarding my wounds.

So, what the hell *was* I going to do with the rest of my life?

An unfamiliar panic set in.

With an urgency I had rarely known, and that Jay had certainly not witnessed, I began amassing catalogues from various training programs. At first, I considered any job that would allow me to work at home, setting my own schedule. While the idea of tax preparation, grant writing, and bookkeeping didn't exactly blow up my skirt, I pictured long morning walks over Corona Heights or Buena Vista before settling down to business. But the idea of public service also drew me. Despite Jay's debacle, I thought of teaching, or more exactly, the summers off.

"I don't think so," said Jay, flipping through a recruitment brochure.

"Why not?" I said, a bit hurt.

Catching my tone, he looked up.

"It's not that you wouldn't be good at it—but you'd have thirty kids climbing the walls. Think about it, Mr. Party Boy. You don't like it when we have more than six for dinner!"

I trailed after him as he went to the kitchen, started washing some dishes.

"Maybe technical writing?" I said. "I could make your dinner and revise documents, all at the same time."

He held a plate under the running faucet, looking dubious.

"I don't know," he said. "When I met you, you were in love with books, but they weren't manuals for computers or medical equipment. Besides, you'd have to drum up business all the time."

"So, what the hell do I do?" I demanded, as if he could answer it for me.

I was surprised by his reply, which sounded more like something I would say to him.

"Wait," he said. "More will be revealed. I have faith."

He set the plate carefully in the rack, then stood reflectively for a minute with his hands under the sudsy water. It hit me that we had traded roles—that here he was, advocating an inner listening that required patience, even slowness, so different from his own restless tendency to act, to move. Such switches aren't unusual, I know, for couples who have been together for a while, but for us it was a first.

I remember the scent of him standing beside me in his clean T-shirt.

One weekend, a month or so later, I was helping him rip out an old linoleum floor at his property.

"Destruction suits you," he said, coming up to me, catching a bead of sweat from my chin on the back of his hand.

"How about some lunch?" he asked.

We took our sandwiches up to the roof. Fog was rolling into Golden Gate Park, but the house was above the clouds on a sunny hill near Kezar Stadium. We lazed on an old army blanket, flipping through a stack of books on paint and wallpaper that Jay had checked out of the library. Suddenly it popped into my head that I hadn't set foot in a library since moving.

"Why not?" asked Jay idly.

"I can buy the books I want now, I guess."

"We should get you a card," he said, noting that the Castro branch was closer, but he preferred the one in Noe Valley. He enthused about the two-story building, going on about the Spanish-style brick and terra cotta, the decorated high ceilings and a wide marble staircase built during the Carnegie era.

"Of course, you would know all that," I said, tousling his hair. "But what about the books? Did they have what you wanted?"

"They had these books," he said, patting the stack. "And a good-looking guy at the desk who could translate the Latin over the front door."

"Which of course you had an urgent need to know," I said, watching him peel an orange.

"Life Without Literature Is Death," he said, grinning. He offered me a segment, then popped it into his own mouth when I shook my head.

"I guess I should have been a librarian," I said, setting my heavy-rimmed safety glasses low on my nose, looking at him over the top of their paint-spattered lenses.

Leaning toward me on the blanket, he initiated a kiss, but soon began to tug playfully on my sleeve.

"What?" I said, breaking off.

"Did you hear what you just said?" he asked.

It seemed totally true. I should have been a librarian.

We began to talk with excitement and relief, not unlike that which welled up in me each time I climbed the steps to the public library when I was a kid. In that time when my family owned hardly any books, the library was, quite literally, the whole world to me, the most cosmopolitan place I knew. I can still recall the inner hush that would swirl through my body when I entered the big quiet room full of stacks and tables and chairs and people, who for the most part would just let me be.

As we finished tearing up the floor that afternoon, a rush of memories spilled out of us both. I told Jay about my mother's mother, who stole me away from the store at least once a week during the summer when I was a kid. Even though her characteristic muumuus and red slip-on canvas shoes usually embarrassed me in public, when we were at the library, I didn't care. All sorts of quirky enthusiasms seemed to be tolerated or even encouraged there. And the librarians had a quality that attracted me. Though I didn't know the word then, now I would call it contemplative. They were humble, helpful, calm.

It was my grandmother's idea to start leaving me there for the whole day, once a week. I'd head for the card catalog, spend hours playing detective, tracking down current interests—trilobites, Civil War photos, Michelangelo's muscle men, Greeks in togas, National Geographics with naked people from anywhere. And there was one whole afternoon I sat cross-legged on the cool linoleum of a poorly used aisle as I perused Gore Vidals's *The City and the Pillar*, scandalized and titillated by this story of a young gay man in the forties.

Jay laughed, remembering how he had moved on from the Hardy Boys and Tom Swift Jr. to thorough searches of medical texts for diagrams of penises. One particularly nice specimen was found balled up in his trouser pocket by his mother collecting the wash.

"I was just worrying about granddad," he'd lied, alluding to the old man's prostate problem.

How delicious they were, those secrets that led us deeper into ourselves and away from our parents, or so it seemed.

I've always marveled at the seeming randomness of conversations like the one we had on the roof that day. Jay could have easily been distracted, could have been silently making a list of supplies as we talked. But he was fully there. I wonder how long it would have taken me to find my path if he hadn't caught my comment that day. Just a month or two later and it would have been too late to apply to the last class of library students admitted to Berkeley.

For those next two years, I felt a great deal of gratitude toward him. While I covered my tuition with some savings and a scholarship, he insisted on paying our living expenses with money left over from his first renovation. I felt awkward at first, accepting it. Felt compelled to cook and clean. But he was true to his word—he didn't see it as a trade—just something he wanted to give me. I had never had the luxury to just be a student, he noted, and he wanted me to have that.

I reveled in it, soaking up experience in several types of libraries during my practicums. I liked the other students and librarians, a
diverse bunch with far-ranging interests. I soon found myself making
a few buddies, bringing them home for study sessions. I kept a pot of
stew ready for those occasions, knowing Jay would be pleased to enter
the fragrant cottage and find both company and dinner waiting. After
a day of working with his hands, he was always eager for a verbal romp,
a wider world. While we had made many acquaintances in the city, we
both still hungered for deeper friendships. At school, I struck gold for
us both, especially with Michael, and then Betsy.

Michael was a year ahead of me. With his dark beard and eyes he
looked like a rabbinical student, and in fact could have been, given his
spiritual interests, his inquiring nature, his familial bent. He was very
close to a Jewish lesbian couple, with whom he intended to have a child
as soon as he found work after graduation. He also loved country-western
dancing, massage groups, flowing silk nightshirts, and talking about
foreign films in a mock-pretentious way while slightly under the influence of a few tokes.

Jay connected immediately with his warmth. It was a double bonus
when Michael turned out to have impeccable taste in home decorating.
Soon he was joining us on trips to renovators' salvage yards in search
of Edwardian hinges, doorknobs, sink pedestals. His eye for detail was
more than an interest in fashion or form. There was something deeper
and more intuitive—an attempt to divine the true spirit of a home,
which in the end really had little to do with stripping out decades of bad
linoleum, shag carpeting, or architecturally inappropriate fixtures. He
described himself as having just exited a period of bitterness after the
loss of a ten-year relationship with another man. He was playing the field
now, enjoying variety, he said, but what he most wished for was a man
with whom he could happily and comfortably read in bed. He respected
history, he said.

It was a respect that he extended to our relationship as a couple. He seemed to enjoy getting us to tell our tale. He was a sucker for love stories, he said. As we obliged, unfolding our romance for him during those dinner-time study-breaks, Jay and I fell for each other all over again. I can see now how those conversations were an island, an oasis, in a city and time where gay coupledom was not the most celebrated aspiration either inside or outside the community. But Michael celebrated us. Selfishly, he claimed, to give himself hope. Yet those talks gave us an arena in which to become us, more fully. After he left, we would fall asleep in each other's arms, murmuring contentedly about our time with him, sending out our wish that he could find some man to appreciate his beautiful lips, eyes, and spirit even half as much as we loved each other.

At spring break, Michael invited us for the first time to Rancho L'amour, a rambling cabin he rented in the Sonoma foothills with a group of longtime gay and lesbian friends. Each April they hosted an egg hunt and bonnet contest, and he wanted us there, he said, to help him mix his old life with the new. We felt touched, as well as a bit shy about being newcomers, but shortly after arrival, we found ourselves skipping, silly and en masse, through the green fields, our kitschy bonnets heaped with plastic fruit, flowers, and baby dolls contributed by our new pals. Dogs and children nosed in the tall grass for eggs; we admired their beauty. Afterward, there was a huge potluck, followed by charades on the wrap-around porch.

Though we had yet to make our own history with people there, Jay and I soaked up the ambiance of familiarity, neither of us realizing how much we had been missing such a group since we had left Michigan.

At one point, as I wandered into the kitchen for a drink, I came across a knot of women fixing a drip under the rusty sink. As I listened to their conversation, I realized they were comparing notes on sperm banks and adoption agencies. Michael was with them.

"We're so glad to have Michael!" one of the women was saying, as she slid her arm around his waist. "Or at least we hope we have him. He has to be a good boy and play safe."

Giving her a squeeze, he nodded at me and grinned, introducing me to the woman with whom he hoped to have a child.

Then he led me out to the garden by hand.

"Better watch out," he said good naturedly, "or they'll be after you for a specimen, too."

"I should be so flattered," I said, appreciating his ease and closeness with women. At school, female classmates often called him "girlfriend."

As we entered the tangled back garden, a stolid woman with a thick prickly mane of black hair straightened up from weeding. Her stunningly blue eyes seemed to widen for a second as she took us in, obviously reluctant to have her quiet time interrupted. I felt an instant kinship with her.

"This is Betsy," said Michael, with an obvious pride.

As she and Michael conferred about a house matter, I ambled over to a stump where a book lay open at its spine, a pinecone set in its crease. Basho: *The Narrow Road to the Deep North*.

"Know it?" she asked.

"I nodded."

She wiped her face, very red from the heat. We said a few words, nothing much, just simple things about the garden, my becoming a librarian, her becoming a therapist, but there was a spark.

Michael and I wandered off to find a cool place to sip our drinks. Jay joined us, and I was surprised when Betsy pulled up a chair too. The heat was breaking, shadows lengthening. The four of us looked quietly out into the meadow. A few adults and kids tossed around a frisbee in the golden light as an old dog watched, panting. I thought about Michael bringing a child into this world with his friend.

"If I could paint," I said, "I'd paint this."

"What's this?" asked Jay.

I gestured toward the field, unable to put my feelings into words.

"Are you an artist?" asked Betsy.

I shook my head.

"He can go straight to the underlying ecstasy without need of religious or artistic technology," said Jay, taking my hand.

Michael cocked his head, considering me with an attractive playful detachment.

"I can imagine that," he said, raising an eyebrow.

I looked away, reddening from the attention. Out of the corner of my eye I could see Betsy observing all this with an inward look.

"I know that urge," she said, ignoring Michael and Jay, picking up on the wistfulness of my remark. "There's beauty tossing around out there in the field, and you want to do something to be part of it. I wish I were an artist, too."

"But you are!" said Michael. "Look at that beautiful trestle table on the porch. She made that yesterday with only handheld power tools."

"Yeah, but don't look too closely," said Betsy. "I still can't get that damn key to fit in the tenon properly."

Jay jumped up, going over to the table.

"I wondered who made that!" he said, running his hand over the freshly sanded fir.

Betsy trailed after him, complaining. Soon they were headed for the tool chest in Jay's truck. Michael and I cleared the table while Betsy and Jay went to work, knocking out the key and clamping it on the edge of the porch so they could plane it into a wedge shape for a tighter fit. I can still see their dark hair shining in the sun as they bent over the wood together.

And so began the closer friendships of those years. Tools were traded back and forth, projects shared and admired. Having kindred spirits to cheer him on, Jay fully embraced his identity as a renovator. Betsy's voracious reading and introspective tendencies made her one of my favorite talking partners, while she and Jay spent many companionable hours assisting each other with woodworking projects. That spring day at the cabin was the first of a number of lovely holidays spent in the countryside.

ⵡⵡⵡ

By the time I graduated, Jay and I felt more at home in the city than ever. We had others to nurture, others by whom we were nurtured. I was thrilled when both Michael and I scored jobs in the San Francisco public library system.

My first night home from my new job, I enthused to Jay all through dinner, gabbing happily about a gay man named Walter who had presented himself to me as my orientation guide. Along with Jay, I envisioned cultivating a whole circle of collegial friends with whom Michael and I would meet for rambling conversations over dinner or drinks.

Within the week, I realized Walter would not be a candidate. Just standing next to him made me tense. I had never met anyone so addicted to detail, in both speech and appearance. I felt him constantly hovering nearby, making sure that I would choose the right style paper clip for the job. If I didn't, he would pounce, happy to exercise his superciliousness in long-winded explanations of which "attachment devices" he preferred and where he liked to store them. I was relieved when my supervisor Connie tipped me off that Walter had been self-appointed as my guide and had no official capacity over me.

"You're doing fine," she told me. "Just ignore him if you want."

Nevertheless, he started popping up in my dreams, officiating my activities as if both our lives depended on it.

"I know enough for now!" I shouted at him one night in a dream. "Could you just move on?"

It was a strange but welcome coincidence when I came to work the next day and found that he was out with a flu. Relieved, I stretched into the work in my own way during his absence. When he finally did come back, he kept to himself, barely noticing me. It was a pleasant surprise, one that made me question my first impression of him. He looked shaggier than I recalled, and had grown a beard, which gave him a thinner, edgier look. He seemed preoccupied and withdrawn, rather than intrusive. Maybe my natural anxieties about starting a new job had skewed my sense of him.

I didn't think much more about him. There were others to befriend, and many moments of contentment with my tasks. I loved working the reference desk, loved the spirit of the hunt there. A new sense of mastery grew in me, not only from helping others, but also from my daily dip into the world's ten thousand things—everything from Japanese bullet trains to the lifecycles of whales. Of course, there were also the ten thousand moods of those who approached the desk, but the golden light slanting through the tall windows, the smell of books, the rules upholding quiet and civility more than compensated. With a decent paycheck and benefits, I felt quite bountiful.

As soon as I had earned enough time off, I decided to surprise Jay with a trip to Kaua'i. I'd noticed he'd been sleeping longer, fighting a few colds. "No big deal," he said, but I knew he needed a break from constant physical work. Michael had raved about a Japanese-style country house run by two gay men with a contemplative Buddhist bent. As he described the blue-tile roof, the black-bottomed pool, the peaceful gardens, and lovely woodwork, I knew it would be our place.

Borrowing Michael's snorkeling gear, I hid it in my closet until one morning when Jay was in the shower. I still had a few more details to iron out before I actually invited him, but on impulse I dragged out the gear to make sure it was in working order. I had strapped on the flippers and was struggling with the goggles when Jay unexpectedly came traipsing through, towel around his waist.

"What's all this?" he said, stopping short.

I jumped up, the goggles fogging my view.

"You weren't supposed to know!"

"Know what?" he said. "How into rubber you really are?"

I laughed, realizing how silly I must look in my plaid pajama bottoms and gear.

"This isn't the romantic set-up I had imagined," I said. "But I'd like to take you to Kaua'i, at your convenience. If you'll come. My treat."

He raised his eyebrows.

"For real?"

"As soon as you can make time."

He leaned forward to hug me. It was a shy embrace, which I received in kind, suddenly feeling very florescent in my lime-green gear. Both of us had to shift to manage a kiss. Stepping on my fin, he muttered in a sexy-mean voice, "I'm sick of rubber."

I pulled off the goggles, letting them drop as he locked his lips onto mine, kissing me aggressively, hard, with a frustration we both understood and had visited before. I didn't know where he meant for this to go, but then he released me suddenly, fastening the towel more securely around his waist. He looked very pink.

"I have an appointment with a plumber this morning," he said, placing his hands on my chest, as if to sooth the savage beast. "But I'll see *you* in Kaua'i . . ."

Later, in the shower, it crossed my mind that a year ago Jay would have speeded up the action before heading out the door, not slowed it down. But he'd been working very hard, as in fact had I. We could both benefit from a break, I thought, tilting my face into the hot jetting water. Neither of us had ever snorkeled in the ocean, but I could picture that blue other world, its beauty, its flashes of gold.

30

WE COULD SEE THE BLUE ROOF gleaming from the highway. Trees tossed in the late afternoon breeze, greeny-gold. Jay doffed his baseball hat and waved it out the window of the rental car, whooping.

As we came up the walk, I let out a long low whistle at the sight of the pool. Fringed by volcanic rock and exotic plants, it seemed invitingly bottomless, dark. A feral-looking cat darted out of the bushes, hissed, then herded us to the door.

We stood for a few minutes in the foyer, waiting for someone to greet us. A carpet of water lilies floated in a sunken pool. Jay went immediately to a Japanese lamp glowing on a low table. He was enchanted by the pleasantly yellowed shade printed with sutras. A devotional calm came over us both.

A beefed-up Australian guy named Mike led us to our room. He was standing-in for the new owner, he explained. "Just got out of the Merchant Marines," he added, running his hand over his brush cut, as if that would clarify something.

Jay and I exchanged an amused glance as we followed him to our room. He stopped just outside the door.

"You'll have the run of the place for a few hours," he said. "I have to go to town.

"I'll leave you to your own devices," he added with a wink. "A couple of girls are here too and should be back before dark."

"Great," said Jay, enthusiastic in a way I knew was for my benefit alone. We both cracked up as soon as the guy left.

At a glance, the room was beautiful. Only shoji screens divided us from the lush fragrant forest beyond. Dropping his bag, Jay immediately began testing the screens, sliding them back and forth in their wooden tracks, admiring their smooth glide. I stood beside him, staring out, my muscles unknotting in the humid heat.

"What's that?" I asked, pointing to an iron chain that dropped from a corner of the overhanging roof to the forest floor.

"Downspout," he said.

I flopped on the bed, pulling him down beside me.

"Now how did you know that?" I asked.

"My woodworking magazine."

"Of course."

He slid his arm through mine. Too hot to stay very close, we lay with our arms and legs just touching, him staring at the wooden beams above, me fingering the rippling indigo print beneath us. The only other time I had seen such cloth was in Japantown, at a rustic artisan shop that sold antique kimonos.

"Maybe they need those chains to keep the house from floating away," I said dreamily. "Think of all the couples who've fucked themselves silly here, drifting off in each other's arms . . ."

But Jay was already gone, snoring lightly. I could have easily joined him, but I needed a drink of water. I rolled on my side. At eye-level was an ashtray full of cigarette butts.

I stared, noting the nightstand was covered with dust and tobacco flecks, too.

Quietly, I went to get a washcloth, thinking I would tidy up this one forgotten area before Jay woke.

There was toothpaste in the sink, hair in the shower.

Just then I heard a truck engine turn over.

Remembering Mike was about to leave, I rushed out of the room, through the house, but was too late.

Asshole, I muttered to myself. Must have put us in the wrong fucking room.

For a few minutes I just stood in the hall, fuming at the closed doors to the other rooms. Wanting the best for Jay, I began pushing the doors open with a surprising belligerence looking for a clean space. Not a single bed was made up.

I stalked back to our room and stood in a corner, trying to contain myself. Jay sensed something, opened his eyes.

"It's lovely here," he said, stretching. "I could sleep a million years under this roof."

He held out his hand to me.

I took it, but shook my head.

"What's the matter?" he said, focusing.

"There's butts in the ashtray and hair all over the place," I blurted.

I was surprised to hear my voice shake. I had wanted everything to be perfect.

Jay sat up, scratching the back of his head.

"What time is it?" he asked. "We did get here a little before check-in. Maybe he'll finish when he gets back."

"That's ridiculous," I said. "He could have just said so."

Jay padded around the room, investigating.

"Yep," he said. "The bathroom needs a shave."

"We should leave," I said.

He sat back down on the bed, surveying me.

"But we have no idea where to go," he said. "Or if we'll get our money back. Maybe there's some mistake. Why don't we just wait? He said he left cold drinks and a snack. Why don't we go get them and hang out by the pool while we get our bearings?"

His kindness only seemed to inflame me more. This was not how it was supposed to be—him ministering to my bad mood!

"Fuck it!" I wrote in the dust on top of the dresser, spelling out each letter loudly.

"Okay, okay!" said Jay. "But what are we going to do?"

"Leave!" I said, really losing it now. "I just want to leave."

"And go where?"

"I don't know," I said, ripping through my bag for the guidebook.

"I'm not prepared to do that. I need a drink," said Jay. He turned and left for the dining room.

Stunned by my own irrationality, I grabbed some beach towels, trying to reel it in as I followed him.

On the table was a plastic bag of pre-washed baby carrots, a jar of Planter's peanuts, an open can of pineapple juice.

It was Jay's turn to get sarcastic.

"I see he opened the wine to let it breath," he said, taking a whiff, then setting the can aside.

"Not exactly the fresh-squeezed juice Michael raved about," I noted, offering a limp carrot to the cat, who turned up her nose too, but kept milling about. Jay picked her up, both of us petting and cooing as she purred.

"At least some things are just like home," I said.

"I'm sorry you're disappointed," he said.

I flushed, embarrassed.

"I wanted the best for you, but I'm falling a little short. I'll stop acting like a maniac."

We found some ice and water in the kitchen, then took our glasses out by the pool. At least the grounds were in good shape. I wandered over to a little pumphouse disguised as a shrine room. A row of votive candles lined a windowsill, tiny gnats caught in the now-hard wax.

I heard a splash and turned to see Jay diving nude into the pool. Surfacing, he floated on his back, arms flung out.

"Come in!" he called. "Look at the sky with me. No dust or hair up there!"

I stripped and slowly immersed myself. The water was warm, almost body temperature. I breast-stroked toward Jay, then floated crown to crown with him, blue above, dark below. I don't know how long we stayed that way, but I still couldn't let go of my irritation.

Suddenly Jay was there, treading beside me, water dripping from the tips of his hair. I pressed my hand against his belly. Very flesh and blood. He reached across my chest in a lifesaving hold and began to tow me, touring the contoured edges of the pool. Passing beneath huge overhanging trumpet-shaped blossoms, he slowed down, clearly meaning for me to see.

I surrendered to pleasure, watching a bee clamber deep in the throat of the flower, almost upside down on his back in his eagerness to circle the pistils. Jay was watching too, and for a few slim seconds I had an almost eerie sense that we were peering through the same eyes, sharing one mind. Yet, as soon as I thought that this was so, the moment vanished like a fish into dark water, and I felt a not unpleasurable sadness.

We entered a darker nook, out of sight of the house. He let go of me and we hung onto the edge, our legs floating up behind us as we looked at the rocks and plants. It was a perfect place in which to fool around, and we did rub and jostle up against each other, but Jay's energy was flagging. I was tempted to stoke things up with a little rough-housing, but I could sense he was content to let things be for a while. We needed time to recharge, I thought. Shake off the city.

But then my longing got the better of me.

"I want you!" I said, suddenly wrapping my legs around him.

He hugged me as hard as he could without ground under his feet. "There's time," he said.

Back in our room, I touched him gingerly, as though making love to a wounded man. A surprising soberness traveled between us, stirring and tender. Though we didn't fuck fully in the way we once had been able, the moment was raw and unprotected, nonetheless. Frustration and disappointment were right there, on the surface. At first, I thought it was just about the room, but then I realized it was something else, something larger, not even about us, really. I couldn't have quite said what it was at the time, but I can see now we were sensing Jay's waning strength.

Afterward, we lay looking out at the forest, Jay absently playing with my hair, curling a sprig around his finger.

"Maybe the next house I work on should be one we keep," he said. "A two-flat building. We could get income from the second unit."

We began to fantasize what street, what view.

"But before we take on a mortgage together," he said, "we should probably get tested."

He said this matter-of-factly. I found myself matching his tone, but in truth it frightened me too much. I really did not want to think about it at all. Now was our time to feel blessed.

I knew Jay was right, yet something I could not quite articulate disturbed me. It surprised me that it was he who was taking the bull by the horns. This seemed more like my role—me, who in general found it harder to shake off a sense of life's fragility.

Suddenly the vacuum roared to life in the hallway, and we jumped to a discussion of how to deal with our complaints about the room.

As it turned out, we spent the night. Mike apologized with a redeeming shame and humility about his inexperience, accepting our cancellation for the other days, and promising to make things up to us with his great "Aussie" breakfast. We never did figure out what was particularly Australian about freezer-burned waffles and sausages with half-thawed fruit cocktail in plastic cups, but after a good sleep, we could at least feel amused and even a little sympathetic.

I can hardly remember much about the B&B where we stayed the rest of the trip, except for the outdoor shower curtained by flowering vines—but Jay was a good sport about it, and we both got a kick out of the two lesbian owners who sent us off to secret coves with names like "Queen's Bath."

Immobilized on land by the heat, Jay came alive underwater, snorkeling the reefs off the wild north coast. I can still see him, waving excitedly as stingrays, barracudas, even a shark darted by. It was he who spotted that fish whose name I now forget, the shy but dangerous one, poking its long nose from between the coral.

Reveling in the mindlessness of our pleasures, I forgot what we had resolved to take on when we got home. If it did pop into my head during the remainder of our trip, I told myself not to think about it. Yet, I relished the open-ended days of freedom as if they were our last.

On a southern beach at the site of a home that had been swept away by a hurricane the year before, we gathered up a bag of inch-square blue tiles which had been mysteriously spared. After we arrived home, Jay laid them interspersed with white on the cottage's bathroom floor when he retiled it for the landlord. As an anniversary present to me, he looked up what constellations had been present in the sky when we met, and arranged the blue like stars amid the white.

31

WAS I ASLEEP IN MY HAPPINESS? How on earth, with an
epidemic all around me, had I, who had been such a worrier, managed
to go whistling by the graveyard? But I was so happy. Jay and I had truly
mingled our lives. His optimism was contagious.

Back home, we plunged into work, pleasantly pining for each other
during the day. We began to break up our hours by calling each other
at lunch, reopening for at least a few moments that blue spacious feeling
of our time together.

The mood faded, of course, as our work lives returned to full swing.

In my case, I had been assigned in absentia to a project with Walter,
which proved unpleasant in new ways. Over the months we had shifted into
a bland collegiality, but now, I detected an oddly suspicious tone of resentment in him whenever we spoke. More than once, he claimed to have relayed
essential details to me which he had not done, later accusing me of forgetting.
I tried not to let it ruffle me, but during my noon calls with Jay, I carped.

"This can't be personal," Jay would insist, but for some reason, I just
couldn't let go.

"He could at least wipe the snot and crumbs out of his mustache," I
said, still smarting from a day when I had handed him a tissue, trying to

be discreet, only to incur his indignant wrath. He had seemed so meticulous when I first met him, but now I didn't even want to look at him.

But no such luck. He began to intrude into my dreams again. One in particular still sticks in my mind.

It began with only a voice.

"You aren't paying attention to me!" it sneered.

I stood in a cavernous storage room, trying to make out who or what was waiting for me in the dark, but at first all I could perceive was the smell of rotting fruit, an odor I had always hated as a kid in my parent's store.

As my eyes adjusted, I saw Walter, wrapped in a bathrobe, glaring at me. Heart pounding, I woke myself up.

At work that morning, I convinced my boss to move me to a different committee as soon as possible.

Jay, meanwhile, seemed increasingly preoccupied with his renovation project. A city inspector had refused to sign off on a permit when he discovered that the space between the toilet and shower was one inch short of code. Other officials might have looked the other way, but this guy seemed to take pleasure in doggedly enforcing compliance. Sheets of costly beautiful honey-colored marble had to be ripped out and refit.

Jay went into high gear, working long hours, eating on the run, coming home late. Sex was out of the picture. When he began to sleep past nine in the morning, I dismissed my concerns, telling myself he was spent. He did seem uncharacteristically panicked, but I wrote this off, too, as being due to the pressures of his project.

I went about my business, occupying myself with work and friends. Michael and Rachel were about to have a baby, so Michael and I buddied around together, hand painting nursery furniture and cooking large batches of soups and casseroles to set aside for Rachel.

When the inspector finally did sign off on the project, Jay and I went out to dinner at Zuni Café, a favorite hangout then, to celebrate. His face seemed brighter than of late—animated, I thought. We had both drunk more than we were used to. At one point he dropped his eyes to his hands then looked up at me, then off to the side, then back at me.

"I love you as much—no, more—than ever," he said, his voice cracking, as if it almost hurt to say it. Surprised by the sudden solemnity, I pressed my knee against his under the table.

"I'm sorry. This is taking me . . . time," he said, meaning the house, I thought. He had continued to be over there several nights a week, even after the inspection.

"What's the rush?" I asked. "Could you pace yourself now?"

He gave me a blank look. He seemed to be struggling to formulate what he wanted to say, then visibly changed course, shrugging.

"The house . . . ? My feelings about it have changed," he said. "I don't like being over there anymore. I just want to be done with it, sooner than later."

There was a weariness in his voice I hadn't noticed before.

"Nothing has changed between us, has it?" he asked. Again, I was surprised. He rarely asked for reassurance.

"I'm happier than ever," I told him. "I just wish I saw more of you."

"You may be seeing more of me than you'd like all too soon," he said.

At the time, I didn't hear anything cryptic or leading in his remark. I did notice a little catch in his voice, but I liked the fact that he was being so emotional. He seemed open, as if the depletion he felt from the project had also loosened him.

When he called the waiter and insisted on paying the bill, I let him.

~~~~~~

My happy oblivion came crashing down on a wet misty night a week later.

I was driving home on Market after having dinner with Michael. Jay had said he would be late. I was enjoying the soft fuzzy glow around the streetlamps and the sheen on the road. Walking up Market was a man who looked like Jay—a man with another man. I drove by, telling myself that it must be a guy with the same jacket. He looked too thin to be Jay. But a few seconds later, I turned around and came back up the street, scanning the pedestrians. There they were, waiting at a red light. It was definitely Jay.

I ducked into a loading zone, hidden behind a wide truck, heart pounding as traffic rushed by. I sank in the seat, ashamed to be spying. It's probably nothing, I told myself. Most likely Jay needed to get a sandwich or some hardware, and was just making small talk with a stranger at the light. Suddenly they were on the walk next to me. I looked away, trying not to be seen. There was the sound of spray flung up from tires and beyond, the unmistakable tone of Jay's voice. I couldn't hear the words, but I knew that music, and it was serious. I looked in the mirror. They had stopped. The other man was listening to Jay intently, staring up into his face. To make things worse, the guy wasn't even particularly attractive. I thought they might break off at any moment. But they didn't. The other man touched Jay's elbow, then reached for his wallet, took something out and handed it to Jay, who looked at it and shoved it in a jacket pocket. Then they both disappeared into a door I couldn't see from where I was parked. Just like that.

A dark fury loomed up in me. I tried to cling to my confusion, making excuses, inventing other possibilities as I gripped the wheel. Suddenly a half-dozen men spilled from the door, their breath floating up into the night air as they stood in a circle, talking. Another man slipped behind them and went inside. Be sensible, I told myself. A new café or bar must have opened. Perhaps Jay was getting dinner with a tradesman or possible helper. He sometimes did that.

The guys on the sidewalk broke apart, drifted away. I started my engine, waiting for a gap in the traffic to pull out, then I backed up, searching for the door. The lettering on the glass was discreet but clear. It was an agency that ran support groups for those recently tested positive.

It seems absurd now, but I drove away up Market and stopped in at Safeway. It was what I had planned to do, and I did it, carrying on with a crazy insistence as if nothing had or would be changed. Inside, I roamed the aisles, trying to keep ahead of the rising panic for my own life as well as Jay's. With no idea of what I needed, I scanned the shelves, looking in truth for something that would never be there. My circle of vision seemed to shrink to a few feet in front of me; everything else was incomprehensible. Under the fluorescent lights, people's faces looked strange.

Was he sick?

Why hadn't he told me?

How long had he known?

Edging past an elderly couple, a terrible aloneness rushed into me. I felt I no longer knew him. All I wanted to do was get home, crawl into bed. Short of breath, I made for the door.

Fumbling with my keys at the car, my fear suddenly gave way to a memory of that night at Zuni, how Jay had stumbled over his words, then asked for reassurance. Remembering that catch in his voice, a horrible image rose in my mind of him locked inside a block of ice, trying to speak, but lips frozen, blue, partly open. And I had sat across from him, chatting happily. I could barely stand it. Starting the engine, I cranked up the heat and headed back up Market for that door.

I waited for an hour in a metered space just outside the door.

Over and over my mind traced the letters of a parking sign. The traffic light ran through its cycles of red, slow, and go. I thought of the virus that might be running through its own cycles in my blood that very minute. Yet in the light of the streetlamp, the skin on the back of my hand looked gold. I knew then I had been deceiving myself, trying to distance myself from the suffering around me, believing our love was blessed, that we would be immune. I sat watching the mist fill up the arc the wipers had made. My personal happiness seemed no more than a drop of that dew, shining, light-filled, small. By morning, it would evaporate.

I suddenly wanted to pray, but to whom or what? I held my face in my hands anyway, asking for courage. And humility too, for I had failed badly. Jay was obviously not well, but I hadn't wanted to see that. I hadn't wanted to know the truth about either of us. I gripped the wheel, struggling against self-pity and fear. I could already feel them stealing in between us, threatening to divide. I didn't want to yield another inch.

I got out of the car. I wanted to be standing, door open, when Jay came out. He was one of the last to exit. I leaned against the fender, staring at my shoes, trying to be unobtrusive as the other guys left. But I felt as though they could see right through me, know if I was one of them. My heart was still pounding.

The man who had been with Jay went by alone. For a moment I wished that the scenario before me was the one that I had first imagined, that it was he who was my opponent. But he had probably only been trying to help Jay. I should feel grateful, I thought, but I couldn't. Not yet.

Jay came out, chin tucked into his pulled-up collar, eyes on the pavement. He would have walked past me.

"Jay," I said.

He glanced up.

"Let me take you home," I said, hand on the door.

He stared at me with the look of a lost animal, confused, and ready to bolt.

"Please come."

With a visible breath, he cast a sideways glance up the street, in the direction he had been going.

Then he got in.

I drove.

He began to weep.

I took his hand.

Neither of us could speak.

We sat across the room from each other, him sunk into his chair, me with Emily on my lap. I had never seen him look so ashamed.

"How long have you known?" I finally said, breaking the stunned silence.

"Just a few weeks," he said, barely audible.

I stared at him. What had he been thinking? I felt myself flush.

"Why did you do this alone?"

He lifted and dropped his shoulders, tears in his eyes.

"Stupidity. It just seemed that I must have been the one to catch it first. Those trips to New York, Key West. And if you are . . ."

He broke off, struggling to regain his composure. I started to rise, but he put up his hand.

"If you have it, it's probably my fault," he said, in a dry whisper. "It only seemed fair that I should test first, so I could get my shit together and be there for you when you got tested . . ."

"Oh Jay," I said, setting Emily aside. I went to him, kneeling down, wrapping my arms around his waist. He put his arms around me too, but turned his face as if he were trying not to breathe on me.

I hugged him tighter. "It's not your fault, it's a virus!"

His hands stayed limp and unmoving on the small of my back. I pressed my cheek against his chest, wanting the comfort of his heartbeat, hearing instead the gaps between. He was barely breathing.

"I wanted to tell you," he finally said. "I promised my group I would tell you this weekend. And I did try, twice. But each time, you were in such good spirits. And then, I just wanted things to be normal . . . for a while more."

I straightened up, looking at him. He met my eyes, and suddenly, a memory came to me of the last time we had made love, shortly after we returned from Hawaii. We had begun matter-of-factly, two tired men relaxing each other before falling asleep, but as Jay released, he had opened his eyes, and I saw for an instant something like sadness, concern, even pity come into them. He had taken my cheeks between his hands, studying my face for a moment as though he were memorizing it, then he went off to the john for a towel. I had fallen asleep, not questioning, his tenderness dousing any flicker of fear.

"We're both right here, right now," I said, gathering him into my arms again. "We'll do this together, right?"

"The truth is, if I could keep this from you forever, this whole fucking virus, I would," he said hoarsely. "Without me, you could go on . . ."

"Don't!" I said, getting up off my knees, fighting a wave of panic. "Come here," I said, holding out my hand to him.

He stared up at me, not moving, so I took him by the wrists and pulled him up. We embraced stiffly in the little circle of lamp light, the sense of doom we had each worked so hard and long to evade filling the corners of the room. We were both shivering now.

"This is what we are going to do," I said.

Leading him by the hand to our claw-foot tub, I drew a bath.

"We're getting in this, together."

But neither of us could sink into our bodies, the bodies that might betray us.

We struggled to arrange ourselves around the faucet, our limbs tense, awkward, in the way.

I squeezed hot water onto his shoulders and chest, trying to stoke the warmth of past times, but his goosepimples did not go away. I felt afraid to look too closely at either of us, knowing even the usual freckles and moles would disturb me.

This too shall pass, I tried to say, but cut myself off.

"I'm sorry," said Jay. "I need to get out."

We left the water steaming in the tub.

We spooned each other all night, waiting for the gray light of a morning that was slow to come.

32

Jay was waiting for me on a bench under tall sparse trees when several weeks later I came out of the health center with my test results. Holding his baseball cap between his hands, he looked up at me with a careful face. He could tell, just from my expression.

Numbly, we walked up 18th toward Castro, arm in arm. The little red neon light at Orphan Andy's beckoned. We slid into a booth, ordering greasy burgers and fries that neither of us could finish. At a nearby table a burly guy with a tattoo of a violet at the base of his skull was talking quietly with a very thin man. I looked away.

Jay reached for my hand. "There are survivors in all epidemics. People who carry a disease without it breaking through. We just have to find out how to do our best." His eyes were burning with determination. I stared at his face, clinging to his optimism, wanting to feel it too. It had been in scarce quantity since that horrible first night. True, he had spent his days buying a computer, getting online, learning how to research treatments—but when it came to actually making an appointment with a doctor, he'd balked. "One step at a time," he'd said, wanting to wait until my test was over.

Now we were clearly at a next step. All I could see before us was a yawning chasm. I sat pushing a cold French fry through the ketchup, trying to draw a line, any line, against the powerlessness I was feeling. I pushed my plate away.

"Let's go to Mount Tam," I said suddenly. My body was tremulous and my thoughts scattered—I felt as though our future had just vanished—but we could at least do this, right now. Be together, with the smell of spring grass, and a bigger view.

He shot right up, offering to drive. Crossing the bridge, an unfamiliar giddiness welled up in me. Maybe Jay was right. Maybe we could give grief the slip, one hour at a time.

On a secluded bluff overlooking the sea we sat on a rock, watching the green grass whorling on the hills below. Jay's hair twirled too. He put his jacket around me. I rested my chin on his shoulder. Everything was vivid— each blade, each breath. It seemed impossible that we could disappear.

"Let's come back," said Jay.

"Every Saturday, if you want."

A turkey vulture circled a nearby crest. I knew what was down below, yet to him, death was fuel. I forced myself not to turn away, swinging out on his big drifting arcs.

"We could be scattered here," said Jay.

There was a long silence between us, then he added, "When we're eighty, of course."

He stood up, gazing out to sea. A mist was rising, blurring the horizon. A far-off freighter evaporated, then a sailboat, then the coast below.

I stood too, shaking myself out, watching Jay, who was swinging his leg in a semi-circle, brushing the blue tips of lupine gently with his toe.

In the weeks that followed, I sleepwalked through my duties at the library, drifting from task to task, unable to give my full attention to anything. I felt like a prisoner inside myself, though of course I knew Jay was in the same state of shock.

But I couldn't bear to think about his mortality now. It was too much to absorb all at once. I felt drowsy and dull much of the time, except at night, when I tossed and turned with anxiety.

Jay, on the other hand, had moved out of his withdrawal and seemed to be hurtling himself into making things easier for me. Though he continued with the renovation, he was often home before me. I would arrive to find him banging around the kitchen, getting our dinner. Unsettled from what had been mostly my domain, I would pace, ripping through junk mail, trying to keep my mouth shut as he struggled with the cooking.

When the plates were finally on the table, he would often be disappointed with the results. I would try to reassure him, saying that it was good just to have him home, but he barely heard me. He'd keep spinning on the details of what he could have done differently. Or apologizing. If it wasn't the limp pasta, it was the sock he'd lost in the dryer, the unemptied strainer in the sink, the night out at his support group. He also began to nag. Had I washed my hands before eating? Did I run the water for five seconds before getting a drink from the filter he'd recently installed?

I wasn't used to Jay acting like this. It all rolled over me at first, a strange tide I was unable to comprehend while submerged in my own glazed mood. But over the years I had come to rely upon frequent and daily infusions of his confident optimism. One night, as Jay stood at the stove cussing over a stir-fry, my frustration broke through.

"Just stop!" I said loudly, above the hiss of onions. "If you're pissy all the time, it's not helpful. I could give a shit if the rice burns or the beans aren't done. Could we just eat in peace?"

He slammed down the potholder.

"Fine!" he said. "Then you cook."

He stalked rigidly out of the room, leaving the wooden spatula sticking out of the pan, close to the flame. Grabbing it, I shoved the onions around, listening to the sound of tap water running in the bathroom. Snapping off the burner, I followed him, knocking lightly on the door.

"Can I come in?"

"At your own peril."

I opened the door. He was drying his face with a towel.

"Apparently everything I touch turns to shit," he said, not looking at me, hands twisting inside the towel.

I leaned against the door jamb, arms crossed. I wanted to reach out and comfort him, but I was sick of his remorse. It was making me feel guilty, too.

"If you say you're sorry one goddamn more time . . ."

He wrinkled his brow in confusion.

"I don't know what the fuck else I'm supposed to do," he said, still wringing the towel.

"What do you mean, what you're 'supposed to do'? You're not 'supposed' to be doing anything. Except be with me. But if that feels like such a chore . . ."

"You know that's not it," he said, glaring back at me now.

"Then what the fuck is it? I feel like you're more concerned about doing your damned duty than about me."

"How the hell can you say that?"

He turned away, staring out the window. After a pause, he spoke, still facing outdoors.

"Don't you blame me?"

"For what?"

Jay shrugged.

I looked at his face in profile. I shook my head, trying to be patient. But when he looked away, I couldn't contain myself.

"No, Jay. Like I said before, it's a virus, not a fault. But do you have to be such a fucking drag all the time?"

Startled, he locked eyes with me, face flushed, jaw twitching.

"You try being in my shoes!" he blurted.

"*Your* shoes?" I said hotly. "What makes you so sure *you're* the only culprit? It's not like I didn't have a life before you, you know! You're not the only fuckhead around."

"Obviously," he shot back, as I marched off to the living room.

After a few minutes he came in, hesitating before me. I remained hunkered over on the couch, elbows on my knees, face in my hands.

Awkwardly, he sat down on the other sofa cushion and let out a sigh. I knew he didn't know what to do, but finally he reached over and hauled me down, head on his thigh. He had done this many times before, but there was a tentativeness, a questioning in his fingers as he ran them through my hair. I could tell he was unsure if he was doing the right thing.

But it was exactly right. The negative spell had been broken.

~~~~~

Despite everything, some semblance of order returned. Bills arrived, laundry piled up, the fridge needed cleaning. Instead of annoyances, our chores became anchors holding us in place. If we had obligations, perhaps we could stay in this life. Each time I pulled on a sock, in that small moment of touching the world, there came a confirming voice, murmuring yes, yes, you are here. I knew Jay was feeling the same.

Still, there was always an undercurrent of fear beneath the now shaken and tentative joy of our routines. Whenever I briskly climbed the library stairs, hefted a stack of books, or sat at my desk, phone cradled against my ear, there was another voice, one that said, "*You can do this now, but . . .*"

Then I would think of Walter. My coworkers and I frequently followed around behind him now, finishing tasks he had left undone.

"Maybe he's just going through something," people would say, not wanting their suspicions to be true.

But in my gut, I knew. I remembered who he had been in those first few weeks of my job, just before he had begun to slip away. No wonder he had seemed so controlling. I now recognized in myself that same effort to hold the world in place. Concentrating on the feel of the paper under my fingers, a draft of air at my ankles, I made great efforts to return to each task at hand.

For a while, I wanted to tell someone. Not a stranger in a support group, or a therapist, but someone close to me—yet I was afraid of how it might change things between us. Jay was less ambivalent. He didn't want us to tell anyone we knew, not until we had to. I could respect that, for a while. Like him, I wanted us to go on in some semblance of the usual for as long as possible. But I didn't share his sense that saying it aloud would somehow give energy to the virus, make it full-blown. For me, it was too real already. I wanted the comfort of telling Michael at least. Jay acquiesced, but as it turned out, it would be nearly a year before I did so.

The next time we saw Michael, it was two days after the birth of his son. Trunk full of flowers and food, we drove up to the Sonoma home of his co-parent Rachel to congratulate him. He greeted us with his bundle, beaming. As he loaded the baby into my arms, I stared down speechless at the red squinched-up face. Already Noah had the beginnings of a curly top, just like Michael. Settling into a rocking chair, I glanced over at Jay, who was watching me with tears in his eyes. Hurriedly he tried to wipe them away on his sleeve, but Michael saw him.

"What saps!" he teased, chucking Jay playfully on the chin. "You're both totally choked up!"

He loved it.

I closed my eyes, rocking Noah in the chair. This must have been how Jay felt that night at Zuni, locked inside his secret. Except I wasn't alone. Jay was beside me, down on his knees, clucking at Noah, carefully keeping his fingers away from the infant's grasp. His other hand was firmly around my ankle, steadying me in our shared knowledge.

"Welcome," I whispered, as the three of us huddled together, staring down into the baby's bright-eyed gaze.

Ironically, we told a vet before we told a doctor. We knew that for our own sake we should test Emily for the bacteria that causes toxoplasmosis, so we made an appointment. When the vet asked what symptoms she was having, we both blanked, staring at each other, feeling foolish and rather exposed.

"That's okay," she said, sparing us. "Sometimes it's just a good idea, even without symptoms. Are you wearing gloves and masks to clean her litter?"

We nodded.

"Too bad you can't be *our* doctor," I said. I liked her manner.

She laughed, but Jay looked away. He wanted me to shut up, I thought.

But on the way to the car, he started talking affectionately to Emily.

"How did you like having the whole damn family with you at the doctor?" he asked, tickling her through the bars of her cage.

Suddenly I got a lump in my throat. The vet had perceived us as family, intuiting our needs. It was a seemingly small thing, but it shifted something, at least for that day. As we drove up Valencia, Jay began to hum a little. I hadn't heard him do that since well before the test.

~~~

It would be at least six months, though, before either of us saw a doctor. It took us that long to gather our thoughts and courage. We kept urging the other to go, but both of us hesitated to make an appointment. Jay at least had practical reasons. As long as he was buying his own insurance as a self-employed person, he wanted to keep the stain of infection off his record, in case he needed to change carriers. Besides, he argued, he felt healthier now. We were eating more, and together, every night. We both gained weight, so I spent more time at the gym, working it off. The extra muscle seemed to appeal to him. We found our way back to some intimacy, enough to convince me that Jay was no longer flagging.

Meanwhile, he announced that after he rid himself of the house, he wanted to find a job with benefits. While it saddened me to think of his career path cut short again, I was relieved by any plan that would get him out of the stirred-up filth of attics and crawl spaces. It couldn't be good for his immune system. He, himself, seemed willing to move on. Which is not to say that he was joyful about it, but once again his capacity to go forward without a lot of backward glances carried him.

Already he was playing out some possibilities. The owner of a hardware store he used was thinking of hiring someone to put together a home repair referral service, along with a marketing newsletter. When the owner met Jay, he was convinced it was a fit, given Jay's combination of teaching and renovation skills. Jay would have to work the floor part-time, but advising customers on their projects appealed to him. Best of all, the store believed in him sufficiently to wait until he had finished his renovation.

Who knew if our plan would hold, but it was comforting to act as though it might. He poured himself again into the work on the house, trying to finish up. I went to the library each day, grateful when I simply forgot our predicament and could help a student find a resource or bring order to their search.

One evening, after a friend spoke highly about a new gay doctor at UCSF, Jay nudged me to make an appointment.

"You go first," he told me, promising he would follow as soon as he obtained group insurance, or if he showed symptoms.

By now, both of us were entertaining a weak fantasy that perhaps at least one of our tests had been wrong. Neither of us had had all that much sex, after all. And we had been safe with each other, for a long time. It just didn't seem fair. We knew this wasn't about fair, but there were false positives. Why couldn't we be among them—at least one of us? I wanted to bargain, curse, shout.

When I went to my first appointment, I didn't tell the doctor I had been tested. There was enormous relief when he saw no clinical signs. He did, of course, suggest a test, "just for routine reasons."

In the weeks before the second results came back, Jay and I lay side by side at night, reading aloud from a book on visualization, conjuring a wild but organized pack of black and silver wolves to streak through our blood streams, devouring the virus like so many chickens. He remained determined that a key, a potion, a cure would be found, and that we would be there for it, could in fact be part of helping to find it, simply by taking care of ourselves with our best wisdom. Jay especially liked a practice that involved picturing a protective blue bubble all around the body like a second skin.

But I knew he had his doubts. Some mornings, I would catch him with a hand-mirror, searching his back. Wordlessly, I would turn him toward the window, inspecting him in the morning light. And when he insisted on drying me off after a shower, rubbing my back hard with the towel, I knew what he was doing.

My moments came when I was riding home from work on the train. Catching sight of my face in the window's reflection as we went through a dark tunnel, I would study myself. Did I appear tired? Gaunt?

I looked surprisingly like myself. Just a man riding home from work, waiting for my stop, just like everyone else.

But when I stepped off the train, that sense of waiting didn't go away.

33

"THERE ARE SOME THINGS WE CAN DO," the doctor told me, when I went for my follow-up. It hit me like a ton of bricks. Not only was I positive, my T-cells were headed south.

As the doctor leaned forward, hand on my knee, I noticed he had beautiful skin, olive-complected and a bit ruddy too. But there was stubble on his chin. I wondered how many hours in a row he had been working. I didn't want to think about what he had been telling me. He was saying he was going to take good care of me, no matter what. The kindness almost dissolved me, but I wouldn't let it do that. Crying would make the diagnosis true. Suddenly I realized he had stopped talking and was just looking at me.

"Are you still here?" he asked, touching my elbow.

I shrugged, then despite my efforts, I began to cry.

It would be a long time before simple joy would come to me again.

I didn't call Jay, not right away.

He had wanted to go with me to the appointment, but I wanted to do it alone. Still, I reassured him that as soon as it was over, I would walk down the hill to his property.

Yet that afternoon, when I came out of the medical center into the ocean air sweeping through Parnassus Heights, I turned into the wind and headed toward the sea. I have no idea how long it took me to get there, except at first it was a long straight road through ugly avenues. I passed at least three phones, but each time, I just kept going. On some level, I knew Jay would be worried, but I strode along, nothing making much sense anymore, my arms and legs swinging, the car bumpers glinting, and the trains rumbling by. I had an impulse to just step out in front of one. If it were going to end, why not now? Better to go like my parents—quickly, without being a burden.

But that was when I went looking for a payphone to call Jay.

"Where are you?" he asked, confused by the street noise in the background.

"Judah and 21st. I just need to walk."

There was silence on the other end. If there were good news, clearly, I would have been bursting with it.

"Let me pick you up," he finally said, clearing his throat.

"I think I still need to walk," I said, but my voice wavered. He paused, waiting for me to change my mind, no doubt. I stared up the street at some boys laughing as they opened a pack of cigarettes. For a moment I did want Jay to come fetch me, but I stalled, starting to shake.

"Bill," he said, his voice a little too loud as he tried to surmount the panic creeping in. "We are going to beat this thing. We're going to find out what we can do and do everything we can."

"Everything we *can*," I echoed, a hint of anger in my voice. His hopefulness, which usually I loved, suddenly felt flat and useless. Selfishly, I wanted to grab him and shout, "Can't you see? Nobody's getting out of here alive!"

I kept my mouth shut, but I was shaking my head. I felt obstinate and perverse, dragged by a force beyond all habit of care.

"I don't know why, but I just need to keep moving," I told him. "I'll be home in a while."

"Okay," he said, hesitantly respectful. We lingered a second, saying nothing. An image flashed through my mind of him standing by the phone, hand behind his neck—an everyday posture he would assume when talking with his helpers, trying to resolve how to put something together or tear it apart. The curve of his back, the solidity of his arms as he stood in that stance, unbearably beautiful.

I set the receiver back in its cradle quickly and quietly. A terrible grief swept through me, as if we were already lost from each other.

Dropping down to the park, I found a wooded trail and followed it. Mesmerized by my own pain, I began to revisit every piece of bad luck, failure, and misery that had come my way.

"Of course," I kept muttering. "Goddamn of course."

Spotting a grassy secluded patch behind a thicket, I threw myself down, sobbing as I tugged at the roots of weeds, hands dirty and wet. It was just the sort of scene that would have appalled or frightened Jay, or so I believed.

When I finally stumbled onto the beach, puffy-faced, grass-stained, and spent, I was lucky to find only a few people there, far down at the tideline. I don't know how long I sat. I felt to my marrow that there was nowhere to hide, no sheltering trees or coves or lover's arms that could spare me. Utterly defeated, I allowed myself to do nothing, to simply watch the waves as they crashed one after another on the beach. I was transfixed, until suddenly I *was* the water, sucked back to the ocean, forced onto the sand. A chill went through me, and I began to shake and weep again, yet somehow this time, I felt a strange saving power, a flooding comfort.

I rose from the sand, digging in my pockets for the prescriptions the doctor had given me. I was thinking about Jay, how worried he must be.

He was home when I got there. The smell of Chinese food greeted me when I opened the door. We embraced immediately, the odd relief of exhaustion flowing between us, a slow intimate music. Jay led me to the table, which he had already set, complete with serving bowls instead of just cartons. I pulled out a chair and sat down, watching him bring the chow mein noodles. Jay took his seat, and we glanced briefly at each other, then stared out the window for a long minute, hands in our laps, plates untouched.

~~~~~

I started on AZT.

It seemed like manna from heaven, at first. In those days, no one had any idea how much should be taken, but when I heard that like HIV, the drug could cross the blood-brain barrier, that was enough to sway me. I was particularly afraid of dementia.

Having never taken any meds before except a round or two of antibiotics, I was unprepared for the side effects. Tolerating them seemed a small price to pay, if it made the difference between life and death.

It wasn't long, however, before I was brought to a different understanding.

My manna, as it turned out, gave me a crushing headache most mornings. Unable to stand the light from a lamp or window, I'd stumble around in the dark, cursing under my breath as I tried to pull together some clothes for work. Jay trailed after me, urging me to down some tea and dry toast along with aspirin. Then he'd drive me to work so I wouldn't have to take the train. I'd lean against the door of his truck, eyes shut, enormously grateful, but worrying aloud about his own need for more sleep.

"Forget about it," he would tell me. "I feel fine these days."

But I couldn't shake my fear that he might be worse off than me. Before the test, he'd been so run down, while I'd had no symptoms at all.

He didn't want to hear about it, though. He'd made his decision and was sticking by his plan: no doctors until he got insurance through the hardware store.

The drug had other side effects, too. I felt like a liability. Unable to focus, I screwed up our checkbook, forgot to pay bills, zoned out during meetings at work. When a coworker who had compensated for several of my mistakes asked delicately if everything was okay at home, I blamed my trouble on migraines, but flushed. Did she suspect? Just a week or two before, I had had to buy new trousers in a smaller size. The drug had literally made me lose my ass.

Most disturbing, though, was something invisible, dragging me down.

"I feel like a bag of poison," I told Jay one night, rubbing my forehead, glaring at the pills and a glass of water next to my plate.

"I know, I know," he said softly, crossing his arms over his chest. Suddenly I remembered the previous night, when I had turned from his touch, sunken by pain, physical and emotional. We had both drifted off into an agitated sleep.

I stopped shielding my eyes with my hand and returned his gaze as lovingly as I could.

"I'm sorry I'm such a drag," I said. "You must be lonesome."

He shrugged. "It's just the way it is right now. You need to be poisonous. A real fucker of a host, to get rid of those asshole guests."

I smiled weakly. He raised his mug, clinking my glass, then I downed another dose.

It was just at the point when I began to feel discouraged by the medication itself that Walter re-entered my life in a strangely influential way. I actually hardly ever saw him at the library any more. After blowing up at a ten-year old patron, he had been reassigned to a backroom position. It was rumored that he was doing better there, but in my dreams, he began to reappear night after night, always standing in a book aisle, repeating the same question.

"Is it time?" he would say, reaching up and touching the spine of a book with a baffled look on his face.

I would wake just at that moment, convinced that a finger had run down my spine. Clammy and confused, I would open my eyes, staring at the green glowing numbers on my clock. It was uncanny, the way the dream always culminated just a few seconds before it was time for my alarm to go off, alerting me to take my AZT. I would sit on the side of the bed, swallowing my pills, feeling strangely prompted. At some point my disturbance at being woken again and again in this way began to subside, transforming into an unexpected affection toward Nurse Walter, as I now thought of him. It was as though the old Walter had somehow found a new employment for his meticulousness. I pictured him wafting from house to house in the Castro, supervising medication schedules with a zestful punctiliousness. When one day I actually ran into the real Walter in the hall, I surprised us both by giving him a big grin.

"I've been dreaming about you lately," I blurted, by way of explanation.

"I doubt it," he said, eyeing me suspiciously over the top of his smeary glasses.

"No, really," I said. "You wake me up and remind me to take my pills."

He screwed up his face.

"I don't think so," he said, sounding confused. He started to move past me, but then something seemed to come to mind, and he hesitated.

"I'm, ah, I'm sorry about the meds," he said, rubbing the unshaven side of his face.

"For what?" I asked. "The dream helps me. Reminds me."

"That's not what I meant," he said, looking me over from head to foot before he pushed through the doors to the storage room.

It was only after he had disappeared that I realized what had just been acknowledged between us.

Jay and I ploughed through that first year with blinders on, like a team of horses. He stuck to his goal of finishing the renovation of his property so he could get it on the market and begin his job at the hardware store. I mostly went to work and laid low.

While we hadn't exactly given up our dream of owning our own home, we stopped talking about it and began to fix up the cottage. We still liked to go on rambling walks through the city, but Jay only occasionally commented on the houses, and when he did, the tone of his voice was curbed. Increasingly, we talked about the birds, or flowers, or trees. Lively, but neutral, things.

We avoided Castro Street. There were still hot young men cruising around on weekends, but tottering between them were emaciated wraithlike figures with canes, walkers, wheelchairs. More and more, we simply left town on Saturdays, hiking alone at Point Reyes, Muir Woods, Mount Tam.

"I feel like a traitor," I told Jay one afternoon, as we stood on a bluff in the Marin headlands, gazing back at the city.

He shrugged, then walked away down the trail.

Annoyed, I followed.

"Did you hear me?"

He kept walking, then muttered something.

"Could you speak up?" I asked.

He turned and faced me, holding his hands out to the side as if accused.

"Could we just go for a walk and forget about all that for five minutes? I need to be able to walk around the side of a goddamn hill and not always know what's waiting for us just around the corner."

Stung by the sudden bitterness in his voice, I slid our pack off my shoulder and dumped it on the ground.

"Okay!" I said. "I'm sorry."

Rummaging for water, I offered him a bottle.

For a second he just stared at it, then eyes flashing, he took it, cracked it open and dumped it over his upturned face.

Biting my tongue, I watched the water stream off his chin, wetting his shirt. Why was he acting like such a pig? I'd never seen him do that before. Capping the bottle, he handed it back to me.

We stood and glared at each other. In the past, we would have had this out, then as the air cleared, settled into a new balance. But now, we each pulled back, as if the expense of energy would be too much. He moved aside on the trail as I fiddled with the pack, redistributing the weight. Then he reached for the pack, giving me a faint apologetic smile, but his eyes had yet to soften.

It was my turn to shrug now. We trudged on down the hill in the direction we had originally intended, silently nursing our hurts. The first rains of the season had moved through a few days before, and there were new green shoots pushing up between the straws of old grass. I remember looking at them, feeling nothing.

Something had to change.

34

"WE NEED TO GET OUT MORE," I told Jay, waving an invitation to Michael's fall equinox party that we had left buried in a pile of mail for days.

"Celebrate Balance!" screamed the orange flyer. "Half-light! Half-dark! Come as you are!"

"Yippee, a party in a petri dish," Jay answered, marking the date on our calendar.

Since Noah's birth, Michael's gatherings featured whole armies of babies and toddlers careening about with slobbery little mouths eager to taste the world. We'd hunch in a corner, hoping to fend off germs and concerned about Jay's hands, which were often banged up from work. We'd cover them in Band-Aids, but he usually spent the party with hands jammed in his pockets, shoulders up to his ears. I hated to see him that way, given how much he actually liked kids, and missed teaching. More and more, we made excuses not to go, hoping that Michael wouldn't take offense, but consumed as he was with parenting, he barely seemed to notice.

This time, though, we went because we wanted to, drawn perhaps by the memory of an expansiveness we had felt in earlier years when we'd romped in the spring grass, making new friends, celebrating the openness that spread up and over the hills surrounding the cabin.

As we set off in the morning, the sky was leaden. Something in me was leaden, too. No matter how much light talk I tried to make with Jay in the truck, I couldn't shake my mood. We had yet to tell Michael about our situation, so every time I saw him now, I felt the weight of what was still unsaid.

When we got there, nothing was as expected. It had begun to rain. Everyone, children and all, was crammed in the cabin around the fire. Of course, Michael greeted us warmly, and for a few hours we hung around talking with acquaintances, but my face felt hot with the effort. Wondering where Jay was, I wandered out into the fine mist and spotted him with a man I didn't know on the otherwise-empty deck of the pool. I strolled over. They were thick in a conversation about real estate. I listened, staring at a bright green scum floating on the surface of the pool. The guy was wearing a neatly ironed Oxford blue shirt, but hooked into the weave of his expensive-looking sweater was a button with that quote that was everywhere then: "I Came to Live Out Loud." He had that youthful eagerness to have his expertise acknowledged, but many things about him seemed to imply that his work life might be over. He was taking a break from selling, he said.

We knew what that meant.

"It's great being around all the kids," he enthused.

In actuality, the three of us were huddled in a half-rain well away from the maddening crowd. I almost laughed. But then I realized he was in earnest.

"Joy is the biggest healer," he added, launching into a lengthy diatribe about his recent decision to withdraw from all medication and trust his body to recover its own healing brilliance. Jay bent over and started fiddling with the rotted leg of an upturned deck chair.

"There is no proof AZT will work," the guy continued. "We don't know if AIDS will kill everyone, but we know AZT is killing some."

He pulled out a joint and lit it, offering to share. I shook my head; Jay just kept messing with the chair. Fearful that the topic would follow us back into the house, neither of us was saying anything about our own situation. We did not want Michael to find out this way.

"I probably shouldn't do this," he was saying. "I never used to do any drugs. But I need a little joy, however I can get it."

He took a big toke. Jay caught my eye, then nodded toward a hawk circling above the trees. Together we began to speculate about what kind it was, glad for an excuse to change the subject. Of course, the guy turned out to be a birding expert. I stopped giving him eye contact, though I was well aware of him standing next to me, trim and compact. His energy was so odd—the tidy solidity of his appearance, the floatiness of his spirit. As he rambled on and on, I drifted off into a fantasy of sliding my hand inside his chinos, massaging his dick as he talked, making his speech come slower and slower until finally he was forced to a stop.

"I have to get out of here," I told Jay, when the guy went off to take a leak.

We said a hasty goodbye up at the house. Michael didn't question our departure. In the car, Jay didn't question me either. He flipped through the radio stations, finally settling on a game, which was odd, since neither of us liked sports.

I slumped back in the seat, taking in the rise and fall of the energetic male voices without really hearing the words. I found myself drifting back to my father, the way he would insist on broadcasting games through the entire store on dark winter afternoons. For some reason, that made me think of his ear, the way the top of it flattened out oddly, the curve sheared off by a piece of shrapnel. It wasn't ugly, just unusual. Our barber encouraged him to grow his hair over it, but he had just grunted and waved him off. He could not have cared less about what other people thought of him.

I sat up, shifting uncomfortably, suddenly aware of a tightness in my chest. Jay sensed my perturbance.

"What is it?" he asked, turning down the radio.

I shrugged. The feeling of constraint seemed to be taking over my entire body.

"I can't do this anymore," I said in a whisper. I was not quite wheezing, but almost.

Jay pulled the truck to the side of the road.

"Just drive," I told him. "I'm all right."

"This isn't all right. What is it?"

I stared ahead, trying to understand. He turned in his seat to look at me.

"I'm sick of not being myself anymore," I finally said, in a voice pulled from deep inside my chest.

Jay looked perplexed for a second, then shook his head.

"You're still you," he said, almost adamantly. "And I still love you."

I stared into his fierce stubborn eyes, then reached up, massaging his neck. Even though he seemed more able than me to mingle and chat and forget our circumstances for an afternoon, he was tight, too. This is what this disease could do, I realized, kneading his muscles harder. It didn't just kill with germs. It could hollow us out from the inside first.

"I have to tell Michael," I said. "I can't pretend things are okay anymore."

Jay drew back, staring over the top of the steering wheel.

"You know if we tell him, Betsy will know. Pretty soon everyone will know."

"I disagree. But I can't care about that anymore," I said. "We have to start acting like *we* know."

Jay exhaled, blowing out his cheeks.

"Okay," he said. "I'll tell Betsy. But she and Fran are going to Guatemala any minute to adopt their baby."

"Life goes on," I said. "What we're going through is part of it, too."

I sounded so clear, I surprised myself. Would I still feel that way when I finally spoke with Michael? I looked up through the wet windshield as a few stars popped out between the clouds.

"Valley of the Moon," I said quietly, as though saying an incantation. I had always loved the name of this place.

"Let's get out," Jay said impulsively, opening his door. The damp air rushed in from the vineyards.

We hopped out, climbing over a low stone wall. Feet in the mud, we stood watching banners of fog stream across the stars, our arms draped over each other's shoulders. Jay suddenly laughed, and with a sweep of his arm, gestured toward the dark echoing outlines of grapevines draped over their supports. There were hundreds of them, marching up into the black hills. When we got back into the truck, I felt warm and cold at once.

~~~~

I called Michael within a few days and asked him to meet me at a quiet Thai restaurant in the Castro.

"A bit much with the kids on Saturday?" he teased.

I paused awkwardly. "Not really," I said, hearing myself adopt the same bland voice I often used now to deflect scrutiny. "We were both just tired."

"Well, I'm ready for adult company," he said, taking me at face value.

We made our plans and hung up, but my discomfort lingered. Would he be angry when he realized how long we had kept him out of the loop? Did he even sense the distance that had grown between us? I had been in a fog for months, unable to share much of interest or depth.

Determined to change that now, I rehearsed all week how I would tell him, deliberately choosing a restaurant that would be mostly empty at that hour.

At the last minute, though, he left me a message at work, saying he was desperate for a burrito at his favorite taqueria on Valencia. Would I mind just meeting him there? Since Noah's arrival, he hadn't been near the Mission.

"By the way . . . ," he added, obviously excited. "I got the job in Petaluma. I can move closer to the baby."

I sat at my desk, putting away my pens, shutting down my computer, fighting off a sinking feeling. He was going forward in life. He was going on. I didn't want to go into this conversation resenting his health, but at that moment, I did.

As I rode the train to 24th Street Station, I kept reminding myself, it's not him, it's not me, it's the fucking disease driving this wedge.

I felt calmer as I came up out of the station onto the street, though that sinking sensation came back to me the minute I saw the line outside the taqueria. Just tell him after the meal, I told myself. When you go for a walk or a drink.

Suddenly I felt someone grab my sleeve.

"Hey! Been so long you don't recognize me now?"

There was Michael, right next to me, pulling me into line with him. I had almost walked right by.

"I came early," he said, obviously eager to see me.

I could hardly look at his eyes. They were so warm. They were often that warm.

"Congratulations," I told him, shaking his hand, genuinely happy for him now.

He beamed, launching into the topic of his new job. I was grateful to listen, but soon the words were sliding through my mind without traction. I struggled to find engaging questions, but I felt far from his enthusiasm for the future.

He sensed something.

"What's the deal?" he asked. "Do you think it's a bad idea? Do you know some dirt I don't know about the system?"

I shook my head. "Sounds great," I said, but my voice was strained.

"So how are things going for *you* at work?" he asked, pushing his glasses back up his nose and looking squarely at me.

"Fine," I said, starting to describe a new project, hoping to deflect any concerns he might have that I was jealous. I wasn't, at least not about the job.

But after we'd found a table and settled in with our food, he stopped unwrapping his burrito and again fixed on me. I had just made a comment about how great it was going to be for him, being closer to Noah.

He crinkled his brow in response.

"Okay, now I get why you're being such a mood queen," he said, looking visibly relieved. "You're all weird and pissy because I'm moving."

"Maybe," I said, shrugging, but something in me relaxed too. We both chowed down in silence for a while.

"You'll get over it," he started up again. "You guys can get out of town on the weekends and come stay overnight. We might see even more of each other. It's only an hour away, tops."

"True," I said, continuing to shovel in my food, wondering if once he knew, he would be so quick to invite us—especially if he had the baby. Would any of us rest easy?

Suddenly I realized he had stopped eating and was staring at my plate, which was now empty except for a few chips.

"What's the problem?" I said, staring at it.

"How can you eat like that and still have such a skinny ass?" he asked.

I turned scarlet.

It took me a second to get that he was only ribbing me in a brotherly way. But in that second, I saw his eyes narrow. He put down his fork, reached for his beer, and looked away.

I realized that up until that moment, he really had had no idea.

He shook his head almost imperceptibly, as if to clear his mind, then he tried again, tried to maintain the direction he had intended to go.

"It's not fair," he continued, grabbing a slight roll at his own waistline, but the teasing tone was almost gone now.

"That seems to happen to a lot of parents," I said, nodding toward his belly, trying to buy time too. "Maybe because you eat what the baby doesn't finish?"

"He's still nursing," he said flatly. "I haven't put on any weight."

We both had stopped eating now and were looking out the window.

"I've been meaning to tell you for months," I said. "On behalf of both Jay and me."

He looked down at his hands, absorbing this.

"If this is what I think . . . ," he said, searching my face, then looking away.

"No," he said. "No. Not you guys. I thought you would be the safe ones. I'm so sorry. I had no idea . . ."

He looked white as a sheet now, as if he had pulled in deep away from his face. I found myself suddenly wishing I could change the subject. It was unnerving to feel responsible for how shaken he was. I was grateful now for the hubbub around us, the comforting color and noise of people jammed in around little tables with friends and family. I could feel it again, the colors and the noise.

It was he who suggested we get out of there. As we wandered away from the busier sidewalks and headed toward the broad swath of Dolores Street he asked me the expected questions about how long, how bad, what treatments. My answers sounded courageous, even to myself. I felt solicitous toward him. I could tell he was afraid.

Still, he was making an effort to be caring and careful with me.

As for me, after all those months of containment, I suddenly felt almost giddy. When we got to the white-washed adobe walls of Mission Dolores church, I stopped at the statue of the Virgin Mary and had a strange impulse to leave at her feet the key to my parents' store, which I had kept on my key-ring all these years.

Michael looked up into the big looming branches of the pine hanging over the wall from inside the old Mission cemetery, still absorbing all he had heard, while at the same time, I found myself riding the crest of a release more powerful than I would have imagined.

We walked down to Walgreen's, where Michael bought ointment for diaper rash and I refilled my prescription.

～～～

Things were moving.

Jay had a prospective buyer for his property and a start date for his job at the hardware store.

Betsy had also taken things in stride when Jay had told her.

People were calling us more.

We were calling them back.

We even began to talk about taking a trip, as soon as Jay closed on the house and before he started work. Maybe Hawaii again, we decided.

The guidebooks were out on the table and a reservation on hold when Jay got a call from his mother. His parents would be passing through on their way to a chartered tour of the islands. Could they stop by en route for a brief visit? The date fell right in the middle of our tentative time away.

"I bet she's dragging him," Jay said, with a puzzled half-grin on his face as he hung up the phone. "She says he wants to see the house, see the work I've done before I sell."

He stared out the side window into the neighbor's yard, pulling at a hair on the back of his neck. He always referred to his father simply as Him now. During the years we had been together, they had barely spoken. Their phone conversations consisted mostly of a few grunts punctuated by mortgage figures or construction details, usually prompted by Jay's mother, who was almost always on the line too.

"How would you feel about postponing our trip?" he asked.

I didn't like it. Who knew if and when the opportunity would come again. But the same was also true about Jay's visit with his father. There was a good possibility that some healing could take place. I didn't want to be selfish.

"It would be a different sort of holiday," I finally said. "A holiday from stuckness. That's worth something."

Jay stared down at his shoes, then shook his head after a few moments of consideration.

"If we do this, we can't have any expectations at all. We certainly can't count on it being good. Would that really be all right with you?"

"I'm not going to resent *you*," I said. "I can't make any promises about how I'll feel toward them, but I'll behave. If you want them to meet me, that is. What would you do with me when they come?"

"What do you mean, '*do with you*'?" he asked, lifting an eyebrow.

"Remember that story Betsy told us about making her old girlfriend sit on the couch in a pink sweater when her parents came?"

"You can wear a pink sweater if you want," he teased, collaring me around the neck. "If that's your fantasy, I'm not going to disown you. I own you! And I order you to be yourself."

"Really!" I said, starting to undo his belt.

He pushed me away playfully.

"Actually," he said, "I doubt that they will even agree to come to this house. My guess is they'll want to go to dinner out by the airport."

Even so, for the two weeks prior to their visit, we both went into a whirlwind, sprucing up the cottage and putting the finishing touches on his property.

35

THINGS WERE UNDERSTANDABLY TENSE on the day of their arrival. I went to work, but it was hard for me to keep my mind on it. Each time I thought of Jay greeting his parents at the airport, I would picture a protective bubble of blue light around him. This was the visualization he always gravitated to when we practiced them together. Who knows if my efforts that day helped him—I continued to worry and check my phone messages. The plan was for Jay to call and let me know if it seemed like a good idea for me to join them for dinner. He wanted to play it by ear.

"Just stay cool," he told me, as I left that morning.

The day would prove to be outstanding for other reasons, as well.

Just after my lunch break, I heard a stack of books hitting the floor, along with some muttered cursing on the other side of an aisle. I went to investigate, expecting an inebriated street person, but there was Walter, two bags of groceries at his feet.

"There's no more room here for my milk!" he cried out, the old supercilious tone in his voice almost reasserting behind the panic and despair.

"You assholes have totally fucked up these shelves. Where the hell am I supposed to put my groceries?" he demanded. "You haven't left any room for me!"

"I'm sorry, Walter," I said, approaching slowly. I could see the outlines of several egg cartons and cereal boxes protruding from a shelf. "Maybe we should ask Marsha . . . I bet she'll have a better place."

"Yes," he said. "Marsha better have an idea. I demand to speak with her."

She wasn't his boss anymore, but he let me help him repack his groceries into the bags, and lead him to her office, where he made his loud complaint, his body odor filling up the close quarters. Without missing a beat, she nodded, made note, and assured him of her willingness to help. Before releasing me to my duties, she stepped out into the hall with me, thanking me for the way I had handled the situation. Surveying me for a moment, she paused. Clearly, I was shaken.

"Why don't you take the afternoon off?" she said.

"Why? It's all right."

"I know it's all right," she said. "But it's slow today, and there's only a few hours left on your shift."

"It's not particularly slow," I told her, surprised to hear my own resistance. "Since when do we send people home for that reason?"

"Last week you asked for the day off, but I couldn't give it to you. Now I can. So why don't you get out of here? I know Jay's parents are in town."

She was only trying to be kind, but I suppose I felt thrown into a league with Walter. Not the old Walter, not Nurse Walter, the Walter of visitation, but the flesh-and-blood Walter was clearly departing his mind, and was soon to be sent home, permanently.

I didn't want to go first.

I went to my desk, called Jay's machine, told him he could find me at home, then dallied, taking an hour to clear out.

I was sitting at the kitchen table restocking my slotted vitamin box with its weekly supply when I heard the door open.

"I'm here!" I called, startled.

258

"I know!" answered Jay gayly. "We got your message and came by to see the cottage."

We. Things must be going well. I rose just as Jay entered the kitchen. His mother peered timidly out from behind him.

"Look at that old stove!" she said, without acknowledging my presence. "It even has an old-fashioned stovepipe, just like we had in the thirties!"

She glanced at me, smiling nervously, then reached out and touched the stove with exaggerated interest. Given Jay's sturdy height, she was surprisingly petite in her wrinkle-free beige raincoat cinched at the waist. But there was a wave to her hair that I recognized.

"Did you see this stove, Phil?"

"Yeah, I can see it," said a gravelly voice from the living room.

I looked around the corner, and there He was, Jay's father, a stocky well-built man, shorter than I'd imagined, with heavy eyebrows and a head of crinkly gray hair spilling over his forehead, fifties' style. He nodded at me briefly, then turned toward the window, staring up at the roof of the front building as if that was what he was here to examine.

"Want some tea, Mom? This would usually be your time for a cup of tea," said Jay, trying hard to please.

"We won't stay," she said, clutching her raincoat around her, but when Jay pulled out a chair, she perched on the edge of it.

"So how much would these buildings go for?" his father suddenly demanded from the living room.

"He could use a drink, too," chimed in Jay's mother. "He never drinks enough and it's so dry in Arizona."

"I don't need anything," he said. "This place would probably get more than that house of yours we just saw," he added.

Jay opened the fridge and got out an Anchor Steam.

"It would probably go for $350,000," Jay said, holding out the beer to his father.

His father snorted. "How ridiculous. These houses are totally ridiculous. What a ridiculous place to buy a house."

"A lot of people like to live here," Jay said, setting the beer down on the end table and returning to the kitchen, where he busied himself running water for the tea. I could see the heat rising up his neck.

"I suppose so," said his mother. "How long have you lived here?" she said, addressing me.

"I moved here a year or so after Jay."

"Where did you come from?"

Mars, I was tempted to say. I'm an alien who abducted your son.

But at least she was struggling to talk to me.

"I'm from Detroit," I said.

"Where do your parents live?"

"They don't," said Jay quietly, cutting her short as he set down her cup of tea. She raised her eyebrows, looking embarrassed and confused.

"That's okay," I said, turning to her. "They died when I was nineteen."

"I'm sorry," she said immediately, glancing at me then dipping her spoon into her teacup, stirring it thoughtfully.

Turning red, I fumbled with the box of tea biscuits. I suddenly felt as if I had confessed a dangerous liability with implications for her son. Once again, an irrational shame that my parents had died returned to me, this time mixed with my fear of what Jay's parents would think, if they knew the whole truth of our situation.

"Have you had any kind of contact with them since?" she said, pausing, as if gathering more thoughts.

"Mom, they're gone," said Jay, openly frustrated.

"I'm sorry, I'm not making myself clear," she said, undeterred by his impatience as she went on to explain, but this time it was Jay's father who cut her off.

"The pocket doors in here work," he called to Jay from the other room, rolling the heavy wood panels back and forth in their track, oblivious to our interaction. "I don't see why you can't just look at these, Jay, and see how to get those ones at your property working."

Jay's mother rolled her eyes at Jay.

"I'm still stupid as ever," Jay volleyed back.

"Oh, don't say that," said his mother. "You know what he's like." Then she turned to me. "After my mother died," she said, "I could always feel her breathing down my neck whenever I cleaned. And there would always be one more smudge or speck of dust that I knew she would have gotten, but I just didn't seem to have time. I did the books for the business, as well as looked after the kids. She just never understood what that was like. But still, I felt like she was around, in my life."

"I never knew that," said Jay, pulling up his chair. "Did you think she haunted our house?"

"It wasn't like that," she said. "It was just something inside me. And then one day it was like she just left. I had a dream that I saw her standing on a chariot surrounded by clouds. She was in a long flowing gown. She looked like she did in her wedding pictures. I knew she was in heaven then."

"Did you feel sad she was gone?" asked Jay.

"No," she said. "Why would I feel sad about her being in heaven?"

She looked at the clump of jasmine dangling down over the window from the roof above. "That's pretty," she added.

"So, did you have any experiences like that?" Jay asked me, pointedly prompting a return to her original question.

She loosened a button on her coat and sat back on the kitchen chair, turning her gaze to me. I could hear Jay's father in the living room, ferociously tumbling the change in his pants. I lowered my voice.

"All I can remember right now is how someone used to call the house a few months after they died, and they would never speak. I could just hear breathing. It was probably a crank caller, but I liked to imagine that it was my mother, dialing me up just to hear my voice."

"Who knows?" said Jay's mother primly. Her tone was so strange. It was as if we were talking about the weather, yet here we were, down to the core of my pain.

"Here's a few pictures of our family," she said, opening her purse and laying a booklet of photos on the table. Slowly she flipped the pages, pointing out to Jay the snapshots and school photos of his two nephews. "This is our grandson Wayne and this is Jerry." From there she went on to wedding photos of a former neighbor girl in Michigan, and baby photos sent by a distant cousin Jay had never met. I was aware of Jay swallowing several times. Later, I realized she was flipping through pages of a history from which he had been excluded.

Yet painful as this must have been, it was also clear that those divisions were forgotten by her, at least for this moment. Here she was, at our table, and by showing me the photos, she was including me.

There was an awkward pause.

"Quite a family," I finally ventured. "You sure did a great job with this guy here. Isn't Jay's house wonderful? You should have seen what a mess it was before he did his hardwork-cure."

His father came to the kitchen door, a gnarled hand on each side of the doorframe.

"We had nothing to do with that," he said. "That's his own deal."

Jay stared down at the plate of biscuits, arms crossed. Understandably, the note of pride in his father's voice seemed lost on him.

"He could have accomplished all that faster if he'd come into the business. That teaching thing was a detour. But he always did have to do things his own way."

"Unlike other people around here," said his mother, dropping the booklet of pictures back into her purse and snapping it shut. Jay picked up our fat green English teapot and stood with it poised over his mother's cup.

"More tea, Ma?"

"That's enough," she said, spreading her hand over the cup. "We should go soon."

Jay just stood there for a second, pot in his hand, arm extended, gathering himself with a look of inward concentration on his face. I stared at him unabashedly, struck by his poise under fire. Suddenly I could see how the affable good nature I loved in him and usually ascribed to a sunny temperament was even more of a victory than I had realized.

"I supposed I should check the weather," said his mother, reaching for the newspaper. "I can't believe we're going to be in Hawaii tomorrow. It's so damp and chilly here."

She picked up the top section, exposing my vitamin box. Jay and I exchanged a look. There was no AZT in the box—but it was crammed with an extraordinary variety of supplements. As his mother opened the paper, I reached over and moved the box to a shelf behind me as smoothly as I could.

"Who's the health nut?" she asked just as smoothly, without peering from behind the paper.

"Both of us," said Jay. "We like to work out."

His dad snorted from the other room.

"Have you seen those get-ups people wear nowadays just to go for a walk? Big fat guys with that sticky material gripping their flab—what do you call it, Mother?"

"Lycra," said Jay's mother. "Is there a weather section?" She reached for the rest of the pile. "I wonder what it will be like in the morning, when we have to leave. I'm trying to figure out what to wear."

"You won't have to be outside more than a few seconds. We'll be in a taxi," said his father. "Anyway, people pay money for those running outfits. Do you have one?" he asked, eyeing me directly for the first time.

"Wouldn't be caught dead in one."

"You're trim, at least," he said, standing up to study something on our mantle.

"You guys don't need a taxi," inserted Jay. "I'm coming to your hotel in the morning to take you to the airport. Remember?"

"Honey, I'm sure the hotel has a van, don't you think?" said his mother, standing now too, gathering her raincoat around her. "You don't have to run all the way out there to the airport. You need your energy."

"Yeah. For the workout," added his father. This time the affection in his voice was audible.

But Jay and his mother were still absorbed in their dance about the logistics.

"Your old man?" he said, nodding at a photo of my father in his army uniform.

"Yeah. Jay told me you were a sailor in the war."

"He did? Where did your father serve?"

"Germany and France. On the ground. He was shot crossing the Rhine."

"I never saw action like that," he said. "I was on a tub of a boat. A fishing boat, actually, pressed into service. Hardly twenty of us on it, and it sprang a leak. Spent most of two years dragging its ass back from the Philippines to San Diego, with stops for repairs in Hawaii."

"So, you've been to the Big Island?"

"Can smell it in my dreams."

"Tell him what they said about those old dreams of yours," piped his mother from the kitchen.

He shook his head, rolling his eyes as if he would shrug off the invitation, but then he started to talk.

"Went to the VA for my regular appointment. Some girl comes in the room before the doctor does. Says they're doing a study on trauma. Did I have any trauma from the war? Nope, I said. Not unless you count almost dying of boredom. Lots of make-work, swabbing decks, and looking at waves and stars. 'Hurry up and wait' was our motto. But you probably heard that from your old man, too."

"I did."

"But then she asked you about your dreams," said his wife.

"Yeah. First ten years of our marriage, I was always waking both of us up with a start. It was always the same damned dream."

"Not just waking up—you'd almost be panting. And not about me."

A blush crept into his face.

"I told the girl I did have a dream. One dream, over and over. Huge waves tossing our boat, and I'd be trying to go below, to get my wallet, but water would be pouring down the hatch. That's when I would always wake up, just before the boat turned over."

"So, were you really in a storm like that?" I asked.

"Yeah. Two times, we were almost done in by typhoons. The first time, the skipper actually told us to prepare to abandon ship. We would have been goners. I tried to get below to find my wallet, but water kept slamming down on me as I hung onto the ladder."

"You were about to lose your life, and you were worried about your wallet?" asked Jay.

"I'd lost my dog tags, Knucklehead. If they couldn't identify my body, my mother wouldn't have gotten any money. I wanted her to get some money."

Jay's mother appeared in the door.

"Like father, like son," she said. "During that same time period, while his father was still having those dreams, Jay kept waking up just before dawn, saying he'd had a bad dream about a big tornado. I never knew why a tornado. He'd never seen one. He was only four or five."

"Yes, I did," said Jay. "In *The Wizard of Oz*."

"I think he got the theme from his father," she insisted to me. "He was picking up on something. But he would never wake us. It would still be dark, and I would hear him in his room, pushing his train around on its track. I'd get up and ask him what he was doing. On one side I had the father, on the other, the son. Both of them would tell me their dream, but neither of them would admit they were afraid."

Jay and Phil glanced briefly at each other, both shaking their heads and rubbing the backs of their neck, the same slight grin on both their faces.

"I still want to know what happened with the boat," I said.

"Things just calmed down. Boy, were we glad to see the stars that night. And all those monotonous little waves. I thought I would never complain again."

Phil looked out the window. Late afternoon fog was blowing through the bamboo.

"Better get back to the hotel," he said, picking up his jacket and checking the inside chest pocket, presumably for his wallet.

"Why don't you let us take you to North Beach?" said Jay. "You love Italian food."

"Thank you," said his mother. "But he's already checked out the menu at the hotel coffee shop. He has his eyes on a Reuben."

"I'm sure we could find one at North Beach. And you could see the hills. We could drive down Lombard Street," I said. "The famous squiggly one."

"We can do that next time," said his mother, buttoning the top of her raincoat.

I bit my tongue. There might not be a next time, I thought.

"Before you go, I want you to see something Jay did," I said determinedly.

Jay raised his eyebrows, but I led them to the bathroom.

"See those blue tiles? We found them on a beach in Kaua'i. Hurricane Iniki had come through the year before, and they were all that was left of a fancy house that had once stood on the site. Jay installed them."

"What a unique design!" said his mother.

"They're constellations," I added proudly.

"I'm glad there's some rhyme or reason," said his father, leaning into the stall, running his palm across the surface of the tiles.

"What made you pick those particular constellations?" asked his mother, turning to Jay.

He looked at me over her shoulder, hesitating, obviously debating whether or not to tell her they were the stars present in the sky when we'd met. But then his gaze shifted toward his father.

He was rubbing his thumb over two tiles that stuck out slightly. It was a small error, but it had bothered Jay for years. Phil straightened up, clearing his throat as if he were about to comment. I felt a wild urge to say something, anything, to divert the conversation.

But Phil merely turned toward the window, looking up through the dark leaves of the plum into the late afternoon sky.

"There's no stars like stars over the ocean," he said, almost wistfully. "You haven't seen stars until you've been in the Navy."

He let out a sigh, seeming lost in his own musings.

This was as good as it could get, I thought.

"I don't know if they were happy to see us," said Jay, after he had returned from driving them back to their hotel. "But they were thrilled to eat white-bread sandwiches just like they'd make for themselves at home."

He shook his head, rolling his eyes just like his mother.

"I guess I should be happy that at least gastronomically they're easy to please."

He didn't mention all the knocks from his father.

"Actually," I said, "I liked your dad. He's passionate."

"Passionate?" Jay screwed up his face, incredulous.

"Yeah. He's critical, but he's engaged. Did you see how he threw off his jacket, rolled up his sleeves, and huffed and puffed around the living room? I can see where you get your ability to throw yourself into things."

"Really?" Jay asked dubiously. "But he never even set foot in the kitchen, except on his way to see the tile."

"He didn't have to! He didn't miss a beat of conversation. We know his hearing's good."

We both laughed.

"I guess so," said Jay. "But he's so rude."

"That, too," I said.

36

AT SOME POINT THAT NIGHT I WOKE to find Jay's arm tight around my chest. "What's going on?" I asked.

"Nothing," he said, but I could feel him thrumming.

"How come it feels like you're pushing trains around the track, then?" I said, remembering his mother's story.

He gave a little laugh.

"I don't know," he said. "I guess it just bugs me that I chickened out."

"On what?"

"On telling my parents the whole story about the tiles. About us."

I rolled over, taking him into my arms.

"There's still time. You did more than enough for a first visit. Anyway, they looked me in the eye, and saw us together. We even talked about dreams and heaven. Who would have guessed?"

As he lay with his head on my chest, I ran my fingertips up and down his back.

"I don't know why, but I'm thinking about Eddy again," he said. "What a big mistake it was for me to not come out to him."

I paused.

"It was a no-win situation, Jay. You can't evaluate the past from the perspective of the present."

He sighed.

"I don't want my parents to know about the HIV. Even if I'm on my death bed. Just tell them some other diagnosis that makes sense."

"Don't you think they'd guess what's behind it?" I asked.

"Probably, but as long as no one says the words, they should be all right."

"Okay," I said.

As I stroked his hair, he stretched out beside me and fell asleep. I stayed awake for a while, just watching him breathe.

"Look!" he said the next morning, pouncing on me as I struggled to open my eyes.

"What? Where?"

He flopped down next to me, on top of the covers. He was already dressed. The clouds of the prior night seemed to have vanished.

"I can't believe this!" he said, flipping through an old National Geographic. "I must have read this article about Venice thirty times when I was a kid!"

Propping myself up, I peered over his shoulder at photos of half-submerged bikes, archways, and streetlamps. *November 3, 1966,* said one caption. The worst *acqua alta,* the highest tide on record.

"I remember those shirt cuffs!" he said, stopped by the image of a lone man in a dark suit, water up to his thighs, wading across a flooded plaza with his hands clasped behind his back. Those brilliant white cuffs made an impressive chevron against the backdrop of salt-marked crumbling grandeur.

"Where did you get this?" I asked, sitting up.

"My mother brought it. She found it in an old drawer. When I was a kid I really wanted a subscription, but in those days you had to be nominated. Then my mother met someone at the beauty parlor who could sign me up."

The sight of a gondolier leaning on his oar, his trim body silhouetted against the humid glare of a lagoon, silenced us both for a moment.

Jay continued the story. "I was so impressed. I thought you had to be an explorer or professor, not some lady your mother finds in the neighborhood, not a kid just catching on to some strange new sensations below his belt."

"And what did you imagine the Society would do to you if they found out you were an imposter?" I teased, reaching for him. "Send that man with a big pole in his hands after you?"

"You wish!" said Jay, checking me with an elbow to the ribs.

We continued to leaf through the pages, reading about the daily ebb and flow of the Adriatic, the high tides at full moon, the *risalta salina* or salt rise, eating into the soft stucco and brick above the sturdy marble foundations.

"The rate at which Venice is going is about that of a lump of sugar in hot tea," I read aloud.

"Says who?"

"John Ruskin, apparently."

"Yeah, but didn't he die about a hundred years ago?" said Jay. "So much for him! Look at these buildings! They're beautiful."

He was staring at a palazzo of rosy stucco, obviously weather beaten, its large wooden shutters hanging crooked on their hinges. Bright flags snapped above the roofline; an attractive little boat waited at the door.

"Venetians made their own ground out of a fluid world," we read.

Seized by those words, we knew we would visit as soon as possible.

37

A MONTH LATER I FOUND MYSELF WAKING UP at the Hotel
Seguso from a deep oblivion fueled by jetlag. As I listened to the long
curtains billowing in a strong breeze, I thought for a moment that we
had set sail. I could hear choppy water smacking, and somewhere below,
a woman's voice speaking an unfamiliar language in a gentle tone. A
child was murmuring soft consents, and as the repetition of the waves
and of the requests wafted through me, I slowly realized I had limbs
to stretch, and so I pushed with my arms and my legs a little. The cells
of my body seemed not to have arrived yet, at least not in their usual
configuration. I felt strangely floaty, as if part of me were still spinning
somewhere above the blue Atlantic and had yet to recongregate around
my bones. And yet my bones were there; they seemed to be rising from
deep dark waters despite an unfamiliar heaviness in their core. It seemed
more as if I had been to the other side rather than just sleeping. For a
few moments I had no idea who or where I was, but nevertheless I felt
infused with a sense of being supported by something I couldn't find
or see—it seemed to be everywhere around me. I knew it had nothing
to do with me, in any personal sense. It was bigger than that. Until that
moment, the love between Jay and me had been the most buoyant force

I had ever known, and there was nothing small about that love. It's just that suddenly I glimpsed the larger sea around us both.

I lay in the bed watching the white curtains stream in the breeze. I couldn't tell if it was late morning or early evening, but I could hear music, and a boat engine, idling. The music was coming from a water taxi, I realized, and the song was "Hotel California," which made me want to laugh. A chandelier of clear glass, old and elegant, came into focus. I was amazed I hadn't noticed it when we'd arrived. But hot and tired, we had stripped off our clothes and lay with our backs pressed against the cool terrazzo floor, fingers barely touching, wash cloths on our chests.

I turned my head and looked over at Jay. He was still asleep, lips slightly parted.

Suddenly an image swam into my mind. It was of Jay, standing naked before a window in a square of white light from the moon or maybe a streetlamp, a long drape wrapped around his waist, knotted just below his belly. The other curtains were lifting and twirling beside him, as though he were raising or lowering a sail. It was a beautiful picture, his body strong but relaxed, his belly open, his whole being lucent as he reached between the curtains and pulled the window partway closed, then rubbed his thumb down a long silvery streak.

I had no idea if this image was a memory or dream, but there was something oddly familiar about it, a sense of *déjà vu*.

I rose quietly and rummaged through my pack for the massage oil I had brought. I wanted to lay my hands on Jay, to anoint his body, to wake him to this floating world.

~~~~~~

"We're walking on water, you know."

Jay stepped to the edge of the Fondamenta, looking back at me, then into the mist swirling up from the lagoon.

"This was all built on a salt marsh," he said, kicking his foot gently against the base of a wide marble stair.

Leaning against the fat column of a stately abandoned building, I closed my eyes, concurring with the marvel in his voice. My whole body registered the push of the sea into the canals on each side of us.

"You look like a masthead, the way your hair is blowing back," he said, snapping a photo of me, then sitting nearby.

That was exactly how I felt. Though we were on a tip of land, it seemed as if we were the ones who were moving, cutting the waves with our prow. We ate our breakfast, some pastries we had bought along the way, as we continued to stare out into the lagoon, not talking much, just feeling the winds that seemed to have blown all the way from the Middle East centuries ago. I pictured sailing ships from Byzantium that made me think of Jay as a boy pouring over old maps in his shiny new magazine. Now here we were, his dream become manifest. I handed him my cup of coffee, which was cold now, but neither of us cared.

Having deliberately left our guidebooks behind, we spent the rest of the morning meandering through the Dorsoduro, following this canal or that on a whim. It became a sort of game.

"This way!" said Jay, taking off down a narrow corridor. "I lead. When I stop, you have to guess what I've led you to."

He stood for a moment on a small bridge, then reversed direction and came back over the canal, taking a right, his eyes scanning the light filtering down between the buildings. Was he following a butterfly or bee? Suddenly he stopped opposite an antique shop, pressing his back against the wall, head cocked. Above us, the sound of a piano wafted from an open window, trailed by eager if untalented chords from a cello. A teacher and child?

I raised my eyebrows, pointing above.

"Got me."

"They sound happy together," he said, smiling peacefully as he continued to listen. I closed my eyes, feeling the sun on my arms. His lack of bitterness at the loss of his own teaching career never ceased to amaze me.

"Your turn for the hot pursuit!" he said.

I wandered along a narrow canal, searching. The water was dark and still, mirroring almost perfectly the upside-down reflections of the buildings on the opposite side. For a brief flash, walking there along that seam's edge, I felt dizzied. It was as if there were two cities, one the liquid dream of the other. Which came first? As we stopped on a small stone bridge and peered over, I saw Jay, the dark top of his head, reflected there.

Sticking my hand in my pocket, I pulled out some coins.

"Make a wish," I told Jay, giving him half.

Without hesitating, he flung them into the water. I followed, watching the concentric ripples from our coins intersect.

"What did you wish for?" I asked.

"Just this, as it is, right now" he said, grinning. "And you?"

"All this, forever."

"Well, I guess we've got our bases covered, don't we?"

"So on with the pursuit," I said, descending the bridge and cutting through an alleyway to a wider canal. Turning down the walkway, I spied an ancient chapel on the other side, its exterior wall stripped away for renovation. It was perfect. There were scaffolding and workmen everywhere; in the canal, a boat was loaded with tools and materials. I stopped just opposite, idling by a streetlamp.

Excitedly, Jay began to rattle off questions. Was it that tool, arch, heap of busted-up marble?

"No, no, and no."

After a dozen tries, he gave up.

"So, tell me!" he said, his eyes still riveted on the worksite.

I strolled ahead to three dusty café tables under an awning.

"Let's get a ringside seat. If you still can't guess after checking out the boys in work boots, maybe I'll tell you then."

We took our seats, and a waitress appeared with menus. Shielding our eyes from the bursts of dust swirling in from the chapel, I understood why we were the only patrons, but Jay was unperturbed. There would be fancier restaurants and more famous sites, but he was so happy that afternoon, watching those guys pry apart the layers of history hidden in the chapel. As we lingered, sipping chianti, enjoying a pasta primavera with a deceptively simple but memorable sauce, he filled me in, pointing things out about the materials and probable order of events as they became clear to him. Though I'd brought him armloads of books from the library before we'd left home, I hadn't realized how much he'd actually learned about Venetian preservation techniques. There was a glow to his skin that made him seem so full, so ripe—*complete* is the word that comes to mind. Of course, I had always known that his calling to renew and restore was deep, but it was so pleasurable to see it in this grand dignifying context layered with the spirits of centuries and peoples. We couldn't have come to a better place.

"Okay, now I get it," he said. "It's the whole chapel."

"Nope!" I said. "*You* might be into that chapel, but this was my turn to be in hot pursuit. What am *I* into?"

He started scanning some guys unloading heavy bags from a boat.

"Let's see, I'm not sure what your type might be these days . . ."

"I'm into *you*, you idiot. *You*, all riled up and passionate about what you love."

That sense of stumbling upon unexpected egresses stayed with us throughout the trip as we wended our way along the canals and pathways, peering into half-hidden courtyards, private gardens, little neighborhood bars unmentioned in guidebooks. We laughed at the hours we spent sipping prosecco and simply eating, savoring huge slices of artichoke hearts sautéed in olive oil and garlic, or surprisingly mild, black risotto flavored with squid ink. We returned again and again to a wood-paneled trattoria-style place called Corte Sconta, which served big tables of Italian families in a courtyard each afternoon. There was a set menu, of which you were informed by a woman who seemed to own or run the place—no if's, and's, or but's. She was beautiful—tall, large-boned, very distinctive in her fitted black dress, stylish without being flamboyant. On our first visit, Jay tried to tell her that we didn't need any salad.

"Even American men like our salad. You will see!" she said, turning away with a small confident smile.

"She looks just like that Bellini we saw today at the Accademia, only older!" Jay whispered, flipping through his guidebook and turning it so I could see the *Virgin of the Small Trees*.

He was right.

But we didn't eat the salad, much to her chagrin. "Very fresh," she kept insisting. "Yes, we can see," said Jay. "Very lovely. But I have a medical condition."

She frowned playfully, obviously disbelieving.

"And you?"

I nodded.

"All you American men. You will have heart attacks. But I will give you extra dessert anyway."

On our second visit, we had to pass up the shellfish. Difficult to do in Venice. But we knew the ropes by then. We knew that the only water we could drink was bottled, and that we must peel the fruit. We were acclimated to these measures, performing them almost as mindlessly as we brushed our teeth.

One evening, as we sat in the cool and dark of the Santa Maria della Salute church listening to vespers, I had a sudden moment of realizing I was following each note without a thought or a care. I took a deep breath, feeling the gift of simply being in a body. In my hand was a little packet of postcard reproductions we had bought that day. Even the bag was beautiful, with its dozens of tiny red stars and globes printed on tissue-thin white paper. As I sat there rubbing it between my fingers, I realized how different I had felt ever since we had come here. I had fallen in love with the body again, despite all its betrayals. Neither of us could stop looking at people—on the streets, in paintings, or on pedestals. We would lose ourselves for hours in the museums. The Accademia was right near our hotel, and it was there we became fascinated with Bellini. Such gorgeous men with lots of personality. Venetian citizens, portrayed as Christian saints. I was enthralled with the incredible detail, the sensual yet restrained aesthetic with which the fabrics of dress and decor were painted.

"You're just a spiritual materialist," Jay would tease, buying me handfuls of art cards in the museum shops. Later, we would sit on a bench under some trees, cards in our hands, making a game of finding a Venetian who most closely matched the face of a virgin or saint.

Jay and I were so different in our approach to museums. It seemed like it would have been me, the librarian, who would be parsing all the details, but he was the one reading the fine print while I drifted in and out of images that drew me, in no apparent order. It might be the faces that struck me, their similarity to the people we saw on the street, or who waited on us. It would be Jay who remembered something about the context of the painting, especially if there were some allusion to the enormous and disciplined efforts of the Venetians to preserve both their independence and their architecture against the storm-driven tides of nature and politics.

"Look at this," he murmured one morning, nudging me and pointing out in his book a paragraph about Titian's painting of St. Sebastian that was somewhere in the Santa Maria della Salute. We were in line outside, waiting to view the art in the daytime. "There are always survivors in any plague. This city had Black Death, again and again."

I read the text, something about how St. Sebastian had been shot by Roman crossbowmen for ministering to Christian prisoners and the plague-stricken. Having healed his own wounds, he became a champion of those seeking to beat the plague. In the painting, he stood at the feet of St. Mark with a bevy of doctor saints. Though pierced by an arrow between the ribs, he stood on strong legs, looking to the side, his sturdy torso exposed above a knotted drape.

A sense of *déjà vu* came over me once more. This was exactly how I had seen Jay that night in my floaty reverie, the first night in the hotel, with the drapes billowing out. I must have seen this book before leaving home, I thought, looking at the cover, but I had no memory it.

As we moved past the actual painting in the church, it was me this time who was searching for words of explanation. I took the book from Jay and continued to read. *Sebastian's wounds were so associated with plague spots that the arrows directed at him were made to hit the points where the bubos of the plague were most common—especially the lymph glands in the throat, armpits, and groin.*

"He seems no worse for the wear," Jay whispered in my ear as he stared up at the painting.

It was true. If anyone seemed troubled, it was St. Mark, whose face was darkened by shadow. Sebastian looked strangely at ease, lost in his own beautiful thoughts as the doctors Cosmas and Damian consulted each other. For a second, without really thinking about it, I leaned slightly against Jay as I looked, feeling an urge to just rest my hand on his belly. Then the line moved along, and so did we.

38

BACK HOME IN SAN FRANCISCO, the fall rains had begun.

One day, on my lunch hour, I took a walk through Hayes Valley in the fine mist, prolonging our vacation by looking in gallery windows. As I stood at a stoplight, I found myself inexplicably relaxed by the sight of car lights gleaming on the dark, wet pavement in mid-afternoon. I gazed for a few moments, entranced, before I realized that the light bouncing off the wet was reminding me of the canals. Without even thinking about it, my body was right back in that larger flow that had come surging into us in Venice. I had to return to work, but I wanted to keep going. Venice had opened in me a raw appetite I couldn't name, one on the verge of becoming anxiety if not obeyed. Whenever I had a minute, I read any travel article that came my way.

Jay, on the other hand, needed time to settle into his new job at the hardware store. For a few months, he would be helping customers, familiarizing himself with the sorts of questions they had before he took on developing the newsletter. On weekends, he was inclined to stay home and catch up on chores.

"We can still walk the dog," he would tease, meaning me. "We don't have to fly halfway around the world to do that." He started clipping out tips on Marin bike trails, Sunol hikes, Sonoma County vistas.

One night after work, on impulse, I hopped onto the N-train and headed for the hardware store instead of home. In my pack was the unopened envelope of photos from our trip that I had just picked up. As the train came up out of the tunnel, I could see the darkening sky lit from beneath by a sun already dropped well below the line of buildings. Cole Valley wasn't far from our Castro cottage, a thirty-minute walk at most, but there was a hill between us, a hill big enough to hold back the coiling dragons of fog that rushed inland from the sea through the Avenues on many afternoons.

As I stepped from the train, I could feel the bite of damp air in my lungs immediately. But the small shops along Cole Street were lit up yellow and bright; the door to the hardware store was open, with shelves of sale plants spilling out onto the sidewalk. I picked out a pot of rust-colored mums, then wandered up and down the crammed aisles of the store, looking for Jay.

I found him near the back, standing on a ladder, a hooked pole in his hands as he stretched to dislodge some merchandise from a peg. I could sense in my own arms his effort to retain control of the pole. A long-forgotten memory washed through me for a second taking me back to an elementary school classroom that had tall windows capped by a second row of horizontal ones near the high ceiling. The only way to open these was with the aid of a long hook. I relished the job, the heaviness of the pole, its precariousness as I struggled not to crash it into the glass. There was not much room for error. But the teacher, who often chose me for the task, went on with whatever lesson she was giving, ignoring me with the sort of deliberate trust that made her anxiety palpable. When the hook at last came home to the latch-handle, fitting perfectly in its hole, I felt as though I had personally created the humid spring air that came flowing through the opened window, smelling of wet cement and fresh-cut grass.

Coming back to the sight of Jay on the ladder, head bobbing up near the fluorescent lights and smudged plywood ceiling, that apple-green feeling of victory began to fade. While Jay rarely spoke about the career he had lost in Michigan, I still felt bitterness at times. Inconveniently and unexpectedly, it was coming over me now. I watched him descend as a couple appeared at the base of his ladder with a question about a runny Edwardian toilet.

How does he do it, I wondered.

I slipped out of sight but within earshot.

Jay sounded happy as he helped the customers sort out their project.

I took a deep breath, following the tone of his voice. I wanted to hold onto the mood of celebration that had propelled me here, the gladness and relief that he had this job. It did, after all, mean medical insurance. Soon. And no more plaster dust or paint fumes. If he was okay with it, why shouldn't I be? His teaching skills were obviously being called upon in a low-stress way.

When he finished with his customers, I came around the corner with my pot of mums. He raised his eyebrows in surprise.

"Those are standing tall!" he said, eyeing the flowers, then letting his gaze drop. "May I help you?"

For a moment, just that was enough to make me forget the cold breeze pushing in through the front door, the customers sidling past each other in the narrow aisles, cutting through each other's breath space.

"I just wanted to come by and see if you needed anything—a hot latte? Some tea?"

I was putting on a hearty voice to match his own, and for a few moments, I did feel it. He shook his head, crossing his arms on his chest as he beamed at me.

"So, what are you doing here?"

"I just wanted to come and see you in your new job."

"And bring me something hot."

"If not now, later."

"Actually, you look like you're freezing," he said, lowering his voice.

I shrugged. "I'll heat up, walking home."

In fact, apart from the warmth I was already feeling just from seeing Jay, there was an odd sudden heat pushing out from my core to the surface of my face.

"I'm not used to being on somebody else's dime," said Jay, keeping his voice low. "I feel like I should be able to take a break just because you're here."

He glanced away, straightening up some wrenches on a rack.

Something in me eased. Neither of us was used to him working until 9 pm. It was good to hear him say what he did.

"Want me to get you a sandwich?"

He shook his head. "I actually got one on my break."

It wasn't until I walked home over the hill and dumped my pack on the bed that I remembered the photos.

Delaying gratification, I decided to take a shower before looking at them. Afterward, I sat on the edge of the bed half-clothed and opened the envelope.

There it all was again, the floating world, in miniature. The piazzas, a vaporetto, the prominent penises of several men of marble. Jay, leaning out the window of the pensione, waving his shirt at me as I stood below on the sidewalk. The shower hadn't cooled me off. But my sweatiness seemed part and parcel of the warmth radiating from the walkways and canals in my memory.

Soon I came to the photo Jay had taken of me as I had leaned against a column that first morning. Like a masthead, he had said.

The picture looked far different from how I had felt in that moment.

And from how I wanted to be remembered by Jay.

I shoved it into the top drawer of my nightstand and kept going, flipping through the pile quickly.

I wasn't hot anymore. In fact, now I had begun to shiver.

Coming to a close-up of Jay, I hesitated, scrutinizing. He was sitting at the café table near the church renovation project. He was reassuringly pink, but was it a healthy pink? I noticed the crow's feet around his eyes.

He's had those for a while, I told myself, crawling in under the covers. We aren't going to stay the same age forever.

I grabbed the remote, turning on the television, yet nothing seemed to please me. I changed the channel, but couldn't focus on anything.

I didn't want to be that man in the photo.

I pulled it out again.

His face was washed out, almost featureless in the glaring ocean light.

It looked exactly how I felt, every time I got a fucking AZT headache.

I hadn't had one that day, yet, nor did I have many on our trip. I had somehow been able to rise above them, push on through.

I ripped the photo in half.

I wasn't outnumbered yet.

I still had decent blood stats. Before the trip, the doctor had said I was holding my own.

And no symptoms, except from medication.

Except now. I was shivering, which is why I was still under the covers when Jay came home.

I told him why I was in bed.

"Put a sweatshirt on," he told me, handing me his. "It's the fall, not summer in Italy!"

He got undressed and crawled in under the covers.

Both of us stared at the TV. He started to drop off to sleep, then roused himself.

"You're wide awake," he said, curling around me, warming me with his body heat. "Are you worried about this? It takes time, going from one climate to another."

He said this so groggily, I began to relax. We hadn't even put our winter comforter on the bed yet, I realized, poking fun at myself as I got up and dug through the closet for it. Then we both fell asleep with the television on.

~~~~~

I don't know exactly when I crossed the line, but I associate it with a moment a few weeks later, when I was home early from work with a headache. Again, I was watching television. Though the house was damp from having no heat all day, I was laying on top of the covers, sweating. At the time, I wasn't thinking about that. Not at all. Which was a sign in and of itself.

Daytime television then was full of depictions of true crime stories about children who had disappeared and would be found later, dead or alive, but most certainly molested. I had hardly ever watched daytime TV before this, but as things progressed, I found myself slipping into an entirely different country.

That day, I was watching one of those shows. Before, I had always found it odd, if fascinating, when parents would preserve the rooms of their dead or missing children for years. "Just in case," I remember one mother said, as she fingered the Oakland Raiders flag hanging above her son's bed. "He will be so happy to see this."

The father got up off the twin bed and held out his hand to her. The camera kept running as the door closed behind them, then drifted around the room to the son's trophies, his rollerblades, a battered old bear stuffed on a bookcase.

In the past, that would have been the moment when I would have changed the channel, irritated with the obvious level of denial the parents were showing.

But that day, laying on the bed, I just kept watching. Suddenly there was no line between me and those mothers whose children had disappeared but who just put one day after another and kept going, waiting for that vibrant little being to return. My ass was thin, my hair brittle, a river of red bumps was running up the insides of my thighs, itching. I'd even had a little diarrhea, when we had first come home from the trip. I told myself, lots of people get a little upset by having different water.

But of course, that was my own denial.

I was disappearing too, cell by cell.

The doctor ordered more blood tests.

In the meantime, he wanted me to consider trying ddi. According to him, most of my symptoms at that point were probably medication-related. I just seemed to be one of those people who didn't do well with AZT.

I liked the idea that medication was my big problem. My "manna" had become "fucking-AZT," a curse word, said all in one breath. Jay and I both had begun to swear more when we spoke of things related to the virus, as if that could make it get out. Sometimes, I would even catch myself bargaining with it, but then I would use an almost prayerful tone.

"If we could just arrive at a balance, we could both have a long life," I would hear myself saying. "But you can't be greedy. If you have to have it all, you'll end up with nothing."

Then, I would revert to swearing: "Fucking murderer. It's your suicide." As if it cared.

39

JUST A FEW WEEKS BEFORE JAY'S BIRTHDAY, Michael asked if I was planning anything special for him. Embarrassed, I confided that I was having trouble coming up with ideas. "He keeps this file of articles about places he wants to go, but there are so many. Somehow nothing seems right to me—though it's not really about me, is it?" I was trying to keep my tone light, but the truth was, I just wanted to stay home alone with Jay, having candles and a cake, pretending that this was just one birthday in a long life of them. The feeling that this event could be the last was creeping into everything we did now. I don't know if Jay felt it then, but it was beginning to exhaust me. I longed for the mundane, for just a few no-big-deal hours. Such extravagance!

"It sounds like you do have ideas," Michael said slowly. "Maybe you just need a little extra time to decide."

Time or energy? I couldn't seem to get myself over the hump of a number of decisions these days, even simple ones, like what to eat for dinner.

Sometimes, I didn't seem to care at all.

But that was nothing I would say to him, really.

"Let me know if you get any bright ideas," I told him. "I'm open to suggestions."

When he called a few days later to invite us to join him for a bayside breakfast in Sausalito, I was relieved. Jay and I would have our evening at home, but there would be an outing, too. I knew he would be pleased. How could I begrudge that?

"We lucked out!" said Michael, greeting us at the café. Though it was early February, it was sunny and warm, with plum blossoms breaking open everywhere.

He led us to a table outside, right near the water, where we talked and shared photos as we waited for our food. We looked at snapshots of ourselves in Venice, and Michael showed us photos of himself with Noah at home, in the park, on the beach, and just Noah, with his mothers, his friends, his caretakers.

It was hard to believe that Michael was already shopping for pre-schools. He had continued to fill out around the middle, which only contributed to his aura of ebullience, though he did have a few dark circles under his eyes. It was hectic, he admitted, but worth it. His life meant something now, in a way he had never felt before. He hadn't been unhappy previously, but now he felt called upon to stretch, to sacrifice, to mature his focus beyond simply satisfying himself.

I stared out across the water toward Tiburon, where there were opulent houses and a speedboat smashing its prow up and down on the waves. Was I immature, or prematurely aged, I wondered, thinking about the careful balance of rest, exercise, good diet, and attitude that consumed my time each day.

Curbing myself, I brought my attention back to the table, where Jay was showing Michael a kit of child-sized but real tools we had ordered from a woodworking catalog for Noah.

"Is he too little for these?" Jay asked.

"Not with supervision," said Michael, picking up the miniature saw, laying its blade on his palm. "These are so great! He's going to go out of his mind! How did you even find such a thing? Every kid needs an aunt or uncle who has time to track down this sort of stuff."

"You seem to do fine," I said.

"I don't know about that. But a ratio of three parents to one child usually helps."

Michael paused, and looking at his hands, added, "Though sometimes it can be more difficult. Right now, we're having trouble agreeing on the right school, but if we give it some time, I'm sure it will work out."

Tilting back in his chair, he turned his face to the sun, closing his eyes. I took a sip of my fresh-squeezed orange juice and looked across at a young woman reading a book at the next table.

Give it some time.

The same words that my doctor had used when suggesting the new medication.

But lately, I had a sense of things speeding up. I wasn't sure if it was life itself or my life, but ever since the trip, things seemed to be running through me in a blur. At work, just the past week, I had begun writing down book names or numbers whenever people came to me with a request—simple requests, ones I would have been able to hold in my mind not that long ago. I was aware of watching the lips of the person as he or she spoke, noting if they were full or dry or an unusual tint, as if that might help me retain the information better, but even when I wrote down a name, my mind couldn't hold an impression. Little seemed to attach itself. I had an image of pollen falling off a stamen onto the white calyx of a lily, then sliding off. The image was beautiful, but the feeling frightened me. It took so much effort and energy to hold each detail of a moment in place, sharp as a single blade of grass, never mind the whole lawn. All that green that had once accumulated within me in a wide happiness, an assumption of continuity spreading below the level of consciousness.

When did I begin to lose it? I turned back to my conversation with Michael and Jay that had already moved on and was now in the middle of talk about a movie whose name I didn't know, so I tried to content myself with listening. As I looked at their faces, they each suddenly appeared to me as if from a distance, as strangers, as men whom I might be drawn to, men who seemed very companionable with each other. I let them go on that way for some time. There was a bittersweetness to it, as if I had gone somewhere else, by myself, and was looking back at them.

"Should we go for a walk?" asked Michael, shooting me a conspiratorial look. I had no idea what was up, but it was clearly some birthday doings, so I made the appropriate noises.

We wandered together out onto the sunny road lined on each side by warehouses and work buildings. Jay did a double take.

"I thought it looked familiar around here. There's Heath Ceramics!" he said. "Where I got the tiles for the house. They hand-make everything—dishes and tiles!"

"And they just happen to have a factory tour in fifteen minutes," announced Michael, looking at his watch.

"You fox!" said Jay, locking Michael's head in the crook of his elbow. "You had all this planned."

We were both impressed. I loved the sea-green tiles Jay had chosen for his renovation. Now that we were here, entering the showroom, I vaguely recalled that there had been something special about how the tiles had been made, but obviously Michael had picked up on Jay's enthusiasm in a way that I had not. I felt both grateful and envious.

Jay pointed to several long tables where stoneware plates and bowls had been set out by the dozens. "I love these."

That surprised me. The Heath plates were understated, modern—very different from the colorful Spanish plates we had bought together on impulse at Macy's several years before. Brimming with hand-painted apples, grapes, and lemons, those had reminded me of abundance and warmth and a certain gleam in Jay's eye when he was happy. Jay had seemed content to buy them, but now, I could see he was truly enamored of these.

"I thought I knew you!" I teased. "Do you really like these? They seem so, I don't know, basic. Were you just humoring me when we got our dishes?"

"I didn't mind," he said.

"But I thought you liked them."

"They're fine. I just like these too."

"Tell me what you like about them," I said. I really wanted to know. At that point, their charm was beyond me. They reminded me of his mother's beige raincoat.

"They're all handmade," he said, lining up two plates. "They look exactly alike, but they're also each unique in some small way. Yet what you feel is the sameness. It's really hard to create that. At least it's hard for me to do that, when I work with wood. So, all these repeating circles—it just seems like a daredevil effort to me."

I reconsidered the long table.

"Plus, it's made with California clay, by local people."

Michael brought over a pamphlet, pointing to a photo of an old woman at a potter's wheel.

"Now that's a girl who loved going round and round," he said.

The photo was of Edith Heath, now in her eighties. Jay and Michael stood reading the brochure for a few minutes, shoulder to shoulder, while I hovered nearby, keeping an eye on the door where the tour would begin. Finished with the pamphlet, they began to chum around the table together, playfully trying out place settings in various colors. They seemed to have forgotten about me, but now, instead of the bittersweet feeling that had come over me in the restaurant, I turned away, nursing a flicker of jealousy as I pretended to study a display about Heath family history.

"Interesting, isn't it?" asked Michael, coming up behind me. He rarely got on my nerves, but there was something in his tone that seemed to imply he thought I needed help feeling included.

Fuck off, I wanted to say, surprised by my own crankiness.

But I kept my mouth shut, concentrating instead on the price of a pitcher, as if the curve of the numerals could bend me away from my own distemper. Too much, I thought. Feeling piqued like this took too much energy. Everything had its price these days, even a mood. How much would this one cost me in good cells?

"Jay's the one who's into this stuff," I finally said, setting down the pitcher.

Jay and others in the showroom were wandering toward a woman in knee-high boots who had just announced the tour was forming.

"I'd like to get him something," Michael whispered to me hastily. "Maybe that vase he just put down. Would you distract him after the tour?"

The same idea had been forming in my own mind, but more slowly.

"Okay," I said, trying not to feel pre-empted. "I'm going to get him something too."

"Good!" said Michael. "We can team up. Most people have more than one dish."

The tour group started into the factory, and I perversely let them go, delaying myself, almost daring them to go on without me. My whole body felt obstinately leaden. This was what it was going to be like, I told myself. More and more, as the disease fed on me. The fear of not being able to keep up swept through me, but this time, instead of fighting it, I sampled it, standing alone now in the showroom as the group disappeared around the corner, their voices still echoing in the room, particularly Michael's.

It had never occurred to me: Michael and Jay. Not in this way.

Would that be so bad, after I was gone?

Don't do this to yourself, I told myself, even as I edged further into the fantasy. Michael's belly, thick now. Amplitude. Him taking off his shirt, and Jay, some relief rising. Not to see flesh so tight against the ribs.

Stop this, I told myself, my chest constricting. Let them enjoy themselves. I refuse to be a burden.

I began walking slowly now toward the rear of the group, through a room smelling of damp raw clay. By the time I drew up next to the two of them, I was able to nod their way, continuing to regard them as if I weren't present. There was Jay, listening intently to the guide, obviously pleased to learn about processing vats, autojiggers, drying rooms, and kilns. Michael, standing slightly behind, was interested too, but I could see that he was even more satisfied by his own good idea to come here. I didn't like it, but some dark star seemed to be sucking any passion from me. I could feel the dampness of the room rising up through the soles of my boots, chilling my bones, but somehow I no longer seemed to be wrapped around them.

Where was I? The sight of machines, the sound of a blower, the grayness of floors, sheet metal, clay—sensations were streaming through me as the tour moved on, past work stations and machines.

I knew I was sick now, not just in my body, but also my mind.

Spotting a restroom, I ducked into it, splashing some water on my face, looking at myself in the mirror. I was very pale. Grabbing my cheeks, I began to squeeze, harder and harder until my eyes brimmed.

"You're not going to do this to me, you fuckers," I muttered, staring into my black pupils as if they were nuclei of the virus itself.

As I waited for the color in my cheeks to disperse, an inarticulate resolve welled up in me—for what, I didn't know—but when I walked back to the group, I felt propelled by it.

The group was gathered now around a young tattooed Asian worker who was turning a large bowl. He had beautiful smooth muscular arms, angular fingers. As the rim grew wider and wider, everyone stared, mesmerized, including Michael and Jay, who were directly opposite me. They were both holding their breath—I could feel it in my own body. We were all waiting to crest the rim, the whole group, and it suddenly felt very intimate. Everyone clapped when the worker brought it off, so to speak. A little mood of celebration swept through the whole group. Michael turned to talk to a guy next to him, while Jay stood, alone in his thoughts, still watching the young man as he carefully cut the bowl from the wheel. Suddenly the tightness that had been in my chest for hours gave way, as I took it in at a glance: Michael, single, here with us as a supportive friend, striking up with the guy next to him; Jay, concentrating on just being here, in the present, enjoying his birthday; me, angry at my weakening ability to hold onto life. Would there be a way to die without killing the love in me first, I wondered.

Maybe nothing, in fact, had changed inside me since I had been with Jay, I thought. Maybe I hadn't moved from where I had been after my parents died. Had I only filled the hole with the contentments of being with Jay? As I stood looking at him, at the lines of his hair, lips, throat, shoulders, chest, I felt at once as if I knew every inch of him, yet didn't really know him at all. Had I ever really loved him just for himself?

He must have felt me looking at him, for he looked over at me. I held his eyes. He returned my gaze with a slightly mystified expression, as if sensing the sea-change within me.

There was still time to love him for himself, I told myself. I could do better.

40

THAT JUNE, JAY BECAME ELIGIBLE for health insurance. At last he could go to a doctor. But still he delayed.

"You have to respect my intuition about this," he told me, in a discussion that sounded more reasoned than either of us probably felt. "Trust me," he said.

"It's the virus I don't trust," I pointed out. "You should at least get a T-cell count, rather than relying on wishful thinking."

"Well, that seems to be working so far. Don't fix what ain't broke. I promise I'll go when I need to."

He stood and began to tidy up some newspapers. I sat, watching him. He did look better these days, now that he had quit doing so much physical labor. He even seemed happy inside his skin. For a moment, I let myself be lulled, just to savor the feeling of all being well.

But I knew this was dangerous.

"Jay, I need you to go," I said, summoning my resolve.

He locked his hands behind his head, grimacing.

"You forget that I was sitting right there at your last appointment," he said. "Your own doctor agreed that none of the current medications work well."

He had me there.

And so, I took what was available, and Jay didn't. And paradoxically, Jay appeared healthy, while I didn't. Meds, no meds, new meds—it was all such a crap shoot. Some of our friends swore they were alive because they avoided standard treatment; others died waiting to get into trials for new drugs. Jay had faith in the canniness of his own immune system. How was I to know if that faith in and of itself wasn't the most powerful tool?

I resisted my impulse to pressure him further. He had been respectful of my choices so far and was all for *me* trying any treatment I could, if my doctor thought it made sense. In fact, he was a much more aggressive researcher into the topic than me.

Each day now, I was ripping open packets of ddi, mixing the white sweet powder of hope with plain tap water (filtered, of course). People complained about having to wait thirty minutes after taking it before eating, but I didn't mind. To me there was something subliminally reassuring about watching the clock for that half-hour. Somehow it gave me a feeling that there was time, and it was mine, at least for those thirty minutes. A simplistic fix, perhaps, but it seemed to ripple out into my day, and for a while, I was buoyed up. My T-cells were still above the two-hundred mark, and neither of us had any opportunistic infections—at least, none that we knew about. It was early summer again.

We said the word "again," again and again, savoring it.
Would you like to go for a hike at Mount Tam again?
Dinner at Ma Tante Sumi again?
You want me to slip my hands inside your trousers—again?

We took all the moments of assurance we could get.

〰〰〰

One day, in September, as I climbed up Corona Heights to survey the city, I noticed I was short of breath, but I didn't think too much about it. After a sequence of sunny still days, air pollution was high. Even so, it felt good to be out after work, inhaling the fragrance of the dry grass on the golden hill. It was always a joy to catch a few rays before the fog rolled in. And somehow, because I had been allowing myself to feel more hopeful lately, the clarity of that late afternoon seemed even brighter.

Just recently, I had begun a treatment to prevent pneumocystis pneumonia, or PCP, as it had come to be known. All I had to do was drop by the hospital once a month and spend fifteen minutes in a recliner, inhaling an aerosolized medicine. The room was sunny; the nurses were warm; there was rarely a wait. And the statistics were good! AIDS deaths due to PCP were dropping. Suddenly, there was something easy I could do, with no apparent side effects.

Except one excellent one. Convinced at last that medicine might have something to offer, Jay decided to see a doctor soon. He'd been making calls, talking to friends and acquaintances, getting the latest scoop on whom to go to. I hadn't realized how deeply my worries for him had lodged in my body, until his outlook had changed.

But things were not to calm down for long. In fact, despite my good mood, by the time I made it to the tall steps of splintering railroad ties on the east side of the hill, I was very winded. Soon I would be more worried about myself than Jay.

Yet, as I paused at the overlook facing downtown, my hunger for air in that moment mixed with my renewed desire for more of everything. It was a golden late afternoon. As the angle of the light shifted downward, the blue of the sea intensified. Everything seemed so poised, balanced.

By the next morning we were locked in fog. At work I began to feel something was wrong with the heating system; I was hot all morning. By noon I suspected it was me. At lunch I bought a thermometer and checked myself out. No big deal: 100 degrees. But I thought I better call the doctor. He told me to come in right away and pick up a lab slip.

"Just to be conservative," he said.

When I got there, there was a slip for a chest X-ray, as well as the expected blood work. After the X-ray, I was sent back to the waiting room. A few minutes later, a technician came out and told another man he could go home.

"I hope it's the same for you," the guy said, breaking into a wide grin as he hugged his motorcycle helmet in his arm. "They can't tell you the results, but if they send you home, it's good news."

As I waited some more, I thought about calling Jay, but part of me just wanted to do this without making a big deal out of it. I played out our upcoming conversation at dinner, one in which I would mention almost casually the unanticipated events of the day, and how they had ended well. I had heard other men talk in this way, with a stoicism or courage that I had imagined would escape me, but now that I was sitting here, doing it, I could see that there wasn't another choice, really. I flipped through a magazine, remembering the pan of lasagna I had left out on the counter to thaw, the fresh vegetables I would need to pick up on the way home.

That strange sense I'd been having lately of everything speeding up came back to me again when a physician ducked in, glancing around the room. He called my name. My heart dropped. Did this mean I had PCP? I fumbled with my things, then followed him to a consulting room. Despite my dread, I was taken with how charming he was, so much more comfortable with small talk than my regular doctor. It was almost a pleasure to be led down that corridor by him, even though some part of me knew I would not come back the same, that this was one of those moments that would stand out as the fulcrum between before and after.

"The X-ray looks a little suspicious," he said, closing the door of his office. "Nothing definite yet, though. Have you had a cough?"

"Not really. I have been a little winded, but no big deal. If it weren't for the fever, I wouldn't have thought much about it."

"Well, we'll see," he said. "Maybe there will be good news. We need to do a bronchoscopy to really know."

He pulled out some papers.

"If you do have PCP, you would be a good candidate for a blind test we are doing. We'll have caught it early, and hopefully can nip it in the bud. It's an opportunity to receive some treatment, regardless, but some people with AIDS have an allergic reaction to one of the medications. You won't know which one you get, but if you take the Septra, and if you're allergic, you'll know it at about day ten. We'll suppress the reaction with Benadryl, and get you through this."

He sat back, watching my face carefully. His warmth and confidence flowed into me. He wanted to help. I signed the papers at once, then used his phone to call Jay.

I don't remember our conversation at all now, except that I encouraged Jay to finish his shift. I had no doubt that he was there for me. We agreed that there was really nothing he could do here yet—he couldn't sit through the test with me. Better that he hang on to his sick days.

"Just tell him to pick you up," the doctor said. "You won't even remember the test."

As I put on the gown, crawled onto the cart, waited to be wheeled to the procedure room, I was full of energy, almost tremulous. A fluorescent light above me was on the fritz, making an awful buzz that seemed part and parcel of the agitation inside me. At some point I just got up, walked over, and turned it off. How could I be sick? The sense of fatigue I had been living with off and on for the past few years was suddenly gone, was burning up in the fire of adrenaline rushing through me. When they finally came for me, I was even jovial with the aide, joking with her as she wheeled me down the hall to the procedure room. It seemed silly to be riding like that, IVs in my arm. I thought of an illustration of Gulliver

I used to look at as a kid. All the Lilliputians scaling those giant limbs, tying him down with what seemed like threads.

The next thing I recall was being told by a woman in scrubs that I had PCP.

"But how can you tell that without a test?" I asked her groggily. She put her hand on my shoulder.

"It's all over," she told me, smiling.

"It can't be, not that fast!" I struggled to sit up.

"Yes. I mean, no. The test is all over. You were awake the whole time—but the drug makes you forget."

Laying back, I said the words aloud, testing them against my inner sense. "I have PCP."

Still dopey, I actually started to laugh. "Isn't that a veterinary drug teenagers used in the seventies? I was never into that."

"That's good," said the charming doctor, who I suddenly realized was standing at a nearby counter, writing.

He came over and peered at me, smiling kindly. "People who don't do drugs have better immune systems. You seem in pretty good shape to beat this thing. I have a feeling you're going to perform well on the medication, no matter which one you get," he said, handing me my first packet of pills.

"So, hang on tight," he said, eyes bright as he closed his hand over mine.

I stared up at him a second. My regular doctor was such a cold fish, even if he did seem to know his stuff. I knew nothing about this guy's reputation, but based on eye contact, I was willing to meet him anytime, anywhere.

"Can I see you again?" I asked. I knew he knew I was flirting a bit, and I guessed he had seen this before, over and over. An attempt to joke in the face of bad news.

"I will definitely see you again. In fact, as soon as you can get dressed. And you're going to be back here every two days so we can monitor your liver. But your regular doc will continue to be your primary care person."

"You mean, I'm going home?"

"You're getting your ass out of here, so you can get some rest.

"You're the same person, in the exact same condition that you were in when you walked in the door," he added. "With this medicine, we're just calling in more troops. Here," he said, reaching for his phone and plopping it down in front of me.

"Call whoever you need to, so you can get going."

As soon as we got home, Jay installed me under a mound of quilts in the bedroom. Neither of us said the word "AIDS," but we both knew what my doctor had confirmed: that having PCP meant that I now would qualify for that diagnosis.

Michael showed up shortly afterward with a bag full of Chinese takeout. I had no memory of calling him from the hospital, but evidently, I had.

"I'm not surprised," he said. "You told me three times you had PCP, then you explicitly asked for hot and sour soup."

"I did? That's nervy, not to mention particular. All I can remember is the doctor."

"He's been talking about him all the way home," said Jay, teasingly rolling his eyes as the two of them began setting up tray tables next to the bed.

"I don't need to eat in here," I said, shoving the covers back. "I'm still the same person I was this morning."

Jay straightened up, surveying the scene. "You're right," he said. "I'm going overboard. But now that we have this all set up, can we just go ahead? I'm hungry."

Suddenly I realized they must both be famished; it was quite late. "Of course," I said, leaning back against the pillows, trying to be a good patient as I watched them dish out the food. The more my head cleared, the sillier I felt, laying there unnecessarily rumpled under the bedcovers.

Unable to stand it, I got up, washed my hands, combed my hair. With the lights down low, I still looked reassuringly like myself in the bathroom mirror. The paleness and dull thinning hair that had bothered me for the past few years didn't seem so bad anymore, especially on a night that could have been spent in a hospital. Just a few years before, I would probably have been struggling under an oxygen mask, or hooked up to a ventilator. I took a deep breath, detecting only a slight tightness in my chest. It was no different than what I might have felt after a stressful day. I was so lucky, the nurse had said. "We" had caught it early, before I had grown weak.

Her use of the word "we" had warmed me then and was with me now as I rejoined Michael and Jay, who had turned on the evening news. I pulled up a chair and picked up the bowl of soup they had already ladled out for me. For a while I just held it under my nose, letting the fragrant steam bathe my airways. As we sat crammed in our little circle together, every mouthful, every utterance, was a gift. I had a feeling now not only of having crossed a line—but of going beyond it. This was more, this was extra.

I thanked Michael and Jay for being there, several times. On the third time, Jay rested his chin on his hand and gave me a quizzical look.

"What?" I asked. Suddenly I became aware of both of them gazing at me with intense love and affection.

"We're really glad *you're* here, too," said Jay. "Do you *know* that?"

I nodded. Barely able to meet their eyes, I started stacking the empty bowls.

"I think I should probably turn in now," I said.

"That's a good idea," said Jay, taking the dishes.

For some time, I lay drifting in and out, happy to just sleep, to not think, to take comfort in being home, in hearing the two men I loved most talking quietly in the other room.

When I woke later that night, Jay was curled around me. Of course, I had not forgotten my situation, but for a while I just lay watching the shifting branches of a nearby plum cast shadows on the window screen. A subtle brightness was filling the room, and it filled me too.

Jay was sleeping with his arm over me, and I took his hand, stroking the tufts of hair on the backs of his fingers. In all likelihood, the branches outside the window would outlast us both. I pulled the covers closer around us, trying to reabsorb the spell of the moonlight, but it looked cold now, and my throat felt unusually dry. I realized I had been breathing directly onto our intertwined hands, unconsciously enjoying some relief as the moisture of my own exhalations bounced back to me.

"Jay," I whispered, moving his hand away and letting go.

He propped up immediately, turning on the bedside lamp, then peering over my shoulder. Gently, he tried to peel back the covers from my face so he could see me better.

"Don't!" I said, covering my mouth with a balled-up wad of sheet.

"Don't what? What's the matter?"

"What are you doing in bed with me?" I said, voice muffled.

He paused, still hovering, then spoke in a cautious tone, as if talking to someone much older or younger.

"Well, we're trying to get some rest, and we're giving your medicine time to work . . ."

He slid in behind me again.

"You're stiff as a board," he said, rubbing my chest.

I cleared my throat several times.

"I'll get you some water," he offered.

As he started to rise, I rolled over, reaching for him, catching the back of his T-shirt.

"It's okay," he said, turning to me. Half-exasperated, half-pleading, we searched each other's faces.

"I'm not going anywhere," he said, taking my hand off the back of his shirt and firmly holding it between his.

Neither of us moved for quite some time. Eventually I withdrew my hand.

"Jay," I said. "I don't think we should sleep together. I don't want you to breathe any droplets. Help me find the sleeping bag, then go wash your hands."

I struggled with the covers to get out of bed. He sat back down on the edge.

"This is for shit," he said, hunkered over with elbows on his bare thighs and hands hanging between his knees. "I haven't heard you cough once tonight. Or all week, for that matter. If I was going to get this, I would have it already. These germs are around all the time, and normal people fight them off. My system must be in good enough shape to do that."

"If you think that, then you have shit for brains," I said, my head popping out of my sweatshirt as I pulled it on.

He glared around the room at nothing in particular. "You worry too fucking much. What do you think that does to you? You need to rest."

I glared back at him, incredulous.

"What?" he said, defensively.

"I can't believe you think my attitude is what's making me sick," I said, standing up. I turned my back to him, biting the insides of my mouth as I stared up at a spider on the ceiling. My breath sounded loud in my ears. I'm just ticked off, I told myself, noting that my heartbeat was loud, too.

After a few minutes, Jay leaned forward, wrapping his arms around my waist, drawing me to him. I hugged his hands to my belly, letting out a deep breath as he pressed the side of his face against my lower back.

"Just for tonight . . . Can we just lay down and try to get some sleep?" he said, in a tone close to exasperation. "Tomorrow we can figure this out, we can call your doctor and find out if this is something we even need to worry about."

I turned toward him, hugging his head against me.

"I'm not going to be a cad and let you be in here all by yourself," he said, getting up and going to wash his hands. Then he crawled back into bed, holding out a freshly-scrubbed paw to me. I raised my eyebrows. He stared at me blankly, then realized what he was doing.

"Okay, I really do have shit for brains," he said, shoving his hand under his armpit. "At least I'm warm," he said, casting an inviting look as he turned and faced the wall.

I lay down too, pushing my back up against his. After a while, he reached behind, tucking his hand under my hip. I reached over, too, sliding my hand under him. For a long time we floated that way, holding each other up. Just as I was about to drift off, I heard him murmur, almost inaudibly, "I'm not letting you go anywhere without me."

Then, like a freezing man in a blizzard, unable to resist the allure of sleep, I let myself descend.

For the next ten days or so, I slept in, head buried in a mound of pillows. When I woke, I would pull Jay's pillow to me and press my cheek against the cool cotton, inhaling his scent, reassured that I still could.

Then I would rise, strip off the pillowcase, and toss it in the hamper.

Jay would already be at work. He tried to act like he wasn't anxious about leaving me, but he called frequently. When I would probe how he was doing, he would veer off into telling me how things were at work, then returned as quickly as possible to the topic of what I was doing. So, I told him what was on the news, or what I had excavated from the freezer for our meal, or what photos I was digging out of our drawers, intending to put them into albums. Our conversations seemed superficial, but apparently left us both feeling more balanced.

After his call, I would lay around in bed again, feeling more torporous than ill. It was strange not to get up and go to work. There, at the reference desk, I had become accustomed to answering other peoples' questions. Whether they wanted to know about antique clocks, or the history of rubber tires, I was someone who could point them in the right direction. Now, the questions I faced came from within me. Would I ever get well again? When I did, what would I be doing with my life? Should I still be a librarian? Was there something else that would be important for me to do?

I stared out the window for long lost moments, watching drops of rain form on the birch tree like glass buds. Some would hang for a long time; others would be flung off so quickly, it was as if they had never been.

41

Jay and I continued to sleep in the same bed. My doctor had said there was no proven reason not to do so. That's what they believed about PCP in those days. The handsome nurse with lustrous dark eyes at the drug trial clinic concurred. "Affection is good for combating infection. Just be safe, okay?" I enjoyed a little fantasy about him taking his own advice.

"I'm going to be your person here at the study," he went on, looking at me from under a shock of glossy black hair. "Whatever you need, you come to me first."

I blushed. Then he snapped on his gloves, getting ready to draw blood, and my little scenario vanished as quickly as it had come.

Rolling up my sleeve, I turned my head the other way.

At home, the word "snuggle" entered our vocabulary. It was both embarrassing and tender.

We told each other that we were too fatigued to do much else. That it was good to build up some chi.

Yet, as we waited to see if my medicine was going to work, we were each filled with a strange sense of being on the move, a sort of blind excitement—almost decisively ignorant of the direction in which we were going.

I went to the clinic almost daily. Each time, Jay offered to drive me, but I insisted that I could take myself. We both knew without saying that it was best for him to hang on to his sick time at work.

After a few days, I began to walk to the clinic, then take myself out to lunch at the Cove, or Café Flore. Not wanting to worry Jay, I didn't tell him. I liked getting around on my own steam, at least for an hour or so in the Castro. I wasn't doing anything juicier than getting some protein-supplement drinks, but truth be told, I liked having a little secret, something that was just me, mine. I was surprised when after a week or so, the clinic doctor told me that I was ready for a few ten minute walks per day. He was not pleased when I informed him of my adventures.

"Ever heard of just giving it a rest?" he said. "Why don't we see what happens if you let your body do the work for you, instead of you trying to control everything. You need to get better at doing nothing."

I turned red. He had my number. Walking up the hill to the hospital had become my way of checking the tightness in my chest, of gauging the progress of my treatment.

Visitors began to come. Knowing that they were taking time out of their busy day, I felt awkward, more lazy than sick.

"Get over yourself," said Betsy, waving me off as she dumped a bag of *People* magazines on the couch.

"I must be in bad shape, if you're bringing me these," I joked. Betsy was my friend with whom I shared a love of Basho and Japanese death poems.

"They're left over from my office waiting room," she said flatly, not taking the bait. Triviality was not her forté, but she went on to do her best to engage us both in tidbits of sensational gossip. An unfamiliar role for her, it was nonetheless touching.

"Superficiality suits you more than I would have thought," I teased, rescuing us both by getting up to make tea. Her face colored with relief and vitality.

"Well, now that we've dispensed with that, how *are* you?" she asked, with the authority of real interest. Stolid in her chair, she seemed willing and capable of waiting forever for my answer, no matter how uncomfortable it might be for either of us.

I shrugged. "Waiting to see if I'm going to be allergic to the medicine."

"That's a drag," she said, looking down at her hands, respecting my vulnerability.

"It must be hard to rest," she ventured.

"Actually, I'm tired of it," I said. "I feel guilty, sitting home, playing with the computer, doing a few little chores."

We paused, watching the honey spiral from the spoon into her tea.

Giving me a soft half-glance, she pressed on. "I've been thinking about how young you were when your parents died. Death is so unreal for most of us at that age. But you must have felt it in your bones, right down to the marrow. I didn't catch that chill until my hysterectomy. I haven't been able to shake the feeling ever since."

She flushed. I knew it was difficult for her to say this sort of thing, especially to a man. It had been her partner who dropped hints about Betsy's past, something about a drunken father and a blue couch. I had felt so trusted, even privileged, when Betsy had asked me to be the one to give her a ride home from the hospital after the surgery. She was obviously ill at ease alluding to her problem even now, two years later. Yet, on my behalf, she was pushing through that discomfort, refusing to let it stop her. I wished she knew how beautiful she was.

Undoing the cellophane on a box of cookies, I held it open to her as she continued.

"I guess what I'm wondering is, given everything, do you find yourself bracing all the time?"

Her question went straight to my heart. As I sat tracing the lines on my palm with my thumb, memories kept rising. How Jay and I had each learned of our diagnoses, our hikes up Mt. Tam, many ordinary days. It was easy to prey upon any moment of pleasure, clinging to it as though it were the last. It was true that my history had left me all the more prone to doing so. Even then, right there, I was casting my eyes around the kitchen, touching on the blue fruit bowl I had given Jay all those years ago, in Detroit. To the left, my mother's pitcher; the photos on our fridge; Jay's father's beer stein. All these things we had saved, despite how fragile they were.

I looked at Betsy, shrugging. "I don't know. Something is different now . . ."

Betsy wrapped the string of her tea bag around the spoon, squeezing all she could out of the bag as she waited.

Suddenly I remembered my first night with Jay—our eyes meeting over the escargot at Thom and Clive's, our ride through the snow to my flat, the friction of his chest on my back. The one moment I would never choose to forgo was either one in which he in all likelihood had passed the virus to me—or the only occasion in which we had both been HIV-free.

Unable to sit any longer, I stood up, clasping my hands behind my head, stretching. I was not going to let this moment collapse into regret. There was a sign in a cottage window up on Lower Terrace Street. "Life is sexually transmitted." I called it to mind, holding it as a shield.

"Am I always bracing? Not anymore. Not all the time," I said, leaning against the counter, letting the words find me. "I guess now it's more like learning to live with things that can't be undone."

Betsy looked straight at me then. Both of us were still. I thought of the blue couch in her life, the blue bowl in mine. I imagined that we were each feeling the current of change in ourselves and each other, that very instant—one that must have been underway for a while, but was still untested and fragile. In the tenderest of ways, we each said nothing, giving the other room to grow.

"Thank you," I told her, stumbling around for words.

"I better go," she said, picking up her coat. Then taking three cookies, she gave me a closed-lip smile over her shoulder.

Heartened by my own visits with friends, I urged Jay to get in touch with some of the guys from his former support group. Perhaps he would be more inclined to air out some of his own concerns with other people.

Initially he brushed off my suggestion, joking that he was less stressed than usual because I was home now, doing the housework.

But he did make a few calls. It turned out that a handful of members still met. They were delighted to welcome him back. He began going to their gatherings, after which he came home and reported on the various health strategies that they vetted or embraced. Soon he was filling a bowl each day with a newly revised regimen of vitamins and supplements.

"Aren't you proud of me?" he asked one night.

I nodded.

But a few days later, when he came home with a bottle of colloidal silver, I began to grow uneasy. Though a number of positive people had begun taking it for its alleged antibiotic properties, putting metal into the soft tissues of the body just didn't make sense to me.

"It wouldn't be on the market if it were harmful," he said, pouring some into a spoon. "It's just a supplement, not a drug."

"Which means it probably isn't even tested for safety," I argued. "How can you have faith in that, yet be so skeptical of other medicine? At least drugs are subjected to some sort of trial."

"Silver is a *noble* metal," he said, striking a mock-dignified profile. "You should remember that from middle-school science class."

I stared at him, appalled by his light tone. I spoke stiffly.

"If I recall my chemistry properly, if a substance is noble, doesn't that mean it doesn't change? When are you going to go to a real doctor?"

I hadn't meant to be so cutting, but it was too late. I couldn't take it back. I knew he had just said what he'd said to be flip, so why was this getting under my skin?

He turned away, tipping the spoon into his mouth, then wiping his lips on his shirtsleeve.

"Well, then," he said sarcastically. "Since silver doesn't change, maybe it will at least make me more reliable for you."

After which we each took off for a separate corner of the house.

Busying myself with meaningless chores, I fumed, wishing I could straighten things out alone, as he was likely to do. But eventually, I went to him, saying that he had been nothing but steadfast, especially over the past few weeks.

He frowned at the clock he was tinkering with.

"No big deal," he said, in a casual, perfunctory tone designed to put things to rest.

Unable to let myself off the hook, I stood awkwardly, hands in my pockets, staring down at the tiny screwdriver he was twisting.

He glanced up. "Really, it's okay. We're each doing the best we can, in our own ways."

He lowered his brow, focused now on pulling off the face of the clock.

Was that really all there was to it for him?

I felt ashamed. I hadn't meant to hurt him.

Or had I?

I didn't like feeling blown off when it came to decisions about his medical care. I wanted some control. What happened to him, happened to me. He had promised to see a physician, but now that I had PCP, he was apparently steering away from that again. Was I just supposed to bite my tongue? I'd read those stories about powders and potions from

God knows where being tainted with bugs and road dust and antlers of who-knew-what endangered species.

I leaned against the counter, arms crossed, lining up my toes to a seam between floorboards. He might be able to lose himself in fixing a damned clock, but I could not deny what was happening so easily.

Something in me began to distance.

42

A FEW DAYS LATER, CELIA, my British friend and colleague, dropped by. As we talked at length, I felt guilty about enjoying such conversational intimacy with her, while I was feeling so estranged from Jay. Greeting me in her usual manner, touching her cheek to mine, she stepped back, holding me at arm's length, frankly examining me. Lady Celia, I had dubbed her, the Midwesterner in me impressed by her posh accent and cosmopolitan tastes.

"So far so good," I told her, shaking myself loose and leading her to the kitchen table.

"I see," she said, adjusting her silk scarf over one shoulder of her black cashmere dress as she settled herself. She wasn't one to immediately affirm or contradict what you said about yourself. If I said I felt like shit, or a million dollars, she would just continue to look me up and down.

Left to stew in my own juices, I used to suspect her of mild cruelty, but eventually I learned to relax. She was, in fact, highly opinionated about many things, but she expected and wanted contradiction. She liked to be brought up against the edge of someone else's thinking, as a way to refine her own views. Making sharp-edged distinctions was her way of amusing herself and others. It was almost a sport for her, nothing personal. She was not without caustic sarcasm at times. But because I could see that she did this to protect a sensitive and passionate temperament, I could forgive her and even allow myself to be swept into the spirit of it. Underneath it all, she mostly just wanted to be enjoyed.

It wasn't long, however, before I was deep into my most irrational complaints about Jay.

"Actually, I'm quite pissed off," I said.

Celia egged me on. While not necessarily believing its vicissitudes, she was comfortable with anger.

I went on and on: the group was a bad influence on him, clearly violating my sense of what he needed. He was mine, and I wanted to keep it that way for as long as possible. But if he was going to keep following stupid death-defying routines, well, fuck him. Why did he always have to stress me out by being such an ignoramus?

"But don't you want him to be death-defying?" said Celia, skewering me with a twinkle in her eye.

"Fuck you, too," I said. "You get me all pumped up, then prick my balloon!"

"Oh good. I'm glad I was effective."

I laughed. I should have remembered that conversation rarely moved forward with Celia based on agreement. Otherwise she never would have stayed so long in her relationship with a woman for whom she seemed to feel passion but with whom she shared few companionable views or domestic routines. There were terrible rows. From time to time, each walked out on the other in restaurants, at the theater, even at social dinners with friends. Somehow, they always managed to come back together again.

"Here, I brought you this," she said, placing on the table an impeccably wrapped gift—Japanese washi paper, folded seams, a sprig of rosemary. "I thought you might be hungry for something that was a little sophisticated but that wouldn't take too much work."

I blushed. I never thought of myself as sophisticated, at least not in the way that she was.

But the book was one I had looked at before, in a local shop. *Van Gogh: The Complete Paintings*. On the cover, an orange setting sun blared through rows of willows, turning the twisted trunks blue. Suddenly I was taken back to that night years ago in the Valley of the Moon, when Jay and I had stood in a muddy vineyard trench, arms draped over each other. As we gazed at the entwined vines marching off into the dark by the hundreds, a chill had run through me then, too.

Quickly I moved on, flipping through the pages until I was stopped by *Orchard in Bloom*, its greens and rusts and vibrant yellows of April coherent on the page, easily absorbed, reminiscent to me of nothing except spring.

Celia spoke in a low gentle voice. "I thought you might be feeling rather shredded. And Vincent's paintings often seem a little shredded to me. I wanted to remind you that people see something beautiful in that, too."

And then she paused.

At a loss for words, I stared down at the page. I was grateful for the gift, of course, but even more for what she said.

"Jay is really there for you, isn't he?"

My eyes grew bright with tears. Realizing that what she said was true, I felt a prickling under my skin, then a wave of nausea, even guilt. While he was going off to work each day, pulling my weight as well as his, I was lounging around, bad-mouthing him, enjoying my visits with friends more than my evenings with him. Yet I resented the few hours he spent with guys from his group.

Celia tried to assuage me, saying that this crisis had opened up many couples to a larger community. I said I didn't feel like we were being opened up. I felt like we were being overturned and dumped out, our intimacy diluted or diverted. Later that afternoon, I called to apologize to her for my defensiveness.

"I'd feel the same way," she said. "It was my way of trying to be cheery."

"Something we're both so good at," I noted.

We shared a laugh filled with self-knowledge.

~~~~~

My relief was to be short lived.

On the tenth day of treatment, my prickliness became physical. What started as a warm tingling at the base of my spine spread rapidly into a full-blown rash. I now knew that I had been receiving Septra, not the new medication. This reaction was not uncommon, but I needed to get to the clinic for an antidote.

I called Jay at work.

"Oh no," he said, when he came in the door. Taking me in at a glance, he quickly averted his eyes.

Was I so hideous?

Checking my arms, I began to feel queasy.

"Where's your knapsack?" he asked. He was rushing around now, gathering up water bottles, snacks, my toothbrush, pills, and a razor.

I stood watching him, fists balled up inside my sleeves. Would all of this even be necessary? It hadn't crossed my mind that I might be hospitalized. In fact, I felt pretty sure that the clinic could deal with me, but clearly, to him, I looked bad.

"Here," he said, handing me a sweatshirt. I pulled it on, wishing I could just stay inside, covered up.

"I'm glad at least one of us is on the ball," I said.

He held the door open for me. "My group deserves the credit," he said. "Somebody made up a checklist for us to keep in our wallets."

I stopped short, turning even redder. The very people whom I had resented in the past were suddenly there in the living room, invisibly helping. What a prick I had been.

Still, what I wanted most just then was for Jay to have been able to look at me.

At the clinic, we waited for what felt like forever as the nurse checked the results of my recent tests.

"Why the fuck don't they do something?" Jay muttered. "All they have to do is take one look at you."

Under the fluorescent light of the exam room, my rash appeared even rosier. I kept digging my nails into my palm as if all my urges to scratch could be concentrated into a few square inches. But it only made me sweat, salting my already inflamed skin. Glancing at me briefly, Jay handed me a tissue for my forehead. Otherwise, he sat hunched forward, elbows planted on his thighs, magazine curled up in his hand as if he might need to bat someone or something away.

Finally, there was a knock on the door. Mario my handsome nurse with the glistening black forelock entered. He stuck out his hand to Jay, flashing his beautiful smile. Mario, with skin so fresh and gold. Jay, his sturdy lean legs stretched out in front of him, crossed at the ankles, scruffy boots tilting up in unintentionally sexy defiance. My clinic dream boy in the same room with my boyfriend! It was such an unexpected meeting of worlds, I forgot my own body for a few seconds—a welcome, if disorienting, relief.

Then, Mario began talking in extra-kind tones.

"Okay, Mr. Bill," he said. "We know from just looking at you that your liver is having a fit with the medicine, but now it's official. You must have been feeling really crappy these past few days. Nausea?"

"Not until a few hours ago," I said.

"Good. If you can hang with it, the doctor wants to treat you right through this. Keep you on Septra, but zap you with Benadryl to cut the allergic reaction. All right with you?"

I nodded.

Jay interjected, suspiciously eyeing the file on Mario's lap.

"What's the alternative?"

Mario bypassed the question.

"If he sticks with this regimen, he'll be done in another week and a half. His lungs already sound pretty clear."

I took a deep breath, glancing at Jay. He was staring at Mario.

"You're gonna get your boyfriend back," Mario said. "He looks like a werewolf at the moment, but he's a brave pioneer. Not everyone is willing to sign up for these clinical trials."

"I bet!" said Jay, now flat-out glaring as he made a rebuking little snort.

"Jay!" I said. I had never seen him be so mean to a stranger, at least not since the fire. "Mario is only trying to help."

"I know that!" he said. "I'm not stupid!"

As he struggled to regain his composure, Mario and I glanced at each other, then at our feet. There was a long pause. Then Mario began again, speaking softly.

"Actually, just to set the record straight, people are literally dying to get into trials like this," he said. "It's pissy for both of you to have to go through this, though. I'm really sorry."

The whole tenor in the room shifted. Jay shrugged, the tension in his body collapsing into exhaustion, maybe despair.

"So, let me ask you, Jay. Are you being treated? If your immune system is compromised, if you don't know what your situation is, you're more at a risk. Pentamidine inhalation is making a huge difference in terms of prevention. It's one of the few things we know works. I would be happy to make you some referrals."

Jay's face tightened up again. "I have my own advisors," he said, his voice going brittle and dry.

Mario had heard from me that this wasn't true. But it was clear that as long as Jay could not admit the need for help or comfort, nothing was going to get through. Mario turned to his chart notes, concern for us both written all over his face.

I fought back my tears, making a tentative move to take Jay's hand. He was folded up in his own arms, face ashen and glazed over. I knew then that it was viscerally coming home to him, perhaps for the first time, that both of us were going to die. If not now, then later, there would be nurses, medicines, a cold, fluorescent light flickering over a bed.

It was me who led him from the office.

The Benadryl was worse than the PCP, or so it seemed. The mere sight or smell of food was nauseating. Fatty, rich dishes would especially send me around the bend. I began to lose weight, though it did not become a spiral of its own momentum, at least not yet. Michael and Jay worked together to package up little containers of bland food that I could take out at will during the day and put in the microwave—a loathsome appliance we bought especially for the occasion. I pushed myself, trying to eat what they had prepared, and also to come up with dinners for Jay that would be tolerable for me to cook.

"You don't have to do this for me," he told me one night, stopping midway through his dinner of halibut with dill sauce.

"Yes, I do. I want to do it for you, but it's also good for me to do what I can. So, it's really for me," I said.

He eyed my barely touched plate of white rice.

"It really looks like it," he said, with a kind sarcasm.

"Don't look if you don't like what you see," I said, the words popping out of my mouth, seemingly nonsensical and coy.

Yet it was an odd thing to say. Jay glanced at me with a confused smile, then down at his plate. I could see that he was stung.

I didn't understand. And then the anger and fear bled through: *Don't look if you don't like what you see.* Suddenly it was all too obvious how much I still resented him, wanted to shame him, for not looking at me when I first got my rash. And now, he clearly felt terrible about something. He was just sitting there, hands flat on each side of his plate, cheeks reddening. I froze, afraid to reach out to him, afraid to hurt him further. I hadn't understood at all what it must be like to see one's beloved mottled, like a bruised plum. It was my turn to hang my head in shame.

When I looked up, he was still flushed but he was also gazing at me, waiting for me. Both of our faces were heated and bright with unhidden remorse.

When the infection and drug reactions finally cleared, it felt as if something between us cleared too. A cautious jubilance welled up in me, sweeping Jay into its stream. On his next day off, he proposed a drive to Bolinas, where we sat in the truck on a broken-topped lane near the lagoon, watching a seal flip and splash in the golden light of mid-November.

Even though I knew I was now probably more vulnerable to PCP, I felt surprisingly hopeful. I had met a dreaded foe and survived. Though my T-cells had dropped to double-digits, my primary care doctor noted that a number of his patients were doing inexplicably well with similar levels. Maybe I would be one of them. He was usually so understated and conservative, I believed him. Even during the PCP, I had never broken a fever over 100. If Michael and Jay hadn't been there to help, I could have done it on my own. Not only was I a victor, it seemed, but for the first time, I felt deep in my bones something that would once have come more naturally to Jay. Maybe I could be a conqueror, too, if only I could hang around long enough.

So that day, we were having a picnic in the truck, talking about this and that. As the water level in the lagoon dropped slowly, pulled by an almost imperceptible tide, my anxiety level dropped too. Conversation lapsed comfortably, and for a while we did nothing but watch the seal pop in and out of view as he made his way toward the open sea.

"I want to make an honest man of myself," Jay said quietly, out of the blue.

My heart skipped a beat, though somehow, I knew, he would not hand me bad news in this moment.

"I lied to Mario," he said. "I didn't have my own advisors then, as you well knew. But I did make an appointment, and I've had a couple of inhalation treatments . . ."

For once, I knew not to say anything yet. Jay drummed his fingers on the steering wheel for a few seconds, then unrolled the window, pointing to a heron lifting up on big wings.

I let out a sigh.

"Now I feel like I can really breathe," I said.

43

"WHY AM I SO EXHAUSTED?" asked Jay, after a few weeks of prophylaxis.

I had been worrying, too. He had the look of a beaten dog whenever he came home from the clinic. Yet nothing in his medical picture explained how badly he was feeling, not at that point. Though his tests showed that his T-cells were on the low side, things were much better than we had anticipated.

"Maybe it's stress," I said. "You've been worried, you've been carrying so much for us both."

He didn't deny this. Stripping down to his underwear, he lay on top of the covers, too tired, it seemed, to crawl underneath. His hipbones looked sharper than I could recall, his face seemed gaunt. I wondered how long he had been like this.

I lay down on my side next to him, placing my hand over his heart.

"Jay, I'm better," I told him firmly. "I'll be back at work soon. And you're reducing your vulnerability to PCP."

There was a pause. Neither of us voiced what must have come into both of our minds immediately: I'd gotten sick even though I'd been doing the prophylaxis.

Yet he didn't argue or go away. He curled up to me, hands between his knees, head on my shoulder. As I ran my fingers through his hair, I could feel him sink even lower.

"It's the beginning of the end . . . ," he said, in almost a whisper.

I stopped stroking his hair.

"You've been running your own war for a long time, with very few allies," I said as gently as I could.

"Yeah," he said. Then after a pause, added, "And you're Mr. Go-with-the-Flow."

There was that spark of chiding humor I loved and missed.

I was still a bit weak, but one morning as I watched the pale sunlight fan across the kitchen floor, I thought, that's me. My energy wanted to come out from behind the fog I had been in for almost two months. It was time for me to go back to work.

My internist cautioned against it. There were worse things than going on unpaid leave or disability, he told me. In the meantime, didn't the library allow workers to donate their own leave time to a colleague?

I understood his concerns, I said, but I was willing to take the risk. If anything happened, I wouldn't blame him.

He took off his glasses and squeezed his forehead. How many times a day did he have to deal with patients who couldn't or wouldn't take his advice? He looked tired, even lonely. I wondered if he himself was sick—if he had anyone at home to look after him. I was so lucky.

"It's not just the money," I said. "It's my turn to look after Jay. If I get back into the swing of things, maybe he will take care of himself for a change. As long as my energy holds, I'm up for that."

The doctor leaned back, surveying me.

"Well," he said finally, in a hesitant voice. "It can be medically advantageous to strengthen the spirit, too."

We smiled awkwardly at each other. I had never heard him use a word like "spirit." He seemed surprised, too, and even a little pleased.

I left his office like a horse out of the gate. At last I would be free of the narrow little box in which I had been living for the last two months. I could finally let in how much I had been missing the stimulation of the library—the casual conversations, even the commonplace irritations, with patrons whom I would never otherwise meet or care about. More than I knew, I had been missing my coworkers too, the book-talk we shared over lunch, the jokes, the gossip. Especially the gossip. For some, it was a high art, raised from the domain of liking or loathing, to an opportunity for bringing imagination and depth to the understanding of human foibles. I wanted back inside that hum and buzz.

And then there was the literature itself—the millions and maybe billions of words and pictures. In my anxious focus on my own body these past weeks, I had barely cracked a book, resorting instead to the distracting chatter of daytime TV. I looked forward now to the happily silent spaces of the library, cushioned by scores of shelves from the agitations of outside noise and inner fear. I longed for steadying work—the research into which books to acquire for the collection, which to weed out. It was a small power, but it was mine, and I liked it.

Watching the streetcar rumble by as I walked home from the doctor's, I pictured how I, too, would be riding the train within a day or two, pressed in with other commuters until the doors opened and I hurried off to the library.

Well, not exactly hurried.

I would have to leave more time, now. A wave of trepidation passed through me, but I cut it short, promising myself I wouldn't be foolish. Just as the doctor had admonished me to do, I would get my ass home whenever I felt fatigued; I would balance myself in whatever ways were needed.

Jay voiced no objections or support for my decision.

As I stood in front of the mirror on the morning of my return, I caught sight of Jay watching me as I adjusted my collar. I noted aloud that after weeks of hanging out in sweats and pajamas, my shirt with its thin stripes and ironed creases felt stiff.

"Good," he said, wrapping his arms around me from behind. "I like stiff."

It had been a long time. We held each other's eyes in the mirror as he unzipped my fly and I reached behind.

Every minute I was late was worth it.

Jay wanted to drive me, but wanting to resume my ordinary routines, I insisted on taking the train. We compromised, and he drove me the short distance to Castro Street Station.

As I fed my quarters into the turnstile, I remembered how clumsy I had felt when I had first tried to use public transportation after arriving here from the Motor City. That had been nearly a decade ago, yet I felt something akin to that now, even though I had been out of commission for only two months. Back then, there had also been pride—pride at having made it to this noble city. Re-entering, I felt that wonder all over again. The light of the train shone first on the dark curved wall of the tunnel, then emerged, round and bright.

I stepped into the car, happy to be part of the surge. As the train left the station and began its rush through the unlit zones, I stood in the aisle, gripping the handrail, looking around for an open seat. For a few moments, I enjoyed the gentle sway of the car, but then an unexpected and irrational fear that I would be knocked off balance began to creep in. As soon as a seat became available, I slipped into it.

By the time we reached Church Street Station, I began to relax a little and look around. A heavy-set bearded guy was leaning against a pole, reading the newspaper. A young Latin man across from me was dozing, suit jacket folded neatly on his lap, mouth relaxed into an "O." Neither of them was doing anything to call attention to themselves, but I enjoyed keeping them in view. This ride was probably no big deal for them, I thought. Just routine—an interstitial time between one place and another. Who knew what they were really up against in their lives—but whenever I glanced at them, I felt anchored. I wanted things to be simple for me again, too, in the way I conjectured it was for them.

Then the guy with the beard coughed. One dry quiet hack. He covered his mouth with his hand, then grasping the pole again, returned to reading his newspaper. My cheeks grew hot, hotter than I remembered them being when I was sick.

Fortunately, my stop was next. Getting out at Civic Center, I rushed through UN Plaza. Behind me, pitched on a thin greenway that stretched to Market Street, were the tents of the AIDS Vigil. Ailing protesters ate, slept, and sometimes died there, in public, come rain or shine.

Not this, not today, I thought, keeping my eyes on the dome of City Hall, the lane of plane trees leading to it through the plaza.

Rounding the corner, reaching the library, I pushed through the tall heavy doors and stood for a second in the foyer, looking up into the grand central staircase. The golden if age-dimmed light of the Piazzoni murals on each side filled the air, rising up off the vast California foothills and oceans portrayed there. To some, the subtle colors seemed as stale as leaves beaten down and leached of autumn brilliance by December rain, but to me they effused a light I wanted in my bones. To be aged someday: I would take whatever I could of that experience.

Then I hurried to the restroom, where I would wash my hands many times that day, and on those that followed.

My wish to both welcome the world, and to be welcomed back, revived instantly when my colleagues greeted me with open arms. Cheeks were pressed against mine, a vase of flowers appeared on my desk. No one inquired directly into the nature of my illness—that just wasn't done—but of course most people knew by looking at me what was going on. Despite the physical shine that Jay had left me with that morning, I was pale and thin.

At first, I was given a light load—shortened shifts at the reference desk or in the stacks; longer time in the little office I shared with six others. In an unconscious stroke of brilliance, my supervisor asked me to spend more time than usual weeding out damaged or rarely used books. It could have been an especially macabre task at that time—all those broken spines and tattered yellow pages! Yet it was satisfying to separate the whole from the irreparable, to immerse again in things—literal physical things—that could be cleaned up, redeemed, or discarded without major emotion.

A deeper relaxation than I had felt for some time flowed into me. Colleagues were always floating around doing research, shelving books, working a desk. The familiar whoosh and clank of a custodian wheeling a trash barrel, the hush of shoes on a floor, the sound of a cart—the engagement of my senses with these quiet familiarities, reassured me by their presence that I was there, too. Somewhere within me were deep reservoirs of calm that over the years had merged with the rhythms and waves of my own body.

As the weeks went by, coworkers kept telling me that I looked good, that I looked like myself. At first, I felt quite jocular, tossing off comments like "Who else am I supposed to look like?" I wanted to believe them, and so, for a while, I did.

But soon, I saw how they glanced at each other after they had complimented me, assuming that I wouldn't notice. They were telling me what they thought I needed or wanted to hear. That sense of being a tourist I had felt at the train turnstile came back to me, but this time in the form of feeling like an alien in the world of the well. I fought against it—I told myself that it wasn't just me who was having a hard time being mortal. In fact, I noted, what were any of us doing, choosing to work in a grand old building with broad marble steps and classically sculpted busts staring out of little alcoves in the lobby, and books written centuries ago, moldering in the stacks? You have to be at least a little worried about things falling into disuse and decay to dedicate a third of one's day to preserving what too would fall to dust, perhaps later than sooner (though with the steep budget cuts that had been prevailing since the late 1980s, and the rapid development of the computer era, it seemed it might be sooner rather than later).

Nonetheless, despite my attempts to maintain perspective, I couldn't keep myself from the fear that mortality was more true for me than for them. Self-pity reared its ugly isolating head repeatedly. If I weren't careful, I could go crazy, trying to fight it off, then feeling sorry for myself for how tiring it was to defend myself against.

Then things began to pick up speed. Of course, they would—they had to—but I also wanted this. I breezed from meetings to back rooms to public desks, arms loaded with papers or books. It wasn't just me who was thrumming—the whole environment was unusually stoked up. As the economy continued on a downward slide, wild talk and rumors stirred people's hopes and fears. Would the Main be reduced to the size of a reference-only collection? Would layoffs and transfers ensue? Or would voters at last approve financing for a whole new building?

"It's like drinking water from a fire hose," my friend Veronica said one afternoon when I came to relieve her at the desk. A dozen students were bobbing about, waiting for help with term papers. She looked frazzled.

"I'm crashing," she said, gathering up her things. "The afternoon slump has got me."

See? I noted. Everybody's energy takes a nose-dive late in the day.

"That's why there's coffee, chocolate, and eclairs," I said cheerfully.

I was right, I told Jay. Working was good for my soul. My spirits were high.

Very high.

Things were accelerating internally, too.

When I was standing in front of a stall at the urban farmer's market during lunch one day, leafing through my wallet to pay for a pomegranate—Jay especially loved them—my eye was caught by a small brown bag full of pears. Despite the opaqueness of their slightly bruised skins, I could almost taste the dull glowing roughness, the butter and grit beneath that yellow-green skin.

I must have been staring in a strange way, because the old Chinese woman behind the table picked up the bag and held it out to me. "Go ahead," she said, smiling. "You deserve."

That experience in the market was a peak, but there were others, too, moments that were subtle, yet radiant. Transfixed each time, I had a sense of in-rushing, a rising heavy fullness in my chest so strong that sometimes I would have to remind myself to breathe.

"I've been having these episodes," I told Celia one day at lunch. "They just sneak up on me. Everything starts to look very high definition. Like I'm seeing the subatomic shimmer behind everything. This ecstasy comes over me—I feel as if I could walk through walls, or mountains. Then my head cuts in and says I'm turning into a nutcake."

She swirled her drink, considering me with level eyes.

"You're not so different than the rest of us. Everybody has such moments."

"Of course! But these are very intense."

"They always are, for the person who is having them."

I flushed, growing irritated. Just a few days before, I had tried to have this same conversation with Jay. At least he had been happy for me, but a blank look had come into his face. Maybe it was just one of those things that can't be put into words, I had told myself. Still, it was a lonely feeling. When it had come up with Jay, I had gone and stood behind him, smelling his hair as I massaged him. He had leaned back, head against my belly. But here, now, Celia was peering at me from across the table, over the top of her reading glasses.

I felt unexpectedly close to tears.

"Yeah, I guess you're right," I said, backing down, wanting to change the subject. "Like you say, no big deal. So, let's move on."

She lifted her eyebrows.

"But it is a big deal to you," she said. "That was your whole point."

"Yeah, that was my point, before you tried to punch out my lights," I said. "So, end of topic."

I reached for the check. She beat me to it, setting it aside.

"Don't get me wrong. It all sounds quite rich," she said, in a conciliatory tone. "Very exhilarating. After such a close call, why wouldn't your body and soul want to celebrate just being here by blasting off a few fireworks in your brain? *Carpe diem, tempus fugit,* and all that."

My stomach turned. Fucking *memento mori* to you, too, I almost said. Even though she didn't deserve such treatment, I closed my eyes, refusing to meet her gaze.

There was a long pause.

Everything in the restaurant suddenly seemed very loud, a hubbub of voices and clanking dishes.

Glancing from under my lids, I could see that she was rubbing her thumbs against each other in a way she used to do before she quit smoking.

"Listen," she said, more anxiously now. "All I'm trying to say is that I've been watching you ever since you came back to work. Bill, you look strung out. I'm worried that you're spending energy as fast as it comes in."

Opening my eyes, I saw she was looking at me with an expression of absolute conviction, but also with unmistakable love. The fatigue that I had been trying to shove down for weeks was surging up now into my throat and against the walls of my chest as if something were cracking open, or breaking down, or both.

Celia was right. In my eagerness to be saved, I was in danger of burning down my own house.

It was December now, and dark when I left work. We were in a drought, but when it rained, the streets were slick with water that the hardened earth couldn't absorb.

I didn't know what I should do, what was right. I had promised myself and the doctor that I would rest or quit when needed, but I hadn't known then how my own restiveness would sweep me up once I was out in the world again.

One night I dreamed I was reading the funnies when the characters leapt to life and began sprinting across the frames. Just as abruptly, they halted. This stopping and starting went on and on, for no apparent reason, until I realized that my own attention was the animating force. Whenever it flagged, the characters fell flat. Eager to share my discovery, I tugged on Jay's sleeve. When he tried to create the same effect, he couldn't.

Waking, I felt bewildered and afraid.

Jay seemed increasingly removed, despite having perked up when I first returned to work. Uninterested in seeing his friends, or reading, or talking much about his day, he went to work, he came home. He was spending more and more time in the basement. At first, I thought it was because things were more chaotic domestically; after work, neither of us had much energy for doing chores. When I tried to talk with him about it, he couldn't explain, except to say that I shouldn't waste time over-analyzing things. In the past, I might have kept pressing, but now there was something in his tone that made me hesitant to really know.

He began to collect and organize things, to an odd degree. First, it was cardboard tea boxes. Once they were empty, he would rip off the lids and line them up in the kitchen drawer as little storages bins for tacks, twist ties, rubber bands. Next he amassed spice bottles, even picking them out of people's recycling bins so he could store hardware in them.

The librarian in me could understand the pleasure of making order; but, he did it with little apparent satisfaction.

When I went down to visit him at his workbench one evening, I found him sorting fasteners with the intensity of a chess player considering where to place his pieces. He barely acknowledged my existence. When he finally interrupted his concentration on his little piles of nuts and bolts, it was to ruminate about whether or not to mix the rusty or bent with the new and shiny.

Sometimes, when he wasn't home, I would turn on the light over his bench and stare, unable to make sense of the complex organization that was in process, but invisible to me. It weirded me out. Though I knew it wasn't true on the literal level, it was as if he were moving somewhere, moving out.

One afternoon, just before Christmas, my colleagues Veronica and Zoe came bustling into the back office with big bags of Thai food for a holiday lunch. It was a welcome surprise. Jay and I had agreed to keep things simple this year. We hadn't been doing much in the holiday spirit besides walking around in the evening, looking at the lights in other people's windows, which suited us just fine. Yet now, as everybody sat around with Styrofoam bowls of steaming noodles in their hands, I was glad to enjoy the benefits of somebody else's efforts. I knew I couldn't eat much without repercussion, but the warmth of the group was good.

Somehow, we got onto the topic of nutty dreams we'd each had about work, so I shared a recent one of my own. It was striking to me because nothing much happened in it. I was just sitting there, in a chair, in a perfectly white and empty space, that somehow I knew was the library. Even more strange was the fact that I was naked, except for a long strand of linked paperclips that draped from my neck all the way to the floor.

"Maybe you've missed your calling as a designer," said Angela.
We laughed.

"Or maybe you just need a new tie," teased Zoe. Then, in a more serious vein, she offered another interpretation.

"I'm remembering those pictures you see of DNA, those twisting helixes. Maybe you're forming some new DNA, stronger than steel, in your immune system."

The mood in the room subtly downshifted as people nodded and looked my way, hoping I would appreciate the healing image and accept their collective good wishes.

"I like that," I said, complying, but secretly, I was relieved when Veronica, unable to contain herself, burbled up with laughter.

"I remember Bill's first day of work," she said, her warm, brown eyes dancing. "Poor Bill was taking his first shift at the reference desk, and he hadn't been there more than five minutes when crazy Walter began to fuss at him about the proper way to manage his paperclips."

As the laughter died down, somebody chimed in, "What has become of good old Walter? Does anybody know?"

There was an awkward silence. Zoe cut in with a quick and quiet no, and the group followed her lead, hastily moving on to the topic of someone else's dream. Even so, I felt naked. A mantle was being passed, I realized.

That night, when it came time to leave, I stayed in my chair, just sitting there, staring at the piles of professional journals, the paperwork, a few books. The "stuff" of my work life. Suddenly, I began ferreting out my personal things—special pens, a toothbrush, photographs, an uneaten apple. Opening my briefcase, I dumped them in, pulled on my coat, glanced one more time around the room. On the wall was a picture I had forgotten to take down. It was just a greeting card, one that I had framed, a fresco of a woman in a toga, excavated from the ashes at Pompeii. It had been hanging there for so long, I had stopped seeing it. *Flora.* Departing with her basket half full, she turns to pick a long stem of starry white flowers.

I hadn't walked through the tent village of the AIDS Vigil in several years, but that night, on my way home, I did. The tents were saggy and slick with rain; a wet wreath hung crookedly on one of them. As I stood awkwardly, just looking, not knowing what to do, both then and with my life, a guy pushed open a tent flap and stuck out his hand to test the weather. Spying me, he stepped out.

"Can I help you?" he asked.

"Is there anyone here named Walter?" I heard myself say.

It was a silly question. Of course, I knew Walter wasn't anywhere that night, except in me.

But it seemed important for me to ask.

When I finally arrived at home I sat in the dark, my coat still on, until Jay arrived. He didn't notice me at first. Quietly, I watched as he flicked on the hall light and hung up his coat, wet hair shining. Bending to unlace his boots, he seemed neither hopeful nor resigned, cynical nor numb—but just simply himself, present, there in his boots.

None of this would be remembered by anyone, I thought.

"Is something the matter?" he asked, when he realized I was there.

I shook my head.

"Just taking in the moment," I said inexplicably, but he seemed to understand.

44

I BARELY REMEMBER THE NEXT FEW MONTHS, except that I was often at loose ends. Aside from medical routines, I had no schedule, and without work, no guaranteed camaraderie. Besides Jay and a few friends, no one expected anything of me, for better or for worse. If I enjoyed myself, or felt lost, either way, the open-endedness unnerved me for quite some time. When I became too exhausted, as I often did, it was easy to fall prey to a sense of not existing at all, but thank God, rest helped.

By the time spring came, my reservoirs began to replenish, enough so that I started to wonder if it had been a mistake to go on disability. But when I saw the grayness of a full day's work on Jay's face, I stopped second-guessing myself.

Soon, a powerful urge to reorganize my space swept me up. Noticing objects that I had stopped really seeing years ago, I vowed to get rid of what no longer served my life as it was—or wasn't—now. "Oh! Great Liberator of Space," Jay dubbed me, as he watched clutter disappear into new filing systems, storage boxes, giveaway piles. It wasn't all a breeze—I did unearth a few artifacts of old pain. Yet when I came across papers related to my parent's accident, I discovered that some things really do heal with time. The bitterness that I had once felt had vanished, replaced by a greater sense of their presence inside me.

"Look at everything you've done," said Jay one night, as he surveyed the living room. "It feels lighter in here."

He didn't just mean the house; he had his hand on my chest.

"It's calmer," he added. "More open."

I reached up and squeezed his wrist, and for a while, we stood listening to the bamboo clacking in the wind against the cedar shakes. I was feeling that spaciousness, too, yet there was something else as well, a little ache in my gut, a hollow emptiness I couldn't quite put into words in that moment.

The next morning, my progress came to a screeching halt. Every inch of my desk and drawers had been reviewed and renewed. Now, only the closet was left. I opened the door, surveying what was front and center. Did I really need nine ties? So many pairs of khaki pants? What about those shoes? For a long time I just stood there, unexpectedly stymied. What's the big deal? I asked myself. Just decide.

Draped in the heavy lead of its own knowing, my body refused, forcing me to admit what once again I was trying to deny. Unlikely to ever return to work, I would have no more need for most of those clothes.

It would be weeks before I was finally able to set them out on the curb, but when I did, they vanished by morning.

~~~

There wasn't much choice now, except to give depression its due, yet when I finally did, it began to lift.

Nevertheless, the same question I had been struggling with all along continued to hammer in my ear.

So, what now?

Sick of stewing in my own troubles, I decided to volunteer. I made it most of the way through a training to become an HIV hotline operator, but my doctor insisted I stop.

"If you're doing this just to prove that you're not dead, then you're not doing anybody a favor, including you," he said, trying to soften my surrender. "You still don't have any big deal symptoms besides side effects, but you've lost some weight, you're anemic from the AZT, and as for the ddi, we're not seeing any positive results yet."

He sat back, watching my response.

Trying not to glare like a caged bear, I tightened my face. "So now what?"

There was an uncomfortable pause.

"Uh-oh," I said.

He shook his head. "No. Things are not that different from what they have been." Yet clearly the weight of our conversation had shifted.

"So, what is it you're trying to tell me?"

"What do you need me to tell you?" he asked.

I drew a blank. "I don't know what to do," I finally said.

"With what?"

I turned red. "With my time."

He set aside my file and leaned forward.

"Well, I'll put it to you flat out," he said, using the tone of someone speaking to a young child, or a recent immigrant. "Now is your time to do nothing but really love *you*."

As I headed home, the ground of my life was once again shifting under my feet. This time, instead of collapsing into fear, or sorrow, I seethed. "Love *me*?" I argued with the doctor in my head. "Is that all there is now? I don't want to love just me." I wanted to be out and about in the world, to be part of it again. I was sick of feeling held back, held in. While on some level I still knew that loving oneself and loving the

338

world didn't have to be mutually exclusive, I wasn't feeling the magic. At that moment, it was easier to blind myself with anger at the doctor's word choice than to take in what he was really saying about my health.

With no idea where I was going, I tromped around the backside of Davies hospital, ripping the tips of stems off the long hedge lining the sidewalk. Across the tracks of the N-line was Duboce Park, and an empty bench. I headed there and sat down. Leaning forward, I rested my head in my hands. A motley assortment of dogs was mixing it up, rough-housing on the lawn in front of me. Watching them play, my anger began to dissipate. I took a few deep breaths and let my mind go blank as I just followed the fast legs, whipping tails, flying leaps across the green, to the north end of the park, where I could see a large and stately Queen Anne-style house. The windows were large and shiny, some were curved. It was easy to see inside. The building was so well-preserved it seemed as if at any minute a Victorian lady might come into view, moving about the sunny dining room in a long white dress, placing a vase first on the large, polished dining room table, then trying the sideboard instead. In and out of the airy room she went, sometimes out of sight, her inner directions unknown to me and perhaps to herself. Just doing the next thing, she seemed calm, and content. Of course, I recognized her as someone who had once lived inside me, but whom I had lost, for a long time.

Let me start again, I heard myself entreat. Deep within my chest, the words came welling up, seemingly from the beyond. Later, I would remember they were from an ancient Gaelic poem. But in that moment, they became my own. Wash my mouth of bitterness, I prayed. Let me start again.

And so, I did.

Slowly, I learned to right myself whenever I fell into believing I was a lost soul.

Walk, an inner voice told me, and so I did, almost every day. This foot, that foot, this block, that block, my life began to ripple outward, moving past the constrictions of this headache or that anxiety. As my arms swung in their sockets and my feet rocked me gently from side to side, the pleasures of aimlessness stole back into my life. Body engaged, I could let my mind go, running from tree to tree like a happy dog following his nose.

Particular trees became my friends: the skinny silver-bearded palms in Mission Dolores Park, the wide magnolias on 18th, weeping bottlebrushes, Monterey pines, and especially, the gingkoes—presumed to be the longest surviving plant species—blazing yellow in autumn along Eureka Street. Collectively, they pinned the earth beneath my feet, stretched it firmly over the hard bones and sandy bellies of the city. The sense of everything shifting and of chasms constantly opening under me gradually slowed. I began to trust the life-force again, in a way I hadn't in a long time. It was all of matter of perspective, of course. The world was no different than it had ever been—but I was growing in my ability to take things tree by tree. "We look at the world through billion years-old water in our eyes," I heard a scientist say on the radio, and I thought, I needed to remember that.

And I did, one day, when it became clear that I really was learning how to shift myself from lostness to looseness. It must have been May by now—the ornamental cherries were in bloom. I was standing still, gazing up into the blossoms, when I heard a door push open, and saw a very old woman in a wheelchair looking out from her apartment building's entryway into the same tree. The skin on her face was paper thin. Clearly, she was not long for this world, yet that wasn't stopping her from letting the light of those blossoms shine in her eyes. Catching each other's eye, she gave me a beautiful smile. It seemed almost as if we had joined in a moment of worship. For days afterward, I felt a friendship with her, as if she had christened my newfound life. Whenever I walked past that place again, I remembered that moment, and how we had blessed it together.

340

Supported by an inner vitality, I was more able to meet the ups and downs of my physical health. Lucky me, since those vicissitudes were becoming more pronounced. My T-cell count actually improved a bit, but my feet began to cramp and burn, at first only at night, then off and on during the day, too. Like many patients, I was developing neuropathies, probably due to medication. I wasn't yet like the young men with canes who could be spotted on Castro Street at any given hour, but there were occasions when I couldn't walk three blocks. Hobbling down the street, my mind would spin with fear. If things got worse, how would I continue to shop for our food? How could I help Jay?

In the past, I would have worked myself into a panic, or despair, but now I would tell myself to stop, and I would do just that, physically. I would literally make myself turn around and look for the nearest tree. Pausing there, I would touch the bark, exploring the rough patches and in between, the smooth. It didn't make the pain in my feet go away, but somehow, I spared myself some misery. Somewhere deep within the thick fibers of the wood, sap was flowing. Pain wasn't everywhere.

But now I was to face another challenge altogether.

A white line appeared along the side of his tongue. It was the color of milk, seemingly innocuous, but we both knew what it meant: the onset of thrush, his first opportunistic infection. There were medications, ones he actually took. None of this prevented him from going to work much of the time, but it was clearly becoming more and more difficult.

Quietly, he worked out a part-time schedule with his employer, who was more than flexible. Allowed to go in at mid-day and leave early, if need be, Jay was home more often now. He could sleep in, hang out in his bathrobe, take time to eat a bigger breakfast. Neither of us had much of an appetite, so it was slow-going for us both, but we could egg each other on. We had only recently gotten a video player, so watching a comedy while we ate was a helpful distraction.

It was also undeniably an oddity. We would ordinarily never turn on the TV during the morning or a meal. I loved Jay being home, doing those things with me, but his presence was also an auger that was discomforting.

One day, as I was coming up the steps with a bag of food, I was surprised to hear voices inside the cottage, followed by a burst of charged, elevated laughter. When I put my key in the door, it stopped abruptly, then I heard Jay, talking low. Slowly I pushed open the door.

Sitting in the chair facing the entryway was a buff young man wearing camouflage trousers and a tight T-shirt. His hair was dark and cropped and his skin was a beautiful color. Elbows resting on his knees, he was leaning forward in his chair as if he might roll into a tackle or curl up any minute, yet he also held his shoulders straight with an appealing naturalness. He met my eyes with a bright look, but there was something surprised and anxious about the way he was twisting his thumb inside the fist of his other hand.

"Hi," Jay said nervously. He was standing in front of the fireplace, arm on the mantle. He looked oddly vulnerable, as if he needed that mantle to anchor him.

"This is my partner, Bill," he said, keeping his eyes on me. He seemed edgy, as if asking something of me, but I had no idea what he wanted. For a split second my imagination ran wild—just as it would have done years ago—but all of that was now highly unlikely. This guy was in the bloom of youth and health.

"This is Edward," said Jay. "He's been in Kuwait. Just got discharged, a few months back. They trained him to be a cook there. Now he works near the airport, cooking for an airline."

"Yeah. And too bad for the passengers," the guy said, with an eager smile. As I took off my jacket and laid it on the couch, he jumped up to shake my hand. I noticed his palms were sweaty.

"He saw your boxes of used books out in the yard, waiting to be taken to Phoenix Books. He offered to drop them off. His girlfriend grooms dogs someplace near there, when she's not with the baby."

Now I was really lost. "How old is the baby?" I asked inanely.

"Well, actually she's three, but she's not my baby," he hastened to add. "We're all just living together," he said to Jay now, as if clarifying something. "We're just friends now; we help each other out, more like family. She took care of my dog when I was overseas."

Emily was brushing up against his shins just at that moment, making him hers. Already won over, he was petting her in long firm strokes as she shamelessly pushed her hips up against his hand.

"Look at Granny," said Jay, and we all laughed, letting off some tension.

"Can I get you guys something to drink?" I said to Jay tentatively, studying his face. I was really asking for a clue—did he want me to get lost, or play host—but he just stared at me with a look I couldn't read. He seemed almost as mystified as me.

The guy stood up suddenly. "Thank you very much, Bill," he said, as mannerly as if he were talking to an officer. "I don't mean to interrupt your evening . . . but maybe I'll come back sometime?" he said to Jay. "I'd like to make good on my offer."

Jay put his hand on the young man's shoulder. "I'd like that too," he said, with a surprising tenderness.

Edward turned to me, shook my hand vigorously, raising his eyebrows as he gave my hand one last meaningful squeeze. "I'm sorry," he said haltingly. "I don't know what else to say, except that I'm very, very sorry. I'm glad to see you guys are still doing so well, or, I mean, like, doing well together."

That was how Eddy, a.k.a. Edward now, re-entered our lives.

"He just showed up out of the blue," Jay explained. "I'm as surprised as you." He was hugging himself around the middle yet standing very stiff. He seemed dazed, or dazzled, or maybe both.

"How the hell . . . ?" I said.

"He was just waiting out front in a car and jumped out when I came home."

"Has he been stalking you, or what?"

"No. He moved here after he got discharged in San Diego. An army buddy already up here helped him get the job. He said he had a hunch I probably had moved here, so he looked me up in the phone book."

"Yeah, I bet. In 1984, this was a great place for gay men whose houses had been burned down by kids who accused them of molestation."

Jay furrowed his brow. "He said he wrote me a letter, but then on impulse he decided he just wanted to see if I would recognize him, and what my reaction would be when I realized who he was. If I looked like I hated his guts, he said he would have just have turned tail and left me alone. He's scared shitless."

"So, what is your reaction?"

Jay sat on the couch, clutching his knee.

"I have no idea," he said, shaking his head, but with an amazed little smile.

"He said he thought he'd never be able to make things right, ever, in his whole life, but maybe he could somehow make things better for us."

"Better."

"Our situation wasn't lost on him," he said, rubbing his cheek. "All he had to do was look at me. He said he could at least do chores for us . . . he offered to take the books, or bring us groceries . . . Not buy them, just shop."

I couldn't believe what I was hearing.

"Jay, we can get a volunteer, if we need to."

"We do need to. I don't want you to do it anymore. And *he* has volunteered."

"I can do my own damn shopping."

"Bill, he is my opportunity to make things right, too. I failed him. I still feel like I fucked up by not being up front with him about who I was."

"*Your* opportunity to make things right? No, he burned down your house, and now you are *his* opportunity. For what? That's what I want to know."

"I can understand you're scared, but you haven't heard the whole story. What he told me about where he's been."

"Obviously he's become some kind of upstanding citizen, but I don't care. I can't trust him."

"We can give it some time."

"Fine, but I will not forgive him."

"Bill, don't begrudge me this. Please. There is still a place in my heart for him. There always has been."

45

Eddy didn't call. One month went by, then two.

"Maybe he just needs time to digest it all," Jay hypothesized.

As far as I was concerned, he could take forever. The whole thing still smelled of cold ash to me.

Yet, as more time passed, and still no Eddy, I began to relax. There was an atmosphere of expectancy in the house again, a spring to Jay's step. Gradually Eddy became Edward in my thoughts—in absentia, I could at least grant him that.

All of that was soon to be sidelined, anyway.

One night in early October around 1 am, I heard Jay get up and open a window. A warm front must be moving in, I thought, kicking off the blanket before I fell back to sleep. Later, hearing the crack of an ice tray, I surfaced again briefly, realizing I was thirsty, too, but not enough to pull myself from the deep. Just before dawn I finally came to, the covers in a tight swirl around my body. It was cooler now. What a hog, I thought, dragging part of the blanket out from under me. When I reached to spread it over Jay, I was surprised to find him gone.

Calling out, I heard a vague answer from the living room.

"In here. I was too hot."

I found him on the floor, a heap of gray in the dim early light.

"What are you doing down there? That can't be comfortable."

"I have the sleeping bag," he said, without moving.

"I thought you were too hot."

"I'm freezing now."

A wet plastic bag slid onto the floor when I tried to place my wrist on his forehead.

"Frozen peas," he said weakly. "Or they used to be. The blackberries and peaches are under my pits."

I pushed my hand under his shoulders to help him sit. His T-shirt, the comforter, even the rug, were drenched.

In the ER they took him quickly behind the scenes, double doors swinging.

I started to push through.

"No," said a nurse, stopping me with a hand up to my chest. "Someone will call you," she said, pointing to the rows of linked chairs in the waiting room.

I hesitated, then turned down a hall instead, searching for a phone. I thought of Jay's parents, but I knew he would be furious. Maybe Michael or Betsy? I picked up the receiver and inserted a coin, then stared blankly at the buttons. The only number that I could remember was the one for my parent's store.

Eerily, I called it anyway.

Back in the waiting room, the image of Jay flat-out on a gurney kept rolling through my mind. Unable to keep still, I approached the admissions window over and over, asking, then demanding, to know something, anything. He could be delirious by now, or worse. All those bright lights, bleating monitors, strange faces. How much longer could he cling to the belief that if he just let things be, they would take care of themselves?

It was hours before they sent me to the ICU.

A nurse intercepted me in the hall, handing me a mask and gown. I stood fumbling with the strings, unable to take my eyes off the official quarantine notice posted on the closed door behind her.

"These too," she added, holding out shoe-covers and a puffy cap.

I stared at them blankly.

She pointed to her own hair-net.

"Better a wealth of caution," she said. "Until we get more information. We're waiting for the results of his chest X-ray, TB test, a bronchoscopy."

"TB?"

"It often travels with PCP."

Seeing the look on my face, she touched my arm.

"We don't know anything for sure yet, but he's in good hands now."

I flushed. It was hard for me to give up my patient, but I knew it was for the best.

"Go on in," she said, gently pushing the door open for me. "Just press the call button if you need me."

There really must be some mistake, I thought, entering the room. This patient had an oxygen mask clamped over his mouth and nose; his hair was darker than Jay's.

I turned to go.

The man made a noise, muffled and raw.

I spun around.

Eyes wild and pleading above his mask, he was beckoning me, his forehead buckling just like Jay's did when he was trying not to cry. As I moved quickly toward him, I could see his hair was darker because it was damp with sweat.

"It's okay . . . it's okay . . ."

How many times did I say that to him and to us both?

It felt so lame, and yet so right. The words came with conviction, with love, from someplace bigger than my fear. For a long time I leaned over him, stroking his hair as I attempted to steady him with my gaze. He was on the edge of panic, picking at his covers, rubbing his feet together.

"It's the fever," said the nurse, renewing the ice packs tucked around him. "Plus, he's fresh from the bronchoscopy."

Jay looked from her to me, then rolled his eyes. "Fresh?"

It was almost the first thing he'd said. A little sarcasm, and my heart leapt.

"Well!" said the nurse, crossing her arms in a mock-nursey pose. "If you're with it enough to be a smart-aleck, you're with it enough not to rip out your IVs."

Gingerly she checked the IV insertion in Jay's arm, then started to untie his wrists. Suppressing a grimace, he studied the bad art on the wall.

"Are you in pain?" she asked, stopping.

He shook his head, but his whole body was tensed.

"Is there anything I can do for you?"

"No," he said, pointedly closing his eyes.

Pausing, she looked across at me.

"Sometimes people feel spooked when they wake up with a mask on," she whispered. "He has calmed down considerably since you arrived."

Together we gazed down at him, waiting.

"Jay," she finally said, tapping him lightly on the shoulder. "I'll be back to torment you some more later. In the meantime, I have a strong suspicion that what you need now more than anything is Dr. Love."

Sweeping the curtain around us, she left.

Jay peered cautiously behind me.

"She's gone," I said.

He glanced my way, then continued staring with big glassy eyes at something just past my shoulder.

"What is it?" I asked, half-turning. All I could see were curtains, olive-drab with gray spangles.

Suddenly he started kicking at his covers.

"Get this thing off!" he blurted, yanking his mask. "It's suffocating me!"

I caught his wrists.

"No, Jay! It's oxygen."

"I don't care," he said, wincing as he struggled against me. The IV needles were obviously digging into him.

"Fuck," he said, sinking back. "I can't believe you're not going to help me."

"I am helping you. It just doesn't feel like it."

There was a short tense silence.

"You don't understand," he said fiercely.

"What don't I understand?"

His eyes darted from me to the curtains.

"They're following me," he whispered.

"The curtains?"

"They were in the emergency room, too."

I wiped my forehead on the sleeve of my gown.

"It's just a hospital, Jay. Those same curtains are everywhere."

He scrutinized my expression, obviously wanting to believe me, but still confused. I waited on the edge of my seat, aware of the perspiration forming beneath my mask. He took another peek, shaking his head a little as if to clear it.

"I can see why you'd be scared, though. Those curtains are ugly as sin," I said, risking a little levity.

When he spoke again, his voice was hoarse but he sounded more like himself.

"I'm sorry," he said. "I was so frightened."

"It's okay, Jay. Your temperature is very high."

Dropping his gaze, he held my hand, stroking the back of it.

"I thought they were the last thing . . . ," he said haltingly.

"The last thing?"

He looked up at me, his eyes fever-bright.

"The curtains. Laying in the emergency room, I thought they were the last thing I was ever going to see."

Reaching up, he traced the outline of my lips beneath my mask.

Fingers intertwined with mine, he finally fell asleep.

Now there was nothing to do but wait. Hands dangling helpless between my knees, I studied the lines of sweat on his face, the slack or tension in his jaw, the flicker of his eyes beneath their lids. According to the nurses, he seemed to be holding his own, but there were alarming gurgles in the back of his throat, a wheeze deep in his chest. As the fear of suffocation began to spread in my own chest, I struggled against a selfish urge to wake him, just to prove to myself that he could be woken. Trying to regain my own steadier rhythm, I covered my ears, lengthening my breath, imagining I could send it into him. I kept this up for quite some time. Whether it helped him or not I have no idea, but it calmed me, and for one wonderful moment we actually did align, breathing in time with each other, just as we had done countless times before as we'd fallen asleep together or made love. All the comfort of our years together came swirling back into me, and I closed my eyes, riding that current as long as I could.

Then he wheezed, and I lurched back to reality.

I couldn't keep my eyes open any longer.

Urged by a nurse, I finally hauled myself over to the scuffed-up recliner by the window. It was hard to admit, but Jay and I now needed the care of others in a way we never had before. She brought me a blanket and an unclaimed tray of food, which soon filled the room with the smell of cold gravy—a strange mix with Jay's sweat—but something in me eased.

Loosening my mask, I tried to settle into the chair. Running my thumb along a cracked seam of the arm, an eerie feeling came over me as I thought of all the people who had sat here doing this very thing, wearing a one-size-fits-all depression into the bottom cushion, despite their distinct shapes and the sizes of their grief. Then the heat came on, lifting a few hairs on my head, making me wonder how many prayers, curses, promises, and lies were still circulating in the air around me. *Everything will be okay, please God, everything will be okay.* For a second, I almost wept, feeling all of this awakened in myself.

But the next moment that wave broke, and I was alone again, staring out the window at the wide city with its glass and concrete laid out before me in orderly grids and tangles. Somewhere behind the hospital the sun was sinking, yet it was still here, too, in the shimmering pink faces of tall buildings to the east. The view was magnificent, better than any I had ever seen before in the city. Instinctively, I turned toward Jay—this was one of those moments when ordinarily we would have exchanged a glance—but of course he was still submerged, his face a sheen of sweat.

PART FIVE

46

Days, then weeks, ticked by. I stopped believing he would ever come home. Not after a month, and him still tethered to IVs. And then a new infection, starting in his arm, at the site where a shunt had been installed, supposedly to make things easier.

Hah!

But there is always room for hope, or so said the medical people, lifting their eyebrows and looking meaningfully into my eyes each time they said it. He *will* go home, a few of them added, emphasizing the *will*.

Despite the standardized eye contact, I almost believed them.

But Jay himself had lost hope. Due to the new infection, his raging fever came back, spiking dangerously. It did eventually drop, but it would never be normal again. Night sweats continued to plague him, soaking his sheets, disrupting his sleep. With plenty of time at 2 am to contemplate the various possibilities for his own demise, he either shut down so completely he was barely verbal by the time I arrived in the morning, or the nurses reported that he had rung the call bell obsessively all night, requesting trip after trip to the bathroom whether he needed it or not. When I asked him why, he'd turn red, and aside from saying (of course) that he didn't want to make a mess, he could rarely add more.

One morning was different, though. He seemed particularly shaken. He'd been startled awake several times by loud voices in the hall, or maybe his own cursing, and he couldn't explain why, but the sight of headlights twinkling as cars came and went on the bridge in the dark disturbed him so much he had begun to shake. He rang the bell, but nobody came for what seemed like forever.

"I can't stand this," he said, close to tears. "I'm nothing but a pain in the ass to other people now."

"No, you're—"

"Yes! I am. And I know those nurses are telling you all about it out in the hall before you come in that door."

I started to shake my head, but he shook his more vehemently.

"Don't, Bill. Don't mess with my sense of reality. The hard fact is that I'm here in this damned room and you love me yeah, yeah, yeah, and you're pouring your lifeblood into being here for me, but at the end of the day you still have to leave, and it's one more nightmare." He looked about to cry. "I lay here, and—"

He bit off the end of his sentence.

"No one understands," he said abruptly. "I do try, you know. I don't want to bug people. When that loudmouth woke me up last night and I got wiggy about the lights, I looked at those cala lilies that Michael left on the nightstand, and I tried to go right inside one of them and disappear. They even seemed to bend my way, as if they wanted to make it easier for me, as if they wanted to give me mercy and comfort, but I couldn't get across the dark to them, not even in my imagination. And when someone did come, and asked me what was the matter, she thought I was nuts, I'm sure. I *was* nuts. All I could do was point and say 'those lilies,' even though she kept asking me how she could help me. Finally, she threw out the lilies and washed the vase."

"Ready for something new?" she had said brightly, setting it on the window sill.

I sat speechless, fingertips pressing against my mouth as I watched him wrapping a little string around his finger, this way, that way. Somehow, I had never imagined that I would see Jay, my Mr. Affable, ever having to be this lonely. Despairing, maybe, but not lonely. Not like this.

"The worst was that no one meant to be unkind," he added, setting the string on the nightstand.

In fact, worse times were on the way, times in which there would be unkindness, and also cruelty. Shame came, bearing its ugly package of humiliation, splitting Jay not only from others, and me, but also from himself. While once he had preferred me to be the one to help him change his gown, get out of bed, walk down the hall, more and more he asked me to leave the room and relied upon aides. Limbs weak and withered, he couldn't stand to look at himself, never mind let me. Though neither of us said the word, he was wasting now. Due to an unknown pathogen in his gut, most things went straight through him. He was still encouraged to eat as much as he could, so we did our best to get as much into him as possible. I brought his favorite foods, as well as my own, which he sniffed appreciatively, and initially, it comforted us to share a mealtime as we usually loved to do. Soon, though, the constant metallic taste in his mouth overrode any pleasure he might have had. We fell into long painful silences, punctuated by awkward attempts to talk about so-called neutral things that, at heart, neither of us really cared about. The news, the gossip, mundane little stories—these were just background music, something on which to float our voices as we tried to offer each other at least a loving tone. But eventually, disappointment struck its chord. Our superficial dialogue—if it could be called that—became worse than nothing, an unbearable pretense. When I began to eat in the cafeteria, neither of us remarked upon it.

It was right around then that along with his hope, Jay pretty much lost his good nature, too. His noblesse oblige, his playful way of making himself the butt of his own jokes, the smooth calming tone he seemed to possess as his birthright—all these were being eaten away from the inside. Not gradually, but in chunks. First, the winsome smile; then, the easy banter; then, the relaxed open-faced way he listened to others. There were still flashes of charm, but now they were tinged with desperation, with fear that he might be ignored or abandoned if he didn't flatter. I had never seen him this way before. Fortunately, it was a phase that didn't last, but unfortunately, what came next was harder. Frightened, terribly ill, forced to accept help from others, he got testy, sullen, even downright mean. At first it was understandable, so clearly circumstantial. But when he began to take swings at people's weaknesses or blind spots, I found myself feeling stunned and angry.

"I don't even know this nasty old man I have to visit every day," I told Celia on the phone late one night. "And I don't want to. I hate myself for even saying so. But the truth is, I'm going in later and leaving earlier. Not because I decided to do that, but I just can't seem to get myself to move any faster."

"Of course, you're angry," said Celia.

I wrapped the phone cord tighter around my finger.

"I'm not even sure if I can keep up with the schedule anymore, never mind with how he's being. I'm about to crack."

And it wasn't just me.

"Jay, this is care, not warfare," a nurse told him one afternoon, growing exasperated.

"Then stop badgering me," he replied, ungiving.

"Listen!" she said, sitting down eye-to-eye with him. "It's no secret. I know the last thing you want to be is needy. You and about fifteen other guys on this unit. Well, let me tell you. Dependence is not the same as dependency. So, work with me."

"You don't even know me," Jay muttered.

After she left, I lost it. "Look, you dumb-shit. We need these people. Our lives depend on them. And I want you to fucking show them a little of your light, and your respect, even if you don't feel it, because we want them to *want* to come in here. We want them to do more for you than just make a duty call. And if you won't do it for yourself, then do it for me, because I need to be able to go eat and sleep and not worry myself sick about who is looking after you."

"I don't need this from you," he said, turning his face to the wall, jaw hardened.

I stood up to leave.

He made no move to stop me.

Hesitating, I picked up a magazine that had fallen from his bed. Smoothing the cover, I held it out to him, which only made things worse.

"I don't want that," he snapped.

"Fine! Neither do I!" I said, letting it drop to the floor with a thwack. As I stalked toward the door, he spewed out something low under his breath.

"What?" I said, spinning around.

He glared back, but soon his face crumpled.

"I can't stand what I'm doing to you . . . ," he said, his voice shaking.

Before he even finished his sentence, and only later hearing the regret in his tone, I fired back. "Good! Then quit! Cease!"

I shudder now, remembering that.

A few days later, he was back at it again, nastily deriding an aide who instead of hurrying out, set aside his mop and paused, listening quietly until Jay interrupted himself.

"Where are you from?" Jay asked.

My mouth dropped. He had downshifted his whole tone, and actually sounded soft, even respectful—almost normal.

"The Philippines," the guy answered. "Where are *you* from?"

Jay flushed. "Evil," he muttered.

"Pardon?"

"I'm evil."

The aide cocked his head. "Why evil?"

"It's evil to be ungrateful," Jay whispered, almost inaudible.

The worker stuck his hands under his armpits, frowning. "You don't have to say that."

"Yes, I do," said Jay. "I need to say I'm sorry."

The aide covered Jay's hand with his.

"You're forgiven," the man said. "And I'm sorry too. It's easy to get things wrong when you care for people."

All three of us looked from one to the other. Jay's lip was trembling. The aide had barely left the room when Jay finally broke down, burying his face between my shoulder and chest.

After that day, the fever of nastiness in Jay's soul broke, even if his literal fever did not. He gained some physical strength, and as he did, he became more like himself again.

Jay being Jay, he was able to convince his doctors, and me, that it was time for him to leave the hospital.

"This is very risky," the doctor said pointedly. "The lung damage is most likely permanent. Do you understand you might not survive another hospitalization?"

"Exactly my point," Jay said, looking determinedly at the doctor. "If this is as good as it gets, then I'm good to go."

The doctor continued to gaze at him sternly.

"I'll do everything you recommend," Jay argued. "Medicine, home-care, whatever. And I accept any and all consequences. No blame."

The doctor looked to me.

I nodded.

"Are you sure? This effects your future, too."

I took Jay's hand.

"I'm here, no matter what," I said, looking into his eyes.

My voice quavered, but as soon as I spoke those words, my heart flew up out of its little box and into the air, singing. Fuck the future; the future could wait. The sun still had gold to spill across our floor.

47

I STOOD WITH MY ARM FLAT against the door, holding it open for him. He took me by the chin as he passed, leading me in. I felt the smoothness of my morning shave; all my expectations for this morning of his return. The rubies and rusts of the tribal rug in the living room flew up at us, spangling our brains with their brilliance. He seemed almost to sway as he looked timidly around, lips pursed together, his right arm held across his body, gripping his other elbow. I had left a window open on purpose; some petals from the plum tree had drifted in. Even the scent of the house had been prepared: Celia had dropped off a still-warm loaf of banana bread that morning; Betsy had brought lilacs imported from God knows where. He wandered around, noting these and other gifts of care—the cleanliness of the house, the shiny windows, a pot of freshly planted flowers. Over and over he asked me who did this or that.

"So many people came forward," I answered, opening the refrigerator and pointing to the containers of soup and pudding. He was still at the window.

"Even the outdoor sills are clean!"

He looked amazed. It was amazing. There were so many things to talk about, but now was not the time. He needed steadying. I put my arm around his shoulders. He leaned his head against me, then turning toward me, let me gather him into my arms.

"When you're shaky on your feet, it's hard to feel upright in your being," he said, resting his chin on my shoulder.

As we held each other, he began to sway again. At first I thought it was because he was weak, and maybe at first it was, but then I realized he was dancing with me, and we started to laugh, stumbling then picking up with each other again, going slowly, deliciously slow, until he had to sit down on the couch, and I pulled off his coat, and as he watched, I danced with it, turning and dipping and brushing up against the fabric. He grinned, following me with his eyes, then with a surprising strength caught me by the seat of the pants and yanked me down. I toppled half-across him, and we wrestled briefly. I was so thin by then, too, but that day I was heavy on him, and it felt good. Really good, he said. And then he pushed me off, saying let me get up, I have to piss standing up in my own bathroom.

When he woke late the next morning, I had been up for hours, creeping around the house, setting things even more right than they already were. Cushions plumped, shoes lined up, tap handles gleaming. Wrapped in his own clean robe, he finally appeared in the kitchen, hands gripping the back of his chair as he gazed out the window. The neighbor's pink camellia was in bloom; two doors down, the magnolia's thick leaves shone.

"Still all here," he said weakly, but with a smile.

Together we stood at the kitchen counter, him watching as I poured yogurt and berries into the blender for smoothies. We were both acting a bit shy, as if it were our first morning together. In a way, it was.

"Do you mind if I open a window?" he asked.

"Of course not, silly. This is your home."

"Such luxury," he said, leaning out. "Fresh air. Thank God."

We were both so hungry for it.

"Who did you say cleaned these?" he said, knocking a knuckle on the glass.

"I forget," I said, my cheeks flushing. "Some people did things when I wasn't at home."

I turned on the blender, hoping to cut off the topic. Instead, Jay laid a hand on my back, talking over the racket of the blender.

"Of course, you don't remember everything. You had to manage so much, and all on your own."

I broke into a sweat. Little did he know how much I was managing things in that very instant, things that weren't mine to manage. And I was managing by lying. I knew exactly who had washed those windows. It was Eddy. Eddy the Intruder. The last person I wanted to come crashing into our conversation that morning, Jay's first day home from hell. Or any other morning, for that matter.

I had arrived home late one afternoon to find him up on a ladder in front of the house, scrubbing. He had been calling for weeks, almost since the beginning of Jay's hospitalization. (Of course, he would pick *that* time to get back in touch.) I put him off, two or three times, telling him Jay was out and would call him when he could. But Jay didn't call, because Jay didn't know, and I hoped that would do the trick. Still, Eddy kept at it, ignoring the edge in my voice, so I finally told him, Jay was in the hospital, and not allowed visitors, which was no longer true, but so what. Then the kid asked solicitously if I needed food. Repeatedly. Or a chore done. How hard was I going to have to kick? I said I had plenty of help of my own. I even said flat out, we don't want you around at this time. *We.* A total lie.

But he didn't believe me. Bags of reheatable homemade food appeared at the door, no note attached. I threw them out. I passed them on. When fatigue began to wear me down, I even ate them. They were disturbingly good.

Finally, one day I came home and found him up on that ladder.

"No!" I said, halting in my tracks. "What are you doing climbing all over my house? You can't just show up like this. It may have worked once, with Jay, but spare *me*."

Pail in hand, he came clanking down.

"I'm sorry. I was just hoping to get these windows done before you got home. Especially the sills. I heard about, well, you know, AIDS and pigeon shit. Even the dust from it, blowing in . . . so I thought—"

"I'm well aware of pigeons. We don't have any."

He wiped his sweaty forehead on his sleeve, then pulled a loose cigarette out of his pocket.

"Yeah, well, I found that out when I got up there," he said, rifling through his trouser pockets, presumably for a lighter. Looking embarrassed, he stuck the cigarette back in his pocket.

"I know it's hard to trust me," he said, shooting me an uneasy look. "Why would you? You have every reason not to. I just hoped . . ."

"No," I said. "I don't have time for this."

"I've changed," he said, his voice cracking. "Let me tell you . . ."

"There isn't time," I repeated, making moves to go around him, but something stopped me, and I turned, glaring at him instead.

"I never meant what I did," he said in a rush, holding up his hands. "I was fucked up. It was a stupid messed-up teenage thing."

"Yes. And you paid your dues in a correctional facility for youth, and it was horrible. Jay already told me."

"It was a nightmare."

"It was supposed to be. And now it's over. The End. You are free to move on," I said, eyeing his ladder.

He winced. "I didn't mean for this conversation to go like this."

Flushed, I took a step back. Just get out of this, I told myself, drawing a deep breath. You don't need to be cruel.

"Look," I said, struggling to even my tone. "I know you're just trying to make peace with yourself, so don't let me stand in your way. I really do have to go."

He stared at me, temples pulsing. "I'm not here just to get square with myself. Is that really what you think?"

I glanced up and down the street, starting to feel afraid.

He shook his head, rubbing the back of his neck.

"But, of course, you would," he mumbled. "I was just hoping . . ."

He trailed off.

I paused. It was true that he had done nothing but good works from Day One of his return. He was doing it again, the good soldier, standing here before me, diverting his gaze as if awaiting my inspection. Involuntarily, I ran my eyes over him, taking in the flecks of gold in his brown eyes, T-shirt worked up out of his pants, an inch of smooth flesh showing above the belt.

"So," he said, clearing his throat, bending over his bucket. "If it's all right with you, I'd like to finish that last window before I get out of here."

Tightening my fists, I walked past him without a word and into the house. Damn his sweet ass.

Jay, brown eyes smiling, was holding out his cup waiting for me to fill it. My Lazarus.

Mine.

To love and to cherish.

And why shouldn't I protect him? I told myself, pouring our smoothies. We didn't need Eddy intruding on this moment—or any other, for that matter. Hadn't we suffered enough? Didn't we deserve to be happy— especially today of all days?

Jay took a sip from his cup, gazing at me over the brim.

"We really are in the pink of it," he joked, turning his glass, watching the strawberry seeds drift.

"Yes!" I said, raising my glass, toasting him, toasting us, silently congratulating myself. Yes, it was only judicious of me to keep these troubles with Eddy to myself. Past, present, and future. No need to waste any more time rationalizing it.

We sat down at the table. Tilting back in my chair, I followed Jay's eyes as they wandered easily around the room. The yellow walls, our multi-colored plates, the smoky black of our 1930s stovepipe—even the rumpled hand-towels dangling from their hook—each leapt to life, as if the house had only been sleeping until Jay arrived to wake it.

And now his gaze was resting on me.

"You're pink, too!" he said, questioningly raising his eyebrows.

"Life force!" I said, self-consciously touching my cheek. How I had missed the intensity of his attention, yet now that I had it, I found myself bouncing the focus back to him as quickly as I could.

"And you—you're filling in!" I said, outlining his silhouette in the air between us.

"Filling up, too." Letting out a long sigh, he shifted his chair into the sun, peacefully closing his eyes. In the full natural light, the toll of illness on his face was all the more vivid, yet so was the joy. I leaned back and closed my eyes too, willing every cell in me to soak up the moment, our moment—to have and to hold—

"A hummingbird!"

Suddenly Jay jumped up—he jumped!—to catch a glimpse.

It was right about then that the story I had been telling myself for months began to fall apart.

Returning to the table, Jay eagerly began reading through his get-well cards. As he took in the love and good wishes of his friends, his whole body seemed to loosen and gain strength. Color—good color—rose in his cheeks. One look at his face, and suddenly what I had always known deep in my heart came pushing itself up, breaking through all my fine excuses for my own behavior. Hearing about Eddy's concern and generosity would only amplify Jay's joy, yet I was acting to curb, even kill, their connection.

It was as simple as that.

How could I have stooped so low?

Abruptly I stood. Sensing nothing amiss, he smiled up at me, including me in his glow.

"This is all so wonderful," he said, nodding toward the little shrine of cards he had propped up in the center of our table. "Thank you. You above all. You've given me so much more than I ever imagined anyone could give."

I shook my head, but he kept going, lavishing me with praise for having carried so much, alone.

"I'm no angel," I stammered.

"False humility not allowed. Come here," he said, beckoning with his finger.

One hand on the back of my chair, I wavered.

"I just remembered who did the windows . . . ," I heard myself say, in a thin reedy voice.

Jay cocked his head.

"Actually, I knew all along . . ."

And then I told him everything. He sat back, hands joined, but soon his smile faded as he listened closely with narrowed eyes. Eventually he began clasping and unclasping his hands, unable or refusing to look at me. Though obviously perplexed, then troubled, he didn't press me to explain. I waited for questions, any question, but none were forthcoming.

Finally, he rose, tightening the belt of his robe.

"I'm tired now. I need to go lay down."

His tone was polite, as if he were talking to a stranger.

I hung my head over the kitchen sink, wanting to puke, but nothing came.

Now that the truth was out, there would be no going back.

I had betrayed him, and our relationship, too.

Me, the one who ostensibly loved and cherished him the most.

Would he forgive me?

How could I even forgive myself?

Despairing, I picked up a plate. Fists on both sides, I shook it, shook it until I was red in the face. I had broken everything else—why not this too?

I raised the plate, centering it over the gleaming metal of the faucet.

In the end, wasn't everything unfixable, anyway?

48

AFTERWARD, I LAY ON THE LIVING ROOM FLOOR, gazing up at the radio tower on Twin Peaks. As the late afternoon fog surged in from the ocean, sweeping Mount Sutro from sight, the tower sailed like a red-masted ship above it, upright in the fray. Steady, I told myself, waiting for my own high waves of emotion to subside. Weary now of my own remorse, I wanted so much to go to Jay, to lay down beside him and share some comfort, but I could hear him snoring. Despite all that had just happened, he could actually sleep. I didn't know whether to be relieved or disturbed. But there was no doubt in my mind that he needed it.

We both did.

Curling up on the couch, I tried to drift off too, but no such luck. I tossed and turned, my mind undulating on a single question. If there was no going back, how was I to go forward?

Without premeditation, I picked up the phone and called Eddy.

A woman answered, barely audible over the happy shrieks of a toddler. I almost hung up, then realized she must be his roommate, the friend from high school. The hubbub receded, then Eddy picked up. I said I needed to tell him something. Neither of us seemed to breathe.

"Well?" he said. He sounded frightened too. I presumed it was of me, but then, with unconcealed dread in his voice, he asked if something had happened.

"No, no, nothing like that," I said in a rush, adding that in fact, Jay had been discharged, and was now looking out of his own sparkling clean windows.

"Jay is very appreciative of everything you did," I added, haltingly. "He never contacted you, because I never told him you had come around."

There was an awkward silence. I tried to picture him standing there, in this apartment or flat he shared with his childhood friend and her baby, then realized I had never thought about his life—the life he had made for himself after juvenile hall, the army, cooking school, whatever else.

"I'm sorry," I stammered. "Also, for crashing into your day like this. Please call Jay whenever you want. I'll leave you alone. I can hang up now."

"No," he interjected.

Then nothing.

We hung there, nobody saying a word.

Was there anything to say?

"So . . . ," I said, trying to take charge. After all, it was me who had initiated this call. But now what?

"I'd like to invite you to brunch," I said, as if it were the most natural thing in the world for me to do.

"You did *what?*"

Jay, a steaming pot of basmati rice in his hand, turned around to face me. It was early evening now. Vapor was dripping down the insides of the windows; the kitchen was gray in the fog light. Until that moment, we had been making carefully neutral conversation. Nothing concilia-tory, but no open conflict, either. Yet time was ticking by. The day would soon be over. Unable but also unwilling to keep my mouth shut, I told him about my call to Eddy.

"He said yes," I added.

Pot still in hand, he gave me a long look, his face unreadable. Then he turned away, setting the pot back on the unlit burner with unnecessary caution. He was obviously taking a minute to compose or perhaps curb himself. As he turned to face me again, his slow deliberate movement made me think of the spring afternoon when he had stood in that exact spot, offering to pour tea for his parents. Given the frustrations of that day, his diplomatic restraint had impressed me deeply. But now, as he leaned back against the counter and crossed his arms, the thought that he might feel a need to put up a screen with me, too, both saddened and frightened me.

Unfortunately, it also made sense. The poor guy hadn't been home twenty-four hours and I kept yanking the rug out from under him. As soon as I got off the phone with Eddy, I realized I had done it again. I should have asked Jay before making *any* invitation, never mind this one. As I met his gaze, the happy freedom I'd been feeling since making my call began to wilt.

"I'm sorry," I said. "I should have consulted you."

"That would have been in order," he said, rubbing his forehead. "But I'm not going to complain. What really matters is that you reached out to him."

"You're being very generous."

"Not really," he said, pausing for a second. "Anything else you'd like to spring on me, while you're at it?"

I shook my head.

"Good. So, I guess that's it." Picking up a sponge, he decisively wiped off the stovetop and threw the crumbs into the sink.

Surprised, I held my tongue.

After a while he looked over at me.

"What?" he said.

"I deceived you. Is there anything else *you* need to say to me, to clear the air?"

"No," he said, carefully controlling his face and voice again. "I don't know what more there is to say. You fucked up; you made it better. I'm glad you did."

"End of story?"

"I hope so!"

I looked out the window. It was almost dark now.

"I just . . . I want us to be able to sleep tonight," I said hesitantly.

He stared at me, then shook his head. "You don't give up, do you? Okay! So, you want to know what really bugs me?"

"Yes!"

"What you are doing right now!"

"What am I doing right now?"

"You are trying to manage this conversation, the same way you have been trying to manage me, and my relationships, for weeks. I want you to stop it, Bill. It's only making things worse."

I flushed. That stung, but rightly so.

"Fair enough," I said.

There was a long pause.

"When Eddy showed up again, you could have come to me," he said, softening. "You could have told me. We could have figured things out. Why didn't you come to me?"

I couldn't, I thought, blinking back tears as I tried to shove down the memory of him packed in ice, his chest straining as he struggled to breathe. I turned my face, not wanting him to see my distress, but it was too late.

"I'm sorry," he said quickly, squeezing his forehead. "What was I thinking? What an idiot! Of course, you didn't tell me. How could I forget that I was a raving lunatic half the time?"

Reeling it in, I shook my head vehemently.

"No. No, no, no. Key phrase here: 'half the time.' There was another half. My half. My lunacy. You were fighting for your life, and I thought I was fighting for you. But I was also being a dick-head. There's no excuse

373

for how I treated Eddy, or for lying to you. That's the long and the short of it."

"Well, yes, now that you put it that way, you were a dick-head."

He held my eyes, suddenly understanding how much we needed this moment.

"Yet I have no doubt that I would have done the same things, or worse, if I were in your place," he added firmly.

"I don't think so, but thanks."

We lowered our eyes. It took a few more breaths, but finally we could rest with each other. As we did, my gaze wandered to his scuffed-up slippers, the ones I always wanted to throw out and replace, except I knew he would kill me if I did.

"I love the way you can always find the lotus growing in the mud," I said, looking up.

He put his hands together, playfully bowing to me.

"And I love the way you drag me through it until I find one."

~~~~

After that conversation, my confidence in us (and in my own heart) lifted. What had been closed, opened. In the days that followed, of all the things that could part us, it seemed like Eddy was not to be one of them. The euphoria of being home together and alive carried us both, sweeping aside the weeks in the hospital when Jay had refused to see anyone. No doubt we looked like hell, but we didn't care, not yet, and not caring felt like a good rebellion. Now, when people dropped by, we welcomed them, glad to be well enough to do so. Conversation became not only our main support, but also our sport. Shucked down to the essence, we turned our attention toward life, and took pleasure in friends. More than ever, we looked at them closely, really looked at them, taking in the telling slump of a shoulder, a happy scratch behind the ear, the

374

nervous lift of a chest. We received them as they were, and ourselves as we were, loving the fresh air they brought in on their clothes, and the gifts they left behind. A rainbow spectrum of T-shirts, X-rated comics, a wooden 3-D puzzle of a Phoenician boat. In a brown paper sack from Just For Fun, our favorite card store, a joke bottle of Damnitall, a cure for whatever ails.

Which is not to say we were oblivious, of course. Hardly. The awareness of death was like a snake in the room, a snake that threatened to coil its blue body around us at any time, squeezing the happiness out of any moment. But if we surrendered to alertness, instead of alarm, the room was full of beauty. Not the beauty that comes from arranging things to our own liking, or the small beauty of getting what we wanted, but the beauty of giving the whole heart and mind to this moment, the only moment. We might never look to sea from the window of an Ashbury Heights fantasy home, or spend a golden afternoon in the high-domed reading room of the British Museum, or maybe even manage a stroll from start to finish along the cliff trail at Landsend. It didn't matter to us. We refused to want what we couldn't have. Kite Hill, with its panoramic view of the city, and its public benches, was right around the corner. We could drive there, it was already paid for by taxes; we met some real characters there, both neighbors and dogs. As we watched the low bright fog of spring mornings rise up from the bay, the line between heaven and earth blurred. Sometimes the whole world seemed to be oozing light.

Thank God that was the zone I was in as our date with Eddy approached. Though nervous, of course, I was eager to test my newfound equanimity. Surprisingly, Jay was the one who grew more tense. As I unloaded our groceries on the day before the event, he stood in the middle of the kitchen, jingling the change in his pants, poking around in the bags.

He pulled out a carton of eggs. "Did you check to see if any are broken?" he asked.

"I thought you knew me!" I teased.

He popped open the box anyway. "Seamless," he admitted. The brown eggs glowed in their Styrofoam nests.

"Everything is coming together just fine," I said breezily.

"But, I still can't believe you invited him to *brunch*. I mean, *brunch!* Why brunch? You always hated brunch!"

"Beats me. God moves in mysterious ways," I said, plopping a box of cream-of-wheat in his hands. "Here. Find a home for this."

He made a face. "Are we going to give it to *him*?"

"Of course not," I started to say, but he was already acting out a little skit, facing our imaginary guest as he presented the cereal. " 'Gee, Eddy, how about something beige? We have dry toast too, or plain white rice— all quite delightful if followed by a vanilla supplement drink chaser!'"

I laughed, but gently took the box from him.

"Don't worry. I'm making frittata, plus scones, fruit salad, fresh juice, sausage if he eats it—there will be plenty for him. And if you and I stick to simpler fare, he won't care. We'll probably all be too nervous to pay much attention to the food anyway." I pressed my hand against his cheek. "Besides, it's not about the food," I said quietly.

"Okay," he said, trying to sound reassured, but as I started putting things away again, he stood in the middle of the kitchen, wrapping the frayed belt of his robe around his finger.

"What?" I asked, taking him by the lapels.

"I just don't know what he wants from me," he blurted.

The sudden anguish in his voice took me by surprise.

"He probably doesn't really know, either," I said. "At least not consciously."

"And that's what makes me nervous."

We searched each other's faces. He was biting his lower lip.

"You don't owe him anything, Jay."

"Maybe not now . . . but—"

He broke off.

He seemed close to tears. After all these years, here it was again, the old self-blame, threatening to poison the well of his recovery.

I put my hands on his shoulders.

"He's not a kid anymore," I said firmly. "Even when he was, his needs were too big for any one person to handle. That's not your fault. Besides, it's not like you had the PTA behind you, waving rainbow flags."

"I guess not . . . ," he said, but he was hanging his head. I gave him a little shake.

"Your wish to help him was beautiful, Jay. Nothing and no one can ever take that away from you, unless you let them."

There was a flickering at his temple. It was the ghost of one I had spotted years before, on the night we met. I remembered him sitting at Clive and Thom's table as several guys made ribald fun of his dilemma with the hot student who wanted driving lessons. "Just put your hand on my stick-shift," that sort of thing. Jay had laughed along with the others—he had a wonderful laugh. I was immediately drawn to him. Riveted on his face, I noticed that twitching at his temple as the laughter faded. I sensed that he wasn't just amused by the joking—he was also uneasy. It made me like him all the more. He seemed to respect both his work and the kid.

I gave his hands a tug, pulling us back to the present.

"This meeting has been a long time coming. I'm nervous too. How could we not be? But we're ready."

He looked at me wishfully, then ran his hands over his hair and rubbed his face, giving himself an air-wash.

"So," he said, fresh color coming into his cheeks. "Okay. Yes. All systems go. We give it our best, then let the chips fall where they may."

We knocked fists, thumbs up.

"I'm ready for the worst," he added.

"And what might that be?"

"He turns out to be a bore."

49

EDDY ARRIVED ON THE BUTTON, carrying a pan of oven-fried potatoes big enough to feed a battalion. "Lightly salted, with very little oil," he said, handing it off to me. As I headed to the kitchen, he and Jay awkwardly shook hands, until Jay held out his arms, and they gave each other a stiff A frame hug.

"Oh here," said Eddy, letting go of Jay as I re-entered the room. He stuck his hand out the front door, picking up a container that he presented to me.

"Sweet potato soup for when you guys need—" He stopped. "When you'd like some."

"How did you know I'm the cook?" I asked, attempting a joke. "Are we that obvious?"

He cocked his head, playing along as he looked from one to the other of us.

"Yes," he said.

"You and I have that in common," he added, giving me a hesitant grin.

"Well, from what I've sampled, your cooking, unlike mine, is definitely not common."

He bent his head, waving off my compliment. Airport and army cooking was hardly high-class, he said, but I noticed there was something

378

about his eyes, a slight tightening, that made me think of a snail, the way they can pull back their eye stems when touched.

I pressed on anyway.

"What you left on our steps was definitely not assembly line. In fact," I added, ironically, "everyone I gave it away to said it was fantastic. When I finally got over myself and tried some, I started to regret being such a prick."

Turning red, he nodded and looked out the window. He seemed pleased.

Jay moved us along to the kitchen and offered him a chair.

Leather jacket creaking, he lowered himself, hands on his thighs as if pinning himself to the seat. His cologne, however, was definitely roaming.

"It's good to be here," he said awkwardly, his eyes scanning the cupboards and doors. Like a cat, I thought, looking for escape routes. He even licked his lips. Jay and I exchanged a glance, staying quiet.

"It's good," he repeated, as if testing the words. Given the circumstances, it struck me as an odd thing to say. He had barely sat down. "Let me take your coat," said Jay. The guy was clearly sweating inside his armor.

"I'm okay," said Eddy, rolling his head around the edges of his collar as he made himself sit back. Underneath the cologne, I caught a whiff of tobacco. Seeing the smooth skin of his neck, I realized he was about the same age as Jay and I had been when we met. Yet Eddy had been to war. With a cook's knife, but still, to war, in Kuwait. I glanced down at his hands. Sturdy fingers, twisting around each other.

"I can't believe I'm here," he said, glancing at Jay. "I can't believe that you are letting me *be* here."

"Well, you're letting us be here, too," Jay said quietly, trying to hold his eyes. Eddy gave a shrug, but a polite one.

"Oh," he said abruptly. "The potatoes need reheating." He stood up, watching as I slid the pan into the oven, then Jay stood up too. We talked about food for a few minutes, then the conversation seemed to run out of steam.

Soon we were all just standing around in the kitchen.

Feeling my eyes on him, Eddy gave me a tight smile, and I smiled back, feeling fake, and nervous. Maybe it was all going to go flat, I thought. The milk of human kindness souring already?

Oh, stop, I told myself. Stop always putting a slant on things.

And then I knew this was my moment, my obligation. It was up to me to shatter the brittle air.

I went ahead and apologized. To both of them, in front of each other. That seemed important. I had interfered and resolved never to do it again. Whatever business they had with each other, I would do my best to make way for it. And if I fell short, they would call me on it.

Jay nodded with solemnity. Eddy's eyes were on him. I kept my eyes on Eddy, waiting. Outside, robins were peacefully announcing their territories.

"Me too," said Eddy, barely audible.

There was a long pause. I nodded; Jay nodded.

Then I pulled out two chairs, pointing to each one.

"Sit," I said. "While I play cook."

As they carefully found their way with each other, I moved quietly around the kitchen, slowing my preparation time. All ears, I followed every word, absorbed not only in Eddy's story, but his ability to tell it without affectation or self-pity. His discomfort was right out there, so raw and real that after a while, it actually began to set me at ease. By the time I served up the food and sat down with them, we were all deeply engrossed. The more I learned about Eddy's path to this day, the more my civility turned into respect, and later, even warmth.

Eddy took off his jacket and rolled up his sleeves.

"A ship?" asked Jay, nodding toward a tattoo on his bicep. Eddy stuck out his arm so we could both see it. No dagger or snake or dragon with dripping jaws; simply the USS Constitution in full sail.

Jay cocked his head. "So, tell . . . why this? And why the army?"

After Jay's house burned and he had left town, Eddy had gotten a job at a gas station, then stole from the till. He ended up in Maxey Boys, a "reform" school. They had a program in which WWII vets from the VA teamed up with punks from the school to do projects like digging up sod and planting gardens for nursing homes.

"I was standing around leaning on my shovel—believe it or not, I had never used a shovel before, and didn't want to, either. I wanted a smoke. This old Navy guy, Jack, comes up and starts digging right next to me, then gives me a shove with his shoulder, on purpose, but not mean. 'Look, meathead,' he says. 'I'm sure you've got experience shoving things in somewhere, so get busy.'"

"Hearing an old guy talk that way spun me out. 'Why you turning red?' he says to me. 'I was a real meathead, too, you know. In the Navy, in Frisco. Visited some real sweet places down low in those valleys, if you know what I mean!' he says, giving me this big, wicked grin. Then he showed me his tattoo. I had never heard of the USS Constitution . . ."

Eddy squeezed his arm, making his bicep bulge. The sails of the ship filled. "A few years later, I got me the same tattoo . . . ," he said, then looking embarrassed, he rolled down his sleeve. Over and out, I thought, expecting him to bail, but I was wrong. He took a deep breath.

"So, Jack and I, we kept being put on the same team, week after week. He kept kicking my butt, telling me he knew I had the capability to help my crew do well. Being around him, I started to grow a heart. The old guy actually looked forward to seeing me. One day he told me his secret. He had accidentally shot another sailor in a cave on Okinawa. Said he had only told two other people in his life, and now me. He wanted me to know that even though he thought he couldn't go on, he did. He went on and became a fireman, and had a chance to save a life, too. Took care of his family, and didn't fuck around.

"'I don't know why you're in here,' he said to me, 'but I know where you can go. And unless you do something bigger than yourself, you're gonna stay nothing.'"

Eddy paused.

"That's when I decided to go into the service," he finally said, looking at Jay. "Enlisted as soon as I got out of Maxey. The army decided I would be a good fit for the culinary school in Fort Lee, Virginia . . . I was there when Jack died. His wife found my address in Jack's top drawer and wrote to me. I went to the library on base, found a picture of the USS Constitution, ripped it out, and went up to Baltimore one weekend, looking for a tattoo artist . . . And if it weren't for you, I might never have gone back into a library," said Eddy, flashing Jay a grin.

Jay bent forward in his chair.

"I heard this guy on the radio say there are two kinds of men," Jay said to Eddy. "There is the kind who is a man for himself, and the kind who has learned to be a man for others. I don't really have the right to say I'm proud of you—but I am. I am honored to know you."

Struggling to control their feelings, they both looked to the side.

Then Jay stood up and clasped Eddy's hand, saying he'd love to visit more another day.

I was not prepared for how suddenly, despite the bigness of that moment, he had crashed.

As he left the room, Eddy and I exchanged an uncomfortable glance.

We were allies now, companions in care and concern.

PART SIX

50

I TRY TO REMEMBER "WHAT HAPPENED" next.

On days when the sun shone and Jay and I walked around in it, I could feel my bones drinking. Let's get drunk, I'd say, as the morning sun struck the top of the neighbor's house.

Happy, happy man, he'd answer, lifting the collar of my jacket up over my cheeks. Then he zipped up his own coat and I see now how I had no idea what he was really feeling. Later, I would know what he was feeling was a secret. Lips pressed together in a thin line, that I took for a quiet smile.

When he told me I should go away for a long weekend and that he would ask Eddy or somebody else to look in on him, I took that as a good sign. His attitude seemed to suggest that I should take it that way, too. I thought there was something confident and forward-looking in his tone.

So, I agreed to go away for a long weekend, with Celia, up 101 North, to a cabin on a ridge overlooking Anderson Valley. Celia and Marionne had rented it before, so it came pre-approved by tough critics. Huge tub and a big view of the valley as you soaked. Celia made a pasta sauce with sardines which was supposedly heart-healthy, and we both hated it, but it was worth a laugh. Afterward we ate Guittard chocolate bars that gave me digestive problems, but what else was new? They were delicious.

During the day, Celia lay outdoors on a recliner, reading in the sun, while I sprawled nearby in the long March grass, thinking of the word "loafing" and conjuring up Walt Whitman and Jay's love for him, which made me love Whitman even more, because I loved Jay, who loved him. I lay in the grass and thought about calling Jay, but I didn't, because it seemed more important to just let him be, and to embrace this gift of "taking some time," as he put it. I did take time then to comb the grass, to braid it, to chew little bits of it, and to hope the cows or wild pigs hadn't come close enough to the cottage to pee on it.

Celia and I left on Monday morning. Gazing out the car window, I wondered how Jay might have been changed by our time apart, and if I would smell like sun and green hills to him. I remembered our first night together in the city, when he had picked me up at the airport. The scents of eucalyptus, greasy tools, ocean air, petroleum whirled up around me as I climbed into his truck. The familiar and the strange, mixing. Like an impulsive teenager, he rushed us through the Avenues as best he could—stop sign after stop sign—to a gravel lot above the old Sutro baths, invisible in the dark. And we parked there. Laughing. How deliciously familiar he had seemed, yet also more in and of himself. As we moved together, I found a different rhythm in him, in us. It may have been awkward at times, even silly. Yet also, irresistible.

And maybe now, after another time of being apart, there would be a new mystery.

I spotted Edward's car as soon as Celia turned onto our street. Lately it relaxed me when he came around; I liked how he pitched in, helped us out, cared. And I was glad that "Eddy" was gone. Edward was competent and caring.

As we came up the stairs to the house, I halted, staring at the bedroom window in front of me. Plywood had been nailed over the bottom half. Through the upper half of the window, I could see the bed, neatly made up, though a few shards of glass on the quilt lay winking in the sun.

Behind me, Celia, carrying my bags, halted on the stairs. "I'm going in with you," she said quietly, but there wasn't time.

The door opened and Edward waved us in with a swipe of his arm. I was relieved to see Jay, in his chair. But he was slouching. Edward sat down on the couch, sweating and clasping his hands.

Celia took one look and announced, "Perhaps I should go." No one contradicted her, including me.

At the bottom of the stairs she whispered loudly, "I can come back in a few hours." I waved her off. "Well, keep riding the waves," she admonished, cheerily, then added, almost sternly, "Call me."

When I returned to the living room, Edward and Jay were sitting where I had left them. They both seemed to be holding their breaths, and soon I was holding mine too. The room was dark and airless.

"So, are you gonna make me tell him?" Edward said to Jay. "Because I will, if you make me. I will tell him."

My stomach turned over. No, I said to myself. No, no, no. But what I should have known, or been able to guess, I didn't. And what I was so sure of, had no truth to it at all.

Jay glanced at me, pressing his lips together in an attempt to look impassive.

"So, you really are going to make me be the one to tell?" Edward said, glaring at Jay before turning to me again. "I'm really sorry to be the one who has to tell you," he said, then paused.

Jay did not accept the prod. So, Edward plunged in.

"I dropped by on Saturday. Jay had told me that Lou from his old group was going to check in on him that day, but I figured a little extra support wouldn't hurt. So, I stopped by early."

Jay was staring down at the pattern in the carpet, as if waiting to see how Edward was going to fit things together.

"Anyways, from the window on the porch I could see Jay laying flat out on the bed. Not end to end, but across it. His hands were folded across his chest. He had a bag over his head. Plastic bag. I broke the window so I could get in. Thank God he jumped right up. He was moving kind of dopey, but he was up. I ripped off the bag, which he'd just wrapped around his neck with duct tape and yes, he helped me but still I shoved him down and called 911."

He darted his eyes at Jay. "You cussed me out for calling, didn't you? You're still cussing me out. This time, for telling Bill. Well, too bad."

Jay shut his eyes and shook his head. I was too stupefied to say anything. Edward went on. I barely heard him, but later I was able to piece together the story.

Edward had held onto Jay until the ambulance arrived. After pumping his stomach, the hospital had almost kept him in a locked ward, but discharged him when Edward promised he'd stay with him at home.

"He convinced those shrinks that he wasn't going to do anything to himself and that what he did was a big mistake, which it was," said Edward, fixing Jay in his stare.

Jay didn't want anyone to call me. He told both Edward and the shrink that I needed this time away.

"I thought it was the only damn thing that he said that was true."

Edward insisted that Jay should tell me when I got home. Or that he would tell me, if Jay didn't. Jay had wanted to wait until I'd been home a few days and settled back in, but Edward wouldn't let him. Edward's voice almost cracked at the end of his story, but he didn't lose his military bearing. He was in charge. Jay wasn't. Everything was different now, in so many ways.

I stood up and thanked him. Thank God for Edward. As for Jay—of course I wanted to do or say something, but nothing came to me, nothing felt right. "How could you?" I whispered, standing up, intending to—what? I leaned over him as if I might hug him, or grab his shoulders and shake him, but I saw the fear in his eyes. Not fear of any physical violence (he knew I wouldn't really lay a hand on him), but fear of me simply coming close. He was afraid of being close. The closer I came the tighter his breathing. And the more I saw how white he was. White as a ghost. He had gone somewhere and been led back in ghost-whiteness. There was a sheet over him. Something he had pulled over himself to keep me off. Or to keep away another day.

I backed up without touching him. We stared at each other for a long minute; I felt like I had never before seen the expression he was wearing. Was he that unhappy, and why didn't I see it?

51

I WOULD LIKE TO THINK I SPOKE LOVINGLY to him those next few days or weeks, coaxing him back into his life, and our life together, but I was so numb, too numb. Blank. Blanker than I had ever been, at least since early on, when I first endured the news of my parents' accident. I seemed to have an ice block for a heart, and another block in my brain. In the blinding white of shock, I could see or think nothing in particular. Nothing was familiar. Including Jay. He was a stranger to me now. What had made him do what he did? Depression? Anger?

As for him, he talked, trying hard to have a soothing tone. How many times before had I heard his genuinely soothing tone? I knew the real thing, and this wasn't it. This was fear. This was despair. Maybe even manipulation. Eventually, when he began to say stuff about how he had just wanted to spare me, I erupted.

"Spare me? What the hell did you think you were sparing me *from?* Or *for?*" I stared at him exasperatedly.

"Okay!" he said, throwing up his hands. "So, I wanted to spare *me* from my own fucked-up body! But I was also trying to spare you from having the lifeblood sucked out of you. Can't you see? If you can keep your energy, at least you might have a chance!"

"A chance? For what? What do you think it would do to me if you had succeeded?"

"You think I was being a coward," he said flatly.

"You said it, not me. I never said that."

"No, but you didn't have to. I know when you're guilt-tripping me."

"Really? I'll be damned! After all these years, you can tell!"

He snorted, then glared out the window.

"Don't push me away!" he said.

"Push *you* away!?!" I said, incredulously. "Look, you could have at least talked to me before you did it. And if I couldn't talk you out of it, you could at least have invited me to sit in the goddamn living room while you drank your Kool-Aid! Did you really think you could just check out and that that would somehow *spare* me?"

Jay twisted his mouth as if he might cry, but he didn't. "That wasn't my intention," he said. "I didn't want to push you away. In fact, I tried to involve you. I took the Hemlock Society pamphlets and fanned them right out on the living room table, for God's sake. But you said, 'Could we put those away? Don't ask me to read them. I don't even want to see them!' That's what you said. You wouldn't even read them, never mind talk about our situation!"

This was true. I had left them, and him, alone.

He stood up, shoving his hands in his pockets as he paced back and forth.

I sat still, horrified. "Well, can I say it now?" I finally said. "I would want to be somewhere close by, if not in the same room. And before that, to be together. Knowing . . ."

He closed his eyes, color rushing to his face. "No," he said haltingly. "I couldn't have done it that way. I would have lost my nerve. And you could be arrested for assisting me."

I gathered a big breath, letting it out slowly. So many different things I felt. So many things.

He narrowed his eyes, studying me. "And in case you're getting any bright ideas," he said, "I don't need to be talked out of it again, right now, by you. It was a big mistake. I know that, and it's over. Okay?"

52

For weeks, I questioned myself, over and over. What clues had I missed? Could I have seen it coming? I kept coming back to one moonless night a few weeks before he made his attempt. Something had woken me. When I opened my eyes I saw Jay standing at the window, staring up through the black budding branches of the trees. "What's out there?" I asked him.

"Nothing. Stars." He cracked the window, then got back into bed.

"There were so many more in Michigan," he added wistfully. "At least in the old days."

We lay spooned together.

"Too much light pollution now," I said sleepily.

"I used to look at the stars as a kid," he continued. "I thought I was so clever, thinking we were no bigger than fleas on the back of a giant behemoth."

"And now?"

"Now I'd be happy to be a big fat flea, instead of a big fat nothing!" he said. We both laughed, but he hugged me tight, and we were silent for a long minute. "And you?" he finally asked, following the whorl of my ear with his finger. "What did you make of the cosmos while I was busy being a flea?"

I closed my eyes, remembering a night when I was maybe ten and laying on our dark lawn. My mother was sitting beside me, a newspaper spread out beneath her. The grass was already wet with dew. I pointed up at the Milky Way. 'What's on the other side?' I asked. 'More stars,' she said. Practical, as usual. 'And beyond them?' 'The beyond.' 'And beyond the beyond?' 'Oh, go on,' she said. 'That's beyond me.'

"Then she got up," I said to Jay, "Shook out the front of her slacks and went inside. And I felt terror. All those stars!" I rested my head on Jay's shoulder. He stroked my back. We were quiet for a long time.

Then Jay told me about when he saw dinosaur bones for the first time, on his third-grade field trip to a museum in Ann Arbor. A huge toothy skeleton reared up right in the entry hall, its spine as pointy as a picket fence. When he got close, Jay wriggled under a rope, determined to touch a bone. "Get a couple million years under my thumb," he told me. The student teacher pulled him back. But instead of scolding him, the teacher knelt down, put a warm arm around Jay's shoulder and said, "That's something, huh?"

Together they stared up into the big gaping maw. Jay could smell the teacher's aftershave; he could hear him breathe. All these years later, Jay still sounded entranced. Jumping out of bed, he started rifling around his top dresser drawer in the dark. "Somewhere in here is something I bought at the museum store that day!"

Coming back to bed, he turned on a penlight. In his palm lay a pill-bottle from the sixties, one with a facsimile of a clock dial on the lid. Jay popped off the top, then poured into my hand a little heap of tiny sand-colored disks marked like wagon wheels, minuscule whelks, and other funny-shaped fossils, each smaller than an oat. "Presents from the underworld!" he said. Ants in South America had heaved these tiny fossils up and out of their mound.

394

We were so close. Nothing at all was pointing me toward what he had planned to do. So many years together, and here we were, lying around, wondering about stars and bones and wonder.

Shortly thereafter, Jay sent me off to Anderson Valley with Celia.

～～～～

The day before Celia and I left, I came upon Jay folding my clothes for the trip. At first, I assumed he was just making room for himself to lie down on the bed, which was cluttered with things I intended to pack. Unobserved, I paused in the doorway, watching as he ran his hand slowly up and down the inside seams of my jeans. Next he picked up my burgundy sweater, bunched it up around his face, and held it there, breathing with his eyes closed. Then he quickly put everything in a bag and zipped it up.

That evening, he had tried to be clear. I am now convinced of that. He sat down on the bed and patted the chair next to the nightstand, inviting me to sit. Or should I say, commanding me. I hadn't seen him use such straight posture in a long time. He used a firm tone, almost severe, but also loving. Later, in memory, another word would present itself: *resolved*.

"Being apart is for the best," he began. "Forget me and go have fun with Celia! It will be good practice—" He cut himself off.

"Practice for—?" I started to say.

He took my hand. Eyes closed, he brushed his lips against my knuckles. His black lashes shone. I must have sensed something. I got down on my knees, resting my chin on his thigh. He stroked my hair for a while in a way he had never done before. Then he pushed me back, looking deeply into my eyes. "We have to begin to say goodbye," he said.

"We'll only be apart two nights," I said, stupidly refusing to understand.

"What I mean is you must go forward. You must take care of yourself. I want to help you. Remember that, okay? I want to help you."

"I know," I said, totally missing the clue. Instead I was thinking about how he had insisted on covering the entire cabin rental for both me and Celia.

He released my hands, then sat back.

There is so much I failed to hear that day—yet somewhere in my brain, something was recording. Later, I realized, there were clues, but I hadn't really taken them in. And now I understand that I was deceived. Not so much by him, but by my own hope. I was too afraid to see his despair.

In actuality, he was often far more balanced than I thought he was. I had pegged him as an optimist, but when his house burned down, when he lost his job, when we each were diagnosed and fell gravely ill, he understandably fell apart. Almost daily. And it was me who kept hoping, sometimes beyond all reason. Me, who argued on behalf of current medications; me, who kept the faith that new and better drugs would come along.

Only now do I realize how courageous and loving it was for Jay to attempt to end his life. Not only to spare himself some pain, but also to spare me. He didn't want to drain me any more than he believed he already had. I came to see that it was more than escape, more than despair, more than the failure of his spirit. Even if it was each of those things, too. So, I have shifted my thinking about Jay. If, at first, I felt angry at him for the attempt, I can now see that he was even more honest than I had ever realized. And that night in bed, he had only his love for us both, and his little bottle of fossils. What was beyond that, he didn't know. He rarely speculated.

53

Aᴏᴛᴇʀ ʜɪs ᴀᴛᴛᴇᴍᴘᴛ, ᴀɴᴅ ᴍʏ ᴛʀɪᴘ, he felt sicker. Wheezy, starving, occasionally incontinent. One day I watched him as he tried to reattach a window lock on the partially rotted sash. Finally, he just sat down. I raised my eyebrows.

"Improvement isn't endless," he said flatly.

I was not about to give up. If passion was no longer possible for him, then maybe at least the memory of it could return to him. Maybe I could help him remember. After all, hadn't his sense of wanting once been something other than despair, or grasping? He had been beloved, and loving, with never a Big Thought about the meaning of it all, or other gaseous cogitations. Or if he did muse, it was clear that at base for him there was nothing to do but love, in an everyday sort of way.

And for him, love could be base, and delicious, all at once.

I brought him a single white gardenia floating in a little bowl. On another afternoon, I sat on the edge of the bed and massaged his feet while he said a few sentences about the pointlessness of it all. I didn't argue. I just felt my hands on his calves and how blood was rising to the surface, driving out an iciness in his bones, and there seemed to be nothing more that was needed or could be said. No point to be made or taken. Just hands on skin.

And if on some days that proved to be too painful or irritating? Something else. There had to be something else. I reassured myself that when the time came, I would know what it was. Just maybe it would be enough to bring him back around.

∼∼∼∼∼

One night he drank down a peanut butter smoothie with a straw, then said, okay, you need to take me to the hospital. At the edge of the parking lot, he vomited into a shrub. Too much peanut butter, I thought. Or maybe it was the bananas.

In the emergency room they took him right away. "Not very busy," he mused, as he lay down on the gurney. I thought his color looked good.

Two aides in pale-blue wheeled him away through the swinging doors. Through the smudgy windows, I could see him talking to them. They were glancing down at him, laughing. I was relieved. He was allowing himself to receive. To be taken care of. Just before they disappeared around a corner, he raised his arm and waved at me. Even though he couldn't see me, he knew I was watching.

Afterward, in the waiting room, I dozed.

They said it was sudden cardiac arrest. Some sort of sepsis too. Crazy, I know, but I wanted to call him immediately and tell him what had happened.

PART SEVEN

Dear Jay,

That day at General. You said, "See you later," and now I think maybe you knew. If not consciously, then in your heart, which was literally failing. Did you know that? I hope not, though I fear you had sensations of drowning. I can barely write those words. I veer away each time an image of that comes. Or sensation.

Let me tell you about the dew instead.

I came home after you died, and along the walk to the cottage six crocuses were blooming. I hadn't seen them before, but there they were, poking their heads up through the crumpled elm leaves plastered in the beds. When had we planted those bulbs? It must have been years ago. Then suddenly! Here they were, returning.

Most people would probably take this as a sign that the dirt of grief feeds. But I could only see a reminder of what is not to be. After all those years with you—and now, those years seem as fleeting as a slender cup of petals lasting only three days. Or is it a week or two—those bent stems of love? But we planted them. We did. We.

When I got inside the house, I opened all the windows and listened to the house breathe. In and out, and out it went. The shades, swaying slightly. The sound of a jay, scrounging beneath the neighbor's shrubs. I lay in bed until maybe noon, listening, growing colder as the dampness rose. The old wooden fence behind us—us, I thought—steamed as it warmed in the sun. The sun was drawing up the dew. Somehow, I had never noticed this before, until my world stopped.

I cannot go on like this, Jay, pretending that it is enough for me to speak to you like this. "Across boundaries," some would say. Darkness, dawn, mid-morning and noon: no matter how hard I try, I can find no clear demarcations where one thing becomes another. It's not that I fail to see the possibility that you may be "here" in some different form—it's just that the line between my grief and my hope is bleary. Is something of you rising with the dew? Then I enter a terrible stillness, one in which I imagine I am always sick, and alone, forever. Perhaps I am depressed, but that is such a small word. "Depressed." This was once my life! Our life!

And you were the man who held up the cat in the morning light so I could see the sun coming through the pinkness of her ears; the man whose big hearty laugh cut the moment free from over-ripe preciousness; the man who then tickled the cat on her belly and made her wake up as herself, all batting claws and hisses.

When I finally got out of bed on the afternoon of The Day After I did something really strange. I put on the *1812 Overture* as loud as I could and left all the windows open. I guess I wanted to blow something up. Or make real the sound of the holes that had ripped through me.

Actually, I am searching for explanations, when mostly I want to tell you all the simple things that no one else would care about. What I ate today, and what I couldn't eat. How I keep losing things—my sweater, my keys, my book—even the soap. And how every time I look at that damned cup in the bathroom, still imprinted by the touch of your fingers and mouth, I see only what I cannot see. What is not here.

Why do I even write?

~~~~~

Dear Jay,

But I won't stop writing.

An arborist came to look at the plum tree last week. It needs to come down, he said. But it still has some life in it, he added, pushing on it, and his grin seemed almost salacious. (I know, I know—for a man in my condition, my fantasy was rather far-fetched.) But desire—yes! It flared like a match lit in a cave. For one second, my whole interior blazed, alive—then the light flamed out. Darkness is here again.

But I caught a glimmer! His chest was broad, and though he was lithe, he was not skinny. Not hollowed out. Strong wood, as you yourself would say. And his spirit, charitable in the best of ways. I felt like he could see that I had known better times, and his smile was his way of saying, "That old young you still shows through." But it's you, Jay, you, who would remember those better times. Those times would be part of your own body's history. And your soul.

I imagine you grinning as I tell you about him.

But it's late now, late now in the telling. I can see with my eye, but no longer with my heart, the sparkle and light on each separate leaf of that tree.

If I let myself be happy about this, will you leave me?

~~~

Dear Jay,

Strange, really strange, to realize that each day of our life together I saw your face much more than I saw my own. And sitting here alone, I seem to have no face at all. I see my feet, my calves, my thighs, my shirt—but no eyes no nose no ears no head. I look around and instead of your eyes or my own, I see the wind blowing the trees, a thin strip of fog running through the city, the tarred roofs of houses. Staring down at my toes this very second, I have no head. Some old Zen book said try this, so I did. Faintly, I hear my heart beating. Maybe there really is a Big Mind. And we are tiny waves upon that sea.

What more can be said?

Tiny, tiny waves.

Beating, beating, beating.

~~~~~~

Dear Jay,

It's strange how I talk to you all the time now. You are inside me again, slipping and sliding. We did this, we did that. Went here, went there.

I remember the time before we were so mixed up together. That edge. That night at Clive and Thom's. In their foyer, at their table. And later, in my car. My bedroom, dining room, kitchen.

My entrance. Yours.

Your skin, your hair, your dick, your mouth, your wide-open yearning places . . .

But now, you come as a phantom, not a possibility.

Not as a young man living out beyond his skin cells.

But oh that first night! Your warmth cast a net and pulled me in.

Then, you went off to Florida and I heard nothing.

Eventually you called, saying you had come home with a sore throat. A sore throat.

And yes, you had thought about me when you were gone.

And now you were calling, you were better than ever.

And if you were to call now, it would be said you were a spirit.

Do I dare believe that?

These are things that haunt me.

~~~~~~

Dear Jay,

I can't forget how you put your hand under my shirt, over my heart, and said Bill, our ways are parting. So, step back. Let me go on ahead. Taking care of me is wearing you down. I want you to rest. So, let go.

No, I said. I don't want to go to Anderson Valley. That's the way I remember it sometimes.

That I said no.

~~~~

Dear What-the-Fuck,

I don't hear you answer.
I don't hear an answer.
I don't hear anything but this goddamn alarm clock.
I don't hear anything but tick tick tock.
And what good is talk?
Talk, talk, talk.
Tick tick talk.
I can't live in these memories. No matter how vividly my mind grows the grass and lupine on Mount Tam, I can't bend a single blade to my wishes. I lay in bed and listen to the heat pour from the duct.

The air stirs but I can put my hand right through it.

Despite what you said, you are not waiting.

~~~~

Dear Sweet Nothing,

In the end we have so little control, don't we?

I remember your fear that hospital curtains would be the last thing you would ever see. And my fear that I would be stuck in some waiting room.

Well, I am still waiting. Waiting until we can be together again. Even though I do not believe in such things.

It was a dream, a fantasy, an illusion. Just like the one in which we both leave this earth at the same time. Dignified by our own clothes, laying side by side, with dahlias on a side-table.

But there is still one way left to me, to honor your own wish to depart in your own way. To honor the wish you abandoned, for my sake, or at least partly for my sake.

I will do what you were forbidden. What I forbade you to do. Except I don't have the drugs. So. The plan.

Dear Jay,

I'm in a hotel now. Lying in bed. I hear a bus grinding uphill. The curtains flap open and closed. Car doors, too. The bridge is lit up like a birthday cake. Down below, maybe a dozen floors below, is the portico.

It's too early for me to get on with it. People are still around, checking in, going out. Up here, me too. I'm going in and out. Sleep, or in-between, or something else.

But I have unfolded your suit. Black. Stiff. The scuba suit you never wore. It is lying on the bed beside me, arms crossed at the wrists. I imagined that when the time came, I would put it on, and it would hold me. And it would warn people not to touch any mess. I have spray-painted on the back of the jacket "Bio-hazardous Waste."

But I don't want to think about that. I want to think about how fine you looked, Jay. How fine you always looked in a dark trim suit.

I see you so clearly. I must be dreaming. How can this be? Out beyond grief and despair, it is after dark, as we said as kids. After dark. And in the center of my vision is a big fat shining star and there you are, at the end of an aisle I am about to walk down.

I stand feasting on the sight of you at the front of the church, your well-muscled chest filling out your tuxedo. A blaze of white shirt—I can almost smell how fresh it is, as if it were line-dried. And the black jacket, almost a bolero, blacker than the darkness of oblivion. Beautiful definition, yes, your body, and your smile, yes! The now-full lips, the bright eyes, the skin ready to sing under my touch. A viola, a bass, a flute, the long drawn-out notes, now sounding the hollows of the chapel.

Where is this coming from? Yes, I am fantasizing, or dreaming, or dreaming deliriously, deliciously. Still, who is playing so beautifully?

Then I notice the pews, the people turning to look at me. Their faces, radiant and welcoming. Michael, Brad, Celia, Betsy and her daughter Grace, Veronica, Mauricio, Zoe, John and Noel, Susan, Ruth. People we rarely see: Amanda, Anne, Michelle. Peter and Lorraine, Greg and Tanja. Even Walter! They are the lilies on our altar; light falls in through stained glass windows. In one a bearded man kneels before another, kissing his hand.

What am I waiting for?

Suddenly the chamber goes silent. I can hear my heart beating. I can see your eyes welling up as you look at me over your shoulder. I can see the gleam in each one, like the warm pennies in the bottom of that small fountain in Venice, tossing in the sun.

And now, you in this chamber, eyes wet again. You hold up your hand—beckoning, cautioning—I can't tell—then putting your finger to your lips—shhhh—you listen, gazing at something or someone to my left. Someone approaching. I turn my head and see an usher. He must be an usher. I hesitate. Do I really need someone to give me away? I stare down at his arm, then glance back at Jay. His back is to me now; he is facing the altar. Waiting, I think.

I look back at the usher, who is still holding his arm out for me. I look into his face and see it is Eddy—no, Edward. Eyes soft, tender, even beseeching. He turns slightly away from the altar, leading my eyes backward with his gaze toward the entry. The door is open. My eyes, unaccustomed to the light, hurt. I almost avert them, yet I notice two people hurrying up the stairs. They are late. A woman who must be young—her hair is blue, really blue, and stiffly pointed. Quite the *Statue of Liberty*. Holding her hand is a toddler. He is jerking his arm up and down and then suddenly he flaps his hand at me, and the young woman laughs, saying yes, he is here. And I know that voice, even though her face in the harsh light is invisible to me. I feel my arm gently taken.

Do I turn, or is Eddy turning me? Or is it all of a piece, a piece of a dream? No matter. If it is a dream, "only a dream," it is still enough to turn me. I hesitate, and glance back at you, but you have evaporated. I make myself look carefully at the place where you were standing. Everything looks natural. The oak of the pews is grainy. The candelabra on the altar shines but needs polish. The feet of the Christ statue are carefully side by side at the edge of his robe. My eyes travel up from the hem to his outstretched arms. His open embrace.

As I roll over in the dark hotel a sheet of light falls in through the open window, and I draw it tight around me as I wait.

〰〰〰

Dear Jay,

I came to this hotel to join you. But as I stand at this window, the window from which I wanted to jump, the image I have of you has changed. It's not your dying I remember, or your grief, or loneliness—or even my own. It's the look of faith on your face as you turned to look at me one more time, before they rolled you down the hospital hall.

"I can walk," you told them. I could hear you all the way down the hall; the door hadn't swung shut yet. Despite your thin waxy skin, the faded hair, the hollow cheeks and shuffle, you were radiant. Something

408

gay and good, a force flowing through you, was shining. And in this darkness, it is breaking through to me again.

Deep inside, somewhere deeper than grief and despair, I know that even though the love between us was so warm and strong, there is a larger current, too. There is More. Some might call it God. Some might call it Love. Whatever it is, I now know that it was underneath us the whole time, bigger than any two people, any one love. Who knows, maybe it was a surge of particles, subatomic waves or quirks or quarks flowing out from every single good-hearted action ever taken in the universe simply catching up with us. And as I remembered the whole span of our love, I felt buoyed up. Suddenly, I wanted to stick around for More.

So, I must go. Home, I suppose. The shrine to you and me must be disassembled. The clothes you will never wear again—it is time to give them away. This bathrobe I have on—it's yours. It still smells like you. I never washed it. Oh stop, you would say. Get over yourself. That's gross. Morbid. Lighten up.

I hear you. I will do my best, on behalf of us both. In a moment I will pick up the phone and call Edward. Something in him, and in me, is unfinished. I will do my best to love him, like we would have loved him together. Very soon—tonight—I promise, I will call him and ask him to take me home.

The twilight now is a soft warm gray. I pull back the drape, open the window. The breeze—it's chilly, but I want it next to my skin. I take off your robe and lean over the sill, looking down. The portico, the top of the doorman's hat, a taxi.

The sleeves flutter and rise as I let go.

EPILOGUE

I WENT TO THAT HIGH CORNER of Dolores Park for the view of the city, the high school, the green lawns—it's popular with tourists, too. The grass gets worn away there, exposing the dirt, that for some reason made me think of Nepal. I've never been there, but Celia has, and she likes to talk about it. About how old the earth seems there, even if it's also a mess. All the ashes, garbage, shit, and bone underfoot. Stale rice, ripped plastic wrap.

Whenever I thought of that, I wondered about who was still here in Dolores Park, buried under my feet. Ohlones? Latin ranchers? Jews? (I'd once read that the park had been a Jewish cemetery, until it got moved out to Colma.) There had been shacks for quake survivors, too. Circus crowds, birds, dogs, teenagers smoking on the footbridge over the J-Church line. Now, the green hills sweep down and flatten into a playground, where there is a facsimile of an old wooden boat on which children play.

I wondered, do the dead walk upside-down beneath us, Ohlones and white settlers mingling with the gay boys who once lazed around in the sun in bikini underwear? Often, I sensed a brother beneath me, sewn to the soles of my feet like my own shadow, except he was a ghost. Even so, we befriended each other.

From there looking toward the East Bay Hills just before sunset I was able to travel backward and forward, and it doesn't matter at all—there is nothing to lose; it's impossible to get lost, to be lost—that sunset is there, and perhaps I can't count on more being ahead, in terms of ordinary reality—but in ordinary reality—I would write off being able to go back and visit other sunsets I have enjoyed. Up there, I was riding the edge where it's all true—a broad expansiveness with no backward or forward; no now or then or before or after; no here or there; no beginning or done—both/and . . .

ACKNOWLEDGMENTS

THIS IS A WORK OF FICTION. All characters are imagined. Specifics of actual places and events—for example, the time of their occurrence—are changed.

At meal time, on walks, or long drives Lynn often told me about authors, events, and ideas that influenced her writing. I wish I could recount them all. I do know that in the acknowledgments for this book she wanted to follow the model of Abraham Verghese in *Cutting for Stone*. So, this is my best effort. She would have done a more complete job. I apologize for my omissions.

"Alma's" story may be based on an actual one reported on NPR, but I have been unable to source it or confirm similarities or differences to the version Bill makes his own.

Alejandro Mazon and the painting described are real. We are grateful to Sidney Brown and Sheila Cohen for creating Bucheon Gallery with a hairstyling chair in the back and showing works directly and indirectly feeding this book, including Mazon's and those of cover artist Susan Synarski.

The reference to waves and troughs is from Alan Watts' teaching *Coincidence of Opposites*.

Bette Midler performed in the Continental baths in 1971. You can watch a grainy video at https://www.youtube.com/watch?v=UOrzpQeJyKI and look for Barry Manilow as her pianist.

The quotation about Saint Sebastian is from *Venice: Lion City: The Religion of Empire* by Garry Willis, copyright 2001, Simon and Schuster, Inc.

The concept of living with fear, like a snake in the room, is derived in part from Krishnamurti. *The Book of Life: Daily Meditations with Krishnamurti*, HarperSan Francisco.

Inspiration and factual information came from our brothers and sisters in the AIDS plague. Ben, Bill, Brad, David, David, Dennis, Eric, Jim, John, Jon, Louis, Mark, Mark, Mauricio, Michael, Mitch, Noel, Peggy, Ric, Steve, Steve, Stewart, Tony, Veronica, and many more who I apologize for failing to name. We are endlessly grateful to you for sharing your stories and technical advice and even more for the courage of your example.

Much of this book was written under the guidance of Susan Griffin, whose no-holds-barred editing was essential to Lynn's bringing her creative vision to fruition. Thank you, Susan.

Claude Summers was among first to recognize Lynn's gifts as a writer. Thank you, Claude and Ted Larry Pebworth. You are pioneers and fed Lynn her first escargot.

Thank you, Karen Straus, for the line, "It's a small life, but it's ours, and we like it," and for advice about the inner workings of libraries.

Thank you, Susan Salisbury for abiding friendship, being the first reader outside our bubble, telling us about the real Hotel Seguso and for continuing to show up in the most difficult of times.

The Collingwood Dog Park and the dogs that play there was a twentieth-century commons bringing folks together who otherwise would not have known each other. Thank you to the people, dogs, and occasional birds who sustained and fed this work through their examples of joy, love, and at times messy conflict resolution.

To Lynn's psychotherapy clients: she loved you deeply and your work together nourished her. You provided her with insights and experiences that shine through in this book. I hope it may somehow find its way into your hands.

Pat Donegan was an inspiration and led the writing group Lynn joined in the 1980s. Later, Lynn facilitated that group, and we acknowledge its members for their sustained creative energy and discipline, including Scilla Ballas, Jackie Berger, Susan Dambroff, Betsy Kassoff, Katherine Lieben, and Laura Horn.

To Beth Ann Rontal Alterman, Scilla Ballas, Zoe Becker, Ricki Boden, Noel Castenada, Veronica Delgado, Cassie Doyle, Barb Eagle, Tony Gillies, Cynthia Goldstein, Leslie Gray, Danny Grobani, Amanda Hale, Kim Haveson, Annette Hess, Clint Johnson, Liz Kalmanson, Betsy Kassoff, Gregg Kleiner, Julia Liebeskind, Leslie Lingass, Cathlin Milligan, Kathy Moore, David Murchie, Anne Ngan, Noelle Oxenhandler, Stephanie Ozer, Ann Carney Pomper, Min Pomper, Yoonie Pomper, Angie Romagnoli, John Rosenzweig, Susan Salisbury, Allen Samelson, Ruth Schwartz, Gloria Shaffer, Gregory Spencer, Tina Stromstead, Steve Suacci, Frances Tobriner, Tatiana Wacyk, Chris Warfield, Robin Westby, John Woodward, and Tenzin Yonten: sharing your energies with us made this book possible. I hope you feel the love coming back to you from both Lynn and me.

Our animal companions: Cubby, Sophie, Brigid, and Annie, our cozy cottage in the Castro Compound and Deki Kang, our Hornby Island haven, provided us and continue to provide me solace and perspective every day.

I am grateful to the folks at 1106 Design without whom I would not have been able to fulfill my promise to bring this book to you.

Lynn commissioned the cover art from Susan Synarski many years ago. I am especially grateful to Anne Ngan for help turning the art into the cover you see. Susan Salisbury, Betsy Kassoff, and Cassie Doyle, dear friends and voracious readers, gave me courage and detailed comments. Their additional eyes on this work were invaluable as I have done my best to bring forth my beloved's creation. I only wish she were here to see it finally come into the world in this form.

Ellen Leonard
Hornby Island, British Columbia
In the time of Covid-19
April 11, 2021

ABOUT THE AUTHOR

June 12, 1954–April 11, 2017

Lynn Crawford was born and grew up in Dearborn, Michigan, where she began writing, drawing, and painting. Her working-class parents did not realize the meaning of a scholarship to Brown and made her turn it down. She went to Henry Ford Community College and then transferred to the University of Michigan—Dearborn campus where she was editor of the school newspaper and literary arts journal and earned a B.A. in English with honors. In the mid-1970s she "ran away with the circus"—Theatre Group of Ann Arbor. In Ann Arbor, she continued writing, attended social work school, met her long-time partner, Ellen Leonard, and began her practice as a clinical social worker. In 1984, she moved to San Francisco where she died in 2017. In San Francisco, Lynn maintained a private psychotherapy practice for over thirty years. She also worked for the Asociación de Mujeres de El Salvador (AMES) where a film of her poem "A Woman in El Salvador, Speaking" spoken by Carolyn Forché was made. Lynn worked at the multicultural Iris Project of the Women's Institute for Mental Health, and volunteered teaching and supervising student interns at the groundbreaking LGBTQI mental health center known first as Operation Concern and later called New Leaf. Her work has been published in *Sinister Wisdom*, *The Bay Guardian*, *Inquiring Mind*, and *Tricycle*.

Lynn studied and practiced Zen and Tibetan Buddhism, shamanism, and Jungian psychology. She read widely, wrote, drew, and laughed regularly. She was a loyal friend and daughter, a great cook, a hilarious wit, and raconteur. Brave, disciplined and generous, beloved by many. It is the greatest blessing of my life to have shared the past forty years with her on this earth and in the beyond. She lived with an open heart. I am confident that in her current form she continues to shake things up.

CPSIA information can be obtained
at www.ICGtesting.com
Printed in the USA
LVHW040854151222
735212LV00002B/752

9 781736 054529